Come Back

Melissa Maygrove

Truelove Press

Come Back

Truelove Press
Houston, Texas
www.truelovepress.com

This is a work of fiction. Names, characters, businesses, places, events, and incidents are either the products of the author's imagination or used in a fictitious manner. Any resemblance of characters to actual persons, living or dead, is purely coincidental.

First Edition
ISBN-13: 978-0-9960397-0-3

Cover design by Carrie Butler, Forward Authority Design Services

Cover photo (couple) by Jenn LeBlanc / Illustrated Romance
Cover photo (cave) by Andrey Bandurenko
Cover photo (sunset background) by mtilghma

Formatting by Morgan Media

A note about etymology: During editing of the original draft, many words and phrases were cut or changed in an effort to eliminate modern language from the text. After much deliberation, the current spelling of the word *okay* was used in lieu of *OK* in hopes it would be less distracting to readers.

To my husband and children, who gave up first place to a laptop and let me realize my dream.

And to my mom, whose relentless corrections of my grammar made me the writer I am today.

I love you guys.

Acknowledgements

So many people helped polish and promote this book, it would be impossible to list them all. The writing community is one of the most altruistic, supportive groups around, and I'm proud to be a part of it. You guys rock.

A few people gave significant amounts of their time, talent and effort, and I'd be incredibly remiss not to mention them.

Carrie Butler – Carrie is dear to my heart and a lady of many talents; trusted CP, NA groundbreaker, graphic designer, and author of the *Mark of Nexus* series. I couldn't have done it without you, my friend.

Loni Townsend – Friend, beta, CP, founder of Stoneword Press, and author of epic fantasy *Thanmir War*. Along with Carrie, Loni pushes me to hone my craft and reminds me not to take life too seriously.

Jennifer McMurrain – This kind lady jumped in when I needed a beta who regularly reads the genre. Her feedback was invaluable. Jennifer is a multi-published author and co-founder of Anna's Legacy, a non-profit agency that delivers gifts of joy and hope to people struggling with terminal illness.

E.J. Wesley – Where do I begin? This guy swims in an ocean of female writers on a regular basis and lives to tell about it. He even managed to beta a historical romance with his man card intact. E.J. is the author of the witty, paranormal *Moonsongs* series, an NA leader, the host of #NALitChat, and an all-around good friend.

Last but not least, my mom – If I'm the 'Goddess of Grammar,' then she's the Queen. She's also my copy editor. She did an awesome job of scrutinizing each and every word. If mistakes persist, blame me.

Come Back

Sometimes a single choice
alters the course of a person's life
forever.

Chapter One

New Mexico Territory
Early August, 1850

Rebecca Garvey looked up at the moon and smiled. Usually the vastness of the heavens made her feel small and exposed. Not tonight. Instead of reminding her how vulnerable she was, the expanse of stars that stretched beyond the line of wagons and into the night stirred feelings of hope and possibility.

The air was still, but the chill of nightfall crept up her back, touching every part of her skin the campfire's heat didn't. Her flesh rippled and she relished the shiver.

She drew her brown wool shawl around her shoulders and stared at the fire enveloping the logs and making them glow. Flames danced on the wood just like the thrill flicking over her heart. The trip west would change her life—she'd known that when she left Missouri—but she never dreamed she'd meet the man she would marry along the way.

Lifting her eyes, she gazed past the campfire at Nathan sitting with his father and some of the men. The fire the men huddled around lit his face with a golden glow and glimmered in his eyes as they met hers. What would it be like to wake to those eyes every morning and see them every night before she went to sleep?

One corner of Nathan's lips lifted, causing his eyes to twinkle even more.

She returned his smile, then turned her attention to her friend who'd joined her on the trunk she was using as a bench.

Charlotte let out a delicate huff. "That's what gave you two away, you know."

"Looking at each other?"

"Not just looking at each other. It's the *way* you look at each other. And the way you walk together and talk at every opportunity."

Heat glazed Rebecca's cheeks. "I enjoy his company."

"Well, thanks to you making eyes at each other, that's no longer a secret."

"I know." Due to a curious mix of piety and gossip, it hadn't been for some time. Once it was clear she and Nathan were sweet on each other, the adults made sure they were never alone. The bulk of their interactions—with always a proper distance between them—was walking alongside the wagons and sitting together at meals.

Rebecca stole a quick glance at her beau while he was deep in conversation, not looking her way.

"Has he kissed you yet?"

"No."

"Held your hand?"

"Once, when he helped me cross a stream."

Charlotte studied her with a skeptical frown.

"What?"

"Maybe he's just toying with your affections."

"No. He's a gentleman." He was—one of the finest young men on the entire train.

"He's been doting on you for weeks. Seems to me, if he were serious, he would have stolen a kiss by now."

Rebecca pressed a hand to her fluttering stomach and chanced another glance. "He's serious," she assured with a smile.

"Oh?" Charlotte lifted her thin red brows.

Rebecca's smile spread into a cat-and-cream grin. "Can you keep a secret?"

Charlotte glared down her nose.

"All right, all right." *Sorry I asked.* "He proposed."

"What!"

"*Shh.*" The gossips had enough to prattle about.

Rebecca leaned closer. "When we were walking together the other day, he told me he's claiming land not far from ours, but he has to help his father build his family's house before he can build his own." Her stomach fluttered again, matched by the rapid patter of her heart. "He told me he loves me, and he said he'd come for me when he was done."

With each word, she fell deeper into the tingly, dreamy state that claimed most of her waking hours. It was a day she would never forget. As they'd walked along the dusty trail beside his family's wagon, Nathan had peered down at her from beneath a shock of wavy, black hair—with those cobalt eyes that never failed to make her tingle from her head to her toes—and asked, "*Will you, Becca? Will you wait for me?*"

She played it coy, but that didn't last five steps more. "*Nathan Keating,*" she'd said with her sweetest of smiles, "*I'll gladly wait for you till I die.*"

"What was your answer?" The utter shock on Charlotte's face drained the joy from the memory.

"I said yes."

"Do your parents know?"

"Of course. Nathan asked my father before he asked me."

"And he approved?"

"Pa said if I waited until we were settled in our new home and if Nathan built a suitable house, he'd allow it."

"What about your ma?"

Rebecca gave a small shrug. "She goes along with whatever Pa says."

Charlotte looked at Nathan, then fixed her gaze on the fire. "You've only known him a few weeks. I hope you're doing the right thing."

"I am." She trusted her father's judgment, but the way her friend stared into the flickering flames sent her spiraling into a whirlwind of doubt. Nathan was the first man to show her any attention. Had she made a hasty choice she'd regret?

"I found something interesting today," Rebecca said, ignoring her misgivings. It was getting late, and she wanted to tell Charlotte about her discovery before they turned in for the night.

"What?" The question was asked with indifference, but that didn't surprise her. She and Charlotte had become friends because they were the only girls over the age of six on the train. They'd been paired by circumstance and had few interests in common.

Rebecca tried a more enthusiastic tone. Sometimes it worked. "I saw some rock formations along the edge of the trail, small white stones arranged in triangular shapes that point northwest."

"And?"

"I bet they mark a path that leads to something." Westward travelers sometimes left signs for those coming after, and the piles of rocks were too symmetrically-shaped to be anything else. "I wish we could stay here one more day. I want to see where they lead."

"You're such a tomboy. What's Nathan going to think of your adventures?"

Rebecca fiddled with the end of her braid hanging over her shoulder. "He doesn't seem to mind. And I'm not a tomboy." *Just because I don't mind getting my hands dirty—*

"No, I guess you're not. But if you want to keep him from losing interest, you should act more your age. You're nearly eighteen." Charlotte tugged Rebecca's braid loose from her fingers and waved the end of it in front of her face. "You should already be wearing your hair up."

Rebecca took it back and fingered it again, wishing it was a lovely vermilion like Charlotte's and not such a plain shade of light brown. "Maybe you're right. But I want to find out where that trail leads, so when you say your prayers tonight, pray something keeps us from leaving." It was an awful thing to ask, but the only way they would have enough time to investigate was if the train met with some sort of delay.

"Will you do it?" she prodded when her friend didn't answer. "Please?"

Charlotte sighed. "Okay, I'll pray." A mischievous glimmer lit her green eyes. "Maybe Old Man Cantwell will break a wheel."

"Charlotte!" They broke into a bout of stifled giggles. If people only knew how they spoke of that poor man.

Melvin Cantwell—or, as he was known to most everyone, 'Mr. Can't-do-anything-well'—had been a drag on the entire thirty-wagon train from the very first day they set off. If it wasn't malfunctioning parts, it was wandering oxen or inadequate supplies. They'd probably be a whole month closer if he hadn't come along.

Of course, it was hard to stay mad at the lonely old codger. He was a childless widower with hopes of making it to California and striking it rich.

Not her. Neither she nor her family was swayed by fanciful tales of wealth and gold. They were there to claim land and make a life. So was Nathan.

"Rebecca," came a stern voice from behind her.

She twisted her upper body and looked over her shoulder. "Yes, Ma?"

Her ma stood in the edge of the firelight, drying her hands on her apron. "It's late. You should be asleep. You've got chores in the morning."

"Yes, Ma."

"Bye," Charlotte whispered and stood to leave. "Good night, Mrs. Garvey."

"Good night, Charlotte. Tell your mother I'll help with breakfast in the morning."

"Yes, ma'am." She hurried off to the next wagon.

Rebecca rose and brushed the dust off her skirt, then headed toward the men.

"Where are you going?"

She halted and turned around. "To tell Pa goodnight."

Her mother eyed her with suspicion. "All right. But hurry up."

"Yes, Ma."

As Rebecca neared, the heated discussion that vibrated from the group in deep tones grew louder. The men were debating which path they would take to California. It had been the topic of discussion for days.

She sidled up to her pa, who had joined in late and was

standing in back of the others, and tugged at his sleeve.

"Rebecca," he admonished quietly, "you know better than to interrupt men."

"I'm sorry, Pa. I came to tell you goodnight."

His eyes softened and he planted a kiss on her forehead. "Shoo, now. Off to bed with ya."

Exchanging a fleeting glance with Nathan, she left for her feather tick in the wagon.

As soon as breakfast was over, Rebecca grabbed her drawing paper and pencil and sat on a boulder near the edge of the trail. She'd done her morning chores in record time. Maybe she could finish a sketch or two before the train left.

She'd barely started drawing when her ma's voice cut through the crisp morning air. "Put those things away. I need your help."

Rebecca flipped her notebook closed and swallowed her frustration. "Yes, Ma."

"I just took up the clothes that were drying. I need you to fold them while I pack up."

With a sigh, Rebecca climbed into the wagon bed and put her things away. She pulled a small crate up to the stack of clothes, sat on it, and started folding. At least she had daydreams of Nathan to dwell on while she worked.

"Becca," came a harsh whisper a few minutes later. "*Becca.*"

She stuck her head out the open bonnet and looked for the source of the sound. Charlotte stood to one side, her upswept hair gleaming in the early morning sun and her emerald eyes sparkling.

"What's going on?"

"Come here."

"I'm folding laundry. Can it wait?"

"No. Leave it."

"But—"

"Leave it. You can finish later."

There was no use arguing with Charlotte. Becca climbed down out of the wagon. She'd appease her friend, then get back to work.

"Where is everyone?" she asked, scanning the nearly-deserted clearing that was usually a hive of activity this time of day.

"That's what I came to tell you. There's an avalanche of rocks blocking the trail up ahead. The men will have to clear it before we can move." She beamed. "You got your wish. We're stuck here for at least a day."

Becca fought the urge to jump up and shout. "Let me finish folding and we'll go."

"No, chores can wait. Who knows where the trail leads? This might take you a while."

"What about you?"

"I'm not going."

Becca opened her mouth to protest.

"Someone needs to stay behind and tell your parents where you went so they don't worry."

"But what about the clothes? Ma will—"

"I'll fold them."

"You will?" Charlotte rarely took on extra work.

Guilt tinged her friend's expression. "I feel bad about the way I spoke to you last night. And for the way I reacted to your news. I should have congratulated you."

Becca stood speechless as Charlotte hung a full canteen around her neck and tucked a small, handkerchief-wrapped bundle into her pocket. "Leftover biscuits. In case you're gone a while." She shoved two empty burlap sacks into her hands. "In case you find something."

Becca gaped.

"Hurry." Charlotte gave her a gentle shove and made a shooing motion with her hands. "Go before your ma sees you and tells you no."

After a beat of hesitation and a glance to make sure she had her knife, Becca grinned and took off on her quest. "I owe you," she called to Charlotte over her shoulder.

Mmm. I could stay here forever.

Becca knelt by the cool, bubbling stream, refilling the tin canteen. The sound of rushing water surrounded her, echoing off the rocks and murmuring up through the trees—such a welcome change from lowing cattle, creaking wagons, and smelly, bickering travelers. After replacing the stopper and glancing at the sun sliding lower in the sky, she sighed, and then splashed her face and took a few sips from her palm. Supper preparations would start soon. If she didn't hurry, she'd run out of time.

She brushed the dust from her worn, cotton skirt and rose to her feet, hoping she hadn't gathered more than she could carry. The wagons had been traveling for months, and fresh food was scarce. The plump onions and potatoes she'd dug were too good to resist.

Becca blew at a strand of hair that had come loose from her braid and settled the canteen strap diagonally across her chest, then bent down and grabbed two cloth sacks full of edible roots. Her arm muscles strained and her back protested the weight. The game knife she'd praised for helping her dig, she now cursed.

Oh, well. She'd find a way to make do. The others waiting back at camp would thank her for the fresh potato soup.

She balanced her load and walked on, lifting her eyes to the west, to the mountains in the distance with their jagged, snowcapped peaks. Each day, fear and elation warred in her chest. Leaving her home in Missouri for the dangers of the long trip west was the scariest thing she'd ever done. Even three months later, being out in the middle of nowhere gave her shivers.

The opportunities that awaited her and her family in California had made them all face their fears. Making a new home would take months of hard work. Years, really. But settling new land would be worth it. They would be blessed beyond their wildest dreams.

As she followed the occasional rock piles on her way back to camp, she had to set the sacks down to catch her breath and get a better grip from time to time. She'd hoped Nathan might come looking for her and help carry the load, but that was a foolish wish. His parents would never allow him to be out here with her alone—hers either.

A wistful smile crossed her lips. She'd have to content herself with what little contact they had, and with the fact their families had chosen the same destination. They'd live miles apart for a time. But then, one day, he'd come for her.

With fond thoughts of her beau lightening her steps, she followed the last of the rocks and rounded the large copse of trees that marked the edge of the clearing. At the sight of the empty prairie that stretched out before her, she set down the bags and shielded her eyes to look around. Where was everyone? Thirty wagons and six times as many oxen and people didn't just disappear.

She glanced down again at the rocks. There must be more than one path. Yes. That had to be it. She'd gotten confused and followed the wrong one back.

"Great," she muttered. "Now supper really *will* be late."

Lifting her bags, she turned to go back the way she'd come and froze. Her heart took flight, and shock stole the air from her lungs. Crates, chests, and other discarded belongings lay strewn along the edge of the clearing—the exact same ones she'd seen earlier that day.

The bags of vegetables slipped from her hands and hit the ground with a sickening thud. She clutched her stomach with one hand and covered her trembling lips with the other. She hadn't lost her way. They'd left. They'd gone and left her behind!

Becca bolted down the wagon trail, crying.

"Ma! Pa! Wait! Don't leave me! I'm here!"

She ran as fast as she could, ignoring the full canteen banging her hip and coughing from clouds of interminable dust. She was young and strong. And fast. The wagons moved slow, barely gaining fifteen miles in one day. If she kept running, she'd eventually catch up.

Fear surged higher as she came upon the site of the avalanche. A jagged bluff rose up to the right, and the cascade of rocks it had poured onto the trail lay parted like the Red Sea.

Her legs tangled in her skirts and she fell, but she pushed to her feet, hiked up her hem, and ran even faster. Tears streamed down her face and sharp pains seared her side, but she didn't stop. She couldn't stop. She was alone in the wild. She couldn't let them get away.

About a mile later, the ruts in the earth formed a Y and

veered in two different directions. Becca whimpered and dropped to the ground. Anguished sobs tore through the ragged breaths that heaved from her chest. Running was useless. She'd heard the men arguing over which route they would take, but she never heard which one they chose.

She lay in the dirt, weeping. What would become of her now? She couldn't survive on her own. If the loneliness didn't kill her, the lack of shelter and food would. She rolled to her back, swiped at her eyes and stared at the sky.

"Why, God? Why did you let this happen to me?"

Silence was her answer—a hot breeze blowing a few high clouds across the sky.

Becca sat up and dried her cheeks on her sleeves. Sniveling like a child would do her no good. She was a woman; Charlotte was right. It was time to start acting her age.

As she rose, she brushed the dirt and grass from her clothes and considered her options. She could choose a path and keep going, but night would fall soon. If she chose wrong, she would be stranded with no food and no shelter.

Winded by exertion and calmed by logic, Becca trudged back up the trail and returned to the spot she had left. Staying put was the best thing to do. When someone's child or ox wandered off, horse-mounted scouts were sent out to search. Surely they would do no less for her.

After dragging the bags of vegetables under the shade of some bushes, she perched on one of the crates and took a long pull of water from her canteen. Her brow furrowed. Her parents would have known she went for a walk. Wouldn't they have sent scouts to search for her before they even left camp?

Maybe they did and the men couldn't find her. She had gone a long way from the wagons.

She took another drink and capped the canteen. There had to

be an explanation. Her parents wouldn't just leave her behind.

At the snort of a horse in the distance, she leapt to her feet to go flag down the scout, but her blood ran cold when he came into view. It was a scout all right—a fierce-looking Indian scout sitting atop a huge stallion—and she dared not wait around to see if he was Apache or Sioux.

Becca crept back into the shelter of the trees before she could be spotted—at least that's what she hoped. The scout had turned his head in her direction just as she'd felt the cool shade of the leaves.

Body tingling with alarm, she turned and fled as fast as she could go, scraping past brush and leaping over rocks and fallen trees. Wind whipped her hair and branches stung her face. Her heart pounded and every muscle in her body burned, but she kept running, farther and farther, through groves of trees and over expanses of bare, rocky terrain.

Something cracked in the thicket behind her.

Becca whipped her head around and looked over her shoulder. Was he there?

Her foot struck something solid, sending her tumbling into a ravine. Sharp sticks bit her skin and her skull landed hard on a rock. Pain shot through her head and white light streaked her vision.

Lying amidst a clutter of boulders and dust, she curled into a ball and groaned.

"Ma... Pa," she whimpered as darkness swallowed her. "Come back."

Chapter Two

Something cold and wet dripped on her face. Becca raised a hand to her cheek and wiped it away. Another drop hit. Then another. She opened her eyes to swirling gray clouds moving across an angry sky.

She lifted her head and promptly lowered it again. "Ohhh." A crippling ache gripped her from the back of her neck all the way to her temples. Pain and nausea racked her whole body. She didn't want to move.

Lightning flickered across the sky and more drops of rain struck her face. She had no choice. She had to find shelter.

Becca sat up and looked herself over. Something dug into her thigh—her knife. The point of the sheath, to be precise, attached by a tether to her waist. She wiggled it free and slid it to the side, thankful the blade hadn't come loose and cut her on her way down. She bunched up her skirts and rolled back her sleeves, then ran her fingers over her face and her scalp. Other than a large bump on her head and several scrapes and bruises on her limbs, she seemed to be all right.

As she rose to her feet, a chill rippled through her. Where was the Indian? The last thing she remembered was him and running away. Listening, she glanced around.

Nothing. Just wilderness, ripe with the heavy scent of rain and alive with the rustling and creaking of a coming storm.

Wrinkling her nose at the way she smelled, Becca brushed the dirt from her clothing and straightened the canteen strap that still hung around her chest, then opened it and took a long drink. Despite the queasiness, her stomach growled as if she hadn't eaten in a week. How long had she been out?

Long enough she needed to relieve herself. Now.

She scrambled up the side of the ravine and hurried to the nearest thicket. Once she'd seen to her needs, she climbed onto a boulder and turned a slow circle to survey the land. Except for mountains and an occasional grove of trees, there was nothing but miles of scrubby, rocky terrain in every direction.

With a sigh, she slumped onto the rock. She was lost. She'd run so fast and so scared, she hadn't paid any mind to where she was going. And now, she didn't even have the aid of the sun.

Thunder cracked overhead, then rumbled and echoed across the land with an ominous sound. Rain pelted her with increasing measure. Finding her way back would have to wait. For now, securing safe shelter was far more important.

She glanced around again, then headed for a thick copse of bushes that was up on a hill and woven with vines. Becca knelt down and crawled inside the protective mass of vegetation. She tucked her skirts around her legs and clutched her knees to her chest, then drew the last biscuit from her pocket and choked the crumbs down as rain fell along with her silent tears.

Becca shivered and hugged herself with her arms. The rain had stopped sometime in the wee hours of the morning. Cold, damp clothes clung to her skin, and her braid lay like wet rope down her back. She shuddered and yawned. The night had been long and sleep had been scarce, but she'd managed to drift off now and then.

She drew aside the rain-speckled leaves in front of her. A pair of does across the clearing dipped their heads, drinking from puddles. When the breeze shifted, one doe lifted her head and perked up her ears. Seconds later, they bounded into the trees with a white flash of their tails.

Becca untangled her legs from the mass of damp skirts and wiggled her way out. The sky was surprisingly clear. Bright morning light filtered down through wispy clouds and reflected off newly-formed streams. She smoothed errant strands of hair from her face and breathed in the clean, moist air.

Standing on the same large rock as before, she scanned her surroundings. Then, using the position of the sun and the mountains to the west as her guides, she made up her mind and set her sights on her goal. It was time to find her way back to the trail and wait for the scouts the train captain would send. Ignoring the damp clothes clinging to her body and the growl of her empty stomach, she set out with a determined pace.

By what must have been at least an hour later, her early morning confidence was gone. She'd walked in the direction she thought led to the trail, but all she found was more untouched land. Pausing to rest on the trunk of a fallen tree, she took some sips from her canteen and mused her misfortune. If she didn't find her way back soon... Her heart sank and her stomach clenched. She didn't want to ponder her fate if that happened. She was growing hungrier and weaker by the hour. The only food she had, she'd left at the side of the trail.

Becca took one last sip and worked the stopper back into the canteen. A faint sound made her cock her head and perk up her ears. Water. It was the sound of rushing water.

The stream!

She shot to her feet. If she could find the stream, she could find the strange rocks, and if she found those, she could follow them back to the site of the camp.

She hurried toward the familiar sound until she stood on the banks of the small creek. Now which way? Upstream or down? She lifted her gaze and tried to recall how close the mountains appeared before. They had been smaller. Definitely smaller.

Downstream it was.

As she trotted along, Becca shook her head and let out a rueful laugh. How ironic. The very same sound that drowned out the noise of the wagon train leaving would be her salvation today.

She nearly shouted with joy when she saw the vegetable patch and the first pile of rocks. If she kept a brisk pace, she'd make it in time to flag down the scouts. She stopped long enough to dig two potatoes and rinse them in the stream, and then she peeled them, sliced them, and ate them as she followed the path.

When she neared the clearing, Becca slowed to a stop. What if the Indian was there? He apparently hadn't seen her, but that didn't mean he'd left or, if he had, that he wouldn't return. She'd have to watch for the scouts and stay hidden at the same time.

After making sure her stash of vegetables hadn't been found, she crouched down behind a large hutch that had been dumped.

17

Having nothing better to do, she busied herself picking the lock of a leather-bound trunk sitting nearby. Her conscience niggled her a bit, but the trunk's owner was long since gone and—whether grudgingly or not—had willfully left it behind. Maybe she'd find something to help pass the time.

When the lock finally gave way, she sheathed her knife and lifted the lid. Musty odors of leather, cloth and paper rose out as sunlight rushed in. Becca ran her hand over the marbled paper lining, fascinated by the swirled hues of blues, grays and purples. Compared to this, her family's trunks were plain. Some weren't even lined at all. With the care and reverence instilled in her from an early age, she inspected the contents and began to lift items out.

Beneath several pairs of shoes and stacks of folded clothes lay a generous assortment of books, including poetry, works of Shakespeare and tales by Dumas. She opened one of the covers and found the name Victoria inscribed in a looped and flowing hand. How strange it was to be sifting through someone else's life.

A gasp escaped her lips as she delved farther into the stack. *Jane Eyre... Pride and Prejudice.* Many settlers were forced to lighten their loads or risk failure on the trip. Still, she bemoaned that anyone would throw such treasures away. Becca lifted out a copy of *Wuthering Heights*, and then replaced the other items and closed the lid. After glancing around at the silent, deserted prairie, she settled herself with her back against the trunk and started reading.

Ten chapters later, the prairie was still silent and the sun was directly overhead. Hair heating and stomach complaining, she marked her place with a blade of dry grass and went in search of food and shade. She grabbed two potatoes and took shelter at the base of a tree. As she peeled them and munched on the crunchy raw roots, she wondered again about the scouts and how much ground they could cover in one day.

Men on horses could travel five times as fast as the wagons. Even if she'd missed them, they could double back a second day. And they would, wouldn't they?

Yes. Even if the others refused or gave up, Nathan would come. He was more than smitten. She wasn't blind to his guardian behavior toward her.

Sending a prayer heavenward for his protection and her safe return, she washed down the last of her lunch with some water and turned her attention back to the book.

When the sun slid lower in the sky, she peeled and ate two more potatoes. Then, when it slipped below the horizon, she crouched down behind the hutch and spread an old wool coat on the ground.

Becca blinked back tears as she bedded down for another lonely night.

Chilling dreams disturbed her sleep all night long, made worse by the blinding darkness and the damp air. Becca awoke as unsettled as she was unrested. And cold. She had no way to start a fire. She shook the dirt and grass from the coat she'd used as a bed and pulled it on. It was tattered and moth eaten, but it was warm.

As more silent hours ticked by, the hazy, disjointed images of her nightmares took on fearsome clarity. No one had come for her because something had stopped them. It was horrid to even imagine, but it was the only thing that made any sense.

Nothing was certain on the trail. Every traveler took the

chance of a mishap—broken wheel, broken bone, the occasional wild animal attack—but once in a while, an entire train would be wiped out. Often by illness, but sometimes by Indians.

Maybe the brave she'd seen hadn't been alone.

Becca couldn't stand the uncertainty any longer. Ignoring the rising fear twisting her insides and choking off her air, she ventured into the open and headed for the cliff that had poured rocks onto the trail. Its peak would raise her high enough to see for miles and learn what she needed to know.

Digging the toes of her boots into the red, rocky earth, she trudged her way up the back of the hill, tripping on her skirt several times as she went. Her muscles burned and her fingers rubbed themselves raw as the incline grew steeper and steeper, but she kept climbing and dragging herself upward. Sucking in great gulps of air and wincing in pain, she pulled herself the last few feet up and plopped onto the edge of the plain that formed the top. She sat for several minutes, catching her breath.

Becca stared toward the harmless east, postponing the inevitable moment of turning around. What if her parents and Nathan were strewn about the prairie, mutilated and rotting?

The more troubling question was what would it mean if they weren't?

Legs quivering from nerves and exertion, Becca rose to her feet. She waited until her muscles stopped twitching, and then she turned around and walked to the opposite edge.

A slow breath blew out between tense lips as her eyes took in the countryside. She focused on the point where the trail split, the place she'd stopped running the first day. Then she followed the upper fork west, as far as she could see.

Nothing but empty land.

Refilling her lungs, she turned her gaze south, praying for peace yet hoping for carnage.

There was no one... nothing. Not even a broken-down wagon.

Becca lowered her head. As she worked to accept the meaning of what she'd seen, her eyes were drawn to the piles of rocks that lay below. Their jagged edges combined with the dizzying distance to the ground would normally have set her stomach to twitching and flopping. The only sensation inside was the raw, disturbing twinge that came with being abandoned.

She lingered a few moments more. Then, numbly, she turned back and began her arduous descent.

Chapter Three

They never came.

Deserted. Unwanted. Left behind. Every day as she worked to sustain her existence, the words echoed, unrelenting, in her mind. But most of all, they haunted her at night—those endless, aching hours when darkness shut out all distractions from the truth.

Her family didn't want her. Nathan didn't want her.

If they did, they'd have found a way to come.

Nathan. The thought of his name made her wince. His betrayal hurt as much as that of her family. No. It hurt more.

Bitter thoughts rose like bile. After he promised to marry her, she'd spent her days in a giddy fog, daydreaming about her future. Their future. Now she chided herself for trusting him. "*Keating,*" she used to recite to herself with a dreamy smile. "*I'll be Mrs. Nathan Keating.*"

She hoped she'd never hear that name again.

Becca rubbed at the ache in her chest that had become a

constant companion. The only thing that hurt more than being left was the reason why. It wasn't for lack of knowing where she was. Charlotte had stayed behind to tell them. It wasn't for lack of food; they had plenty. That left only two things—either they couldn't come back and get her or they didn't want to. Every scrap of evidence she had pointed to the later.

The absence of bodies and burned out wagons had been both a relief and a cruel blow that confirmed her secret fear. Going to the stream alone had made her the subject of rumor. She'd ruined her reputation and lost everyone's respect. Including Nathan's.

Loading the last of her belongings onto a flat sled she'd fashioned from a discarded bookcase and some rope, Becca paused to look at the home she was preparing to leave. A mocking laugh bubbled up her throat. *Home.* But that's what it was—the tiny lean-to dwelling she'd built from branches and scraps of wood.

For the last eight weeks, it had kept her cool in the day, warm at night, and safe from storms. But now, she had to move on. Winter was coming, and her supply of firewood was dwindling. If she didn't find a warmer place to stay, she wouldn't survive the first snow.

After donning a pair of leather work gloves that were two sizes too big, Becca stepped inside the loop of rope and lifted it until it rested across her chest. She leaned against the weight and urged the load forward. The trek was slow and exhausting as she dragged the sled across rocky, uneven terrain, but she kept going. About a mile to the northwest, a larger, warmer home awaited her. The thought of living in a cave frightened her, but—unless she slept unprotected under the moon and stars—night was dark no matter where she was.

She kept trudging forward, pausing from time to time to

adjust the rope and take a sip from her canteen. Her load was heavy, but well worth the effort. She'd gleaned quite a lot from the crates and trunks desperate travelers left behind. If it hadn't been for that, she might not have found her new home. Using chanced-upon candles and matches, she'd investigated several caves until she found one that was suitable—and, she shuddered, uninhabited.

Bats, snakes, and bears were God's creatures, too, but she'd just as soon admire them from a distance. A very far distance.

By the time she reached the entrance, her chest was heaving and her body was damp with sweat. She plopped onto a rock to catch her breath and quench her thirst, but she didn't tarry long. Every moment her flat of possessions lay out here in the open, she was vulnerable. Erasing any clue to her presence was her first priority.

Survival depended on food and warmth, and on staying hidden.

Chapter Four

Eleven months and one day later

'*September 1ˢᵗ*

He visited me again today. While Ma was busy with the wash and Pa was fixing a broken fence in the south pasture, I snuck away to meet him, my golden-haired knight with eyes like the clearest blue pool. I know I shouldn't, but I can't help it. I quiver every time I see him. I have never felt like this before.

When he looks at me, my whole body feels like... like the birds of spring are taking flight in my chest all at once. And his touch makes me tingle, the way the hairs on my arms do when lightning strikes. He barely touches me, tells me we should wait, but sometimes he traces the curve of my face with his finger, making a warm trail that spreads through my whole body and leaves me wanting more. He always leaves me wanting more.

Today, he stared at my lips for a long time. I thought he might kiss me, but he closed his eyes and sighed. When he backed away, I could tell he wanted it as much as I did, maybe more. But he is a good man. He says he wants to do this proper, ask my father for my hand and wed me with his blessing. How can I tell him that never will be? It breaks my heart.

I am so torn.

Should I tell him the truth and convince him to wed me against my father's wishes, or should I keep meeting him and keep living this lie? I don't want to hurt him, but I don't want to lose him. He is my breath, my very life. If I am forced to live without him, I will die.'

Becca closed the diary and set it aside. She'd read it three times through already, and each time, the words pricked her as deeply as the first. She'd felt the same way about Nathan. Reading this stranger's diary gave her muted feelings new life. Painful life. That's why she now limited herself to reading one entry per day—the same day as the one she was actually living. It helped her keep track of the date. And it reminded her never to trust.

She'd resisted becoming embittered, but that battle she'd lost, thanks to a phenomenon she'd never quite understood. People made mistakes—sometimes serious ones—and were readily forgiven. Yet with other poor choices, even the *appearance* of evil caused the offender to be shunned.

Becca emerged from the cave and studied the sky. Winter was coming. Its first chilling storm would be here soon. She ducked back inside, pulled her sled from its hiding place, and left on her weekly quest to find wood. According to the calendar she'd made, she'd been here over a year. The first winter, she'd nearly frozen and nearly starved. Cold, hungry and thin, she'd met spring with dogged determination to plan better.

Dragging the sled behind her, she made her way along a new gathering route, stopping to pick up any usable piece of fallen wood. Wind-raked clouds hovered overhead like a blanket of shorn wool, and dry leaves crunched under her feet as she guided her growing load between gnarled bushes and shedding trees—stubborn leaves still fluttering on their branches.

Halfway back to the cave, she froze stock still when the whinny of a horse rent the air. The horse whinnied again. Hoof beats trailed off at a brisk pace. Then silence.

A whoosh of air left her lungs. Whoever it was had ridden away.

With her heart pounding and her skin stinging with fright, Becca urged her load toward home. This hunt was over. She'd not crossed paths with another living soul since the Indian scout that first day, and she was determined to keep it that way.

As she climbed the last big rise, the sled's rope dug into her gloved hands, but she didn't care. She needed to get home, get hidden. And her path was mostly flat land from here.

A strange noise stopped her in her tracks.

Trembling, Becca scanned the area ahead.

Her hand flew to her mouth and her heart stuttered in her chest. A man lay sprawled on the ground!

She glanced around to make sure he was alone.

Seeing no one else, she steadied her sled on the hilltop and crept closer. The man lay flat on his back with his eyes closed. He wasn't moving. He'd groaned—she'd heard him—but now he looked as if he were sleeping. Was it a trick?

She glanced around again, then picked up a stick and nudged him with it.

Nothing.

She nudged harder.

Not even a wince.

The man—a young man, not much older than she—wore a blue work shirt, light brown trousers and boots. Dust covered his clothes, and scratches marred his forearms.

Becca laid the stick aside, then chewed her lip. Part of her wanted to run, but...

She studied him again. The horse she'd heard must've been his. Yes. That made sense. He'd been thrown. This poor man was stranded and hurt. She couldn't just walk away.

She slipped off her gloves and stuffed them in her skirt pocket, then knelt beside him, wringing her tremulous hands. *Make sure nothing's broken. Tend his wounds.* She'd seen plenty of injuries during her months on the trail, even helped doctor a few, but she wished now she'd paid better attention.

Warily, she reached for his shoulders, pressing down and running her fingers along his collar bones. They were straight and firm, so she turned her attention to his arms. Starting with the right, she wrapped her hands around his muscles—big muscles, even when flaccid at rest—and squeezed, over and over, as she inched her way down to his wrist. Nothing popped, bent, or crunched under her grasp. *Thank goodness.* Now the left.

Becca hesitated. This was the arm that didn't look so good, his forearm anyway. It wasn't crooked, but it was swollen and beginning to bruise. She took a deep breath and did what she had to do. His upper arm was fine, so she braced herself and continued slowly down, past his rolled up cuff. A soft groan came out with his next breath, but nothing beneath her fingers felt like a break.

His hands looked fine, but she checked them anyway. Except for some scrapes and the usual calluses, they were uninjured.

Becca laughed at herself. She was stalling. She needed to check his hips and his legs, but... well... she glanced over both shoulders. It wasn't exactly proper.

Of course, no one was around to see—or to help. No man to take over the task. She was it and this had to be done.

She positioned her hands either side of his hips and let them hover there. Then, with her eyes shut, she pressed in. Nothing.

Opening one eye a bit, she ran her hands around back, then

up where the bones ended just under his waist. Whew. She sat back and slung her hands several times to fling away the tension. And a tingle. Now his legs. *Oh, my.*

Lord, forgive me, she prayed as she reached for his thigh.

Becca checked each long leg as she had with each arm. They were muscled and lean. Even slack with unconsciousness, this man's body impressed her. It was obvious her patient worked hard. And it was obvious he'd look twice as good standing up with his wits about him.

A warm current sizzled through her. She savored it, then chided herself just the same. What was wrong with her? The poor man was injured, and here she was, going all wanton over some unconscious stranger.

If her Aunt Prudence was right, she'd just secured a prime spot in hell.

Becca moved back up until she was next to his arm. His breathing wasn't terribly shallow, but she needed to check his chest. Figuring she'd long since forfeited her ticket to the pearly gates, she slid his suspenders aside and unbuttoned his shirt.

Mercy! Was the bolt of shock from the bruises staining his side? Or from the rippled wall of skin and muscle that was his chest? She had to check his ribs, but she nearly refused. Touching such a manly form would certainly send her over the edge.

Tarnation. What choice did she have? She had to care for the poor soul. Even if it meant sacrificing her own.

Ignoring the soft tufts of tan hair that brushed against her palms, Becca ran her hands over the man's chest and down to his waist. When she pressed the bruises that lay over his ribs, another moan came out with his breath. His eyes fluttered open, then closed again.

She needed to check his back, so she crossed to his good side and tugged at him until he rolled almost all the way over.

A louder moan came out this time.

His shirt was dirty, but it wasn't torn or stained with blood. When she was satisfied she'd missed nothing, she rolled him back and he moaned again.

The man's eyes fluttered open. He blinked several times, then drew his brows together and mumbled something as Becca buttoned up his shirt.

"What did you say?"

"Aa—" He cleared his throat. "Am I dead?"

She angled her head so her face lined up with his. "No. Why would you think that?"

"A... Angel," he said as his blue eyes searched hers.

"What?"

"Yuh... You're an angel."

Becca couldn't keep from smiling. "I'm not an angel." *Ha. Far from it.* If he only knew her thoughts. Besides, angels were male. Everyone knew that.

"I'm dead. Gotta be." He mumbled again, something about 'angels' and 'heaven,' and closed his eyes.

"Mister." She shook his shoulder. "Mister."

No answer. Just the soft snores of an exhausted man.

Becca sighed. She'd let him sleep. He'd probably hurt less that way anyhow.

She pushed herself up and sat on a nearby rock. Lifting her skirt, she tore a wide strip from the bottom of her chemise. His ribs weren't broken, but they were badly bruised, a few of them possibly cracked. She'd bind them—for his comfort, if nothing else.

His hat lay a few feet away and she went to retrieve it. She settled back down next to him and looked inside. No name.

Nothing tucked in the band that she could see, but there was a gouge in the side of the felt. Was it new?

Becca set the hat and the fabric aside. She brushed back locks of sandy blond hair from his face. There was nothing on his forehead, just a scratch on his cheek, so she ran her hands over his scalp. As her fingers slid through the wavy strands, the tension of his features eased. Then her hand brushed up against a bump, and a small groan vibrated in his throat.

She lifted his head as much as she dared and found a persimmon-size lump behind his left ear. She parted the hair and looked closer. No cuts and no blood—good. But the fact he'd hit his head bothered her. Some people went to sleep and never woke up.

Becca swallowed, her throat now dry. He'd woken up and talked to her. That was good, right? He'd called her an angel, sure, but that was only logical. He was out in the middle of unsettled land, with no one for miles upon miles. Waking up to a woman, even one as plain and dowdy as she, would make anyone think the worst.

With that shred of reasoning bolstering her, she set about binding his ribs. He moaned several times through the process, but didn't once open his eyes.

She refastened his shirt and replaced his suspenders, then took a long look at his arm. It probably wasn't broken, but she used the last of the fabric and some sticks to splint it all the same. After she tied the last strip, she rested his forearm across his body and tucked it under one of his suspenders to hold it in place.

Having done all she could for him, Becca brushed off her skirt and stood up. What now? She couldn't take him back to her cave, but she couldn't leave him out here either. She hugged herself and scanned the surrounding sky. A hazy gray mist hung in the air to the east, and the wind was picking up. Just as she'd feared, a storm was brewing. She'd known it since watching the sun rise red that morning.

She'd have to get them both to shelter. And soon.

Chapter Five

Becca hurried back to the man. She'd left him long enough to gather necessary items from her cave, then returned to figure out what to do. The rope and tarp she'd brought could yield a modest tent, but this was no small storm. She looked at him, and then back at the sky. How was she going to keep them both safe?

She waited as long as she dared for his horse to come back, but the animal was nowhere to be seen. Not even a snort or whinny in the distance. Of course, she couldn't have lifted the man onto the horse herself, and he was in no condition to mount up and ride. She'd either have to make a shelter here or... her old home. She would take him to her old, lean-to home.

With a huff of determination and a pang of regret, Becca dumped the firewood from her sled and dragged it over to the man. She rolled him onto his good side again, and then slid the sled under him as far as she could. It took several minutes of nudging, heaving and tugging, but she finally got him centered with a blanket over him and her belongings packed securely around him. She even managed to fit several pieces of wood.

Settling the rope across her chest and through her gloved hands, she leaned into the weight and trudged toward her nearly-forgotten home.

Her hands stung and her legs burned as she dug her boots into the rocky soil and dragged the sled along. The man wasn't small, but even so, his size was deceiving. She hadn't pulled anything so heavy since moving her belongings to the cave. By the time they reached the thicket that concealed her old shelter, she was panting like a dog on a summer day and sweating so much that large, wet patches covered her clothes.

Thank goodness the man was still sleeping. She probably looked a fright.

An angel from heaven—ha. Becca giggled. If he woke to her now, he might think he'd gone the other way.

After pausing to rest and take a deep drink from her canteen, she eased through an opening in the foliage and inspected her abandoned dwelling. She'd ducked into it a time or two when she'd been caught in a sudden downpour, but that hadn't happened for months.

Becca grasped the edge of the wood slab that formed the sharply-slanted roof and tugged. Still sturdy. The sides made of wood scraps and branches were also intact, and they had been strengthened by invading vines. Nice. She peered around inside as best she could with the burgeoning storm clouds blocking out the light, making high noon as dull as dusk. No being— human or otherwise—had taken up residence. *Thank goodness.* Now all she had to do was get the man and the supplies moved inside.

She eyed the dirt floor of the hut. The interior wasn't much wider than an outhouse, and not nearly as tall, but it was fairly deep. If she could get the sled through the surrounding bushes and trees and into the hidden clearing, she could slide it right in. Not only would it simplify the move, it would give them a smooth floor and raise them several inches above the runoff.

Becca had to pull the sled around the side of the thicket to reach a space that was wide enough to accommodate it, but she managed. Before long, she was lining it up with opening of the hut and shoving it inside.

She crouched down and carefully stepped around her patient, arranging her supplies. Then, as the first drops of rain spotted the dusty ground, she secured the large piece of oiled canvas so that it covered the open end of the hut, sealing them in.

Darkness engulfed them and Becca shivered. She was stuck in a small dark space with a large strange man. As soon as the tarp shut out the cold and the wind, his heady scent surrounded her along with her fear. Through odors of dirt and sweat, arose a scent that was decidedly male. Fresh air and leather blended with warm, spicy skin.

Becca knelt beside him and lit a candle so she could check on him one more time. The flickering flame cast eerie shadows on the walls, but it gave off a comforting light. The stranger's face looked less intimidating in the pale glow, rather boyish and peaceful in sleep. The only thing that gave away his age, besides his size, was the shadow of whiskers that shaded his jaw. Becca reached out to touch it, then pulled her hand back. What was she doing?

She sat back on her heels and looked her patient over. His clothes were those of a common man, but they were in good repair. He didn't have a beard—save a day or two's growth—so he must shave. And bathe. The smell of soap mingled with his scent.

The storm arrived. Rain pelted the tiny structure and dripped through the cracks.

Becca tucked the blanket in around the man, then huddled against the wall under a smaller one of her own. With one last glance in his direction, she blew out the candle and plunged them into darkness.

Chapter Six

"Get away from her!" an enraged voice growled.

Becca screamed as an arm landed a heavy blow to her shoulder. Her heart pounding, she scrambled back into the corner of the hut, unsheathed her knife, and clutched the grip.

"I said, get away!"

It sounded like the man. He was thrashing in the dark next to her, but who was he yelling at? She didn't sense anyone else in the room.

"Don't do this." His tone became fearful. Pleading, almost. "No! Rachel!"

Rachel?

"No! No, Rachel, no..." His shouts decayed into sobs.

Becca pressed a hand to her chest and blew out the breath she'd been holding. He must be dreaming. "Mister." She nudged him with the toe of her boot. "Mister. Wake up."

He swung at her again, barely missing the knife.

"Mister! Wake up! You're having a dream!"

"Rachel?"

"No, I'm not Rachel." Becca lit the candle as quickly as she could.

The man squinted and threw a hand over his eyes, then lowered it and looked at her as if she had three heads.

"Relax. You're safe."

He looked around. "Where am I?"

Becca sheathed her knife and wedged the candle safely between two of the branches. "You're..." How should she answer that? "You're in southern New Mexico Territory, just west of the Rio Grande. I found you lying unconscious on the ground. A storm was coming, so I brought you here."

He studied her again—she must only have two heads now.

"Are you thirsty?"

He nodded, still studying her.

Becca lifted her canteen from its resting place against the wall.

"Ahhh," he groaned. He'd tried to sit up.

"You're hurt. Stay where you are." She bundled up her blanket and placed it under his head, then opened the canteen and held it to his lips. "Here. Drink some."

He pulled away and eyed her with suspicion.

"It's just water."

He hesitated, then placed his lips against the spout. After the first sip, he tipped it up and drank so greedily he nearly choked.

"Easy. There's plenty." She gave him his fill and capped the canteen. "Are you hungry?"

He relaxed against the rolled blanket and shook his head, wincing with the movement.

Becca sorted through her things and fished around in a cotton sack. The candle barely gave off enough light to see inside, and it took her a while to find what she was searching for. She pulled out two potatoes and a bag of dried fruit. "Are you sure? I have enough to—"

His eyes were closed. His head lay lolled to one side, and his breathing was slow and deep.

A smile tugged at her lips. His face was lax again—long, brown lashes grazing his cheeks and lips full and round, now that they weren't stretched thin with doubt. *Handsome*, she thought as she settled her back against the wall. He was certainly handsome.

She drew out her knife and peeled a potato, then sliced it and ate as the slowing rain pattered against the roof. She couldn't tell if it was day or night, but she didn't care. They were stuck there till the storm passed anyway.

Becca started to peel the second potato, then set it aside. Better to save it. Once the man got his appetite back, he'd be hungry as a bear. She cleaned her knife, nibbled on some dried berries, and then put the knife and the food away.

After slipping outside to relieve herself, she crouched down and ducked back into the hut, careful not to clomp her boots and jar the sled. The man was still sleeping... and, she frowned, he had both blankets. That was a problem. She didn't fear a freeze, but her clothes were damp and the temperature was dropping by the hour. With the sled covering most of the floor, there was no room inside the hut for a fire, and the rain would douse it if she put it outside.

Becca chewed her lip and pondered her predicament. She finally snuffed out the candle and lay with her back to the man, then tugged at the edge of the blanket and scooted closer still. Aunt Prudence wouldn't approve. Heck, most everyone she knew wouldn't approve, but she was cold. And they weren't here.

As the stranger's heat warmed her spine and his snores

brushed her ears, she decided there was no harm in breaking the rules for the sake of survival. It was prudent to stay warm and dry. And it was nice not to be alone.

"Mmm." Becca nuzzled closer to the warm, solid mass pressed against her cheek. The fabric under her skin was soft and the heat seeping through it was pure heaven.

"Miss." A deep, raspy sound vibrated her face. "Miss?"

She bolted upright and stared into blue eyes fixed on hers. She must have rolled over sometime in the night. She'd been asleep with her head on the stranger's—oh, dear—on his chest! "I... I..." Becca scrambled out from underneath the blanket. "I'm sorry. I—" Heat blazed from her neck to the roots of her hair.

Seeming unfazed by her proximity or her mortification, the man threw back the blanket and attempted to sit up. "Owww." He lay back down, clutching his side and his head. After taking several breaths, he tried again.

"Don't." Becca knelt next to him. "You're hurt. Remember?" She touched his arm, then jerked her hand back and patted the air instead. "You should stay put."

"I need to get up." He propped on one elbow and prepared to rise a third time.

"Mister, please. You hit your head and probably cracked some ribs when you fell. I'll get you whatever you need, but you must stay put."

"I've got to get up. I need to make use of your outhouse."

"Oh." Becca reached for a rusty can in the corner and handed it to the man. "Here. Use this and call for me when you're done." She got up to leave, but the look on his face stopped her. She was back to having three heads.

"I can't use this." Disgust thickened his tone.

"Why not? You used it yesterday."

"I did?"

Becca nodded. "You were in and out of consciousness, and you were in no condition to walk. It was the only way."

"I don't remember." His gaze dropped to the buttons on his pants, and the color of his cheeks deepened. "Please tell me you didn't have to..."

She wondered if her face was as red as his. "No. You were able to do everything for yourself except empty the can."

Embarrassment fled and his brow turned as dark as a thundercloud. If he were more able-bodied, she'd have been scared.

He tossed the can aside with a loud clank. "I'm not an invalid. Help me up." He gritted his teeth in a twisted expression of pain and pushed himself into a sitting position. When she didn't move, he glared at her. "Help me up!"

Becca flinched, but she did as he asked.

Acting as a human crutch—something for which she was a good height, even bent over—she pushed aside the canvas and helped him out of the hut. The man groaned as he straightened up. His face was pale in the morning light and his forehead glistened with a sheen of sweat.

"You okay?" she asked.

He nodded.

He wasn't, but she didn't argue.

The man took a few steps more and looked around.

"There isn't an outhouse. You'll just have to—"

"I get the picture," he ground out.

She tried to walk with him to the thicket, but he pushed her away and staggered there by himself. When he reached the trees and caught hold of one, she turned around and went inside.

The man was gone quite a while, but Becca resisted the urge to check on him. She shoved down the worries rising up from her gut and busied herself laying out some food in the dappled light. She was glad for her new cave home, but part of her missed this place—especially this time of day. Even with the solid roof and the canvas in place, the sun found its way through the walls.

"Miss?"

Becca shot to her feet—*ouch*. She whirled around and rubbed her head where it struck the roof.

"I—" He motioned to the place where he'd slept. "I need your help." He looked weak and paler than before.

Becca hurried to the man's side and helped him lie down. The whimper of a moan that escaped his throat made her wince with him. He must really hurt.

Once he was situated, she gave him a few sips from the canteen. "Would you like something to eat?"

He wiped his mouth with his sleeve and shook his head. "Not right now." When he closed his eyes and rested his head on the rolled blanket again, a shaft of light illuminated his face. He was terribly pale, almost green, and the tiny beads of sweat hadn't dried in the cool morning breeze.

Becca fetched a cloth and returned to his side. She wet it with water from the canteen and proceeded to mop his brow.

His eyes opened and he stared at her. Her hand paused as his gaze traveled from her eyes to her nose to her lips and back again.

"I'm sorry to put you to all this trouble," he said.

A slight smile curved her lips, and she pressed the cloth to his face again. "It's no trouble."

Once his color improved, Becca laid the cloth aside and settled herself against the opposite wall. "Will it bother you if I eat in front of you?"

"Nah."

She pulled some dried fruit from her bag and nibbled on it as unobtrusively as possible.

"My name's Seth," he finally said. "Seth Emerson."

"Nice to meet you, Seth." She took another bite of fruit.

"What about you?"

"Hm?"

"Do you have a name?"

Becca stopped chewing. She bought herself time by taking a drink from her canteen. Maybe it would wash down the lump that had formed in her throat. How should she answer?

Once the stranger was able, he would leave. What would it matter? "Angel."

He studied her, his clear blue eyes filled with questions his lips held at bay.

Becca's heart thudded in the silence. Did he remember calling her that? Did he know she was lying? She looked away and took another sip from her canteen.

"Where am I?"

Now she studied *him*. "You don't remember?"

Seth shook his head.

Becca capped the canteen and set it aside. She told him again where they were and that she'd found him unconscious. Instead of the glazed look he'd given her the first time, his face lined with genuine concern.

"How far away from here was I?"

"'Bout half a mile."

He looked her up and down. "How'd you get me here?"

Becca inclined her head. "The wood you're lying on is a flat sled. I loaded you on it and dragged you here." His mouth fell open and she bit back a grin. Three heads again. Maybe four. "I'm stronger than I look, you know."

He frowned. "Apparently."

"I waited as long as I could for your horse—"

Seth came up off the pillow and cursed. When she stiffened, he blushed and looked at her from under those long lashes of his—a look his mother probably got a lot when he was little. "Beg pardon. I didn't mean any disrespect. I just can't believe I forgot about Cyrus. I musta hit my head pretty hard." He lowered himself again and sighed. "Everything I own was on that horse. All I got now are the clothes on my back."

"And your life."

He looked at her full on now. "You're right," he replied, even though the look in his eyes said he thought his life wasn't much worth saving. He held her gaze, but it looked to be a struggle. "I don't recall thanking you for bringing me here and taking care of me. So... thank you."

Becca set aside the food and brushed off her hands. "Wasn't anything special. I'd have done the same for anyone. I'd be a pretty poor excuse for a human being if I'd left you there—" She swallowed past another sudden lump, then managed a pleasant expression. "Speaking of clothes, I have a spare outfit that's about your size. If you like, you can change, and I'll wash the ones you're wearin'."

Three heads again. *Men.* Did he think she'd put him in a dress?

"Do whatever you wish," she said, pulling a gray pair of trousers and a white shirt from among her supplies, "but today is wash day. You can change and let me do your wash, or you can stay in your grimy things and hold your peace." *And I'll hold my nose.*

"Whose clothes are those?"

"Does it matter?"

He narrowed his eyes. When he held out his hands, she tossed him the clothes.

She placed a basin of water nearby, along with some soap and a cloth. "Can you manage by yourself?" Seth nodded, so she rose to leave.

"Wait. Can you help me with my boots before you go?" He looked like a whipped puppy. Was it really so hard to ask for help?

"Of course." Becca straddled his leg with her back to him and pulled, freeing his foot, then did the same for the other. She set his boots neatly in the corner. "Anything else?"

"No. Thank you."

"I'll be back after a while," she said as she pushed the canvas aside and stepped out. "Take your time."

Chapter Seven

Seth awoke to the sight of the slanted wood ceiling, still surprised by it after three days. He stood and rolled the stiffness from his shoulders, then pulled back the canvas door of the hut only to stop when he saw Angel a few feet away.

She was kneeling on the ground with her back to him, dipping a cloth into a basin of water and washing her face. The soles of her boots peeked out from under the hem of her skirt, and her shirt, still tucked at the waist, hung inside out over her hips. The only thing covering her upper body was the sleeveless top of her chemise. Her honey-colored hair hung in a braid to her waist, and her skin was creamy white. There wasn't much to her at all, she was thin, but the way her muscles shifted and sloped with every move revealed the source of her remarkable strength.

Remarkable. The word described the woman in every way. Angel—or whatever her name was. She'd lied about that, he was sure—was a very big puzzle in a very small package.

Stubborn as a mule and twice as mysterious. Every time he tried to get information out of her, she'd turn mute or change the subject.

Truth be told, he couldn't be sure she *wasn't* an angel. Except for an outpost being built quite a ways to the south, there wasn't an ounce of civilization for at least eighty miles. Why a woman would live alone in the wilderness baffled him. And *how* baffled him more.

As Angel squeezed out the cloth and began washing her arms, a clash of conscience struck. This wasn't right. A gentleman would turn away or make his presence known.

Seth stepped out of the hut and cleared his throat.

Angel dropped the cloth and grabbed for her shirt, stuffing her arms in the sleeves as if her life depended on it.

Way to go, imbecile. You interrupted her bath and embarrassed her in the process.

She glanced back as she pulled the shirt on. A shaft of light lit the fine fringe of her hair, outlining her face in glowing strands of gold—and pointed to a purplish bloom of blue on the front her shoulder.

Seth closed the distance between them in three long strides. "What's that?" he asked, reaching for the bruise.

Angel shrank from his touch. "It's nothing."

"It's not *nothing*, Angel. What happened?" Had she lied about being alone? She was getting supplies from somewhere. "How did you get it?" he demanded.

She pulled her shirt closed and shrank from him even more.

"Did someone hit you?" His blood boiled at the thought.

She nodded.

He'd gladly beat the bastard. "Who?"

She lifted her hesitant gaze until it met his. "You."

Seth's lungs seized at her reply. He wished she were lying,

but the candor in her pale, round eyes told him otherwise. Angel may have lied about her name, about other things she'd said, but she wasn't lying about this.

He dropped to his knees. "How? When did I do this to you?"

She turned away and buttoned her shirt, then faced him again. "It happened the first night you were here. You had a dream—a nightmare, more like. You were yelling at someone and you struck me with your arm."

Seth nearly muttered a curse, but he stopped himself. Now it made sense, why she recoiled from him whenever he showed the least sign of anger.

Angel brushed his forearm with her slender fingers. "It was an accident, Seth. You didn't mean to hurt me. You didn't know what you were doing. In fact, I think you were trying to protect someone. At first, I thought it was me, but..." Her hand fell away. "You were just dreaming."

"Did I hurt you any place else?"

"No."

"I'm sorry for striking you." Seth raked his hand through his hair. "I can't believe I don't remember any of this."

"You hit your head. You were in and out of consciousness for the better part of a day. Don't blame yourself. I don't."

He blew out a breath and nodded a reluctant acceptance, then rose to his feet and offered Angel his hand.

She stood and brushed the leaves from her skirt. "Can I ask you something?"

"Sure."

"Who's Rachel?"

Guilt grabbed his heart and squeezed until a wave of icy detachment pried it loose and shut it down. "No one important." He frowned and walked away, hoping The

Almighty wouldn't strike him dead for uttering the lie of the century.

"Seth."

He kept walking.

Footsteps hurried after him. "Seth, wait."

Fisting his hands, he spun around and glared. "I said she's no one important!"

Angel took a step back.

He closed his eyes and drew a deep breath. What was wrong with him? This woman had helped him. Been nothing but kind. She, of all people, didn't deserve his wrath.

He looked at her again and relaxed his frame. "I'm sorry. I didn't mean to yell. I'd rather not talk about it."

She fiddled with the end of her braid hanging over her shoulder. "I wasn't going to ask you about that. I was going to show you something. A surprise." She dropped her arm to her side and shrugged. "That is, if you'll let me."

Guilt gripped his heart a second time. "Of course I will."

A smile lit her face like the noontime sun. "Good. Follow me."

She led him out of the thicket surrounding the hut, to a nearby stand of trees almost as dense as the place they'd left.

"I don't get it," he said, looking around at the nondescript grove of vegetation. "What's the surprise?"

Angel held up a finger. "Wait right here." With a glance over her shoulder that was as delighted as it was mischievous, she pushed aside some limbs and disappeared into the trees.

Seth waited, staring at the wilderness around him. *Women.* What could Angel possibly be so excited about? If it wasn't September, he'd bet a whole dollar she'd found nothing more than a cache of wild berries or some other frivolous thing. Well, probably not frivolous to her. He still wondered how she found enough to eat.

A rustling noise to his left caught his attention. And the sight of what had made it stole his breath.

There was Angel, walking around the edge of the trees toward him and holding the lead line to a big brown horse.

"You found Cyrus!" Seth practically ran to them. He exchanged a nuzzle with his prodigal companion, and then looked him over from head to hoof. The animal was likely beyond weary of his saddle, and he'd picked up a scratch or two, but he seemed unharmed.

Seth turned to Angel, who was beaming like a parent on Christmas. "Where? How?"

"I went for a walk early this morning and found him wandering near the place you were thrown. He seemed all right, so I watered him, tied him here to graze, and decided to wait till you woke up." She let out a laugh. "Good thing the wind cooperated. One whiff of you, and he might have spoiled my surprise."

Seth grinned and shook his head. "I'm surprised all right. And surprised he let you get that close. Cyrus is a good horse—don't get me wrong—but he doesn't always take too well to strangers."

Angel smiled at the horse. "You didn't give me any trouble at all, did ya, Cyrus?" She stroked his neck and gave him a nuzzle of her own.

Seth took the lead from her, and they began walking back toward the hut. "I still can't believe it. When he didn't show up after a day or two, I figured he was gone for good. I thought I was going to be stuck out here forever."

Angel wasn't beaming anymore.

"I'm sorry. I didn't mean it like that."

She looked up with a reluctant curve of her lips. "It's okay. I know what you mean."

She didn't say much more the rest of the way. And could he blame her? She'd rescued him and seen to his every need for the last three days—happily—and he'd up and spouted off like he wasn't the least bit grateful. Like he couldn't escape her presence fast enough.

Well, he'd fix that. In return for her kindness, he'd take her from her godforsaken home and bring her with him. A woman had no business living out here on her own anyway.

Chapter Eight

Seth resettled the game bag strap biting into his shoulder as he hiked back to the thicket hiding the lean-to. He'd spent most of the afternoon hunting and enjoying the solitude. He'd been on his own quite a while. The time alone felt familiar.

So why did he miss Angel so much?

She had saved his hide—he'd give her that—but he barely knew her. And, as people went, she could be plenty annoying. Most *mules* he knew had less of a stubborn streak.

Looking around, he had to admire her for one thing. The girl knew how to stay out of sight. If she hadn't shown him the hut where she lived, he would never have known it was there.

Still, he didn't like the idea of her being here all alone. As he'd trudged through the woods hunting supper, he'd concocted a plan to talk her into leaving with him. He'd learned how to spot when she was being untruthful. It wasn't foolproof, but a little muscle near her mouth tugged at her lips when she was about to tell a lie.

Seth smiled. His Angel was stubborn. Little did she know, she'd met her match.

When he slipped through the opening into the clearing, he found her stoking the fire and preparing to cook.

"If you don't mind," she called over her shoulder without looking, "could you wash up and help me clean some fish?"

"I will." He walked closer. "After I clean these."

Angel's eyes went wide at the wild turkey and rabbits he laid at her feet. He could've given her a melon-sized nugget of gold and she wouldn't have looked more surprised.

"I'd have brought you back a deer, but this was the best I could do with my sidearm." Warmed by the wealth of gratitude in her eyes, he wished now he'd taken his rifle.

"Oh, Seth. This is wonderful! I so wanted to make you a special supper for your last night here, but I don't have a lot to offer in the way of food."

Truer words were never spoken. If he had to eat one more meal of potatoes, fish and dried fruit, he'd go insane. But she shared it gladly, and he couldn't fault her for that. In fact, he worried she was using up her winter stores to feed him.

Angel glanced at four small trout she'd caught while he was gone. "Should we even bother with the fish?"

"Sure. Cook it all. We can have a feast tonight, then eat whatever's left for breakfast in the morning. And," he added, "I have flour and saleratus in my bag. Think you could whip us up some biscuits?"

Angel nodded, and he swore he saw her drool.

Her infectious smile spread to his face. "Good. Between the two of us, we'll have one heck of a supper."

Seth prepared the game, then crafted a spit out of wood. He cleaned smaller branches to spear the rabbit and fish, and a larger one to hold the turkey. By the time the meat was done roasting over the fire, Angel had cooked the potatoes and biscuits. She'd even used a little of the dough along with some of his sugar and her berries to make a small cobbler.

Seth retrieved a pair of tin plates and forks from his bag. They served themselves and settled on pieces of felled logs opposite the pile of flickering coals from each other.

"Mmm," Angel hummed as she chewed her first bite—the turkey—her eyes rolling back in her head. "Thmis ms gmood." She blushed. "Sorry," she said once she'd swallowed. "I haven't had meat in a long time."

Seth lifted his canteen and washed down a tasty bite of rabbit. "What do you eat?"

"Fish, mostly. I manage to snare a rabbit now and then, but I don't try very hard."

"Why not?"

Her gaze cut to the side, then back. "I don't like what I have to do to them when I catch them."

"There's no shame in killing animals for food."

"I know. But it's not as easy when you have to do it up close."

"You don't have a gun?"

She shook her head. "Just a hunting knife. And some string and hooks for fishing."

Seth's mouth fell open. "What else do you eat besides fish and the occasional rabbit?"

"Well, potatoes and berries, as you've seen."

He nodded and tried not to grimace.

"In the spring and summer, things are better. I gather wild greens, onions, dandelions—that kind of thing. I also plant my own lettuce and greens, then collect the seeds when the plants bolt. And, of course, I eat fresh berries instead of dried." She bit into a biscuit with a more ecstatic look than the one from the turkey.

Seth narrowed his eyes as he picked up one of his own. "What about grain? Bread?"

Twitch. "I have some now and then." She was hedging.

He started to pursue it, then changed his mind. He leaned back against the side of the hut, stretched out his legs, and crossed his boots at the ankles. "How long have you lived here?"

Angel tossed the turkey bone into the fire and reached for a piece of rabbit. "A little over a year."

He gestured, indicating the general area. "Here?"

She studied him, and then nodded... took a bite of rabbit.

He wanted to barrage her with questions, but he kept it nonchalant. "Where are you from?"

She swallowed, with some difficulty it seemed, and set down the rabbit. Her cheek twitched again, but then she looked him in the eye. "Missouri."

Probably truth, but if he went down that road any further, he might get a lie.

Seth decided to let up. His questions could wait. This poor girl finally had a decent meal in front of her. It'd be cruel to put her off it now. "I'm from back east, too. Ohio, originally."

The line between her brows eased and she reached for the rabbit. *Good.*

He took a sip from his canteen, and then took a bite of potatoes for Angel's sake. Paired with the turkey and rabbit, it wasn't bad. "I'm currently working with some men building an outpost about seventy miles southeast of here. That's why I'm here. I was doing some scouting for them when I was thrown."

"An outpost?" Her brow creased again.

Seth nodded, not sure what to make of her frown. "This seems to be about the spot where travelers get desperate, start dumping excess weight, and run low on supplies—especially those coming from Texas. The men I work for figure locating a store—a trading post of sorts—where the trails from Texas and Santa Fe meet will help the wagon trains and make the three of them rich at the same time."

She seemed to relax a little. "So you're going to work there?"

"No. I'm just making some money before moving on."

"Oh. Where are you headed?" Her inquisitive eyes searched his. Was that disappointment he'd heard in her tone?

Seth spooned some of the cobbler onto his plate. "I'm not entirely sure," he said, leaning back again. "I thought I might go to work for the railroad until I heard several cattle ranches in Texas are looking for hands." He took a bite. *Mmm.* Plumped up and sweetened, the berries weren't bad either. "This is really good."

Angel gave him one of her smiles. Even in the gathering dark, it lit up the night.

Seth paused before taking another bite. He wanted more of those smiles.

While they finished their supper and polished off the cobbler, he entertained Angel with stories about his travels and Cyrus' antics. Her eyes twinkled, and her musical laughter rose with the tiny sparks floating up from the fire. As he glimpsed the real person behind the wall she'd put up, his plan became more than repayment for her kindness, more than a simple act of good will.

She was no longer some random woman alone in the woods. She was real to him now. He'd never intended it to happen, but she'd found a place in his heart.

Angel tossed the last of the bones into the fire. She rinsed and dried the plates and forks and gave them back to him, then placed what was left of the rabbit, turkey and potatoes in a metal tin.

She pointed to the fish. "Think it'll keep till morning?" Neither one of them had touched a single trout.

Normally he would have said no, but a winter storm was coming. "I think it will. The temperature's been dropping all day. It wouldn't surprise me if we have a light frost."

"I'll put it in a separate container just in case." She disappeared into the hut and returned with a second tin, a cloth sack, and a generous length of rope. After sealing the food with the lids and placing the tins in the bag, they threw the rope over a limb of a tree and hoisted the bundle up high.

Seth tied off the end of the rope and pulled the knot tight. "There. That should hold." He turned back to Angel hugging herself and rubbing her arms through her tattered coat. "C'mon. Let's get you back by the fire."

He threw another log on and poked the coals. Angel sat closer to him this time, but far enough away he could see her face.

She held her hands out to the flames and flipped them back and forth.

"Better?"

She smiled at him and nodded, but as she looked back to the fire, that familiar line appeared between her brows. "Do you really think we might get a frost? I mean, it seems a little early for that yet."

"I do. I've been watching the sky and the animals. I'd lay money it'll be snowing soon. And not just a light snow either. Something tells me this area is in for a harsh winter." He was laying it on thick, but if his prediction convinced her to come with him, it was worth the exaggeration.

She nodded again—this time a slow, thoughtful movement, never breaking her gaze from the fire.

Seth shifted his position on the log, angling himself toward her, and nudged back the brim of his hat. It was time to get down to business. "Angel, I'm gonna ask you a question, and this time I want the truth."

Her eyes cut to him immediately, amber flames reflected in their dove-gray depths.

"Are you living out here alone?"

She stared at him for a long moment, then averted her gaze. The slender arms that held her hands out for warmth crossed and wrapped around her waist.

Seth waited, his question hanging like fog in the silence.

She finally nodded, but he could see how much it cost her. He might as well have rubbed salt in a wound.

"All alone—no one else?"

Again, a solemn nod.

"How old are you?"

"Nineteen."

"Are you married?"

Her eyes cut back to him—she hadn't expected that, but apparently it hurt even more.

Still, he repeated the question. He needed to know he wasn't stepping on another man's toes.

She moistened her lips. "No."

"In that case, I have something else to ask you." —if she didn't up and run away before he could. The look on her face was one of pure fear. "Relax, Angel. I'm not going to propose."

She exhaled and gave him a hint of a smile.

"I want to know if you'll come with me tomorrow." Her smile disappeared. "Before you say anything, hear me out."

Her eyes remained wary, but her shoulders relaxed a little.

"I'm amazed you've managed to survive out here all by yourself—truly amazed—but you can't keep living off fish and potatoes. What happens when you can't find enough firewood or food? What happens when your clothes wear out?" She started to speak, but he held up a hand. "What happens when a bear or an Indian finds you? Or even another white man? Not all men treat women kindly." He pointed to her knife. "You don't even have a gun."

She hugged herself tighter and stared at the ground.

He hated scaring her, but she needed to see reason. "Look. All I have to do is go back to the outpost, give my report, and pick up my pay. Then I'll be free to do as I please. I don't have to go to Texas, not right away. I can take you just about anywhere. You said you were from Missouri. I could take you back there."

Something akin to hope glimmered in her expression, then it was gone.

"Do you have family there?"

"I don't want to go to Missouri."

"Well..." He lifted his hat and settled it back on his head. "I could take you to Texas with me. I'm sure we could find a place for you to stay, maybe get you work as a caretaker for children or an elderly widow. Or even as a teacher. If you're good with your studies, you could do that. I hear there are lots of towns in need of teachers for their schools."

She shrugged. "I don't know."

"You're not good with your studies?"

"I do all right. I used to mind class when our teacher was ill. It's just..."

Shit, Seth. Back off. "You don't have to decide all that right now. Just say you'll come with me. We can make plans as we go."

She frowned again and chewed on her lip.

"C'mon, Angel. Come with me tomorrow. Let me take you someplace safe."

She still didn't respond.

"Will you at least come with me to the outpost?"

Twitch. "Yes."

She was lying and he knew it, but he'd done all he could tonight. He'd let her sleep on it and continue his convincing in the morning.

Seth rose to his feet and offered Angel a hand. She followed him into the hut, and they prepared to bed down for the night.

Once he'd removed his holster and hat, he lay down on his side with his bedroll underneath him, his saddle bags as a pillow, and one of her only two blankets as a generous cover while she huddled against the opposite wall.

He couldn't let her sleep like that, not tonight.

She blew out the candle.

"Angel."

"Yes?"

"Come sleep over here."

"...Why?"

"Because you'll freeze if you don't."

"I'll be all right."

"No you won't. I can hear your teeth chattering already."

A long moment later, fabric rustled and boots scuffed against wood.

He lifted the edge of his blanket and waited for her to crawl in. She finally did, but with her back to him and her blanket wrapped around her like a cocoon.

Good thing she couldn't see him grin in the dark.

He lowered his blanket over her, and she stiffened like a sun-dried boot.

"Angel."

"Hm?"

"If I wanted to hurt you or have my way with you, I'd have done it by now." Being mindful of where he touched, Seth wrapped her with his arm and tucked her against him. "You're safe with me. Go to sleep."

Seth shivered under the blanket. The warmth around him had faded. So had the jasmine scent that filled his nose all night long. He opened his eyes to the pale morning light peeking through cracks in the branch-woven walls, and to an empty space beside him. With half a grin, he shook his head and shoved his covers aside. Knowing Angel, the little early bird was probably stoking the fire and warming their breakfast.

He stepped out of the hut and looked around, each breath a white puff in the frosty air. Fresh logs blazed, but the remnants of supper still hung from the tree. Angel was nowhere to be seen.

Oh, well. If she had slept as well as he, she'd probably just awoken. He'd lay money she was off taking care of personal needs... which was the same place he was headed.

Boots crunching through icy leaves, Seth strode across the clearing and into the woods. He chuckled as he walked to *his area*, as Angel termed it. Earlier in the week, by sheer chance, they'd chosen nearly the same spot—at nearly the same time. He didn't argue when she insisted they choose sides.

When he returned, she still wasn't there, so he retrieved the food, sat by the fire and waited, devising a plan to fulfill the offer he'd made last night.

Getting back to the outpost wasn't going to be easy. They'd be traveling with twice the belongings and people, yet with only one horse, and—thanks to the weather—doing it all pressed for time. He doubted Angel owned much, but she obviously drew from a stash of possessions somewhere. He hoped what she was unwilling to part with wasn't more than they and Cyrus could feasibly tote.

Of course, once he bought a second horse and a wagon, they could double back and fetch her things before heading on to Texas, or wherever she wanted to go. For as much as she'd done for him, it was the least he could do in return.

As the sun rose higher in the trees, he pulled the food from the sack and scanned the camp for cookware. She probably kept it inside. He removed the oiled canvas door from the hut, folded it, and set it aside, then turned back around and stepped in.

Seth stood in the open doorway and stared at the dust mote-filled space. Something was different, but he couldn't put his finger on what. The unfettered light streaming in made it look bigger. Emptier.

When he scanned Angel's side of the hut, his heart skipped a beat. Her space was completely bare, except for a canteen leaning upright against the wall and a stack of clothes. Men's clothes.

Hoping in vain he was mistaken, he squatted and lifted the canteen. Full. He sifted through the trousers and shirts. All of them were his size.

Damnation. She'd left. That sneaky little woman had got up and left. But—a rueful sound escaped his throat—not without seeing to his needs one last time.

"Angel." He sighed. "What were you thinking?"

Seth stood and raked a hand through his hair as her

thoughtful defiance fueled his ire. He'd put up with her games long enough.

He gathered his things as fast as he could, doused the fire, and rolled up his bed. He bagged the food, too—breakfast could wait. Within minutes, he had everything packed and secured to Cyrus' saddle. With a last glance around, Seth mounted up and took off. He'd find his stubborn Angel one way or another. She wasn't going to win. Not this time.

Becca sat crouched behind the rocks at the top of a cliff, amid flurries of snow. Bitter wind gusted, chilling her bones and stinging her skin.

For more than an hour, Seth had scoured the countryside calling her name. His search was getting erratic and his pleas were growing shrill, but she didn't answer, didn't show herself. It almost killed her, but she refused to be found.

For a fleeting few moments when he'd held her close last night and told her she was safe, she let herself believe he really cared. But her heart knew better. She'd pulled his body from the elements and taken him in, and he was forced by obligation to do her some favor in return.

It wasn't that she expected him to fall in love with her and make some grand promise after knowing her less than a week— life wasn't a fairytale, and Seth wasn't her knight—but the truth behind his words to her still hurt. In all the plans he suggested for her future, there was no mention of him. Of *them*. If she had let him take her to Texas, he'd have turned around and left her there. She was a stranded female he felt the need to rescue. Nothing more. "*Relax, Angel. I'm not going to propose,*" he'd said.

"*If I wanted to have my way with you...*" —which meant he didn't. It was clear Seth didn't want her, and she might as well face the truth. Nobody ever would.

"Angel!" His desperate cry pierced the wintery wind.

Blinking flakes of white from her lashes, she tugged her coat tighter around herself and peered through a crack in the rocks.

Seth shielded his eyes and scanned the hills, sitting atop Cyrus who was tossing his head and turning an irregular circle. "Angel!" he yelled again. He looked at the northern sky and let loose a curse, then flipped up the collar of his leather duster, tamped down his hat, and spurred his horse into a gallop toward the south.

Becca swiped at the icy trails of tears wetting her cheeks and gulped down her sadness as he rode away. She watched his shrinking form until it was gone, and then she made her way down the back of the bluff and headed for the lonely shelter of her cave.

Chapter Nine

One month later

The weight of the sled she dragged behind her was nothing compared to the layer of sorrow that coated her soul. Of the fourteen months she'd lived here, the last one had been the worst. Even the isolation she'd felt the first weeks after the wagon train left hadn't hurt this much. She'd only known Seth a few days. He'd been gruff at times—downright surly even—but memories of the nomadic cowboy kept running through her mind and tugging at her heart.

As the sled bumped along the rocky ground and she half-heartedly searched for pieces of wood, Becca frowned and pondered the paradox of the man. He had the plans of a drifter, yet he had the manners of someone raised by a respectable family. He wasn't a criminal of any sort—that was evident. And he was educated. She'd seen him read and write. He was healthy, strong, and smart. A young man like that should have better goals.

Of course, he probably thought the same thing of her.

She'd seen the utter shock in his eyes when she told him she lived here alone. And the judgment that followed when she resisted his urging to leave. Her reasons weren't something she'd talk about, but they were good ones. Maybe when it came to his choices, Seth had good reasons, too.

Becca bent down and lifted a fallen branch, a nice one that would burn a long time. She dusted it off and added it to the growing pile on her sled.

Thankfully, the weather had finally let up. She'd have bet her last morsel Seth exaggerated about it to convince her to go, but the storm that hit the next day proved her wrong. It dropped the temperature unseasonably low and covered the hills in a blanket of white. That snow didn't stick, but the next one did.

He was right. It was going to be a harsh winter.

A familiar grove of aspens came into view—their tall, tapered trunks dotted with gray, a single evergreen dwarfed at the base. To anyone else, it was just another grove of many, but to her, it meant she was nearly home. Becca steered her sled north, toward the incline that led to her cave, then bent to pick up one last piece of wood. As she straightened, a noise behind her made her stiffen.

She drew a tight breath, laid the stick down, and eased her hand toward her knife. She knew the sound of a shoe snapping twigs when she heard it.

"I wouldn't do that if I were you," a voice said. Male, but not Indian. And probably not more than ten feet away.

Now she wished she'd held on to the wood.

"Shoo-wee. A woman out here in these hills," a second voice said. "I wouldn'a believed it if I hadn'a seen it with my own two eyes." Also male. And half-drunk, by the way he slurred his words.

Her heart pounded and her mouth went dry, but she refused to give in to fear. Maybe she could grab for the wood and—

"Turn around," the first one commanded.

Becca drew another tight breath and rotated slowly until she was facing the strangers.

Two unkempt men stood a few feet from her, dressed in grimy, tattered clothes. One was tall and thin. Young. His hat sat sloppily cocked to the side, and his grin was just as crooked.

The other one, the one who'd just spoken, was shorter, stouter, and old enough to be her father. His eyes narrowed until their yellowed whites disappeared, and his gaze slid over her like profane mud.

Becca resisted the urge to grimace and kept an even tone. "Are you lost?" She didn't see any horses, and it was too late in the year for a wagon train to be moving through.

The tall one snickered, but the other man's gaze only grew more intense. "No," he said. "We're not lost."

She lifted her chin a notch in spite of the dread twisting her gut. "Well, then. What do you want?"

The older man's lips took on a sickening curve. "What exactly are you offerin'?"

Becca gestured toward the sled, hoping they wouldn't see her hand tremble. "If you need firewood, I can spare a few logs."

The tall one nudged the older man and snickered again. "She thinks we want wood."

Don't show any weakness. "It's all I have to give you," she said flatly. "So take it and be on your way."

The older man's lips went straight, and malice lit his eyes. In one quick motion, he pulled a knife and closed half the distance between them. "You're gonna regret saying that."

"Take it easy, Ray," the tall one said.

"Shut up, Tucker. No bitch is gonna to tell me what to do."

Becca started to go for her knife, but the murderous look in Ray's eyes stopped her. She backed away, then stilled when he reached for the sheath at her waist.

With a swift yank, he tore it from her, breaking the tether that held it in place. He flung it to his partner without looking back.

Ray grabbed the nape of her neck and dug his fingers into her braid with a twist that sent pain shooting through her scalp. "You'll do what I say." He pulled her up against him—his breath hot and putrid on her face. "And don't even think about fighting back." The tip of his knife put a point on his words as it pricked the soft flesh under her chin.

Becca closed her eyes and willed herself to be calm even though her heart raced and her body quivered with fright. The girl in her wanted to crumple to the ground and weep, but the woman stood firm. *Show no weakness.* In preparation for their trip, her father had told her many times, '*If someone threatens you, cooperate. But don't show any weakness.*'

The tip of the knife left her skin, and Ray's hand released its grip on her hair. "Take off your coat."

Becca opened her eyes to a heartless gaze boring into hers.

Ray struck her face with the back of his hand so hard, it whipped her head sideways. "I said take off your coat."

A tear ran down her throbbing cheek and a drop of blood trickled down her neck. Ignoring the invading cold and the tingling pain of her swelling face, she tucked her gloves in the pockets and lay her coat aside. She wiped away the tear, but left the blood.

The tall m—*Tucker's* face had gone from foolish to feral, and Ray's lips once more held a sickening curve. "Take off your clothes."

Becca stood there, frozen, a battle raging in her mind.

'Cooperate.'

No!

'Cooperate.'

Please, Pa. I can't.

'Cooperate, Becca. The alternative is worse.'

Was it?

"I said, take off your clothes!"

Becca flinched and reached for the front of her shirt, but Ray grabbed it before she could. With a growl, he ripped it open, buttons popping like the spat of gunfire.

Tucker moved closer, stealing her attention. Ray shoved her to the ground. She fell hard on her back and skidded in the rocky dirt. "Be ready to hold her if she tries to fight," Ray muttered as he started unfastening his pants. His grip on his knife loosened with the distraction. Maybe she could get it and use it on them.

Becca eased onto her elbow and coiled her muscles to spring up and charge them. If she could knock Ray backward, she could take them both down.

"Get away from her!"

All three of them looked in the direction of the voice.

Seth! Becca scrambled to her feet.

"Pass on by," Ray called out. "You have no business here."

Seth reined Cyrus to a stop and surveyed the scene. His fierce gaze locked on Becca, then shifted to the men and turned deadly. "I'll give you a chance to walk away, but I'm not leaving."

"C'mon, Ray," Tucker said. "Let's go. She's not worth it."

"Don't be a coward," Ray growled. "She's ours and he's outnumbered."

Seth lifted his revolver and leveled it at the men. "This is your last warning."

Tucker dropped her knife and ran off in the opposite direction, but Ray stood his ground. "This doesn't concern you, stranger. Pass on by."

"Go, Angel. *Run.*"

Becca started to back away.

Ray's eyes narrowed in a scowl. He turned and charged her, teeth bared and knife raised to strike.

Becca shrieked when a gun blast split the air and echoed off the hills, and then she fell—knocked backward to the ground under Ray's weight. She shut her eyes tight, waiting for his knife to stab her. Seconds passed. He moaned, and she opened her eyes again.

His face was inches from hers, his eyes blank and a trickle of blood oozing from his mouth.

Becca screamed and began shoving him away.

Big hands grabbed her attacker and lifted him off. He moaned again, but the sound was silenced with a crack as Seth roared and gave the man's head a sharp twist. He tossed Ray aside like a sack of grain and stood there, chest heaving—the look on his face so savage it chilled Becca to her core.

She stared at Ray's lifeless body, then at Seth. He took a step toward her and she scooted away.

"Angel, it's me." He held out a hand. "You're safe." She finally took it and let him help her to stand.

The same hand that touched hers with gentleness had just killed a man, yet when Seth's familiar voice settled over her, her pounding pulse began to slow. The lethal fury that had rendered him unrecognizable was gone. Only sadness and compassion remained.

Until he saw her neck.

Seth reached for her chin.

She turned her face before his fingers made purchase.

He withdrew his hand, but pressed his lips together in annoyance. "You're bleeding."

"It's nothing." She swallowed. "H-he nicked me with his knife."

Seth reached for her again. "How bad? Let me see."

She relented and let him examine her wound.

A low growl rumbled in his throat along with what sounded like a curse.

"Well?"

"It's not deep enough for stitches, but we'll have to clean it real good. And put something cold on that eye." Seth let go of her face and began looking her over. "Did he hurt you anyplace else?"

"I don't think so." Becca followed his gaze to her chest. Blood spattered her from the waist up, and her shirt gaped open. She yanked it closed and clutched it tightly with both hands, thankful her chemise hadn't torn and left her totally exposed.

Seth reached for her arms and she pulled away. "I need to see if you're injured."

"I'm not."

"You're covered in blood."

"It's not mine. Maybe a drop or two from my chin, but—" Becca swallowed back bile.

"Angel..." He drew the name out in admonition.

"I promise. I'm not hurt. I just need to—" She cursed her fate inwardly. "—to wash up and change clothes." She didn't want to walk anywhere alone, but that was the only way to keep the location of her cave a secret.

Strands of hair Ray had yanked loose from her braid flapped in the breeze and lashed her face. She tucked them behind her ear, then gripped her tattered shirt again. "You go on ahead. I'll change my clothes and meet you at the hut."

"No."

"What do you mean 'no'?"

"For one, I'm not about to let you wander these hills alone after what happened, and—"

"I'll be fine."

"No. Just... No. And we can't go back to the hut."

Her churning stomach hit the ground. "Why not?"

"That was the first place I went. The men must've found it somehow. Two horses were tied there, and I saw evidence of a recent fire. That's why I came looking for you. I was worried whoever found your hut had found you, too."

Becca hugged herself tighter and looked away, invaded by a bleak coldness that had little to do with the winter wind.

Seth stepped closer. "Don't worry, Angel. We'll find a place to stay."

"Rebecca."

"What?"

She drew a breath and met his gaze. "My name is Rebecca."

His cheek creased as the corner of his mouth lifted. "All right, then. Rebecca." Her name sounded comforting coming from his lips, just like she knew it would.

Becca shivered and her teeth began to chatter.

Seth left her to retrieve his horse. He returned her knife and fetched her coat from the sled. "There's a small cliff about a quarter mile west of here," he said as he helped her put it on. "We could make camp under the shelter of the overhang, and then—"

"Thanks, but I already have a place to stay."

"You can't go back to the hut. It's not sa—"

"I'm not referring to the hut. I haven't lived there in over a year." At his look of consternation, she added, "I only took you there because... because I didn't want you to know too much about me." Why did admitting it make her feel so awful?

"Oh." He sounded resigned, not angry. That made her feel worse. "In that case, we'll go to your new home. Lead the way."

Becca inclined her head toward the dead man. "What about him?"

Seth shifted his stance, blocking her view. "I'll come back and take care of that. Right now we need to get you someplace safe and warm."

Becca put on her gloves, stepped into the loop of rope attached to the sled, and bent over to lift it off the ground.

"What are you doing?"

"Taking my firewood home."

Seth was beside her in two swift strides. "I'm not going to stand by while you pull that load. What kind of a man do you think I am?"

"I didn't mean to insult you." Becca dropped the rope and stepped aside. "I'm not used to having anyone do things for me."

His expression softened, and the hint of a smile she'd seen earlier returned. "Here." He handed her the rope he'd attached to his horse's halter. "You can lead Cyrus. He likes you better anyway."

Becca walked beside Seth and pointed the way as he dragged the sled like it weighed next to nothing. "Are you working for the men at the outpost again?"

"No. My work for them was done weeks ago."

"Oh." What he'd been doing since?

He didn't elaborate and she didn't pry.

When they were almost there, she started to ask him to keep this place a secret, but he looked at her with those noble blue eyes, and she knew that he would. "I live in a cave now."

"A cave?"

She nodded. "It's just behind those trees."

Seth shook his head when they rounded the copse and the ledge-shielded entrance of the cave came into view. "You sure have a knack for keeping yourself hidden." He stepped away from the sled and looked around. "Where do you want me to put the wood?"

"I stack it inside." Becca led him up a slight incline and into the opening of the cave. In summer, cool shade would have greeted them. Now, in contrast to the frigid weather, a relative warmth pervaded the space.

Around the corner to the right lay the cavern where she stored her wood—a stone niche completely shielded from the rain. Refusing any help, Seth carried in armfuls of sticks and logs, his muscular shoulders bulging and shifting as he worked. Once the new wood was neatly stacked with the rest, he stood the flat sled on end in its storage space nearby and brushed the dirt and bark from his leather duster. "That's an impressive stash of wood."

"Thanks. I learned my lesson last winter and did a better job of collecting it this year." Her grip on her coat tightened and Seth rubbed the back of his neck as uncomfortable silence hung between them. She wanted to be alone, but she had someone else's needs to consider. "Do you need to come in and warm up before...?"

"No, but thank you." He glanced at her clothing, trying not to be too obvious it seemed. "Want me to build you a fire? Heat some water for your bath?"

"It isn't necessary."

"I don't mind. Cold as it is—"

"Thank you, but it really isn't necessary."

A small crease appeared between his brows. "I'll be gone a

while. Are you sure you'll be all right?"

Becca forced a smile. "I'll be fine."

Seth exhaled and tipped his hat. "See you in about an hour." He strode to where Cyrus waited, readied his mount, and swung into the saddle with masculine grace. He was kind; an obvious gentleman—a fact she couldn't reconcile with the brutal act he'd committed.

Apparently he couldn't either. A grim expression hardened the lines of his face as he turned to ride away.

Becca watched until he was out of sight, and then she retreated into the cave. After removing her boots and coat and gathering a towel and fresh clothes, she padded along the smooth, stone path that led to the spring. Even in the relative dark, the rippling blue-green water was visible, a welcome sight.

One by one, she removed each piece of her clothing. Skirt? Wash. Stockings? Wash. Drawers? Wash. Torn, blood-spattered shirt? Burn. Blood-stained chemise? She cringed.... Wash. The thought of wearing it again turned her stomach, but after ruining one to bind Seth's ribs, she was left with only two. She reluctantly placed it in a bucket of cold water to soak.

Becca removed the tie from the end of her braid, combed her hair loose with her fingers, and walked to the edge of the pool. A throaty sigh escaped as she slid into the steamy water. Fed by both a spring and a stream, it was hot but not scalding.

She waded out a few feet—the water level just above her waist and the sandy bottom molding to her toes—then buckled her knees and submerged herself completely. She pushed back through the surface, propelled by the stinging under her chin, but she held the whimper at bay. Slicking the water from her hair, she returned to the side and settled herself on one of two underwater ledges protruding from the spring's wall.

As the water lapped her shoulders, Becca hoped her cares

would vanish with the wisps of steam rising off the pool, but they didn't. She ran her hands along her arms. Instead of feeling silky the way the water usually made them feel, they felt slimy. She couldn't see her body through the foggy water, but the thought of what nearly happened to it—to *her*—sent a blast of truth from her head to her feet and triggered a wave of trembling spasms and choking sobs. She drew her knees up and wrapped them with her arms, her ragged cries distorting as they bounced off the dome-shaped walls. For once, she was glad to be encased in stone and all alone.

Her face dipped too low and she sucked in water with a breath. Coughing and sputtering, she shot to her feet. Her mournful wails turned to angry roars.

She grabbed her bar of soap from its place beside the spring and scrubbed every inch of her skin as fast as she could. Even through the jasmine scent, she could still smell the blood. Frantically, she lathered her hair and arms and chest; scratched and wiped and scrubbed. Would she ever feel clean?

With a final, defeated sob, she threw the soap aside and sank to the bottom of the pool, eyes closed, cocooned by soundlessness.

However detached, sensibility returned as she surfaced and drew in a breath. Seth would be back soon. She couldn't let him find her like this. Becca squeezed the water from her hair. She waded out of the pool and reached for her towel.

Chapter Ten

Seth stared at the entrance to Rebecca's cave, trying to muster the courage to go in. She wasn't the only one shocked by what he'd done. He had no issue with the fact he'd killed a man—saving her life was more than enough justification—but the fury that compelled him to break a neck with his bare hands was a frightening thing to possess. And, he sobered, probably twice as frightening to witness.

Rebecca had gone willingly with him and invited him into her home, but it was clear she was only being polite. Still, as shaken as she was, he needed to make sure she was all right. He knew all too well how traumatizing something like this could be for a woman. Seth took off his hat and walked inside. If Rebecca didn't want him there, he'd stay someplace else; but first, he'd make sure she was well enough to be left alone.

The cavern to the right where she stored her wood was a dead end, so he went to the left. The tunnel was narrow and dark, but he kept going, drawn by light at the other end.

When the familiar scent of jasmine met his nose, he stopped and cleared his throat. "Rebecca, it's Seth. Are you there?"

"Yes," she called. "Come in." Maybe it was the acoustics of the cave, but her tone didn't sound very inviting.

He stepped out of the tunnel into a huge, round room, and his gaze was immediately drawn skyward. Large shafts of sunlight crossed like pale white reeds, shining this way and that, coming through holes in the rocky dome. He'd never seen anything like it—well, once, when he'd torn down an old barn with his pa. But the meager, mote-filled beams coming through that roof weren't as spectacular as this.

"Pretty, isn't it?" Rebecca said. "As soon as I get the fire going, I'll fix us some lunch." She was kneeling near a pile of kindling in the middle of the room, wearing fresh clothes and a damp braid. She was calm, but she was pale. And he didn't miss the high-neck white blouse buttoned all the way up.

Seth followed the shaft of light that was shining on her up to a hole directly above her head.

"Don't worry," she said as if reading his mind. "Except for very windy days, I can build a fire in here. The smoke will rise and go out."

"What do you do on windy days?"

She shrugged. "I don't build any fires."

"What about winter? How do you stay warm?"

"I go deeper in the cave. The temperature doesn't change much there."

Seth was struck dumb. So many assumptions he'd made about this woman and her dwelling were wrong.

Pulled back out of his thoughts by her curious gaze, he lowered his game bag off his shoulder and held up two freshly killed rabbits. "Want to add these to lunch?"

"Um. Yes." 'If you'll do the skinning,' the look on her face said.

"I'll take them outside and get them ready for you. I'll make a spit, too."

"Don't worry about the spit." Rebecca rose to her feet. "I saved the ones you made last time." She crossed the room and fished the smaller one out of a crate against the stone wall, then turned to him with a bashful smile. "Hasn't gotten much use, though."

"Do you have a bucket I can borrow to fetch some water?"

"Wait here. I'll do you one better." She disappeared through a tunnel on the far side of the room, her dark brown skirt swishing around the ankles of her boots. Minutes later, she returned, carrying a wooden bucket, and held it out to him already full. "There's an underground stream that runs through the cave. It's safe to drink."

"Want me to fill your canteen?" she asked when he took the bucket.

"No. But thank you for offering." He'd filled it when he washed up after disposing of Ray.

Seth set the bucket down long enough to dip his handkerchief in the cold water and squeeze it out. "Here." He offered it to her. "For your face."

"Thank you, but I already put something on it."

Seth made a rote move to return his handkerchief to his pocket, then stopped midway, not sure what to do with the soggy cloth.

She gingerly took it from him. "I'll lay it out to dry."

Rebecca knelt near the kindling again. She lifted a pair of spectacles and held it over the pile. She glanced up, then scooted over and aimed one of the lenses so it focused the sunlight into a thin, bright beam. It wasn't long before the kindling began to smoke. With rote, economical movements, she added more kindling and blew the embers into flame, then added sticks and a few small logs.

Seth stood there, staring.

Rebecca rose to her feet and turned around with the spectacles in her hand. "I thought you were going to clean the rabbits."

"I am," he said, schooling his features. He was making a habit of gaping at her like an idiot. "I was watching you start the fire. Do you always do it that way?"

"Yes, whenever it's sunny out. I have to use a bow drill when it's not."

"You don't have matches?"

Her long, brown lashes lowered over her eyes, and the brightness that had finally begun working its way back into her expression disappeared. "I do, but I have a limited supply. I have to conserve them." She crossed the room to the crate and carefully placed the spectacles in a small wooden case.

Seth lifted the game bag onto his shoulder. "I'll go clean these. I won't be long."

Rebecca gave a demure nod. "I'll fix some potatoes."

Seth finished cleaning the rabbits and headed back to the cave, the whole time thinking about Angel, the woman he now knew as Rebecca. A month ago when he'd left to go back to the outpost, he spent the entire trip wondering if she was crazy. Of course, he'd assumed she was living in the hut. Seeing her cave and the ease with which she cared for herself changed his opinion. Well, not entirely. She couldn't survive out here—not long-term—but he was beginning to understand her reluctance to leave. However foolish the notion, the woman was determined to make it on her own.

But how in blue blazes did she get here in the first place?

Announcing his presence, he entered the cave and joined her in the large, sunlit room. "Need help?" he asked as he laid the rabbits on a clean square of cloth she'd prepared.

"No—um, yes." She handed him the spit. "Skewer those while I set up the frame."

Seth went along, but he was skeptical. In the woods, he'd driven the stakes into the ground. That would be impossible to do with the stone floor of the cave.

Rebecca arranged two blocks of wood, one on each side of the fire. The blocks had holes in them—charred indentions that looked like they'd been hewn by a knife and burned by friction.

She glanced at him and blushed. "I failed a few times before I learned to use a bow drill."

Seth frowned inwardly—probably more than a few. Using friction to start a fire was a difficult task, and not very reliable.

Holding one of the blocks steady, she inserted a stake into the hole. When she let go, it stayed standing.

"Well," he said as she secured the other one, "at least they're good for something."

She smiled at him then, and it reminded him how much he missed her smiles.

They took turns rotating the rabbits over the fire while Rebecca tended the potatoes that were baking on hot stones at the edge of the coals. The smells of smoke and game filled the air. And jasmine.

"Can you keep an eye on this for a minute?" she asked.

At his assent, she rose and hurried into a second tunnel a few feet to the right of the first. It was wider, but nearly as dark.

She returned, carrying two small crates, and set them upside down a safe distance from the fire. "I don't store much in here," she said as she sat down and took over turning the spit. "The holes are wonderful for letting in light, but they also let in rain."

Seth pushed himself up and sat on the other crate, rubbing the ache from his knees. "How big is this place?"

"My cave?"

"Mmhm."

"I don't know... probably about the size of a small farmhouse."

His brows shot up. "Really?"

She nodded. "It has several rooms."

"Do the other rooms have holes for light like this one?"

"No."

"How do you see?"

She pointed to an opening over one of the tunnels. "There are shafts here and there that connect to other parts of the cave. On bright days like this, there's enough light to see my way around. On stormy days and at night, I light a candle if I need to see."

"You don't have a lantern?"

She shook her head and her expression fell some. "I spend most of my time in here. Unless it's raining or too cold."

Silence filled the space between them.

"I'll get my plates," Seth offered.

"Don't bother." Rebecca pointed to the crate across the room. "There are plates in there. Cutlery, too."

He retrieved two plates—fine china, no less—along with knives and forks and brought them over by the fire. Becca served them both ample portions of food, but she wasn't eating much.

"I'm shocked," he said, trying to lighten her mood. "I figured you'd eat your rabbit and fight me for mine, too."

Her cheeks flushed a soft pink. "I'm sorry. It's very good. I'm just not hungry."

"I was joking, Rebecca. You don't need to apologize."

Seth set his plate aside. His appetite wasn't much better. "Those are awful fancy plates for a cave," he said, gesturing at hers. Maybe if he got her talking it would distract her from the day's events. Heck, who was he kidding? Distract them *both*.

She swallowed the tiny bite of potato she'd just taken. "China's heavier than tin." At his puzzled expression, she added, "I found them by the trail."

Ah. "Is that where you got the clothes you gave me?"

She nodded. "You'd be surprised what desperate people will throw away."

Seth stretched out his legs. "What else have you found?"

Rebecca set her plate on her lap and looked thoughtful. "I've found all kinds of clothes and shoes... a few kitchen utensils—" She glanced conspiratorially at him. "—people generally hang on to those, and books—lots of them." Her eyes lit up with the last.

"You must like to read."

"I do, very much."

He bet she did. How else would she pass the time here alone? And judging by the look on her face, conversation was near the top of her list, too. *Keep her talking.* "What's the strangest thing you found?"

She knitted her brows, then a flash of enthusiasm smoothed them. "In one of the trunks, I found a wooden leg."

"No kidding?"

"Honest. I couldn't believe anyone would leave something like that behind."

"Do you still have it?"

"No." She ducked her head and glanced at him sideways. "I used it for firewood last winter."

Seth chuckled. "I hope it was a spare."

Rebecca laughed, then her eyes lit up again. "Oh. And after the wagon train that came through in July..."

He didn't hear anything after the word *July*. Seth stared past Rebecca as he processed the implication of what she'd said.

The distant hum of her voice fell silent. "Seth...? Is something wrong?"

He looked at her again. "Do you know when the wagon trains come through?"

"Um. Yes. New things are dumped beside the trail afterward."

"No, I'm asking if you know before that."

She regarded him warily. "I'm not sure what you mean."

He pinned her with his gaze. "I'm asking you if you watch for them or listen for them—if you know when they're here."

She stared at the plate of food in her lap. "Sometimes."

"Have you tried to make contact? Asked to go with them?"

"No."

"Why not?"

Rebecca looked up. "What good would it do? No one would take me."

"Oh, c'mon. No decent, self-respecting person would refuse—"

"Oh yes they would." Now her gaze was doing the pinning. "You said it yourself. By the time the wagons get here, they're running low on supplies. Families barely have enough food to keep from starving before they get to their destination. They're not going to take on another mouth to feed." She collected her plate and stood. "And, even if they would, *I'm* too decent of a person to ask."

With an angry swish of her skirt, she strode across the room and scraped what was left of her lunch into a metal tin, and then she marched out of the cave without looking back.

Chapter Eleven

Seth stood at the entrance to the cave and scrubbed a hand over his jaw. He'd really hit a nerve with Rebecca. She'd stormed out without her coat and stayed gone so long, he was worried. He was about to saddle Cyrus and search for her when she appeared at the edge of the trees and walked into the clearing. Her steps faltered when she saw him, but she continued toward him with her arms wrapped tightly around her midriff.

"I was about to come looking for you."

"I'm fine," she muttered.

Seth readjusted his hat. He rubbed the back of his neck and let his arm fall to his side. "I'm sorry if I upset you. I didn't mean to."

Her gaze flicked away. "I shouldn't have left like that. I'm sorry, too."

"Well, I'm glad you're back." She looked up at him through her lashes, and a smile tugged at his lips. "You haven't told me where my *area* is yet."

Crimson spread across her pale cheeks, matching her red nose. "There's a thicket about twenty yards that way," she said, pointing east. "If that's all right with you, it's yours."

Seth tipped his hat. "That'll do." He started to leave, then silently cursed his lapse. "You must be freezing. I'll stoke the fire before I go."

Rebecca waved him off. "I can do it." He had no doubt that she could.

Seth tipped his hat once more. "I'll be back shortly." He turned his collar up against the chilling wind and headed for the thicket to the east.

When he returned, she was sitting on a crate near the fire with an empty look in her eyes. He cleared his throat and she flinched.

"Beg your pardon," he said, stepping into the room and removing his hat. "I didn't mean to startle you."

"It's all right." She gave a small smile.

"You warming up?" he asked as he joined her by the fire.

She nodded.

"I was wondering," Seth said, keeping his voice easy, "if you had any more of those berries left."

"I do."

"I liked that cobbler you made last time I was here. If I gave you some sugar and the ingredients for the crust, would you make another one?"

She smiled, a real Angel smile this time. "I'd be glad to."

Good. That made her happy, and it would keep her busy. "I noticed some deer tracks while I was out. If you don't mind me leaving for a little while, I'll see if I can get us some venison for supper. How does that sound?"

"Do you really think you can?" From the look on her face, she hadn't had deer in a very long time.

"I think so. I'm a pretty good shot."

Rebecca blinked and the life practically drained from her face.

Shit, Seth. Could you've put your foot any further in your mouth? "Sorry. I, uh, I didn't mean to—"

"What did you do with him?" Her voice was almost a whisper.

"The man who attacked you?"

She nodded, her moist eyes staring into his.

"I—" He wanted to throw the bastard off a cliff to be food for the buzzards, but... "I buried him."

"Where?"

"Far enough away you won't come across the grave." That seemed to appease her.

She exhaled and stared at her slender hands clasped in her lap.

"Rebecca?"

"Hm?" She looked up.

"If I don't go soon, I won't have time to hunt. Will you be all right here alone?"

She sat a little straighter and nodded.

He managed a smile. "I'll get the stuff you need for the cobbler from my bags, then I'll go get us a deer."

Seth sopped the last drop of broth from his bowl with one of the biscuits Rebecca had made. "You make a darn good venison stew." He wasn't kidding. It was so tender and tasty, he'd nearly abandoned his manners. She nearly had, too.

"I hope you left room for cobbler."

"For your cobbler? Definitely."

Rebecca served them both some, and it was better than before. Not wanting to spoil her good mood, he avoided sensitive topics and kept the conversation light. When they'd stuffed themselves sufficiently, he helped her clear the plates and store what was left of the food.

"That's one good thing about winter," he said as he hoisted the leftovers into the same tree as the rest of the deer. "Food keeps." They both rubbed their gloved hands as white puffs of breath dotted their stroll back to the cave.

He entered the main room and set his hat aside as Rebecca added a log to the fire.

"I—" they said at the same time. They both grinned.

"Ladies first."

Rebecca tucked an errant strand of hair behind her ear. "Thank you for supper."

"I should thank you. You cooked it."

"Yes, but you provided most of the ingredients."

"And I ate more than my share. It was a team effort. Let's leave it at that."

She gave a conciliatory nod.

Seth rounded up his courage. He was about to upset the cordial climate, but the sun was setting and he needed to know where he was spending the night. "I, uh." He cleared his throat, more to buy time than from necessity. "I need to find a place and make camp?"

Rebecca's pleasant expression faded. She caught her lower lip with her teeth, and he wished he could read the thoughts going through her head. "You can leave if you like," she finally said, "but you're welcome to stay here. It's going to be a cold night."

She was right about that. "I don't want to impose. Are you sure?"

Half a beat later. "I'm sure."

"Thank you." Seth glanced at the dwindling fire. "Could I ask one more favor?"

"Yes."

"I'd like to heat some water and wash up."

Rebecca chewed on her lip once more. "Would you rather take a bath?"

"You have a tub?" He hadn't had a tub bath in months.

"In a manner of speaking; the cave has a spring."

"Is it warm?" He'd take a potful of warm water over a cold lake any day.

"It's very warm."

"In that case, point me to it."

A crease appeared between Rebecca's brows. "I can loan you a towel, but I don't have any more clothes your size."

"That's not a problem. I have both." Seth retrieved the items from his bags, along with his soap. When he returned, she was scooping some of the embers from the fire into a long-handled skillet. She added a few small pieces of wood and stoked the pile until they caught fire.

"What's that for?"

"The cavern with the spring is dark this time of evening. You'll need it to see." She drew a candle from her pocket and lit it with the flame from the wood, then held it with one hand while she grabbed the cloth-wrapped handle of the skillet with the other. "Follow me."

She led him into one of the tunnels and down a smooth, stone path. Flickering amber light danced on the walls and cast her in shadow. As they descended, the air around them grew muggy and warm. A faint scent of sulfur mingled with wood smoke and wax.

The tunnel opened into a domed room much like the main

one, only the ceiling was solid and low. Under it, a rippling pool topped with a foggy layer of steam was barely visible.

Rebecca set the skillet on an outcropping of rock and placed the rag a safe distance away. "You can put your things over there," she said, pointing to another rocky shelf. "There are a couple of underwater ledges here at the side you can sit on," she added once he'd deposited his belongings. "You can venture a few feet from the edge, but don't get too close to the center of the pool. It's very deep and very hot there."

Candlelight bathed Rebecca's face, softening her features, and reflected like gold in her blue-gray eyes. She'd gone from average-looking to beautiful, and it wasn't just the light.

"Do you have everything you need?" she asked when he stood there like a dumbstruck fool.

"Yes."

"When you're done, bring the skillet. You can use the fire to light your way." The glow of Rebecca's candle disappeared with her into the tunnel.

Seth set his soap and towel near the water's edge, shed his clothes, and stepped into the pool. Air hissed through his teeth—dang, it was hot—then he let out a contented sigh. Soaking in the spring was pure heaven. No wonder she didn't want to leave.

When he reached for his soap, he noticed a smaller bar nearby and brought it to his nose. Jasmine. With a smile on his face, he set it down and lathered up with his own. No self-respecting man would be caught dead smelling like flowers. He was glad Rebecca did, though. It was one of the things he'd remember most about her. And that thought, the fact she would eventually be nothing more than a memory, made his smile fade.

Seth rinsed himself off and soaked for a while, then glanced at the dwindling fire in the skillet. He'd best get out soon, or he wouldn't have enough light to find his way back.

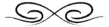

Rebecca was sitting on the ground by the fire when he returned. Her arms hugged her skirt-draped knees close to her body, and she stared blankly at the floor, sending a cold wave of trepidation rolling through his chest. She'd always seemed distant to a degree, but not like this.

"Thank you for the bath," he said, dumping the flickering embers into the fire and setting the empty skillet nearby. "I haven't been in a hot spring since I was a child." He laid his towel over a rock to dry, then took his soiled clothes across to his bags.

"I'll be doing laundry tomorrow. Want me to wash those?"

Sweet Angel. Always taking care of him. "If you don't mind." He handed her the clothes, then proceeded to find a draft-free corner and unroll his bed.

Seth stopped when that familiar crease appeared between her brows. "Are you having second thoughts about me staying here tonight?"

"No, I'm worried you won't be warm enough. This room will be cold by morning." She must not want to waste the wood it would take to keep the fire going.

Conserving was pointless—she was coming with him when he left—but he let it drop. Now was not the time for that discussion. "Good point." He gathered his belongings. "Show me where you want me to stay."

She nibbled her lip, then stood and lit the small candle she'd used before. She led him down the same tunnel she'd gone into the get the crates. They passed three rooms of various sizes, two she apparently used for storage and one that looked like a bedroom. It contained no bed, just a pallet on the floor, but a small oak vanity stood against the far wall.

After they'd gone about five more feet, the tunnel opened into a large, empty cavern. The room wasn't warm, but it was a comfortable temperature. Well, *comfortable* if you wrapped yourself head to foot in a blanket.

"Will this do?" Rebecca asked.

"Yes. This is fine." He didn't like being so far from the entrance, but the other man and the horses were long gone when he checked on the hut. He didn't expect any trouble tonight.

Rebecca crossed to a rocky shelf protruding low on the wall. She tilted the candle sideways, pouring out a puddle of wax, then pressed the stub upright in it as it cooled. "Blow this out once you're settled," she said as she turned to leave. "See you in the morning."

"What about you?" Seth indicated the candle.

"I can find my way in the dark."

"Well, goodnight then."

"Goodnight." She disappeared with a floral-scented swish of a skirt.

Seth rolled out his bed as he always did—bedroll below, blanket on top and saddle bags for a pillow. He removed his boots, but kept his clothing on and his sidearm nearby in case something happened in the middle of the night. He refused to leave Rebecca unprotected.

Lying on solid rock wasn't as comfortable as dirt and grass, but he'd make do. At least he was sheltered from the cold. He blew out the candle, rolled to his side and closed his eyes to drift off. A strange noise made him open them again.

It was Rebecca. She was crying. Her sobs were soft and muffled, but they dug like a knife at his soul. Few sounds were as painful as an anguished woman weeping.

Seth scrubbed a hand over his face. Now what was he going to do? He debated ignoring it, but that didn't feel right. She was upset; he should go to her. But what if he was the reason for her tears?

He ignored the self-loathing that came with that thought and rose to his feet. One way or another, he'd find a way to soothe her, even if it meant leaving the cave.

Several toe-stubbing steps through the dark later, he stood near the entrance to her room. "Rebecca?"

Her sobs went silent. "Yes?" She sniffled.

He started to ask, 'Are you all right?', but she obviously wasn't. "Is my presence here upsetting you...? Do you want me to leave?"

"No." She made a small hiccup. "What m—makes you think that?"

I brutally killed a man while you watched. Hell. What was he supposed to say? "I, uh." He felt useless when it came to crying females. "Would you like to talk?"

"No."

Well.... At least he tried.

Seth stumbled through the dark to his bed, burrowed under the blanket again, and tried to find a comfortable position. He listened for sniffles and sobs, but heard nothing.

He was about to drift off when the hiss of a match being struck echoed through the cave. The pale glow of a candle lit the tunnel outside his room, and a quilt-wrapped figure appeared at his door.

Rebecca's lips trembled and she blinked several times. "I changed my mind."

Seth sat up and motioned to her. "Come here." He took the candle from her and fixed it like the other on the ledge.

She dropped to her knees in front of him and drew a shuddering breath. "I—I—" She hiccupped again. "You're not the r—reason I'm c—crying," she said, shaking her head. "I'm g—glad you're huh—here."

"You are?"

She switched to nodding. "Those men—" Her face pinched with emotion. "Th—They were going to—" She choked on a sob. "You saved my life." She broke down and cried, hand trembling in front of her mouth and tears streaming down her cheeks.

"Ah, Rebecca." Seth drew her into his arms and cradled her against his chest. She buried her face and sobbed so hard she shook. "Shh, Becca, shhhh." He rocked her back and forth, murmuring to her and stroking her hair. She'd been so brave, so strong. The sum of the day's events must've finally hit her.

Her sobs finally slowed to an occasional shudder. "You c—called me Becca."

"You don't like it?"

Her head nudged his chest in a gesture of denial. "I like it. It's just... I haven't heard anyone call me that in a long time." Her body sagged against him, and she made no effort to move. Her eyes were so near closed, damp lashes fringed her tear-stained cheeks.

Seth blew out the candle and eased them down until she was lying in the crook of his arm. She was still cocooned in her quilt—one hand holding it closed and the other clutching the fabric of his shirt.

He pulled his blanket up over them both. "You're safe, Becca. Go to sleep.

Chapter Twelve

Mmm. Seth hugged the bundle next to him and pressed his nose to soft cotton. He loved the scent of Rebecca's soap, but he craved her sweet, female skin more. He nuzzled higher, searching for her hair.

His eyes flew open. What was he doing! He tracked his gaze downward, half flinching at the threat of her reaction.

She wasn't there.

He pushed his blanket aside. Lord help him. He'd been hugging a rolled up quilt.

Seth flopped to his back and stared at the rocky ceiling. One of the cave's shafts opened off to one side and lit the room with a soft, morning glow. It wasn't bright like a window, but gave enough light he could make out the objects around him.

He closed his eyes and scrubbed a hand over his stubbled jaw. What was he going to do about Rebecca? She'd be leaving this godforsaken country and coming with him this time—that wasn't even up for discussion—but where, and what then?

A month ago, he'd seen her as nothing more than someone to rescue, a minor complication to his plans. But now... He'd best not dwell on that thought. Some things were better left undisturbed—the foolish dream of finding a wife and settling down being one of them. He wouldn't settle for anything less than a good one. And once she found out about his past, no good woman would settle for him.

Seth pulled on his boots, then grabbed his soap and shaving kit from his bag and headed for the main room of the cave. Unsurprisingly, Becca was kneeling by the fire, cooking breakfast. "Good morning," he said as he entered the room.

She looked up at him with a bashful shade of pink heating her cheeks. "Good morning." She was probably embarrassed about— "I'm sorry about last night." She half averted her gaze.

"Don't be." He smiled. "That's what friends are for."

She smiled back, but the spark of it was missing from her eyes. Her gaze shifted to his chest and she turned bright red.

Seth held out his arms and looked down. Not only was the front of his shirt wrinkled, but it looked like a handkerchief. A stiff, dry, well-used handkerchief. He looked back up at Becca, who'd covered her face with both hands, and grinned at her when she peeked at him through her fingers.

Her fingers snapped shut. "I can't believe I did that to you," she groaned.

Seth laughed. He set his shaving kit aside and turned to go back to his room. "Don't worry. Thanks to a generous lady I know, I have a spare."

Once he'd changed, he gave Becca the shirt, reveling at her mortified face that still glowed. "Wash it for me and we'll call it even. Deal?"

"Deal."

He grinned and threw her a wink. "I'll be back," he said as he pulled on his duster and reached for his hat. "Don't worry. I won't go far—only about twenty yards to the east."

Seth tapped down his hat and walked out into the cold, clear morning, taking in the sight of the mountains and making his plans for the day. He'd keep the conversation light until after their meal. Then it'd be time to get down to business.

Seth set his plate aside. "Thank you. That was good." Rebecca had fried some potatoes and venison steaks, and heated what was left of the cobbler.

"You're welcome. I'm glad you liked it." Her eyes fluttered closed in an expression of ecstasy as she took a sip from her china cup. "Mmm."

"Coffee good?"

She nodded.

It wasn't, but she'd apparently been deprived of it so long her point of reference was skewed.

Taking care not to drop the dainty cup from his large hands, he took a sip and stretched out his legs. He needed to broach the subject of leaving—the threat of winter weather mostly driving the urge—but he wanted to learn more about Rebecca before he did. Maybe she trusted him enough now to answer him truthfully and not dodge his questions.

He drained his cup and handed it to her, shaking his head in refusal of a refill. "You've got quite a place here."

She smiled mildly and took another sip of coffee.

"When you said 'cave,' I pictured a hole in the side of a hill and not much else."

"It took me a while to find, but it suits my needs."

Dig a little deeper. Something neutral. "Do you have any brothers or sisters?"

The curve left her lips. "I have an older brother who lives in Missouri. I had a younger sister, but she died when I was seven."

"I'm sorry," he said and she gave a slight nod.

He was already treading on thin ice. Might as well plunge in all the way. "How did you end up living in the wilderness alone?"

Rebecca's face took on a pained expression so acute it surprised him. He'd known this wasn't going to be easy, but he hadn't expected such an intense reaction.

She set her cup down and wrapped her arms around her waist.

"Please, Becca. Tell me."

Tears rimmed her eyes, but she blinked them away. "I was left here."

He sat forward. "By whom?" She flinched at his tone, but he didn't care. He couldn't wait to get his hands on the mongrel who did this to her.

The agony in her eyes was palpable. "My parents."

Seth gaped. "Your parents did this to you?"

Becca nodded.

"Why?"

She didn't answer.

He rubbed the back of his neck, then held out his hand. "You were only eighteen."

"Seventeen." The word was practically a whisper.

"My God, Becca. Why?"

"I don't know why. We were traveling with a wagon train headed for California. I found out we were going to be delayed for a day, so I left to go exploring. When I got back to the trail, they were gone."

Seth couldn't believe what he was hearing. "You didn't hear them leave?"

"No. I was too far away, near a stream. The sound of the water must've drowned out the noise."

"Did you try to catch up with them?"

"Yes!" She drew a breath and composed herself. "I ran after them when I realized what happened, but I came to a fork in the trail and I didn't know which path they took."

Oh, Becca. The draining emotion stole the strength from his voice. "No one ever came back for you?"

"No... well. I don't know. I went back to the place we'd made camp and waited. But then an Indian—"

"An Indian!"

She waved dismissively. "He didn't see me. But seeing him scared me and I ran. I hit my head and knocked myself out. When I woke up later that day, a storm was coming. I had to take shelter overnight. And then I got lost. By the time I found my way back to the trail, nearly a whole day had passed." She shrugged. "It's possible they sent scouts and I missed them."

Seth shook his head slowly, lips parted. She was obviously being honest with him, but something about her story didn't ring true. The captain would have sent scouts when they realized she was missing, but why didn't they notice her absence right away. They should have never left.

"What?"

He must've said the last part out loud. "They should have never left. I'm trying to figure out why your parents didn't notice you were missing right away."

She hugged herself again and barely met his gaze. "I think they did."

"What makes you say that?"

Humiliation like he'd never seen lined her features. She rose to her feet and gave an almost imperceptible tilt of her head, an invitation to follow, then led him to the second storage room and walked all the way to the back. In the dim light, he could barely make out the items stacked around the walls.

"I found those sitting by the side of the trail," she said, pointing to two wooden barrels. "They were apparently left there for me."

Seth bent over and inspected them more closely. "What are they?"

"They came from my family's wagon. They're empty now, but they held my rations of corn and wheat."

Nausea gripped him. She was right; they must've known. Even partially-full, the barrels would've been too heavy for horses to carry. They would have to have been removed before the wagons left.

Seth brooded over the facts until his head hurt. Dumping her for lack of food didn't make sense. They'd left her rations behind.

Maybe her reputation had been compromised. That was the only thing he could think of. But even in the face of that, most parents wouldn't leave their only daughter to die in the wild. Something must've prevented them from staying to look for her and from coming back. "We need to find your family. There must be an explanation."

A tear rolled down her cheek and she swiped it away. "If they wanted me, they would have found me."

"But you don't want to be found—you stay hidden. You said so yourself."

"I didn't at first." She swiped away another tear. "For *weeks* I sat by that trail every day, waiting for someone to come." Her chest heaved with an errant sob. "Had they wanted to find me, they would've." Shame and indignation radiated from her. So much pain. He reached for her, but she spun on her heel and ran out.

Seth went after her. She was bitter and ashamed, and probably wanted to be alone, but he didn't want her running off again. He hurried to the entrance of the cave, then drew to a halt and stepped back into the shadows when he saw her sitting on a rock on the other side of the clearing. She was hugging her knees, her face buried and her shoulders shaking.

His muscles tensed, practically hurting with the effort it took to stay put. He told himself it was better this way, but his heart refused to listen to his mind. He was about to give in and go comfort her when Cyrus ambled over to her instead.

The horse nudged her shoulder, twice, then blew out a frustrated breath and nudged her again. Becca shrugged him away at first, but then she lifted her head and swiped at her eyes. It wasn't long before she was hugging the animal's neck and stroking his mane.

Good boy, Cyrus.

Seth watched the pair from the shadows, a little jealous of his mount, if he was honest. Just like last night, he glimpsed the frightened girl inside the brave woman, and he wanted to be the one she turned to for reassurance. Heck, for everything.

Let it go, Seth. You're not what she needs. Not long-term, anyway.

Rebecca must've sensed his presence. She looked over her shoulder and met his gaze. Turning back, she gave Cyrus one last pat, then she got up off the rock and walked toward the cave.

When she reached him, Seth tipped up her chin and wiped away the traces of tears with his thumb. "Parents don't up and leave their children behind. There has to be an explanation."

She pulled her chin from his grasp and glanced away, then

turned her weary eyes on him. "Can we talk about something else? Please?"

Seth let out a sigh as she brushed past him into the cave. He'd get to the bottom of her abandonment eventually. For now he just needed to convince her to leave.

"Lunch about ready?" Seth asked as he walked into the large, domed room. He'd given Rebecca some time alone while he tended to Cyrus.

"Just a few more minutes." How she managed to sit on a crate and look as poised as if she were on a settee in some fancy parlor, he didn't know.

He set his hat aside and took off his coat. "What's on the menu?"

"Potatoes and steaks again. I hope you don't mind."

"Nope. Not at all." He smiled. "Meat and potatoes is always good eatin'." He settled himself on the other crate with his back against the wall, legs stretched out, watching Rebecca cook and trying not to stare. Her braid swept back and forth as she moved, the tip of it grazing her narrow waist. Despite her bulky clothes, he could see she was slim. Too slim. He could also see the vestige of curves a few pounds would nicely round out.

He made it through the meal without bringing up anything that would keep her from eating. She still wasn't back to her old self, but she ate a reasonable portion.

Rebecca set her fork down and dabbed the corners of her mouth with her napkin. "Do you think it's safe to go looking for wood?"

He bought himself a few moments chewing and swallowing

his last bite of steak. "Yes. And actually, that reminds me of something I'd like to talk to you about."

Seth set his plate aside and took a swig from his canteen. "I'll help you gather wood if you want, but you don't need to do that anymore." She opened her mouth to speak, but he held up a hand. "You're not safe here. And, while you've done an unbelievable job of surviving for the last year, without livestock, crops, and a reliable way to renew your supplies, you won't last."

She stared at him, then looked down at the fire, hurt and rebellion warring in her eyes.

"Becca," he said softly. "You know what I'm saying is true."

She didn't respond.

Seth leaned forward and tilted his face so he could better see hers. "When I leave this time, I want you to come with me."

Her lips pressed into a thin line, and her chest rose and fell with several breaths before she looked him straight in the eye. "Why did you come back for me?"

That sat him back.

Why? Because I admire you. Because I care about you. Because I'm beginning to dread the thought of life without you. He shoved his foolish feelings aside and gave her the only answer he could. "Because it was the right thing to do."

Her face flinched at his reply, and some of the spark left her eyes. "Why do you care what happens to me?"

Was she serious?

"Because you're a human being—in need. And because... because I *do*." He shouldn't have to justify himself to her. Rescuing her was what any decent person would do. Yet she stared at him with such disappointment in her eyes, he felt like he'd just failed a test.

Without a word, Becca collected their dishes, washed them,

and put them away, then turned away and walked toward the tunnel.

What just happened?

Seth stood and raked a hand through his hair. "Um. Would you like me to try and get us a turkey for supper?"

"Do whatever you want," she muttered. "I'm going to my room."

Chapter Thirteen

Becca finally dragged herself from her bed where she'd lay curled in a hopeless ball for the last few hours. She was so forlorn, she couldn't even bring herself to cry.

When Seth had come back for her, she began to think he really cared. He'd held her last night when she cried, stroked her hair, and called her Becca. Since then, he'd joked with her and tried to cheer her up. More than once, she'd caught him looking at her with longing in his eyes. Had she only seen what she wanted to see? Assumed feelings that weren't really there?

Maybe she had. She'd seen the same in Nathan—even had a promise of marriage—and he'd still gone off and abandoned her.

Smoothing her clothes and tucking in strands of hair that had come loose from her braid, Becca returned to the main room. By the slant of the light, it was nearing time to start supper. She gathered her pans and the spit, and then proceeded to stoke the fire. Seth would likely be back soon with a turkey.

And what would she tell him then?

She scooted back against the wall, hugged her legs, and propped her chin on her knees. She wanted to send him away and keep living on her own, but he was right. She wouldn't survive. The problem was, she wasn't sure she wanted to. A familiar numbness had settled over her, just like those early, dark days—days she'd stared bleakly at the empty prairie and contemplated bringing about her own demise. Or at least not doing anything to prevent it.

She was at that crossroad once more, and this time she knew what her decision would be.

Boots thudded on the ground outside, drawing her out of her thoughts. Heavy footsteps trudged to the entrance, but something about them wasn't right.

Becca stood as the foreign sounds came closer. When a strange groan echoed through the tunnel, she backed away and placed her hand on her knife.

"Becca." The word was a feeble entreaty.

Seth!

He stumbled from the tunnel hunched over and barely recognizable. His left eye was swollen, his face was bruised, and his hands were covered in blood. He dropped the game bag he was carrying and began to list sideways, losing his footing.

Becca rushed forward and caught him.

"Help me off with my coat."

She did so and gasped. Blood saturated his shirt, which was slashed nearly in half. Beneath the gaping flaps of fabric lay a long gash that went from his middle all the way around his right side, under his ribs. The skin was flayed open, cut an inch deep in places. "What happened?"

He started to sway, so she lowered him until he was sitting on the ground. He closed his eyes and ran his tongue over dry lips. "On my way back from hunting, I was attacked."

Becca shivered and glanced back at the tunnel.

"Don't worry. He was alone. I wasn't followed."

"Who attacked you?"

He studied her for a moment. "The man who ran away yesterday."

Becca's hand flew to her mouth and tears pricked her eyes. Tucker. As long as she lived, she'd never forget that name. "Did he get away?"

Solemnity swept his features. "No."

"Good." It was an awful thing to say, but she didn't care. And Seth didn't seem to mind. He just stared at her with a look that was somewhere between astonishment and relief.

He gestured to the hole in his shirt. "I need stitches. Can you patch me up?"

She'd been sewing for years and she'd seen it done before. "I think so." Something dark glistened near her knee—blood! Seth was bleeding so much, it was pooling on the floor. "I'll get some rags. Don't move."

He closed his eyes and nodded.

She hurried to gather everything she would need to care for his wound, then helped him remove his shirt and positioned him flat of his back. She quickly rinsed her hands and placed a folded cloth over the gash in his side.

"Ahh," he groaned when she pressed down.

"I'm sorry. You're really bleeding."

"It's okay," he rasped. "Do what you need to do." He reached for his coat and pulled a shiny, metal flask from one of the pockets.

"What's that?"

"Whiskey. I keep it for medicinal purposes." He must. In all the time she'd spent with him, she'd never seen him take a drink or smelled liquor on him.

Becca lifted the cloth. A bright red stream ran over the edge of the cut and down his side. She repeated the process two more times, holding firmer pressure, but it didn't help. "It's not working. There's a place the keeps bleeding no matter what I do."

Seth's eyes were closed. When he opened them and looked at her, they were bleak. "You're going to have to burn it." He inclined his head toward her waist. "Take your knife and stick the end of it in the fire. Get it as hot as you can."

She shied away and shook her head.

"You have to, Becca. You have to, or I'll bleed to death." Fluid sloshed in the flask as he tossed back a swallow. "Just do it. We can't waste any more time."

Hands shaking, she unsheathed her knife and held the tip of it in the flames. When the knife was so hot it was practically glowing, she returned to him and knelt by his side. "I don't know if I can do this."

"You have to. Hurry—before it cools." He clenched his fists, closed his eyes, and gave a single, sharp nod of his head.

Becca steadied herself by placing her free hand flat against his side, and then she pressed the tip of the knife into the cut, right to the source of the blood.

A tortured cry ripped from Seth's throat through clenched teeth as flesh sizzled and smoke rose. Becca gagged as much from the act as the smell. She held the knife there—did what she had to do—but that didn't stop her heart from breaking or tears from running down her face.

By the time his groan quieted to a stifled sob, the bleeding had stopped. "I'm sorry," she whispered as she wiped her eyes and set the knife aside.

Seth's throat moved with a tight swallow, but his jaw stayed clenched and he didn't speak. Sweat beaded his pale, lined brow.

She rinsed the gash with some of his whiskey, eliciting another agonizing groan from him, and then patted it dry and readied her needle with thread she'd wet with spirits, too. After taking a breath and willing herself not to be sick, she positioned herself to sew up his wound. "Are you ready?"

"Do it," he ground out.

Becca pierced the skin and drew the needle through the other side.

Seth flinched. He exhaled as she tied the first knot.

The gash deepened toward the center, and her next few stiches grew hesitant. Even though she warned him each time, she could tell her lingering was only hurting him more. She steeled herself and finished the rest with quicker, deliberate motions.

He barely uttered a sound, but his jaw was stiff, his face was pale, and his fists were clenched tight enough to break bone. A shudder went through him when she finally called out, "Last one."

Becca put away her needle and pressed a cool rag to his face, wiping away the perspiration and smoothing back his hair. She rinsed it, wrung it out, and laid it on his brow, above his swollen eye. Switching to the pan that held warm water, she wrung out a fresh rag and began bathing him from the neck and shoulders down. She paused to cleanse his scrapes and cuts and took care to avoid his stiches. By the time she reached his fists, his hands had relaxed and his fingers lay open. One at a time, Becca lowered his hands into the water to loosen the caked-on blood. She gently bathed every crease and callus until the last trace of red was gone.

His pants were another story. He'd bled so much, a soaking

stain extended to the knee of his right leg. They would have to come off.

"I'll be right back," she said as she rose to get fresh water and more supplies. "Don't move."

Seth nodded without opening his eyes. He looked so exhausted, she didn't fear any disobedience.

Becca returned and knelt at his side, then folded a blanket in half and centered it lengthwise over his waist. Reaching underneath, she unfastened the buttons of his trousers and loosened the ties on his drawers. He was looking at her now with tired blue eyes.

"Lift your hips," she said, ignoring her discomfiture.

He did so, groaning in pain with the effort.

She slid his garments down, being careful not to dislodge the blanket. After removing his boots and sliding his pants and drawers the rest of the way off, Becca knelt at his hips and wrung out a warm rag. She started with his left leg since it was mostly clean. Then she switched to his right, alternately rinsing out the rag and wiping away the rusty, copper-smelling haze that coated his skin. She tried not to look at his body—to keep her eyes on her hands and her mind on her task—but his rippled stomach and his long, muscled legs were too striking to ignore. She slid the blanket over as far as she dared and removed the last traces of dried blood. Thankfully, it hadn't seeped any farther.

After she finished bathing his legs all the way to his feet, Becca set the bowl aside and gently blotted his skin dry with a towel. She positioned the clean brown trousers she'd brought from one of the trunks and worked them onto his ankles. They were two sizes too big, but that was probably for the best. He would be bedridden for a couple of days.

"Lift up," she said when she'd gotten them past his knees. He did so and groaned again. "I'm sorry I don't have any drawers."

"'t's okay."

She reached under the cloth to fasten the fly, then removed it now that his body was properly covered. Well, almost. He still needed a shirt. He also needed a warm place to sleep, and moving him was going to be tricky.

"Don't move," she instructed and went to get bedding.

As soon as she'd spread his bedroll out in a covered, draft-free part of the room, she turned to find Seth trying to sit up. "Wait," she called as she rushed back to his side. "You'll pull your stitches loose." Sure enough, he almost had. Three of them had torn the skin, and tiny trails of blood were trickling.

"Damn." Seth lay back with a moan as she held a cloth to his side. "Are you gonna have to redo them?"

Becca lifted the cloth and looked them over. "No, but stay put while I find something to bandage this."

He nodded and held the cloth in place. "I still have the strips of fabric you bound my ribs with. Will that do?"

"Yes. Where are they?"

"In my room, in my bag."

"Are they clean?"

"Yes."

Becca retrieved them. Rolling him slightly, she slid the long strip of cotton under his back and tied the ends to hold the folded cloth in place over the wound. He was shivering now, his flesh covered in tiny bumps. Taking care not to disturb the stitches, she helped him on with two shirts—first cotton, then flannel. She buttoned them both but left the tails loose.

She frowned as she eyed the distance to his temporary bed. There was no other way to do it. She was going to have to drag him. And she couldn't pull him by his arms because of the stitches. She went and got a tarp.

Becca knelt next to him. "Roll to your good side," she instructed, bunching the tarp along the entire length of his body.

"Why? What are you going to do?"

"Move you to your bed over there. You can't walk, so I'm going to drag you."

"No. I'll find another way to get there."

"You'll pull your stitches out."

"Leave me here, then."

"I won't be able to keep you sheltered here." She pointed up at the holes.

"I camp outdoors all the time. I'll be fine. Just cover me—"

"You've lost too much blood. You're shivering already. I've got to keep you warm."

"*No.*" He glared at her. "I'm too heavy for you to be dragging—"

"In case you forgot, I've done it before." She planted her hands on her hips and glared back, daring him to refute her claim.

He looked away in disgust.

Becca cupped his cheek with her hand and turned his face until his brooding gaze met hers. "I know you don't like this, but you're injured, and you got that way protecting me. Taking care of you is the least I can do."

The lines around his eyes softened. "All right. But leave my feet free so I can push with my legs and help you."

She helped Seth roll to his side and stuffed the tarp beneath him, then spread it out when he rolled back. Standing at his head, she gathered the end in her hands and slid him across the floor, canvas scraping against stone with each push of his heels.

Once he was fairly centered on his bed, she removed the tarp, placed a pillow under his head, and covered him with a quilt and two blankets.

Becca stoked the fire and offered Seth a drink from his canteen. "Do you need anything else?"

He blotted his mouth with his sleeve. "No, thank you."

As she capped the canteen and set it nearby, panic hit. "Where's Cyrus?"

"He's okay. He's outside." Seth closed his eyes and groaned. "There's a deer on his back, and he's still saddled."

Becca stood and sheathed her knife. "I'll take care of it."

Seth muttered a curse. "Just drag the deer a safe distance away and leave the saddle on. One night in it won't kill him. I should be feeling well enough tomorrow to take it off myself."

Becca frowned at him. They both knew that wasn't true. "I'm capable of removing a saddle, Seth. I'm also going to dress the deer." She nearly gagged at the thought, but chose to ignore her revulsion and do it anyway. With Seth unable to hunt, they needed the meat.

"Do you know how?"

"Yes." She'd helped her father several times on the trail.

Becca glanced at the fading light as she pulled on her coat and gathered a few rags and some rope. She went to pick up the game bag and could barely lift it off the floor. "What's in here?"

"Three rabbits and two turkeys."

Great. At least they were already dead. She only had to stomach the butchering.

Becca braced herself and hoisted the bag over her shoulder. "I'll be back as soon as I can." She peered down at Seth as she would a recalcitrant child. "You had better behave while I'm gone."

Becca trudged back to the cave with a bag full of rabbit and turkey slung over her shoulder. By the look of the sky, a winter storm was well on its way. The deer she'd hoisted into the tree would freeze tonight, and the smaller game she brought with her would stay plenty cold in a trunk toward the front of the cave.

Before returning to unsaddle Cyrus, she checked on Seth, relieved to find him peacefully sleeping. He looked so boyish when he was at rest, such a contrast to the hardy man he was. Becca warmed herself by the fire, then gloved her raw hands and went back to care for the horse.

Seth was awake when she carried the saddle inside, so she held it firm and tried not to stumble under its weight. She set it down and walked over to him. "How are you feeling?"

"I'm sore."

She could see in his eyes and the lines of his face he was more than sore. "Want some whiskey?"

"Nah. Not yet."

"Let me check your wound." She knelt by his side and removed her gloves.

Seth grasped her hands and held them up, his brow creasing as he rubbed at the chafes and inspected the cuts. "I'm sorry you got stuck with all that. A woman shouldn't have to do a man's work."

She folded his blankets down. "I didn't mind." And truly, she didn't. "Now Cyrus is happy, and we have enough meat to last for a while."

"Well, as long as Cyrus is happy," he groused.

Becca laughed and lifted the hems of his shirts. Small spots of blood stained one end of the bandage, but they were dry. "Looks good." She smoothed his shirts back down and handed him his canteen. "Drink some water." She was no expert at caring for the sick, but she knew frequent drinks of liquid were a must.

"C'mon, drink," she urged when he stopped after two small sips.

He hesitated, then turned the canteen up and took several deep swallows.

"That's better." She capped it and set it aside.

A hint of pink crossed his pale cheeks. "You wouldn't happen to have a chamber pot, would you?"

"I do, but I doubt you could position yourself to use it." Becca ignored her nerves and kept her voice even. "What's the nature of your need?"

"I, uh, need to relieve myself."

She retrieved a can much like the one he'd used at the hut. "Use this."

Seth took it from her without argument, but she could tell it cost him.

"Do you need my help?"

"No."

"I'll step outside, then. Call for me when you're done."

Once she'd stoked the fire and checked on Cyrus, Becca made herself a temporary bed along the same wall as Seth's, to be nearby in case he needed something during the night. She removed her boots and sat near his head, watching the blankets covering his chest rise and fall with easy movements. He'd dozed the entire time she cooked supper, awoken long enough to drink some broth and a few sips of whiskey, and then he'd fallen back into a sound sleep again.

Careful not to wake him, she smoothed the locks of hair covering his forehead back away from his face. Light brown lashes fanned out over his cheeks, and his mouth lay with lips slightly parted. His skin was still pale, but it was dry and cool; and it was smooth, which meant he was free of pain.

She wrapped her knees with her arms and gazed at him. Who was this man? Where had he come from? She'd been so busy hiding her own identity that she hadn't asked about his. She sighed and slid under her covers. Her musing was pointless. Once she nursed him back to health and sent him on his way, none of it would matter.

Rebecca opened her eyes and stared into the dark. Someone had called her name.

"Becca," Seth said again.

"Yes?"

"I'm cold." The flaming logs had dwindled to a clump of glowing embers.

Becca hurried across the room and added some wood to the coals, all the while chiding herself for letting the fire burn down. She wasn't used to keeping one going all night. She'd stayed warm under her blankets; having lost so much blood, he must not be able to.

Once the logs caught and erupted into a blaze, she returned to check on Seth. She crouched down and tucked his covers snugly around him. "Do you need anything?"

His eyes glittered with firelight as he peered up at her. "No. Sorry I woke you."

"It's all right. I didn't mean to let the room get so cold."

She checked his blankets one more time, and then crawled back under her own. After a while, she drifted off to the sound of crackling wood and soft snores.

"Becca."

"Hm." Why was he calling her again so soon?

"B-Becca."

She opened her eyes and pushed the quilt off her face. Pale winter light shone through the holes in the ceiling, filled with floating flakes of snow. Hours had passed. It was morning.

"B-Becca, I'm c-cold."

After stoking the fire, she knelt at Seth's side. Shivers racked his body, and his teeth chattered like an old wagon on a rough road. Brushing his hair aside, she placed her hand on his forehead. His skin was dry and hot—much too hot. He wasn't shivering because he was cold, and now, neither was she. A fever probably meant infection. And infection often meant death.

The burden fell like lead onto her shoulders. She didn't know much about doctoring, and she held this man's life in her hands.

Seth looked at her with dull, listless eyes. "I'm s-sick, aren't I?"

"You've got a little fever. That's all." She lifted his head and held the canteen to his cracked lips. "Drink some water."

He took several swallows and laid his head back down. "You're n-not a very g-good liar."

"I'll be right back."

Becca fetched a clean rag and filled a bucket with a mixture of hot and cold water. She wrung the rag out and wiped his face, then folded the blankets back to check his wound.

A wave of heat rose from him, and he shivered violently.

Becca peeled back the dressing. The stitches were undisturbed and the edges were closed, but the skin was beginning to turn red in places. She lingered, buying herself time to think. What would her mother do?

"You've been s-starin' a long t-time. It mu-must be bad."

"No," Becca said, replacing the bandage. "Not bad." She managed a smile as she covered him back up. "I'm going to gather a few things. I'll be back shortly."

After checking a book on herbs to reassure herself her memory was true, she donned her coat and went in search of what she would need. Her choices were limited by the season, but she found a willow growing near a stream. She scraped off some bark, then brushed aside the snow in a field nearby and began gathering handfuls of green.

"I was-s beginning to g-get worried about you," Seth said when she returned.

Becca emptied the precious bounty from her apron into a shallow, wooden bowl. "It took me a while to find what I needed."

He eyed her harvest. "W-What's that?"

"Willow bark and chickweed. Willow bark for your fever, and chickweed for your wound." Becca put some bark in a pot of water to simmer, then made a poultice with some of the chickweed and applied it to his injury, securing it in place with the bandage. Once the bark had steeped long enough, she strained some of tea into a cup and added sugar.

She helped Seth raise his head again. "Drink this."

He glanced at her, then took a tentative sip. "Ack. It's bitter."

"I know. But it will bring down the fever and help with your pain."

He grudgingly took another sip and grimaced.

"Are you hungry?" she asked when he finished the tea. "I could make some biscuits."

"No, but thanks."

She wrung out the rag and wiped his face again. "What about some soup?"

Seth shook his head.

She tilted her head to the side and frowned. "You need to eat something."

"Maybe some broth."

Becca checked the herb book again, and then gathered some edible greens from the woods. Determined to help Seth get well, she chopped them finely and added them to the rabbit soup she'd reheated from supper.

Once she'd fed him plenty of broth and coaxed him to take a few bites of meat and potato, she settled back with a bowl of her own. "Feeling any better?"

"Come to think of it, I am." He'd moved his arms from underneath the blankets, and he wasn't shivering anymore.

She felt his forehead and breathed a sigh of relief. "Your fever's coming down."

Seth touched the area over his bandage.

"Something wrong?"

"It feels warm."

"It's supposed to. The chickweed heats up as it draws the infection out." She lifted her cup and took a sip of water. "Tell me when it gets hot, and I'll put a fresh poultice on."

"Hot?" The look on his face was priceless.

Becca spent the rest of the day caring for Seth, offering him water, broth, and willow bark tea, and changing his poultice. By the next morning, he was free of fever and the redness was gone from his wound. But he was growing restless.

Once she'd cleaned up from breakfast, Becca chatted with him as she secured his bandage and helped him change shirts. It was obvious he appreciated the care, but she could see the toll this was taking on him. No one liked being an invalid, especially a man.

She straightened his blankets, folding them down at the chest. "Is there something I can do to make you more comfortable?"

"Nah. I'm just getting stiff from lying on the ground so long." She didn't doubt that. She suspected boredom wasn't helping either.

Becca smiled and patted his arm. "Hang on. I'll be right back."

She sifted through a pile of books in the first storeroom. If she could keep him resting one more day, he'd be able to start getting up and walking around. She gathered a few she thought Seth would like and carried them back to his bed.

"I thought you might like to read." She read off the titles to him and he chose *The Three Musketeers*.

Seth took it from her and read for a while, but then he set the book down and sighed.

"Finished already?" Becca joked as she carried in wood for the fire.

He flashed a small smile, but the look in his eyes betrayed it.

She added a log to the fire, and then she sat against the wall near Seth's pallet and positioned him so that his head and shoulders were elevated on a pillow in her lap. It hurt him to move, but once he got settled, he seemed more comfortable.

"Show me where you left off," she said as she picked up the book.

For the next couple of hours, she read to him. He was more peaceful than he'd been in some time. The fire kept them warm while flakes of snow drifted through the roof and melted as they fell to the floor. Thoughts of him leaving pricked her heart from time to time, but she ignored them and basked in the comfort of his presence.

"Don't stop," he said, interrupting her reading.

She was about to ask 'what?' when a jolt of self-awareness sent a blazing blush across her face. She'd been running her fingers through his hair!

"Please, don't stop." He was looking up at her now. "My pain goes away when you do that, and I almost forget I'm hurt."

The sincerity in his soft blue eyes drew the heat out of her cheeks and filled her with a different kind of warmth. She dragged her gaze back to the page, and then she smoothed the hair at his temple and combed her fingers through his silky locks as she read.

Chapter Fourteen

Seth looked up from the leather halter he was cleaning as Becca entered the tunnel and turned into the first storage room. He gulped as a bolt of heat raced through his veins. Even from the back, the sight of her affected him. His body stayed on alert, simmering with want whenever she was near. For more than a week, he'd watched her go about her chores, felt her tender touch as she cared for him, and grown more attached to her by the day. And they still had weeks—maybe months—of traveling to go. How was he going to say goodbye to her and walk away?

Just tell her the truth and you won't have to. She'll leave you.

Humbled by that dose of reality, he set the halter aside and headed for the storage room. After being nothing but a burden for days, perhaps he could do something useful.

Hmph. Not likely, his conscience prodded again. He was still weak and forced to guard his healing side. But it couldn't hurt to try.

"Need help?" he asked.

Becca looked up from the stack of books she was returning to a wooden crate and smiled. Just smiled. She didn't look startled the way she had when he first arrived, flinching every time he entered a room. That ounce of progress made him happy.

"No thanks." She stood and smoothed her skirt. "I'd offer you another book, but I think you've read them all."

"I think you're right." She'd read to him for countless hours while he recuperated, and then he'd read to pass the time. If the men he worked with ever got wind of some of the books—the girly titles—they'd never let him live it down. Well, maybe, if they saw the woman the books belonged to, heard her read a passage or two. Becca's sweet voice made anything sound good.

Seth scanned the room. In all the time he'd been here, he'd never come in. Crates filled with everything from shoes to quilts lined the walls, along with several trunks and a desk with an old organ stool for a chair. The desk looked as though it got regular use. He started to ask why she kept it in a storage room instead of her own, but an upward glance answered his question. A large shaft off the main room opened into the ceiling of this one. The lighting was better here.

"What's that?" he asked, walking closer and fingering a large, bound book sitting off to one side. It was flat, like a ledger.

"It's nothing. Just a sketch book."

"Mind if I look?" He glanced up when Becca didn't answer right away.

She shrugged. "If you want to." She was fiddling with the end of her braid—something she only did when she was nervous or uncomfortable.

Her discomfiture fed his curiosity. He lifted the cover.

The first page was blank, but a pencil drawing of a sparrow perched on a branch was centered on the next one. The drawing was so detailed and accurate, it looked real. He turned the page.

A sketch of the mountains spread across this one, complete with snowy, cloud-draped caps and trees lining a stream at the base. He might as well be looking at the real thing. The skill of the artist was exceptional.

On the next page, a woman stared back at him. Her features were comely, her lined eyes kind, and her face oddly familiar. She was an older version of Rebecca.

Seth looked up at her, working to find his voice as realization dawned. "You drew these."

"Yes." She was staring at the picture, not him, the longing in her eyes palpable.

"This is your mother, isn't it?"

She nodded.

Seth looked back at the sketch and paused, his eyes lingering on the benevolent ones staring back at him from the page. He didn't want to cause Rebecca pain, but letting a wound fester only made it worse. Opening it hurt. But opening it meant the healing could begin.

It was his turn to tend wounds.

He picked up the book and gestured toward two trunks sitting side by side along the wall.

Becca took a step back and glanced at the door.

Don't run.

She looked at him again. Her shoulders slumped, and she sat on one of the trunks.

Seth sat next to her and opened the book so that it lay across his lap.

The next few pictures after the one of her mother must have been of her life before she left home. One was of a barn. Another, a window looking out a girl's room. And another, a man fishing from the bank of a pond. Even in profile, Seth could see the resemblance. "That must be your pa."

Becca nodded, her lashes glistening with unshed tears.

Seth pulled his handkerchief from his pocket and handed it to her.

A half a beat later, she took it with a muttered acknowledgement.

He nudged her and muttered back, "Better that than my shirt."

A bashful smile spread across her face.

That's better.

The next several pictures depicted life on the trail, the last of them drawn from the perspective of someone walking alongside a wagon, watching a single line of shrinking prairie schooners curve and disappear into the distance. She'd even managed to capture the dust.

Seth slowly shook his head. "Becca, these are good. You're very talented."

She just shrugged, dismissing his words as if she didn't believe him. Could she not see the quality of her work? Not hear the honesty in his voice?

He tipped up her chin and looked into her eyes. "I'm serious. Your drawings are some of the best I've ever seen."

Now a battle raged in those blue-grey depths. Disbelief warring with a bid for validation. For worth.

The familiarity of their position sent a tremor of heat from the tips of his fingers to the soles of his boots and drew him like an ant to sugar. Before he did something he'd regret, Seth let his hand fall away from her face.

Her gaze dropped to her lap and the handkerchief she held in her hands. Disbelief had apparently won.

Vivid colors surprised him when he turned the page. The

other pictures had been drawn in shades of gray, but not this one. The laughing young lady whose face filled the page boasted lightly-freckled cheeks, sparkling green eyes and a head full of wavy red hair—a mixture of copper, scarlet, and gold. "Who's this?"

Becca wore a pleasant expression, almost wistful. "That's my friend Charlotte."

"From Missouri?"

"No. She came from Kentucky. We met on the wagon train. I didn't think she liked me at first, but we eventually became friends."

Seth studied the picture. "Why didn't she like you?"

"She..."

"She what?"

Becca shook her head. "I shouldn't. It isn't nice."

"C'mon. Tell me." He leaned in and whispered, "I won't breathe a word. I promise."

Becca gave a quick upward glance. "Oh, all right." She looked up at him through her lashes. "Charlotte's rather haughty. You know. One of those people who thinks they're better than everyone else, that they shouldn't have to get dirty or do any real work."

"Ah." Seth nodded. "I see."

"She wasn't so bad. She pitched in. And she was lots of fun—we laughed all the time. She just didn't like the same things I did."

"Like what?"

Becca shrugged. "Gardening, fishing, those kinds of things."

The lady sitting next to him may be able to hunt and butcher with the best of them, but she was no less refined. And haughty she was not. Not anywhere near.

Seth flipped through a few more pages of landscapes and animals. "Why are some of your pictures in color and others not?"

"I found the sketch book and pencils first. I didn't find the pastels until later."

The picture on the next page made him smile. A blue-eyed, towheaded child not more than two grinned back at him, with rosy cheeks and wispy curls framing her face. He turned to Rebecca, expecting a similar reaction.

She wore a smile, but the tears pooling along the edges of her lids belied it. "That's Emily," she finally said, "my sister."

He should have known. "How did she die?"

"She caught a bad fever. Momma cared for her night and day—we all did—but..." She dabbed her eyes with his handkerchief.

"Aw, Becca." Seth put his arm around her shoulders and tucked her to his side. The action sent a throbbing ache through his wound, but he didn't care.

Becca clutched the handkerchief in her lap and drew a shuddering breath. "We buried her on a hill behind the house. I used to visit her grave every day and talk to her. I miss my home and my friends in Missouri, but the worst part was leaving Emily behind."

Seth gave her shoulders a gentle squeeze. He waited until she regained her composure, and then he turned the page with his free hand. The most pompous-looking female he'd ever seen stared down her beaky nose at him. Pursed mouth, severe hair, close-set eyes with a skeptical glare—now *that* was a haughty woman.

He was almost afraid to ask. "Who's she?"

"That's my Aunt Prudence."

Fitting name. Although 'Pretentious' would have fit even

better. Seth stifled a chuckle.

Becca outright giggled.

"What's so funny?"

"I was thinking about what she'd say if she saw us right now."

He raised a brow.

"You know. Sitting here alone like this, *un-chaperoned*." She'd drawn out the last with a nasal tone, apparently imitating her aunt.

Seth grinned. Then he promptly removed his arm from around her shoulders and cleared his throat.

The spark of humor left Becca's eyes, and she scooted away. Those tiny few inches felt like miles, but he forced himself to tolerate it. Soon it really would be miles.

He flipped through several more pages, enjoying both the art and the commentary, truly amazed at the talent Rebecca possessed.

They both grew quiet when he turned the next page. Drawn in shades of blues, browns and grays was a portrait of him atop Cyrus in the base of a valley—the sky ashen, the land filling with snow, and the tails of his duster flying in the wind. His hand shielded his eyes as he looked up in the direction of... the artist. It was the day he tried to take her with him, the day he he'd searched for her to no avail.

"You were watching me," he said, looking at her.

Becca's gaze dropped to her lap, to hands nervously twisting his handkerchief. She didn't speak; merely nodded.

He looked at the picture again, recalling how she'd run and hidden that day. He didn't ask why, because he already knew the answer—she didn't want to be found—even though he didn't fully understand it. He didn't scold her either. What was the point?

With a heavy sigh, he shoved his annoyance aside and turned the page. The next picture was also of him. In this one, he was sitting by the campfire, smiling. The next was him sitting on a rock, reading, and the next was of him asleep in the hut.

He looked over at Becca again.

Now she was staring up at him through her lashes with a tentative look on her face.

He smiled at her and kept turning pages. Him tending Cyrus. Him fishing with her homemade lines. Him injured, eyes closed, lying under blankets in the cave. He didn't miss the feminine hand on his forehead—her hand. He also didn't miss the fact he was the subject of more of her drawings than anyone else, even members of her family. What did that mean?

"It's easier for me to draw people if the image is fresh in my mind," she said as if reading his.

"Makes sense." It did, but it stung. Even though he and Becca had no future together, the idea she favored him meant a lot.

The next one showed Cyrus stealing some work gloves out of his back pocket with his teeth. Seth scowled and shook his head. "So *that's* what happened." He'd frequently reached for them only to find them on the ground. "Stupid horse."

"Ha. He seems pretty smart to me."

Seth laughed. "I shoulda known you'd take his side." He turned a few more pages. Regrettably, they were blank.

"That's the end," Becca said.

"They really are good." He peered into her eyes, wishing she'd believe him, and wishing their time together didn't have to end. When his gaze was drawn to her soft, pink lips, he forced himself to turn away.

He lifted the sketch book to close it, and a crinkled page fell out. One edge was uneven where it had been torn from the book, and the drawing was smudged. It looked as though it had been crumpled into a ball and smoothed back out. A tall, young man stood alone by a wagon, his dark hair blowing in the wind and his piercing blue eyes enlivened by the smile on his face.

"Who's this?"

When Rebecca didn't answer, he turned and looked at her.

Her face was blank. "No one important," she said flatly. Her gaze lingered a moment more on the drawing, and then she stood and strode from the room.

On closer inspection, several small spots dotted the surface of the portrait, the color washed out of their centers and concentrated in dark lines around the edge as if water had dripped on the page.

Rain? No. Becca was too careful with her things to let that happen.

It had to be tears.

Seth slid the page back in and closed the book. The smiling man by the wagon might not be important to her now, but at some point in her life, he was.

Becca left the cave and went for a walk with Cyrus. As she led him to a nearby field to graze, she turned her face up and let the sun bathe her cheeks with warmth. She hadn't bothered putting on her coat. The weather had taken a turn, bringing spring-like conditions.

Plucking a few blades of grass, she sat on a large rock and watched Cyrus nibble, wondering if Seth would follow her and question her about the drawing. She should have thrown it away. Unlike the others, the pleasant memories it stirred no longer outweighed the bad.

The familiar trod of Seth's boots approached, his left step slightly heavier than his right, especially now that he was injured. He'd told her he was as good as healed, but she knew better. He still favored his side, and his stamina hadn't completely returned.

He stopped a few feet away—hatless—studying her from under the lock of golden hair that swept sideways across his forehead.

"You forgot this," he finally said, holding out Cyrus' lead line.

"Don't need it." She squinted up at him, the curve of her lips more a reaction to the sun in her eyes than an actual smile. "He follows me around like a puppy."

Seth's arm dropped back to his side, the coil of rope still in his grasp. He inclined his head toward the rock she was sitting on. "Mind if I join you?"

Becca scooted over and motioned to the empty spot beside her.

They sat there in silence, staring out at the prairie while the breeze fanned their faces and stirred the ruffles of her skirt. That was fine with her. She didn't feel like talking.

Seth shifted his boots in the dirt and fingered the coil of rope in his lap. He didn't say anything, but she could feel the tension building the longer they sat there. Directly, he looked up at her. *Here it comes.* "Who is he?"

She tossed the grass aside, never breaking her gaze from the line of trees in the distance. "His name is Nathan Keating." She stood and took a few steps, keeping her eyes on the horizon and her emotions locked away. "I met him on the wagon train. His family's wagon was near ours in the line, and our parents became friends. They were planning to claim land near each other and build farms. Nathan was, too.

"A few weeks into the trip, he began paying attention to me—doted on me quite a bit, actually. He eventually made his intentions known and asked me if I'd marry him once we got to California. I said yes." Becca turned and faced Seth. "He was my intended."

His eyes widened, and what little color had returned to his cheeks over the last few days drained away.

She stood there, waiting for him to respond. When he didn't, she turned away again. The breeze took on a mournful sound, and the prairie seemed emptier than ever before.

"Was," Seth muttered. "You said he *was* your intended. Don't you mean *is*?"

Becca lowered her head with a sardonic smile only the ground saw. "Let me ask you something." She faced him again. "What if the woman you planned to marry was left behind? What would you do?"

His brow darkened. "I'd do whatever it took to find her."

Exactly.

Her point made, Becca left for the cave.

Seth rose and caught hold of her arm. He stepped in front of her and his gaze locked with hers—irises dark and turbulent. "He doesn't deserve you."

Her grip on her emotions slipped with a sharp intake of breath.

Seth slid his arm around her waist, drawing her flush against his large, taut frame as he cradled her jaw in his hand and tilted her face up to meet his. His breath feathered over her mouth, and his lips touched hers with a softness that surprised her. He lingered there, then slowly lifted his head.

Becca stood speechless as his eyes searched hers. A flock of sparrows took flight from a nearby tree. The brisk beat of their wings matched the flutter of her heart.

He'd given her a kiss. Her first kiss.

A small crease appeared between Seth's brows. He released her waist as the hand on her face fell away.

A big brown nose came out of nowhere, bumping his shoulder and knocking him sideways. With an angry snort, Cyrus wedged himself between them and glared at his owner.

Seth glared back. "What in the—"

Cyrus snorted again and stomped his hoof.

Becca patted her champion's broad neck. "It's okay, boy. He wasn't trying to hurt me." Cheeks heating, she eased around Cyrus, avoiding Seth's gaze. "I'll go start lunch."

Seth handed Rebecca his empty plate. "Thank you. Breakfast was very good."

Her smile did little to allay the uneasiness that both weighted and electrified the air. She hadn't gone back to flinching when he entered a room, but renewed awkwardness marked every interaction they'd had since he kissed her in the field the day before.

When he'd learned she was betrothed to someone on the train and the gutless fool hadn't moved heaven and earth to retrieve her, he'd been so consumed with rage he was ready to track the cretin down and beat some honor into him. Worse, his insides twisted in knots at the thought of her with another man. As if he had any claim.

Stupid. In a fit of jealousy and lust, he'd done something stupid. And crossing that line had set things back between Rebecca and him. Not only had he started something he had no hope to ever finish, she apparently didn't appreciate his advance. She'd stared at him in shock and fled at the first opportunity. Even Cyrus knew he was out of line.

From that moment on, he'd taken care to be as mannerly as possible and filled the uncomfortable silence by talking to her about returning with him to civilization. She listened, but she wasn't saying much, leaving him to ponder the direction of her mind.

"Rebecca?"

She stopped picking at the food on her plate and looked up at him, warily.

"Have you given any more thought to what I said yesterday?"

She swallowed and set down her fork. "Yes. Some."

"And?" He tried not to sound as insistent as he felt.

Her gaze wavered. "I'm not sure what you want me to say."

He rested his elbows on his knees and turned out his hands. "I want to you tell me where you want to go, and I want you to say you'll come with me."

She stared at her plate and didn't answer, but her posture and her silence spoke volumes.

Seth rubbed the back of his neck. "Look. If you're worried about what happened yesterday, don't be. When I said you're safe with me, I meant it. That kiss—" The kiss that still heated his blood. "I made a mistake. It won't happen again."

Her shoulders wilted and her gaze returned to her lap.

Shit. What did he have to do to convince her? She knew these hills like she knew her own mind. If she decided to hide from him again...

To hell with his pride.

Seth knelt in front of her. He took the plate from her lap and set it aside, and then he gathered both her hands in his. Her whole body stiffened, but he didn't let go. "I'll take you anywhere you want to go, anywhere at all, but I can't wait much longer for you to make up your mind. Winter's coming and we're running out of time." His heart ached as he stared into her eyes. "I'm afraid you're going to hide from me again, and I couldn't live with that, with leaving you here alone—leaving you to die. What do I have to do to convince you to come with me? Tell me, Becca, please."

Seconds ticked by as a new emotion wrestled with her wary detachment. Was it guilt? She wet her lips, and her chest rose and fell with several breaths.

"Please." He rubbed his thumb across the back of her hand. "I'll take you anywhere. Just promise me you'll come."

Her lashes lowered and she nodded. "Okay."

Her cheek didn't twitch, but he needed to be sure. "Promise me you won't hide from me this time."

Her lashes lifted again, and she looked him in the eye. "I promise."

Relief flooded him as a sigh deflated his lungs. "Good. Where do you want me to take you?"

"It doesn't matter," she said softly. "Whatever inconveniences you the least."

"You're not an inconvenience, Rebecca. Far from it." He released her hands and returned to his seat on the crate. "Do you want to go to California?"

She shook her head.

"Are you sure? We could find your parents and find out what happened?"

She flattened a pale hand against her stomach. "I know what happened. They knowingly left me here."

"You could be wrong."

"I'm not. I didn't find any evidence of an attack on the

train—did you?" Her question held a flicker of double-edged hope.

He snuffed it with a reluctant shake of his head. He'd scouted well west and south of Becca's location. If there had been an incident severe enough to keep them from her, he'd have come across the remains of it.

Her chest rose and fell with a shaky breath. "Going to the stream alone ruined my reputation. It's the only feasible explanation."

"But you had a promise of marriage. Even if they suspected that Nathan went with you, he was already planning to marry you."

"Yes, but he didn't go with me. His time was likely accounted for." Becca looked up at him, an eddy of pain swirling in her dove-gray eyes. "If they thought someone *other than* Nathan was involved, it would explain why no one came back for me, not even him."

Seth's face went slack with understanding. By the time he recovered enough to convey his compassion, she had already looked away.

"What about Missouri? You said you had a brother there."

She fingered the cuff of her sleeve. "Traveling north this late in the year wouldn't be easy."

"No, it wouldn't. But I'll do it if that's where you want to go."

She looked up, her expression as tired and bleak as he felt. "Do you need an answer right away?"

Seth scrubbed a hand over his jaw. No matter where they went, they would have to go to the outpost and buy supplies. He wouldn't need to know their destination until then. "I can give you two days."

Becca nodded. She rose to her feet, and he did the same. She was too quiet. That bothered him. But she had a lot on her mind, and he was partly to blame.

He'd give her some time alone.

Seth went to his room and packed by the light of a candle. Becca hadn't decided where she wanted to go, but she'd warmed up to him over the course of the day. And she'd agreed to leave in the morning and travel with him to the outpost, which was a deal breaker for him. No way would he leave her here unprotected.

On his way back to the main room, something caught his eye. A small leather-bound book lay open on her vanity. It looked like a diary. He glanced around the corner. She was clearing the dishes from supper, so he ducked into her room and picked it up. He despised himself for what he was about to do, but he was desperate to know what she was thinking.

'*October 14th*

He kissed me today. It was a simple kiss, just a brush of his lips, but it blazed through me like a grass fire on a windy day. My heart pounded and my knees gave way. If he hadn't held me up, I would have crumpled to the ground.

How is it that such a simple thing can feel so wonderful? I have touched people before and been touched, shaking hands... caring for the sick... a goodbye kiss for my grandmother, but none of that ever felt like this. Every place he touches me tingles with a strange heat that makes my insides shiver and my heart long for more.

I know it is terribly wanton of me to say, but I want more.'

Seth swallowed. His pulse sped and his hands trembled as he turned the page.

'October 15th

I lay awake last night, thinking of him, his golden hair and his vivid blue eyes that seem to see straight to my soul. I can't get him or his kiss out of my mind. It consumes me hour by hour. The mere thought of him stirs me deep inside, and not only in my heart. It stirs me in places I cannot talk about... dare even think about.

I know there is more that goes on between men and women than the caress of a face or the brush of lips, and I know it is wrong, but I want him to do more, to teach me more. If I don't quench this longing, I will surely go mad.'

Seth's throat went dry. He practically shook with desire as he turned the page.

Blank.

He laid the book aside and closed his eyes, and then he gritted his teeth and clenched his fists in a tenuous bid for control. He'd never wanted a woman so badly in his life, and now, to know she wanted him just as much—damnation! It was more than he could take. It was all he could do not to run and bury himself in her body.

Becca's confession had stolen what little doubt he had left about her feelings for him.

He prayed it hadn't stolen his decency right along with it.

Chapter Fifteen

Becca added two more logs to the dwindling fire, and then she stepped back and fanned the coals. Maybe Seth would sit and visit with her a while. It was getting late, but she didn't want to say goodnight. Not yet. She wanted to spend as much time with him as she could before they went their separate ways.

His admission that kissing her was a mistake tore a chunk from her heart, but the pleading look in his eyes when he begged her to come with him had mended it some. He truly cared what happened to her, and he was a good man. She'd be wrong to deceive him again.

And she hadn't. Not really.

What she said wasn't a lie. She would go with him to the outpost. But then she'd send him on his way and return to her cave. She would have the supplies she needed to survive, and he would no longer be burdened with her care.

Her pulse quickened at the scuff of his boots approaching.

His steps paused, then continued until he was standing right behind her.

Becca turned around to Seth peering down at her with the same turbulent eyes he'd had in the field. Before she could speak, he cupped her face with his hands, and his gaze slid to her lips. He leaned his face closer, but stopped before their lips touched. Her skin tingled with anticipation and burned from the heat pouring off his. What was he waiting for?

Hesitantly, she lifted her chin until her mouth reached his.

He kissed her firmly then, covering her lips with his and nibbling the tender skin. A strong arm snaked around her waist while a hand smoothed her hair and cradled her nape. His tongue swept over the seam of her lips. Her knees went weak and her lungs cried out for air. When she opened her mouth to take a breath, his tongue slipped in, startling her and thrilling her all the same. She froze at first, not knowing what to do, but then she gripped his shoulders and imitated his movements.

Seth pressed her to him, his body taut as sundried leather and twice as hard. He kissed her hungrily, and then he tore his lips away, leaning his forehead against hers and breathing in ragged heaves.

She trembled in his embrace, her chest rising and her heart pounding in time with his. The torrent of sensations he'd unleashed left her reeling.

He'd promised not to kiss her again. What changed his mind?

"Ah, Becca," came a husky utterance. "You tempt me so."

Maybe that's all she was to him. A fleshly temptation. Her aunt had warned her to avoid close proximity with men; that familiarity led to sin. It seemed she was right.

Seth rested his cheek against her temple. "Are you upset with me for kissing you?"

She released her grip his shoulders. Her hands slid down and flattened against his chest. "No. I..." Dare she admit? "I like it when you kiss me," she whispered. His arms tightened around her in a comforting hug, and she wished she could stay there forever.

He planted a kiss on her forehead. "I should go check on Cyrus." He loosened his hold, but his voice sounded as unenthusiastic about the parting as she felt.

Reluctantly, she turned out of his embrace and knelt in front of the flames. As she poked the glowing logs, Seth's presence behind her was palpable. She couldn't see him, but she knew he was standing there, watching her.

Long minutes later, he knelt down, his thighs flanking hers and his chest so close to her back she could feel the warmth of his body. He eased his left arm around her waist and drew her against him. His arm shielded her from the fire's heat, but it had a heat all its own.

"Seth?"

"Shhh." His arm slid higher until his hand cupped the curve of her ribs. His breath caressed her neck, and then the fingers of his other hand brushed stray strands of hair aside as his lips pressed a kiss behind her ear.

A soft sigh escaped as her eyes drifted shut. She should be frightened, but she wasn't. All she could think about was the tingle skimming over the surface of her skin and the weighty, liquid heat pooling low—a desperate longing.

He nibbled down the column of her neck until he reached the curve of her shoulder. "Mmm. You smell so good." He nipped the skin with his teeth, then retraced his trail with kisses, ending with the lobe of her ear. "Watching you care for me and go about your chores every day; being surrounded by your scent. I can barely keep my mind off you."

His body was like a rock behind her, tense and solid. He drew a deep breath and blew it out slowly with a groan.

Kiss me again. I know it's wrong, but do it anyway.

As if he'd read her mind, Seth pressed his lips to her neck again and drew on the sensitive flesh. Now she was the one breathing hard. Her body needed something—needed him—but it needed more. That was all she knew. She needed more.

'He always leaves me wanting more... If I don't quench this longing, I will surely go mad.'

Now she understood.

The hand cupping her ribs slid higher, grazing the underside of her breast. His thumb brushed across her nipple, sending a jolt of pleasure straight to her core.

She bit back a moan... was barely aware when his other hand tugged her skirts from under her knee, until he touched her thigh.

Her spine stiffened and she grabbed his wrist.

"Let me, Becca. Let me teach you what you want to know."

She wanted to know, but...

"Becca." The breathy word was as much admonished as asked.

Lord, forgive me.

Becca closed her eyes and released her grip. When Seth's lips pressed another kiss to her neck, she relaxed into his solid embrace. And when his hand dipped under her skirts once more, she let him pull her knee aside, separating it from the other.

They had no future, no *forever*, but she didn't care. Her questions would be answered, and the memory of Seth's touch would sustain her through a life of solitude, however long or short that might be.

His large, callused hand felt surprisingly soft as it traveled up her thigh. Only the thin fabric of her drawers separated his flesh from hers, but her skin was so alive, she hardly felt the barrier. His touch tingled. It burned. It affected more than the narrow trail his fingers traced. It was as if he was caressing her everywhere, all at once. But not like an actual touch, like a longing for that touch.

His fingers reached the top and he paused. Just as with the kiss, he lingered there as if to ask, 'Are you sure?'

Yes. She was sure.

She rolled her head to the side and rested it against his shoulder.

Seth planted a kiss on her neck as he slipped his hand inside the split seam of her drawers. His fingers brushed against her curls and she jumped. "Easy, Becca." He touched her again and eased a finger in between her folds. "Just this... Only this."

His warm, tremulous breath grazed her cheek as his fingers reached the place that ached for his touch. Air hissed in through her teeth and came back out as a guttural moan. Ever so slowly, his fingers moved in gentle circles that made her melt.

Her blood thickened in her veins and her heart raced, pushing it through her body like a raging river after a spring rain. Her limbs hummed and her ears rang with the force. As the pressure and the speed of his movements increased, the world around her shrunk. One by one, everything disappeared—her only awareness was him; the place where he touched. Sweet yearning grew and grew until she thought she'd explode if it grew anymore. Her legs tensed and trembled, and her hands grasped helplessly at her skirts.

Seth didn't stop. He held her tighter and increased his tempo even more. "That's it, Becca. Don't fight it. Hold on to me if you need to."

She grabbed his thighs and dug her fingers in. Every muscle

clenched and every nerve throbbed. Her body pressed against him and her hips began to rise.

He held her tighter.

Time slowed to a stop. Heat sped through her veins. The curl of tension in her belly was all she knew, and finding release all she craved. If she could just... just...

Becca's heart pounded and light streaked her vision as rapture surged through her body and a throaty cry filled the air. She sobbed Seth's name over and over as pleasure rippled from her core to the tips of her toes. What had he done?

As the waves of ecstasy ebbed, the fingers that touched her most intimately slowed to a stop. With one last brush of her curls, Seth withdrew his hand.

She released her grip on his thighs and her frame turned from fencepost to jelly. Panting, she slumped against him like a rag doll.

He was breathing just as hard. "God help me," he rasped. "I want you so much."

She didn't know what to say, but she felt the same want. The fire inside her was banked but not sated. Not completely. She sighed and rested her head against his shoulder again.

He relaxed some, too, although a firm ridge still pressed into her back.

Seth leaned his head against hers until his breathing slowed. He nuzzled her neck. "What will you write in your diary tomorrow?"

"My what?"

"Your diary." A hint of playfulness tinged his tone. "Will you write about—" He squeezed her breast and kissed her ear. "—this?"

"What are you talking about? I don't have a di—" Her spine straightened, its pliancy gone. Becca swallowed as her throat went dry. "It's not mine."

"What do you mean it's not yours?" He chuckled. "Do you have a twin you haven't told me about?" His arms encircled her in a comforting way. "It's all right. You were just writing what was in your heart. I don't think any less of y—"

"The diary's not mine."

Seth's arms dropped from around her. "C'mon, Becca. You described my hair, my eyes—our kiss. I shouldn't have invaded your privacy, but don't lie to me."

Distrust radiated from him so cold it canceled out the heat from the fire, and she winced at the rejection. Wonder and passion left her in a whoosh. She stared at her hands now clasped in her lap.

Seth scooted around and grasped her shoulders, turning her toward him as he leaned to see her face. "Tell me the truth." His voice was softer now, but just as determined, its persistent edge matching the flicker of flames in his eyes.

"I'm not lying to you. I found it in a trunk by the side of the trail. The diary, the writing, it's not mine."

A crease appeared between his brows. His clear blue gaze bore into her, then grew unfocused as his eyes widened and his brows parted and rose. When she glanced at his hands still gripping her arms, he let go.

He looked at her again with a mixture of alarm and confusion. "If you didn't... that means I... Dear God. *Becca.*" He scrambled to his feet, body shaking and eyes pleading. "I'm sorry. I—" An anguished growl grated through clenched teeth as he clutched his stomach and ran from the cave.

Seth could barely make it up the incline as he trudged toward the entrance of the cave, consumed by remorse and sickened by what he'd done. He'd nearly retched up his supper when he left, but even now, hours later, his stomach still churned. Rebecca had taken him in. She'd cared for him and trusted him to protect her. And in exchange for that, he'd violated her.

He could blame it on the diary—he truly thought it was hers—but that was a coward's way out. No matter the reason, he'd crossed a line he shouldn't have.

He paused midway in, still unsure what to say. An apology was clearly inadequate, but he had to make some sort of amends. He half expected her to draw a knife on him. And if she did, he wouldn't blame her. In fact, he would stand there and let her gut him without offering an ounce of resistance. It's what he deserved.

With a labored breath, he continued on inside, his soul as dark as the murky shadows looming over him and quivering along the walls.

His misery doubled at the sight of Rebecca. She was sitting on the ground, hugging her knees and staring blankly into a waning fire. He'd seen that look on one other woman's face; this time, it hurt twice as bad.

"Becca." He'd barely heard the word, his voice was so rough and weak.

She must have, though, because she winced and turned her face away.

"Becca, I..."

"Don't," she said quietly. "Just get your things and go."

He deserved to be kicked out—deserved far worse—but he was torn. He couldn't just leave after what he'd done. He approached her and stopped a few feet away. "I'll leave if that's what you want, but let me apologize first."

She cast him a pained, sideways glance from under moist lashes. "Apologize for what?"

"For betraying your trust and forcing myself on you. For being no better than the men who tried to rape you."

"Did I try to stop you?"

"That's not the poi—"

"*Did I?*" Her words dripped with scorn.

"At first." *But I ignored you and did what I wanted anyway.*

"Did I keep trying?" she insisted, glaring at him. "Did I push you away and say no?"

"No, but—"

"Would you have stopped if I did?"

"Yes."

"Then you're not like them." She rested her chin on her knees and stared at the fire again. "You're not the evil one. I am."

Seth squatted down across the fire from her, his heart riddled with guilt and his arms aching to comfort. He was prepared for her wrath—welcomed it—but directed at him, not turned inward.

She lifted her gaze to meet his, but she didn't move her head. Thin, wet trails glistened down her cheeks in the firelight, sending a spear of remorse through his heart. Long moments passed and she said nothing.

"You're not evil, Rebecca. I'm the one to blame for this. You put your trust in me, and I betrayed it. Betrayed you." He turned out his hands. "I need you to believe that. I can't stand the thought of you blaming yourself for this—you taking on guilt that rightly belongs to me."

Rebecca's brow creased, her conscience obviously at war with his words.

"Don't blame yourself for what happened. *Please.* I don't

think I can watch another woman go through this."

Fresh pain flickered in her eyes. He had better explain himself.

Seth exhaled a heavy breath and sat with his back against the rocky wall, one leg stretched out in front of him and the other bent at the knee with his boot on the floor. He stared into the glowing pile of coals, and then he met Rebecca's gaze and steeled himself to exhume memories he'd spent the last five years trying to forget.

"Do you remember the first night in the hut, when I—" *struck you*. Seth ground his teeth at the memory. "—when I called out a woman's name in my sleep?"

Becca nodded.

"I was dreaming about Rachel, my sister." That seemed to ease her mind a little. He wished something could ease his.

"It was the fall of forty-six, harvest time, and I'd just turned fifteen. Rachel was seventeen. Our crops had done so well, my father had to hire extra help. I'm his only son, and even with Rachel and Ma helping, it wasn't enough.

"Pa didn't like the two men he hired much. They worked hard enough, but something about them bothered him. He told me to keep an eye on them. He also told me to make sure Rachel was never alone with them. Ma, either. "When the crops were all in, he paid the men and told them they could stay one more night to rest up before leaving. I went out to do my morning chores, but then I dawdled for a while. I wanted to check my traps, and I figured it would be all right since the harvest was over and the men were planning to leave."

Seth drew a deep breath and stared at the coals. "On my way back to the house, I stopped off at the barn to put away my game bag. When I walked in, one of the men was dragging Rachel toward an empty stall. She was struggling and he hit her.

I started toward them, but the other man grabbed me from behind and held me firm. He told me if I fought or made a sound, he'd slit my throat. I felt a blade at my neck, so... so I complied.

"The man who had Rachel sneered at me. He pulled a knife and shoved my sister to the ground, and—" Seth swallowed past the swell of emotion in his throat and worked to keep his voice steady. "—and then he raped her while I watched."

Becca gasped.

"I looked away for Rachel's sake, but the man behind me gouged me with his blade and forced me to open my eyes. I focused on her face, hoping she would see how sorry I was. When she finally closed her eyes, I watched the tears roll down the side of her cheek, knowing she was ruined and it was my fault."

Seth looked up at Rebecca. Fresh tears streaked her face.

He looked away again. "As soon as it was over, the men left. Rachel curled into a ball and cried. I wasn't sure what to do, so I went and got my mother." A derisive sound grated his throat. "I let my sister get raped, and all I did was run for my mother."

"You were only fifteen. What else could you do?"

His eyes flashed to her. "I could have obeyed my father and kept an eye on my sister like he told me to. If I had, she'd still be alive."

Becca's jaw dropped. "She's dead?"

Seth scrubbed a shaky hand over his face as images of his sister, pale and gaunt, haunted him. "I don't know for sure. The last time I saw her, she had taken to her bed and refused to eat. Doc Bennet didn't expect her to live much longer."

"How long ago was that?"

"Five years."

"You haven't seen your family in all that time?"

Seth shook his head.

"Don't you miss them?"

He shrugged. He missed them so much he ached, but it didn't matter.

"I'm sure they miss you."

"I doubt it. No one said it, but I could tell they blamed me for what happened. Especially Rachel."

"They didn't try to stop you from leaving?"

"I didn't tell them. I just left. It hurt Rachel to look at me. Every time she saw me, it made her think of the men. I could see it in her eyes. The only chance she had of getting better was for me to leave."

Becca sat there, staring at him with a mixture of pity and disbelief.

Seth cleared his throat. "The reason I told you all this was to say I don't condone taking advantage of women. I know it doesn't excuse what I did, but I truly thought the diary belonged to you."

She hugged her knees again. "I believe you. It's easy to get confused about what day it is out here."

"What do you mean?"

"You kissed me the first time yesterday, on the thirteenth. The kiss in the diary happened on the fourteenth, today." At his perplexed expression, she went on. "I read the entries on the same day of the month it actually is, to help me remember. The fifteenth is tomorrow."

"No, Becca. The fifteenth is today."

"It can't be. I've counted every day since I've been here. Today is October fourteenth."

Seth shook his head. "I left the outpost on the third and arrived here on the fifth. I've been here ten days. It's the fifteenth. I'm sure of it."

She tucked a strand of hair behind her ear and stared beyond him, eyes unfocused. "If it's the fifteenth, that means I've been here one day longer than I thought."

"You said you were knocked out when you fell. Could you have been unconscious more than a few hours?"

"I..." Her voice was almost a whisper. "I must've been."

Seth leaned forward. "I bet they came for you, Becca. You just didn't make it back in time to see them."

Her face pinched with emotion, but she brushed it away with her hand as she swiped at her eyes. "It's late," she said as she rose to her feet.

Seth stood, too, keeping his distance. "I'll go. Just give me a few minutes to gather my things." When she didn't object, he headed for the tunnel that led to his room.

"You don't have to leave," came her soft voice from behind him.

He turned back around and forced his gaze to meet hers. "I don't deserve your hospitality after what I did."

She looked down at her hands clasped at her waist, the fingers of one nervously rubbing the other, then slid her arms around her midriff and lifted her chin. "It was a misunderstanding. Let's leave it at that."

Seth gave a single nod. He still assumed blame, but he wouldn't insult her graciousness by arguing.

He swallowed despite his dry mouth and ignored the tension gripping his body as silence hung between them like a sheet of ice. If his actions caused her to change her mind about their trip... "Are you still willing to travel with me?"

Becca didn't answer right away. Tiny beads of moisture, turned a deep orange by the waning glow of the coals, glistened along her lashes. "Yes." The word was spoken with surety, but so quietly he barely heard it.

"Good. We'll leave in the morning for the outpost."

And he'd wait to discuss the specifics of the trip with her until then. She wasn't the only one who needed time to come to terms with her lost day.

Chapter Sixteen

Becca stared at Seth's back—his broad shoulders stretching the dark leather of his duster, and his hat tamped down on his head—as he led Cyrus with her mounted sidesaddle. She'd just as soon walk, but he'd insisted she ride. The trip to the outpost would take the better part of two days, and the trip back with a second horse, supplies and a wagon, three more.

They'd brought the barest of necessities to get them there, but they'd have plenty upon their return. Once back at the cave, they'd add her possessions and go. Go *where*, she wasn't sure. They hadn't discussed that. Seth had been somber and silent from the time he awoke. He wasn't rude and he'd spoken when needed, but he wasn't himself.

Neither was she. After the existence of the lost day sank in, she'd lain awake most of the night, her reality turned on its end by the addition of a mere twenty-four hours. She'd been unconscious the first day and lost for another. Scouts could have come for her both days, and she would have missed them.

Even if they'd followed the trail of strange rocks, they wouldn't have found her, only evidence she'd been digging vegetables by the stream.

The anger driving her to live and die alone was quickly turning to regret. And longing. Maybe her parents hadn't left her behind after all.

And what about Nathan? Had she misjudged him, too?

She'd planned to replenish her supplies and send Seth on his way when they returned to the cave. Now she wasn't sure. She didn't know what she'd find if she went to California, but hopelessness was giving way to curiosity. She wanted answers.

The day dragged on, sluggish as the stagnant gray clouds that coated the sky, and Becca stared blankly at the faded landscape. Her thoughts turned on themselves like the endless, shifting gait of the animal beneath her. At least the horse was making progress. After hours of dwelling on her predicament, she'd made absolutely none.

She finally abandoned her musings and took note of her surroundings. The hazy drape of clouds skimming the horizon glowed a dull pink from the lowering sun.

"Seth."

"Hm?" He'd been trudging along, apparently as lost in thought as she.

"Can we stop for a while?"

The brim of his hat grazed his collar as he lifted his head and looked around. "Yeah. It's time to make camp anyway."

He drew Cyrus to a halt and came alongside to help her dismount. Becca braced her arms on his shoulders as his hands encircled her waist. When her boots touched the ground, her knees buckled and she nearly went down.

"Whoa." Seth held her steady. "You all right?"

"I'm fine. Just a little numb, that's all." She let go of him when the feeling returned to her legs, and he slowly withdrew his hands.

"I should have given you a break before now. I'm sorry. I lost track of time."

"I'm okay."

He backed up and she took a tentative step, then another, all the while pasting on a smile to hide the fact every movement sent spasms of pain from her shoulders to her knees.

Becca glanced around for a place to relieve herself. There was a small copse of trees to the right, but that was where they'd likely make camp, and none of the low bushes dotting the perimeter would provide enough cover.

Seth cleared his throat. "I'm going to take Cyrus and go find some firewood. Will you be all right while we're gone?"

She pasted the smile back on and nodded.

"I'll stay within earshot. Call out if you need me."

As soon as man and horse disappeared over the rise, Becca hurried to the tallest clump of bushes she could find. She gathered up her skirts and squatted down with a sigh. They hadn't even traveled one whole day. If they went to California together, she'd be dodging awkward moments for two more months.

Once Seth had built a small fire, Becca busied herself heating up some roasted rabbit while he watered Cyrus and set him to graze. By the time she'd plated their food, Seth had returned from a nearby stream with two full canteens.

He handed one to her and sat at the base of a tree, taking a swallow from the other. "The rabbit smells good." His expression was pleasant, but it couldn't mask the discomfiture of the man behind it. It was almost as if they'd started from scratch again, only with scandalous memories making the acquainting worse.

Her stomach roiled every time she recalled her behavior—how she'd given in so easily and behaved so wantonly with a man she barely knew. Yet her body hummed at the memory of his lips and his hands on her. He had made her feel things she never imagined a body could feel, and it only fueled the longing in her heart. How she wished things were different between them.

Becca sat as primly as she could on the ground, tucking her skirts neatly around her. She handed him his plate, then picked up her own.

For a while, they ate in silence, exchanging an occasional glance. Then a crease appeared between Seth's brows and grew steadily deeper, the way it always did when something was bothering him.

He turned a picked-cleaned leg bone over and over in his fingers before tossing it into the fire. "I was wondering if you'd given any more thought to where you'd like me to take you."

Only every minute of every hour. "I've thought about it some."

The crease in his brow that had shallowed deepened again. "Have you made a decision?"

Becca set aside her half-eaten rabbit. What meager appetite she'd had was gone. "You said you didn't need an answer until we got to the outpost."

"I... I don't. I was just curious."

Seth stood and scraped the rest of the scraps into the fire, then traded his plate for his hat and glanced up at the waning daylight. "I'm going to take Cyrus and go to the stream once more before dark. I'll be back in time to make camp."

While he was gone, Becca went about the job of cleaning up. As she washed and dried the tin plates and put them away, the stack of bedrolls pulsed like a burgeoning storm cloud in the fringe of her vision. No longer would she and Seth have separate rooms. She didn't fear him in any way, but camp sleeping arrangements hadn't been discussed.

And what about once they shared a wagon?

Becca put it off as long as she could, then stood over the bundle of tarps, quilts and blankets, wondering what she should do.

How would Seth want things arranged? Would he want their pallets next to each other, or on opposite sides of the fire? If she placed them too close together, that might make him uncomfortable. And—her stomach clenched—make her look wanton. But if she put them too far apart, his feelings might be hurt.

Becca gnawed on her lip and wrung her hands. She hated decisions like this.

Maybe the best arrangement was something between the two. She could angle their beds so they were across from each other, but with their heads facing the same way. Sort of like a V.

She bent over and reached for the rolls.

"Wait," Seth called as he rode up. He reined Cyrus to a stop and swiftly dismounted. "Don't untie those."

"Why not?"

"I've decided not to make camp."

"You found someplace better?"

"No." Why did he have such a grim look on his face? Was the thought of sleeping next to her that upsetting?

Seth snatched up the bundle of bed rolls. "We need to leave. It's not safe here." He kicked dirt onto the fire, then began tying their belongings to Cyrus' saddle. "Help me." He inclined his head. "Grab the canteens."

Becca wanted details, but his urgency was genuine. She did as he asked and held her tongue.

Within minutes, they had everything packed—the only trace of their presence an extinguished pile of sticks.

Seth turned to her and reached for her waist. "Let me help you mount."

Becca backed away. "I'd rather walk."

"It's going to be a long trip, and you're tired."

"I am, but I'm more tired of riding."

He glanced around. "All right. But if we run into trouble, I want you to climb on Cyrus and ride away as fast as you can."

She opened her mouth to protest.

"No matter what, Becca. Promise me you'll get yourself to safety."

"I promise."

"Let's go." He clipped on Cyrus' lead line and glanced over at her as she flanked the horse's other side. "Stay close."

Seth led them east at a brisk pace, occasionally looking back the way they'd come. For now, they could see, but they wouldn't have daylight for long. The sun was quickly setting, and the temperature was dropping. Becca rued the loss of the fire.

"What happened back there?" she finally asked when they'd gone a few miles. Several thumps of horse's hooves later, she still hadn't gotten an answer. "Seth?"

"When I went back to water Cyrus the second time, I noticed tracks near the stream."

"Bear or mountain lion?"

More hoof beats punctuated the silence. "Human."

She sucked in a breath. "How many people?"

"At least two, with horses. But I'm not certain the tracks are fresh. They could have been made any time in the last day or so."

Becca stared straight ahead and pressed a hand to her quivering insides. She kept walking, but she could barely feel her feet touching ground. Her limbs had gone numb.

"Becca?"

She kept walking until the absence of hoof beats made her look to the left. Cyrus had stopped a few feet back and was bending his neck to graze. She turned back to Seth standing directly in front of her.

"The tracks I saw looked like they were made by some Indians passing through, headed west. They're probably long gone, but I don't want to take any chances." He clasped her arms with gloved hands and gave a reassuring squeeze. "I'm not going to let anything happen to you."

Seth collected Cyrus, and the three of them began walking again.

Pale light from a hazy half-moon replaced the purple shadows of dusk, and a deep chill settled in with the night. Becca clutched the collar of her coat closed as she trudged with feet that had gone from being numb with fear to being numb with cold.

She looked over at Seth who strode along with even, confident steps. "How do you know which way to go?"

He glanced up at her as if she'd pulled him from his thoughts and pointed toward the sky where fingers of mist crept across the heavens. "I can tell by looking at the stars."

"Even when it's cloudy like this?"

He nodded. "I can see enough of them to find my way." A few moments of silence passed between them, the steady plod of Cyrus' hooves and the crunch of lumpy prairie grass under their feet the only noise. "Do you need a break?"

"No. I'm fine."

Becca wished Seth would tell her more about the stars—about anything—to make the night feel less eerie and the trip seem less long, but he kept to himself.

Several miles later, the numbness in her feet had spread through her entire body. Her steps slowed and her boots kept catching on the uneven ground. She took some deep breaths and willed her legs to lift her feet higher, but they didn't obey. After snagging her toes and stumbling so many times she lost count, she tripped and fell flat.

Seth was by her side in an instant.

"I'm fine," she assured as she pushed herself up and brushed the gravel from her palms and the dust from her clothes.

"No, you're not. You're so tired you can hardly stand."

She looked into dark eyes lined with concern. "I just need a short rest."

Seth opened his canteen and offered her a drink. After taking one himself, he glanced around as he replaced the stopper. "I think we've gone far enough to take a break. Do you need a private moment?"

"I could use one, yes."

"There's a good spot over there," he said, pointing to a cluster of waist-high bushes a few yards away. "I'll stay here with Cyrus and take my turn when you're done."

Becca made her way across the silvery, moonlit clearing and peeked through the bushes at Seth who kept his back to her the whole time. Moments like this were still awkward, but their discomfiture was beginning to ease. Maybe this would work out after all.

Once they'd seen to their personal needs, the two sat on some large rocks and took another drink of water. Seth kept shifting his attention back and forth from the prairie to her, eyeing her with a troubled expression.

"What's wrong?"

"I'm debating what to do. You need rest, but I don't feel safe making camp."

"I'll be fine. Just let me sit here a few more minutes." She was about to fall asleep sitting up, but she didn't dare admit it to him.

He glared at her sideways and pursed his lips, letting her know he saw through her subterfuge. Then he brooded again, tapping his canteen.

"Come here." He led her over to a boulder that rose a couple of feet above the dirt. "Can you stand on this for a minute or two?"

"Yes, but..."

He returned to Cyrus and swung into the saddle, then rode over to where she stood. After scooting back, Seth reached down and lifted her right off her feet, turned her sideways, and set her in front of him.

Cyrus snorted and sidestepped in protest.

"Easy, boy," Seth crooned.

Cyrus turned his head and sniffed Becca's skirts, then faced forward and gave a resigned blow. When Seth gathered the reins in one hand and clicked his tongue, the horse ambled forward at a steady pace.

"Am I too heavy for him?"

"Nah. He's just being ornery."

Seth's masculine scent and the nearness of his body sent a tingle racing through her. Becca tried to sit up straight and keep from leaning into him, but their position and the movement of the horse made that nearly impossible. At the brush of his chest against her arm, she shivered, thankful a timely gust of wind disguised the cause.

Seth reached behind him and pulled a woolen blanket from his saddle bag. He shook it out and wrapped it around her.

Becca thanked him, still trying to hold her posture straight.

"Does this bother you? Riding double?"

"No." Not in the way he meant.

He studied her for a long moment, the moon reflected as ivory beads in his eyes, and then he lifted his gaze to the horizon and rode in silence, one hand guiding the reins and the other resting palm down on his thigh.

Cyrus' easy steps lulled her, and Becca began to nod off. She swayed in the saddle, catching herself with a jerk just shy of losing her balance.

Seth's arm shot up in response. "You're exhausted." He unbuttoned his leather duster, baring the shirt underneath. "Lean against me and rest."

Becca eyed the blue flannel with indecision. She was trying to maintain a proper decorum, but she was so tired.

She lifted her eyes just in time to see shame cloud his. If she didn't accept his offer, he would be hurt. "Thank you."

He wrapped his arm around her as she settled against him and laid her head on his chest, soaking in the heat that seeped through the fabric. Becca tried to stay awake so she could savor the closeness, but her traitorous eyes grew heavy too soon.

As she gave in to exhaustion, his muscular arm held her firm. "Sleep if you want to. I won't let you fall."

Becca opened her eyes and squinted at the early morning sun. A chill frosted her cheek as she lifted her head, making her shiver and burrow back against Seth. His chest was better than a blazing fire at giving off heat.

"Did you sleep well?" he asked in a scratchy voice.

"I did." His arm loosened its guardian position as she reluctantly pulled away. "I can't believe you held me all night long."

He looked down at her with tired, wind-burned eyes. "I promised you I wouldn't let you fall."

Oh, but you did.

His selfless act had warmed her heart. Now the depth of his sacrifice was practically crushing it.

Becca swallowed past a lump of emotion. "Is the outpost much farther?"

"No. About twenty more miles." He raised his chin, lifting the brim of his hat. "Just over those hills."

"Do you think it's safe to stop for a while?"

"Yeah. Cyrus needs a rest."

Good. She'd make them some breakfast. Then maybe she could convince him to take a nap.

Seth guided Cyrus to a shady spot near some trees.

Becca shifted in the saddle and wiggled her feet, making sure nothing was cramping or numb. Her body felt a little stiff; that was all.

"I'll get down first so I can help you," he offered.

"No need." She clasped his hand for support and slid smoothly to the ground.

Becca turned around just as Seth swung his leg over the back of the saddle and let out a muffled groan. When his boot touched ground, he removed the other one from the stirrup and stood at his horse's side. His fingers gripped the pommel so tightly his knuckles blanched, and the side of his face corded with tension as it had when she'd stitched up his side.

"Are you all right?"

His jaw relaxed as he drew in a breath. "Yeah. Just stiff from the ride." He removed their belongings from the saddle, then led Cyrus over to a grassy area with halting steps.

Becca gathered a few branches and started a fire. She put on a pot of coffee to boil while she heated some biscuits and meat.

"Smells good," Seth said as he joined her by the fire. "I could sure use some coffee." His stride had eased, but he gritted his teeth as he lowered himself to the ground.

Becca poured him a cup. "It's probably bitter. I wish I'd had an egg to throw in."

"I won't complain." He blew at the surface of the oily, black liquid and took a tentative sip. "Ahh."

"And four more for the skillet."

"Huh?"

"Eggs." She sighed. "I haven't had eggs in so long."

Seth's smile became a wince as he leaned back against a large rock.

"Are you sure you're all right?"

"I'm fine. I just need a rest." He wasn't a very good liar either.

Seth took another sip of coffee, swirls of steam grazing his upper lip. "Maybe we'll get lucky and Sam will have some eggs for sale."

"Who's Sam?"

"The man I worked for at the outpost. He was due to get the rest of his shipments last week. He should be stocked and ready for business by the time we get there."

"Oh." Becca handed him his plate.

Seth set his coffee aside and took a bite of his biscuit. "Mmm." He chewed, eyes closed and crumbs clinging to the corner of his mouth. "Youm—" He swallowed. "You make the best biscuits. Even left over, they're good."

Becca rolled her eyes and shook her head. He was laying it on thick. Without milk and lard, they could pass for hardtack.

"What was that for?"

"You and your flattery. Those are some of the worst biscuits I've ever made."

He shrugged. "Not to me. As trail biscuits go, they're superb."

She laughed outright. The man was seriously deprived of decent food.

Becca took a bite of her biscuit and forced it down with the bitter coffee. She lifted the palm-sized lump to take another bite and stopped with it inches from her lips.

Seth's cerulean gaze was fixed on her, his eyes twinkling like gems. "It's good to hear you laugh."

She sat motionless, her heart stirred by his warm regard, until she realized she was staring. Becca averted her gaze and busied herself brushing crumbs off her skirt. "How long until we leave?"

"Cyrus needs to rest and graze. If we leave after lunch, we'll get there in time to get our supplies packed and paid for. Then we can leave for the cave in the morning."

"Are you sure you want to do this?" She grasped the end of her braid and rolled it between her fingers. "A wagon is costly. And I have no money."

Seth took a sip of his coffee. "Don't worry about money."

"But what if my family refuses to pay you back?"

"I hadn't planned on asking them."

"What about your plans? The money you're saving for a ranch?"

"Rebecca." He sat forward, resting an elbow on his bent knee. "I offered to do this of my own free will. I don't expect anything in return." He relaxed against the rock again. "I'm only twenty. I have plenty of time to save money."

Seth eyed her over the rim of his cup. "You mentioned your family. Does that mean you've decided to go to California?"

Becca's hand slipped from her braid and she nodded. "I want to find them and find out what happened."

"Good." A shadow passed over his face, dulling the acknowledging curve of his lips. "California it is."

Under the glare of the midday sun, Seth shrugged off his duster and draped it over his mount's empty saddle. The brim of his hat cast his face in murky shade, but it didn't hide how lack of sleep lined his face and weighted his lids. Becca turned her attention back to the trail and kept trudging along. She'd promised to keep watch—even offered to sit with a loaded gun in her lap—but he refused to sleep. At some point, the stubborn fool would have to trust her. He wouldn't survive the trip without regular rest.

"How much farther?" she asked, stifling the urge to scold him.

"'Bout two miles." He glanced at her. "Are you tired?"

Look who's talking. You're practically dead on your feet. "No."

He slowed to a stop. "I'll help you mount up if you'd rather ride."

"No, thanks."

He adjusted his hat as Cyrus lowered his head and sniffed a clump of grass. "Need a personal moment?"

Becca chewed the inside of her lip. "Does the outpost have an outhouse?"

"Yes."

"I'll wait." She started walking again and Seth did the same. The scent of the sundrenched prairie rose with the heat of the day and filled her nose. No longer damp and dewy, it smelled of wild hay and stone.

"Are you angry with me?"

Yes. "A little."

Not three steps later, he stood in front of her, blocking her path. "Why?"

Becca sucked in a breath and stared up into eyes that were hard and glaring. She knew exhaustion was partly to blame, but the way his gaze bored into her made him look fierce.

She swallowed and lifted her chin. "Because you don't trust me. I've survived on my own for more than a year, and you treat me like a child."

Seth blinked and took a step back.

"You haven't slept in over a day. You're about to fall on your face, yet you refuse to let me keep watch. If we go to California, we're looking at weeks on the trail—*months.* You can't stay awake the whole time."

"I know that, Rebecca. This is different."

"How is it different?"

"I didn't feel safe camping, but it doesn't matter. I'll sleep at the outpost."

"And what about when you don't feel safe camping on the trail? What then?"

His glare was back. All puffed up with reckless male pride, he was practically fuming.

"I know how to use a gun, Seth. A knife too."

"Yeah. I saw how well you defended yourself against those men. You were winning that one for sure."

Becca gasped and her fingers dug into the fabric of her skirt. She wanted to strike him, to wound him as deeply as he'd wounded her, but she turned and walked away. Her heart ached—for her family, for Seth, for all she was giving up—but she'd been kidding herself. This would never work. Tucking her arms tightly around her gutted middle, she headed in the direction of her cave.

Seth muttered a curse. "Becca, wait."

Boots thumped the ground behind her and his hand closed over her shoulder, but she shrugged it off and walked faster.

He grabbed her again.

"Leave me alone."

"Becca, I'm sorry."

She rounded on him and tore his hand from her arm as unholy outrage burned away every last bit of restraint. "You're damn right you are."

Seth's eyes widened.

"How *dare* you blame me for what happened." Her fists clenched as fury tremorred through her body. "You want to know how those men got the better of me that day? I'll tell you. They were able to sneak up on me because I was distracted, not paying attention. And do you know why that was? It was because of you—*you*, Seth. I was thinking about you."

Chest heaving, she glared at him, watching his shoulders wilt and his face grow pale. Her words had hit harder than her hand ever could.

Tears welled as anger abated. And she'd be damned if she'd let him see her cry. "Goodbye."

The salty drops had barely reached her lips when he came up behind her and grabbed her arm. She clawed at his hand, but it wouldn't budge. "Let me go!" She kicked his shins and beat his chest with her fists, but he captured her anyway, holding so tightly he pinned her flailing arms and muffled her protests with a wall of flannel-clad muscle.

"Rebecca, I'm so sorry. Please forgive me."

The naked remorse in his voice drained her ire and reduced her to sobs.

Seth cocooned her in his arms, enveloping her with his familiar scent and the deep timbre of his voice. "Forgive me." His cheek molded to her temple. "I never meant to hurt you."

She sniffled, and her hands, which were flattened to push him away, curled around the fabric of his shirt.

He sighed. "I don't blame you for what happened. And I trust you."

"No you don't," she choked out.

"Yes I do. But I convinced you to travel with me. I'm responsible for your safety."

Becca lifted her head and wiped the moisture from her face. "That's admirable, but it's not realistic. No matter how hard you try, you can't protect me from every possible danger. You'll kill yourself trying."

Troubled eyes studied her from under drawn brows.

"I mean it, Seth. If you're not willing to let me do my part, then leave me here. We'll never make it to California if we don't work as a team."

He sighed again and closed his eyes. When he opened them, they were soft with acquiescence. And dull with fatigue. "You're right." He brushed the ridge of her cheekbone with his thumb. "I know you can take care of yourself. I didn't mean what I said before."

Seth left her and collected Cyrus. "Ride with me?" he asked over his shoulder.

The vulnerability in his voice softened her even more. "Yes."

"Good." He mounted and lifted her onto the saddle. "I need a rest. And Sam would skin me alive if I left a lady to walk while I rode."

Becca sat a little taller and glanced at him sideways. "I'll go along—in front of Sam. But when we're alone, that's another compulsion you'll have to get over." She squirmed and shifted her hips. "Riding makes my backside numb."

"Lord, have mercy," he muttered. "What have I gotten myself into?"

Chapter Seventeen

Becca squinted at a strange brown speck in the distance. "Is that the outpost?"

"Mmhm."

"How many people live there?"

"Just Sam and a couple of men who work for him."

"No women?"

"Nope."

Becca's shoulders sagged. She'd hoped for some female conversation. "Sam's not married?"

"He's a widower. And the men who work for him are single." Seth's stern gaze left the horizon and focused on her. "All three of them strike me as trustworthy, but see you stick close to me. Understand?"

Becca nodded. He was overprotective, but on this, she wouldn't cross him.

She turned her attention back to the south and the outpost, growing larger and larger with each of Cyrus' steps. When they were half a mile away, Seth lifted his arm and waved.

"What was that for?"

"Just saying hello."

"They can see us?"

Seth chuckled. "I dare say Jesse's been watching us approach since we were five miles away." He pointed at a tall, wooden structure to the left of the building. "See that tower?"

Becca nodded.

"He and Andrew take turns sitting up there, keeping an eye out for trouble."

"So, how do you know it's Jesse?"

"He always takes watch this time of day."

Becca smoothed her hair, adjusted her clothes, and wondered what people would think of her. For the first time in over a year, appearances mattered.

As Cyrus ambled into the yard surrounding a new wooden structure that resembled a general store, a middle-aged man stepped off the porch and walked out to meet them. He dressed much like Seth, but he was shorter and stouter with graying hair fringing the bottom of his hat.

Seth handed her down, then dismounted and came to stand beside her. "Rebecca Garvey, this is Samuel Dugan."

Sam tipped his hat. "How 'do, Miss Garvey... Seth." Both his tone and his gaze turned on edge with the second greeting.

"Where're Jesse and Andrew?" Seth asked.

"Jesse's is in the tower and Andrew's over there." Sam lifted his chin to indicate a man with sandy hair and green eyes standing in the doorway of a nearby shed.

"Andrew," Seth greeted.

Andrew responded with a silent nod, but his icy look of reproach matched his boss's tone. For men Seth spoke of with such ease and favor, they seemed none too friendly, and he shifted under their scrutiny.

Sam looked back at her, his face softening. "It's nice to meet you, Miss Garvey."

"Thank you. It's nice to meet you, too, Mr. Dugan."

"Aah—Mr. Dugan was my father. You can call me Sam."

"All right then. *Sam.*" Becca felt another surge in her pulse. She wasn't used to calling her elders by their given names.

"That's better." Sam gestured, indicating she walk with him. "I'd like to speak with you, if you don't mind." Becca looked to Seth. His expression was stiff, but he gave a curt nod, so she let Sam lead her a few feet away.

Sam faced her and held her hand between both of his, the way her preacher used to do when he greeted congregants. "I know you don't know me from Adam, Miss Garvey, but I'm someone you can trust if you need help."

"Um, thank you." She hazarded a glance over her shoulder, unsure what to say. "We came for supplies before heading west."

Sam pressed his lips into a tense smile. "Perhaps I didn't make myself clear. Jesse can see quite a ways from that tower. He told me there was some trouble between you and Seth before you arrived. Seth didn't hurt you, did he?"

"No! We had an argument, that's all."

"What Jesse described sounded like more than an argument. I swear to you, if you're being mistreated in any way, you can tell me. I'll protect you. Jesse and Andrew will, too."

"That's kind of you, but Seth would never hurt me. He's gone out of his way to protect me. He's a good man."

Sam eyed her a moment more, then released a burdensome breath. "I must say, I'm relieved. I was beginning to question my ability to judge a man's character. Seth has never before given me a reason to doubt him, and it was plain as a beak on a

174

bird he was worried sick over you, but I wanted to be sure.

"If you ever need help," he added with a pat to her hand, "the offer stands."

"Thank you. I'll remember that." Becca shifted back and forth on her feet, thankful her skirt hid the little dance. "Is that all you wanted to talk to me about?"

"Yes."

She squeezed her thighs together. "Where's your outhouse?"

"Forgive me for not offerin'. It's over there." He pointed to a spot behind her.

Becca hurried past Seth who stood stock still except for a muscle twitching along his jaw and a stony gaze that followed her every move.

After relieving herself and sending up a prayer of thanks for modern convenience, she opened the pine door and started across the yard to rejoin the men. Sam was speaking to Seth, looking rather apologetic, and the tension in Seth's shoulders had eased.

Andrew reached them just before she did. He tugged off a leather work glove and extended his hand. "Sorry for the misunderstanding."

Seth shook his hand. "Don't worry about it. If the tables were turned, I'd have done the same." He'd no sooner introduced her to Andrew when a shorter, younger man—not more than eighteen—walked up with a rifle in his hand and a broad smile on his face. He had green eyes, too, but they were brighter, and the hair curling out from under his hat was jet black.

"Hey, Seth." The young man looked at Becca, his smile never faltering. "This must be the girl you told us about."

Andrew elbowed him and Sam frowned. "The *lady* has a name, Jesse. This is Miss Rebecca Garvey."

He turned sheepish and tipped his hat. "Forgive my manners, Miss Garvey. It's nice to meet you."

Becca smiled. She imagined Jesse got reminded of his manners quite a lot. Probably as often as he was forgiven. He had a face you couldn't stay mad at for long.

Jesse looked from Sam to Andrew. "Did you tell 'em about the horse yet?"

"*Jesse*," Sam admonished. "These folks just got here. I haven't had the chance."

Seth looked to Sam. "What's he talking about?"

"'Bout a week or so back, a horse came wandering up, saddle and all. I sent Andrew out to search in case the owner needed help, but he never found anyone."

Becca caught a glimpse of Seth. His jaw was tight again.

"What did you do with the horse?"

"We still have him, but he's not worth the feed it takes to keep him." Sam scratched a spot beneath the band of his hat and settled it back on his head. "The gelding and his saddlery looked kinda familiar, like one we saw passing through around the time you left." He motioned at them with his hand. "C'mon. I'll show ya."

Becca trailed behind Seth as they all walked to the paddock. His frame tensed and his steps grew mechanical as he neared.

"You recognize him," Sam said.

Seth didn't respond. He rubbed the back of his neck and woodenly lowered his arm to his side.

Sam narrowed his eyes, then gestured to his men. "You two go back to what y'all were doin'."

"But Sam—"

"Do as I say, Jesse. We'll talk about this later."

"C'mon Jes," Andrew said with a tilt of his head. "I'll catch up with you later, Seth."

"Andrew," Sam called before he'd gone very far. "Show Miss Garvey inside so she can rest."

Becca clasped one clammy hand with the other to keep herself from wringing them. "Thank you, but I'd rather stay."

Seth looked at her with painful indecision.

She stared back at him, silently pleading. Something was weighing heavily on his conscience, and she had a fair idea what. She didn't want to leave him to face this alone.

He closed his eyes and exhaled. "Let her stay."

"You sure about that?" Sam asked.

Seth nodded.

Sam waved Andrew on, and then he propped a dusty boot on the bottom rail of the fence and adjusted his hat. "You know the owner?"

"In a manner of speaking."

"He around?"

Seth's gaze lowered and he slowly shook his head.

"I see." Sam glanced at the horse before returning his attention to Seth. "A few days before you left to search for Miss Garvey, Jesse mentioned seeing a couple of ne'er-do-wells passing through. One tall, one short."

Becca's stomach began to churn.

"They kept their distance," Sam continued, "but they came up later that evening, trying to talk him out of some feed. Did you see them?"

"No."

"Jesse said one was named Ray."

Becca swallowed back the foul-tasting liquid that rose in her throat as Seth's face drained of color. No. This wasn't happening.

Sam looked back and forth from Seth to her. "Jesse said they took off the next morning, headed west in a rush, as if they'd struck gold."

Seth's throat moved with a measured swallow and his eyes turned to steel. "What did Jesse tell them?"

"Nothing, he swears. And I believe him. He's a mite impulsive, but when it comes to the safety of this camp and the people in it, he knows how to keep his mouth shut."

"It *had* to be him. I never saw them. How else would they have known about her?" Seth's nostrils flared with an intake of breath, and then he closed his eyes and pressed his lips into a thin line of regret. "Andrew," he muttered. "They must've overheard me talking to Andrew." When his eyes opened again, they were ravaged by torment and shame.

A tear rolled down Becca's cheek. She brushed it away.

"Miss Garvey? Did those men hurt you?"

"No." Her voice trembled. "Seth stopped them before they could."

Sam muttered a curse.

"They were going to rape her. I—"

"Stop. Don't say another word." Sam eyed the stray horse with his lips curled into a scowl. "If you did what I think you did, those bastards got what they deserved."

Becca looked up from her plate and gazed around the roughhewn, rectangular table at four men shoveling their suppers into their mouths as if they hadn't eaten in a month. Relearning how to use the cookstove had taken some effort, but it was worth it to be revered by a group of soon-to-be- stuffed and sated men.

The corner of her mouth lifted as she forked another piece

of chicken and tried not to jump up and squeal. Sam had chickens. That meant eggs for breakfast.

"Excellent meal, Miss Garvey," Sam managed between bites.

The sentiment was echoed in a murmur of masculine tones from the other three who nodded and smiled, but barely stopped chewing long enough to agree.

When they'd all cleaned their plates, Sam leaned back in his chair and rested a work-worn hand on his belly. "Thanks again, Miss Garvey. I haven't eaten a meal that good in a long time."

Becca dabbed her mouth with her napkin. "I'm glad you enjoyed it."

He regarded her with a boyish smile. "I hate to ask after all you've done, but I was wonderin' if you'd do us one more favor." He gestured to the others. "We could all use a haircut. If I found you a pair of scissors and made these rascals wash up, would you be willin'?"

Becca scanned the expectant bunch of men with mops of unruly, hat-dented hair hanging past their collars. "I'd be glad to."

She cleared the table and washed the dishes. By the time she was done, Sam had moved a straight-back chair out to the porch and found her a pair of scissors and a comb.

Jesse was first in line. He shucked his shirt and wet his hair with scoops of water from a nearby bucket while the other men settled on some upturned crates in the yard and watched from a distance, talking among themselves. Becca tried not to stare at his scrawny chest as he climbed the steps and sat down. His rangy, boyish frame was nothing like Seth's.

"How short do you want it?" She asked as she draped his shoulders with a towel.

He ran his fingers through the thick, damp mass. "Ah, take a few inches off, I guess. Ain't no women folk around, and the lot of us'd starve if we had to earn our keep as barbers." Becca began combing and trimming the ebony locks, wet clumps landing on the floorboards near her feet. "Have you worked for Sam long?"

"He took me in a few years ago when my parents died."

"I'm sorry about your parents."

"They died in a carriage accident. There'uz nothin' anyone could do." He shrugged, but she doubted he was as indifferent as he appeared.

"Do you have any brothers or sisters?"

"No."

She nudged his head forward so she could even up the back, then stepped around front. "What about Sam's children?"

"Irene—she was Sam's wife—couldn't have kids, so I'm the only one. When Irene passed, Sam decided to move out here and build this outpost. He says it's so I'll have something of worth to inherit someday, but I think he needed to get away from the memories that were keepin' him sad."

"Sounds like you and Sam are lucky to have each other."

"Yeah." Emotion finally penetrated the show of indifference.

Becca finished with Jesse. Andrew went next, then Sam. As he buttoned his shirt and returned to his crate, she swatted bits of hair off the chair with a rag. "Seth, it's your turn."

"I'll pass."

She blotted her forehead with the back of her wrist. "You sure? I don't mind."

Jesse nudged him. "Go on. She does a good a job."

"He's right." Andrew lifted his hat. "Best haircut I ever had."

"You do look a mite scruffy," Sam added.

Seth braced his hands on his thighs. He stood and walked toward the porch, setting his hat aside when he reached the low table with the bucket. With a solemn expression, he tugged his shirt loose from his pants and removed it. As he doused his hair and took a seat on the porch, the murmur of male conversation ceased.

Becca winced inwardly. She'd forgotten about his scar.

Sam's face hardened the same way it had at the paddock. Then resignation claimed it as he turned away and gained the attention of Jesse and Andrew.

Becca placed a hand on Seth's shoulder. His muscles were like rocks under her palm. "They're your friends," she said softly. "They'll understand."

After draping his shoulders with a towel, she took her time trimming his sandy blond locks, running her fingers over his scalp in hopes it would soothe him. By the time she made the last snip, his rigid frame had relaxed.

She gave his upper arm a gentle squeeze. "All done."

"Thank you." His reply was quiet and rough.

Seth stood and descended the steps. He dried his hair with the smaller towel hanging near the bucket and buttoned his shirt back on. Without another word or a look in anyone's direction, he picked up his hat and walked away.

Becca stared out the kitchen window, watching Jesse, Andrew and Seth load the last of the supplies into the wagon.

"Don't worry," Sam said from behind her. "He's got a lot on his mind. He'll come around." His boots scuffed the floor, and a chill morning breeze pulled through the sink window as he swung the door open and walked out.

"I hope so," Becca whispered to an empty room.

She went back to scrubbing the dishes, her mind on anything but.

Seth had returned from his lone walk at nightfall, only to usher her into Sam's proffered room and sleep on a bedroll outside her door. She urged him to join the men in the bunkhouse, but he refused. He seemed resigned to protect her—insistent—but he didn't seem happy about it.

At first, she thought the shift in his mood was because the men had seen his wound and found out what he'd done. But as she watched them work together like nothing had changed, a knot of misgiving tied up her gut.

Ray and Tucker learned about her here. If she'd gone with Seth the first time, if he hadn't had to return for her, he wouldn't have been injured. And he wouldn't have been forced to kill.

She was the one to blame.

Becca finished her work in the kitchen and gathered her things. With a last glance at the store, she walked out and crossed the yard to the pile of goods being loaded.

The wagon's bonnet gleamed in the early morning sun. It was no Conestoga, not even a Schooner, but the sturdy conveyance would more than meet their needs. Having no furniture or other large household items to tote allowed them to take a smaller wagon and team; and being able to leave fully stocked of food and feed, with only weeks to go, gave them a sizeable advantage.

When the men finished loading and went around front to hook up the team, Becca peered into the wagon's bed at rows of barrels and crates lining a single sleeping pallet. The sight bothered her, but now for a different reason. She'd become the burden she'd never wanted to be.

Everyone gathered together to say their final farewells. They all smiled, but an undeniable sadness lay beneath. It didn't matter that they'd been friends less than twenty-four hours. A wagon trip west meant they'd never see each other again.

True to form, Jesse spoke first. "Thanks for the haircut, Miss Garvey. The meals, too."

"You're welcome."

"Same goes for me," Andrew said. "Have a safe trip."

Both men's hands twitched alongside their trousers as if debating some manner of contact, then lifted to tip their hats instead.

Sam had no such reservations. He pulled her into a fatherly hug. "I'll be praying for your safety," he whispered in her ear. "But I also have faith in Seth. If anyone can get you home, he can."

When Sam backed away, Becca blinked at the sudden bead of tears in her eyes and noted the sheen in his. "Thank you for your hospitality," she managed.

After a round of handshakes among the men, Seth looked to her with a wan smile. "Ready?"

At her assent, he lifted her onto the wagon seat and climbed up to join her. Then, with a tip of his hat, he gathered the reins, released the brake and started them rolling on their journey.

Becca stared out over the terrain as they jostled in the direction of the cave. The creak of the wood and the constant bumping and shifting of the seat caused her mind to flood with memories—few of them good.

"You all right?" Seth asked over the noise of the wagon and the team.

She gave a small smile and a nod, but her mind went right back to all they faced. And all he'd sacrificed. "I hope you didn't spend all your savings on this," she finally said.

Seth opened his mouth, then closed it again, his expression softening. "No, actually, I didn't." His lips curved and he shook his head. "Sam took up your cause and refused to charge me more than cost. Wait. I take that back." He lifted a finger in the direction of the new bay gelding. "He took a little profit on Zeus."

Becca couldn't help but smile.

"I've never seen Sam so softhearted toward anyone but Jesse." Seth glanced over at her. "If you had asked to stay, he would've taken you in as his own. No doubt in my mind."

Her mouth went dry. "Is that what you wanted me to do?"

Seth's brow furrowed.

"If you've changed your mind about taking me to California, you should have said so—"

"Becca."

"—back at the outpost, before—"

"*Becca.* That's not what I meant. I was just making an observation."

He reined the horses to a stop and engaged the brake, sending a silent cloud of dust swirling up around them. "Are you having second thoughts about traveling with me?"

"No." She shifted uncomfortably on the bench and lowered her voice. "I thought you were having second thoughts about traveling with me."

"Why?"

"You've been quiet... as if something's bothering you," she said, skirting the heart of the matter.

Seth stared off into the distance. "Planning a trip like this isn't easy. I have a lot on my mind."

Something told her he was avoiding truth, too.

He looked directly at her. "Let's settle this right now. Do you still want to go?"

"Yes."

"Then I still want to take you."

He released the brake and spurred the team into motion.

Becca faced forward, gripped the seat, and held on for the ride.

Seth parked the wagon as close as he could to the cave. When they woke the next morning, they added the most essential of Rebecca's belongings and made their way back to the trail. She was pleasant but quiet, and he knew she was reluctant to leave.

"I'm sure going to miss that hot spring," he said, trying to lighten her mood.

The comment gained him a small smile. "Me, too."

Becca tucked a stray strand of hair behind her ear, then fingered the buttons of her old brown wool coat. "I'm curious. Why did you buy a second horse instead of a team of oxen to pull the wagon?"

If something happens to the wagon... "Because they're easier to steer should we have to ride them."

She looked thoughtful, then nodded and faced forward again.

Seth turned his attention back to the horizon, the reality of life on the trail weighing heavier than ever before. He'd pressed her for an answer yesterday and insisted the issue was closed. Now he was having second thoughts.

"Whoa." He reined the team to a stop. "I need to ask you something," he said, looking at her again. "I haven't changed my mind about taking you west, but I worry I was too hasty in gaining your approval.

"I know this isn't your first trip," Seth added when she

turned her puzzled eyes on him, "but it's your first one alone—without the company of other wagons, I mean. We'll have an advantage over anyone finding us—no one expects trains to pass through this time of year—but we won't have the safety of numbers if they do. Whatever happens to us on the trip, we'll have to deal with it, just the two of us."

"What other choice do we have?"

"Well, we could hide the wagon and store the supplies in the cave, using the food to get us through winter. Then, come spring, we could replenish everything at the outpost, join a train headed west, and be on our way.

"I'm willing to do either," he added when she didn't say anything. "I'm leaving the decision up to you."

Becca sat and thought a long time. "I want to go now," she entreated with liquid eyes. "I miss my family."

Seth grazed her cheek with his thumb. "Don't worry. We'll find them."

He urged the team into motion, equally burdened and relieved. On the trail, he'd have to protect her for weeks from every conceivable danger. In the cave, he would've had to protect her a solid six months from himself.

The sight of furniture, trunks, and other belongings littering the side of the trail pulled Seth from his thoughts.

Becca was completely entranced, staring at them.

"Do you want me to stop?"

"No." She turned toward him, her gaze lagging a bit with the movement. "This is where we were camped the day the train left without me."

He covered her pale hand with his and squeezed. He still couldn't fathom what it must have been like for her to go for a walk and return to an empty prairie.

A couple of miles later, after passing between two mounds of fallen rocks, they came to a fork in the trail. He didn't need to check his map—with winter nearly upon them, they were forced to take the southerly path—but the way Becca swallowed and stared at the groves made him think back to something she'd said. When she'd taken off after the wagons, this was the place she stopped running.

Seth glanced back as they veered left and sucked in a breath. Why hadn't he thought to ask her before?

He quickly reined them to a stop and ignored her puzzled expression. "Come with me." He helped her down and led her behind the wagon, then pointed to both sides of the Y. "Look at the ruts. See the difference?" Though the ground was mostly rock and the ruts weren't very deep, the tracks they had traveled were freshly gouged. The other path was pristine.

He watched her look slowly back and forth and waited for her to absorb what she was seeing, but the crease between her brows only deepened.

"Becca," he said, gaining her attention. "The dirt is freshly turned on this side, but the other ruts are weathered and undisturbed."

She looked back at the ground.

"The day you ran after the wagons, didn't you see it?

Her head moved slowly back and forth. "No." She raised her gaze to his. "Believe me. I looked for any sign that might tell me which way they'd gone. Both trails looked the same."

"Exactly the same?"

"*Yes*. Do you think I would have stopped running if I'd known?"

"No." He put his arm around her shoulders and guided her back to the front of the wagon. "I thought you might have been too upset that day to notice, that's all."

She stopped him when he moved to lift her onto the seat, her forehead creased again. "What does it mean?"

"It means the wagons must have split up."

Becca recoiled and her brows rose with incredulous regret. "I could have caught up no matter which way I chose?"

"Probably. But with whom? You said yourself there were people on that train you couldn't trust as far as you could throw them. What if you'd made the wrong choice?"

She closed her eyes and nodded.

"I promise you," he said when she opened them again. "We'll find your parents. I'll get you home."

Chapter Eighteen

November 2, 1851

Becca eyed Seth across the field while she was taking up the laundry from its drying place on a cluster of bushes. The argument they'd had on the way to the outpost had apparently done some good. He still carried his penchant for safety too far, but most of the time, he treated her like an equal partner.

But then what choice did he have? It took both of them working from morning till night to do everything that needed to be done.

Heaving the laundry basket onto her hip, she carted it over to a crate they were using as a bench. "What are you doing?" Seth was standing near a pile of wood.

"I'm breaking up an abandoned yoke I found. It's useless for parts, but it'll make good firewood." He lifted his hat and blotted his forehead with his sleeve. "As soon as I'm done with this, I'll do some scouting, then we'll harness the team and go."

Not wanting to draw attention to a wagon traveling alone,

they were cautious to circumvent populated areas. They also had to avoid terrain a lone wagon couldn't cross. Every couple of days, armed with the map Sam had given him, Seth hiked or rode to the top of the highest hill and planned their path. So far, it was working. They'd only been on the trail twelve days and had already traveled nearly two-hundred miles. With ample feed for the team and no other wagons slowing them down, they often gained twenty miles in a day. The weather had been kind as well. Being farther south, the temperatures were milder.

Becca finished folding the clothes and put them away. When Seth returned from the hilltop, she hurried to load the pots and pans from breakfast while he dumped dirt over what was left of the fire and harnessed the team.

She gestured at his face after he'd lifted her onto the wagon seat and climbed on. "That beard looks good on you."

The skin above the border of sandy blond turned pink. "I let it grow in winter. Keeps my face warm."

"Where are we exactly?" she asked as they pulled away from camp.

"We're about one-hundred-fifty miles west of Las Cruces. If we keep making good time, we'll reach California before the end of November."

Becca gazed out at the landscape. Sheer cliffs lined the path to their right and the Gila River marked the left—all of it turned a fresh, golden yellow by the morning light. "Do you think there's any chance of finding my parents before Christmas?"

"I think so. If they didn't change their destination, or not by much." Seth leaned back and braced a boot against the footrest. "You said they were headed for a town called Blackwater. I'll have to check with the locals once we get closer, but, figuring in weather and such, we could probably make it there by mid-December."

She hoped her arrival would be a welcome surprise. Her stomach knotted at the alternative.

Seth looked over at her. "Is Blackwater where Nathan was headed, too?"

Her stomach tightened more. "Yes."

"You haven't mentioned him at all."

Becca shrugged. "Why would I?"

"He's your betrothed."

"Was."

"You can't know that for sure. What if he still wants to marry you?"

Her heart and her gut clenched at the same time. "I'm not sure I still want to marry him." She stared down at her hands. "I'm not sure what I feel anymore."

When she looked back up, Seth had fixed his gaze on the horizon, his stalwart frame jostling with the wagon as it rattled across the rocky soil.

Armed with empty canteens and a bucket, Becca made her way down the steep bank of a clear, mountain stream that fed into the Gila. If she'd learned one thing on the trail, it was the importance of finding safe sources of water. And plenty of it.

She knelt by the rocky edge and filled the containers, shivering as the chilly current rushed over her hand. The atmosphere all day had been nearly as cold. After asking her about Nathan, Seth had barely said two more words. He'd never been what she'd call talkative, but he'd grown unusually quiet. She spent more hours than not pondering what occupied his thoughts.

Becca gathered the vessels and hurried back up the hill. There were still chores to do before supper. Her boots crunched steadily up the incline, to the stones that marked the upper edge of the bank, until her right foot slid and wedged itself into a deep crevice. The world tilted sideways as she swiftly went down.

The impact forced the air from her lungs and sent her bucket skidding down the embankment, its precious water spilling and seeping into the sand. Becca lay dazed for a moment. She pushed herself up into a sitting position, then adjusted the canteen straps on her shoulder and sighed. She'd have to climb back down and fill the bucket again.

She pushed herself into a standing position. Pain shot through her right ankle like sharp shards of glass. She cried out and tumbled back to the ground.

"Becca?" Seth called from a distance. Boots thudded the ground and he peered over the edge of the embankment.

"I hurt my ankle," she said, trying not to cry.

He quickly angled down the slope and crouched next to her. "Hold on to me." He draped her arm around his neck and caught her about the waist. "Let's get you back to camp."

She glanced back as he hoisted her up and wrapped his arm around her waist. "The bucket."

"I'll come back for it."

Seth held her steady as she hobbled back up to the trail, then lifted her into his arms and carried her to where they'd parked the wagon. After settling her on a crate near the fire and laying the canteens aside, he began unlacing her boot. "Let me take a look."

Becca gritted her teeth as he slipped off her shoe and rolled down her sock. Her ankle was turning a deep red and starting to swell. She flinched and bit back a yelp as he examined it, pressing on each of the bones.

"Did I break it?"

He set her heel gently on the ground and exhaled a dismal breath. "I can't feel a break, but there's no way to know for sure. You'll just have to stay off it."

She let her tears flow freely now. How would they keep going if she couldn't do her share?

"Stay here," Seth said, looking worried and a little ill at ease. "I'll go get something to wrap it with."

Becca wiped her cheeks with her palms and worked to get her emotions under control while he was gone. If she kept carrying on like this, Seth would think she was a weakling.

He retrieved the bucket she'd dropped near the stream and set it nearby, then he dipped a towel in the cold water, wrung it out and wrapped it around her injury.

She shivered when the cloth touched her skin but relaxed as the numbing effect began to counteract the pain.

"Better?"

She nodded.

He slid another smaller bucket over so she could rest her injured foot on it, then prepared to cook supper.

"If you'll help me move closer, I can do that," Becca offered.

"It's okay. I don't mind." His words were genuine, but his smile held a trace of disappointment.

He finally saw her for what she was—a burden.

Becca sat with her hands folded in her lap and watched Seth go about their evening routine, doing both her work and his. Once he had tended to the horses and readied camp for the night, he lifted her into the wagon and helped her settle into bed.

"Does it hurt much?"

"No." Her ankle throbbed, but it paled in comparison to the ache of worthlessness.

After climbing back out, he drew the rear bonnet closed and left for his bedroll by the fire. "Call out if you need anything."

Becca eased herself out of the wagon and balanced on her good leg. She'd heard Seth moving around outside when he first awoke, but now camp was quiet. It was just as well. Using a stick as a crutch, she began to hobble in the direction of the nearest grove of trees. Or rather, hop. She still couldn't stand to bear any weight on her bad foot.

"What are you doing?" Seth called. He hurried to her side.

Becca's cheeks heated. "Making a trip to my *area*."

Seth shot her and her feeble crutch an exasperated frown. "And what did you plan to do once you got there?"

She opened her mouth to argue, but he was right. There was no way she would be able to hold up her skirts and squat down on one leg.

He took the stick from her hand and laid it aside, then grasped her wrist and guided it over his head. "Hold on to me." Once she'd draped her arm around his shoulders, he caught her behind the knees and carefully lifted her into his arms.

Becca blinked back tears as he carried her toward the thicket and her last shred of dignity died. Having a man hold you steady while you relieved yourself went far beyond awkward.

"I made something for you," Seth said as they rounded the edge of the thicket. He turned her so she could see and inclined his head toward the ground.

At the base of a tree, over a freshly-dug hole, sat an upside down crate with the middle two slats missing—just like the one she'd made for him after he was attacked. He'd grudgingly consented to pass water by way of a can, but when his daily constitutionals resumed, he'd insisted on going to the woods, even though he was so weak he could barely make it there and back. Her makeshift outhouse seat had been a godsend for them both.

This one would be, too.

Seth lowered her onto her good leg and helped her sit, arranging her skirts over the crate so that nothing but her split drawers was between her and the missing slats. Her ankles barely even showed.

He squatted down, putting the two of them at eye level. "Will you be able to manage the rest by yourself?"

"Yes. Thank you."

A spark of reward lit his eyes. "You're welcome. Call for me when you're done." He rose and handed her some strips of old cloth from the pocket of his trousers, then strode away and disappeared through the trees.

As he cooked and served their breakfast two days later, Seth's fatigue was beginning to show. He didn't complain about the toll the extra work was taking on him, but he didn't have to. It was written in the lines of his face and the dullness of his eyes.

"How's your ankle?"

"It's much better," she lied. Her ankle still throbbed, especially when she sat with it lower than the rest of her. Be it bitter or not, she wished for some willow bark tea. "If you'll put a pan of water near me when we're done, I can wash the dishes."

"Don't worry about it."

Becca lowered her plate to her lap and felt her spirit sag at his indifference. "I know it's not much, but if you'll let me help, we could get going sooner."

"We're not traveling today."

"Why not?"

"The horses need a rest and I need to hunt." He eyed her from under the brim of his hat, then returned his attention to his plate. "I found a secluded area large enough to conceal the wagon," he added between bites. "Don't worry. You'll be safe."

Becca picked at her food for the rest of the meal. What appetite his cool detachment hadn't squelched had vanished at the news of his departure.

Seth harnessed the team long enough to move the wagon, then climbed inside where she was lying and handed her a revolver he'd bought from Sam. "It's loaded. Keep it with you, just in case."

Becca nodded and set the gun close by.

"Where's your knife?"

"Right here." She pulled it from its hiding place next to her pillow.

"I watered Zeus and tied him to graze. I'll move him when I get back. I'm taking Cyrus with me." He adjusted his neck and shoulders as if he were anxious to get going. "Do you have everything you need?"

Becca glanced around. A full canteen and leftovers from breakfast were within reach, and the special crate sat in the corner over a chamber pot. "Yes."

"Stay in the wagon and don't let on you're inside, no matter what you hear."

A twinge of insecurity sparked in her chest. "How long will you be gone?"

"Depends on how soon I can find game." He rubbed the back of his neck, his gaze lighting on everything except her. "Probably not more than half the day."

"Be careful," she called as he climbed out of the wagon and cinched the bonnet closed.

"I will."

Becca hugged herself as the sound of hoof beats faded away. She knew they faced dangers on the trail no matter whether they were together or apart, but Seth's presence, his unwavering vigilance, gave her a tangible sense of security. And his company filled a need in her so deep, she feared the wound it would leave when the time came for them to part. She was getting a tiny taste of it now, and her very soul was turning hollow.

She needed a distraction. The time would pass more quickly if her mind was occupied. She couldn't do much with an injured ankle, but she could read and she could draw.

Pushing herself into a sitting position, Becca propped against the side of the wagon and retrieved her sketchbook. Her subject was what it often was these days. The man who would be part of her life for the next few weeks, and a part of her heart forever.

Soon she was lost in the task of recreating him on paper—his handsome face, his gentle eyes, the way his muscular frame filled his clothes and stirred her every time she saw him. She often thought back to the night he'd comforted her and held her in his arms as they slept. She craved that closeness, and each time he carried her now, it made her hunger for it even more.

Becca's stomach growled as she put the finishing touches on the third drawing. Judging by the patch of sky she could see out the front of the bonnet, it was high noon. She put her things away and unwrapped her lunch.

As she nibbled on biscuits and bacon, she tilted her head and listened for the sound of Seth's approach. The nook he'd hidden the wagon in had been reassuringly quiet, save an occasional snort from Zeus, but now she longed to hear the clomping of Cyrus' hooves.

Seth hadn't arrived by the time she finished eating, so she reclined on her pallet and tried to busy herself with a book. That quickly lost its charm.

With each degree the sun lowered in the sky, the doubt chewing at her confidence rose. When night fell, fear sent her mind racing and weakened her limbs.

Where was Seth? Even if he hadn't found game, he would have returned by now. Zeus needed tending. She did, too. He'd only left enough food for her midday meal. Not that it mattered. She couldn't eat if she tried. But still.

With a whispered prayer, Becca crawled under her blankets and willed herself to be patient. Seth was strong and smart. If he wasn't here, he had a good reason.

Becca pushed her aching body up from her bed and rubbed her scratchy eyes. The night had been long, and sleep had been scarce. She'd jerked at every sound and imagined every scenario that might keep her protector away—most of which did little to calm her ragged nerves. Still, she wouldn't let go of her faith, in Seth or in God.

A year ago when she realized no one was coming for her, the desertion shook her belief to its very foundation. But, with Seth, she was finding it again. His kindness and his insistence that she not give up was restoring her trust, little by little.

Life was not without trials, and maybe this was one of hers—one that would bring about something better if she didn't allow it to destroy her.

Becca sat up and checked her canteen. It was less than half full, but no matter. She could make do. Surely Seth would return soon, now that it was light.

Bracing herself on the barrels and crates, she hobbled about and searched for food she could fix without the aid of water or fire. Her appetite was meager, but she was weak from going without supper. After collecting some hard tack and a bag of dried berries, she lowered herself to her pallet again.

Becca took a few bites and chewed the dry lumps of mush, sipping just enough water to wash them down, then she capped her canteen and blew out a breath. She could do this. Today was no different than yesterday. No. It would be better. She'd busy herself with drawing and reading, and, before she knew it, Seth would ride into camp.

She tugged her braid loose, brushed her hair, and replaited it, then gathered her art supplies and tried to think of something she could draw that would lift her spirits. The corners of her mouth turned up. Seth falling into the water when he'd tried to impress her by catching a fish with his bare hands—that was an image she'd never forget. With a giggle similar to the one she hid behind her hand the day it happened, she started sketching.

A frustrated blow from Zeus pulled Becca from her thoughts, along with gnawing rumbles from her stomach. The horse was growing restless. So was she. It was well past noon, and Seth still wasn't back.

After forcing down more hard tack and berries, she considered getting out of the wagon and tending to Zeus. The horse seemed fairly docile, but he was new and big. If he took a mind to run while she was leading him, she wouldn't be able to hold him. And Cyrus couldn't pull the wagon alone.

Becca leaned her head back against the taut cloth of the bonnet and sighed. As much as she pitied the poor animal, she had no choice but to leave him where he was.

"I hear ya, boy," she muttered when he stomped and snorted again. "I'm stranded without food and water, too."

She picked up a book, but set it aside before she'd even read a whole page. Something was wrong and she knew it.

She stared at the dimming patch of sky until it turned black, wringing her hands as dread curled its icy claws around her gut. Either Seth had been injured so severely he couldn't return. Or he'd chosen not to.

Becca winced as the pain of abandonment sliced through her, wounding her worse than it had the first time. Clutching one of Seth's shirts to the throbbing ache in her chest, she choked on a sob and cried until she fell into a despondent sleep.

Chapter Nineteen

The sound of footsteps met Becca's ears as she opened her eyes, and dread brought her mind and body to sober attention. Someone had found the wagon.

She eased her knife from under her pillow, then reached for the gun. Her whole body trembled as she lay with the cold steel of the revolver heavy against her chest. Just like the pale morning light that invaded the front of the bonnet, the intruder would find her. It was only a matter of time.

Could she really shoot another human being? To kill?

And what if there was more than one?

Breathing as softly as her rising fear would allow, she focused on the sounds. Maybe she could discern the number of people—the extent of the threat.

Boots scuffed the ground to her right. Then silence.

A low growl rumbled from a man's throat.

Something bumped and jostled the wagon.

"Well, damn."

Becca's hand clamped over her mouth and stifled a sob. Never had she been so glad to hear a curse. *Seth*. Her shoulders shook and tears escaped the corners of her eyes.

Wiping her face, she returned her weapons to their places and pushed herself into a sitting position. He'd come back.

Seth set his tools aside and walked to the rear of the wagon. He'd looked in on Becca when he returned late in the night, moonlight glistening along the tracks of her tears. The thought of her crying herself to sleep had gutted him, but her breathing was slow and deep, so he'd reluctantly left her to sleep until morning. Now scuffling sounds came from inside. He started to open the bonnet, but decided to announce himself first. The woman was armed.

"Becca, you awake?"

"Yes."

When he pushed the fabric aside, he was greeted with the sweetest smile he'd ever seen.

"How's your ankle?" he asked as he helped her climb out.

"It only hurts a little."

Before he could move to pick her up, she threw her arms around his neck and held on tight. A moment later, he returned the hug and tried not to crush her. Leaving her hadn't been easy, but being kept from her damn near tore him apart.

Red-rimmed eyes met his as she pulled away. "I'm glad you're safe. I..." She shook her head. "Never mind. What took you so long?"

"It's a long story," he said as he carried her over to the fire and set her on a blanket he'd put there for her. "One you'll need to be sittin' down for." He filled their cups with coffee, then took a seat across from her and stretched out his aching legs.

Seth paused to take a sip of the strong black brew. "The day

I left, it was nearly noon before I managed to track any game, and I had to go quite a ways from camp to find it. By late afternoon, I had a turkey and a deer. Had I left for camp right then, I would have been back by supper."

Becca lowered her cup and swallowed. "What stopped you?"

"Indians." He watched her eyes round with fear. "Not all Indians are dangerous, Becca."

"I know."

Problem was, it was hard to tell which tribes—and even which encounters—were going to be friendly. He let that fact lie.

"Anyhow" —he took another sip— "I sought out a hilltop to survey my path before returning. Good thing. There was a group of them traveling east through the valley."

"Right below you?"

He nodded. "I was safe, but I was stuck. I couldn't chance being seen—or worse—leading them back to you. I was forced to stay where I was until they were gone.

"I kept watching, and more kept coming. Then they made camp. I had no choice but to bed down for the night."

She'd been sipping her coffee with relish. Now her cup sat forgotten in her lap.

"I climbed back up on the hill the next morning and watched them again. I figured they'd pack up and leave early, but some of them stayed behind. By the time I was sure my path was clear, it was nearly dark. At first, I thought that was for the best, since it would help conceal my movement, but then clouds rolled in and hid the stars from view. I lost my way and had to stop and wait again."

Becca's lips parted and she slowly shook her head.

"Finally, the sky cleared, and I was able to find my way back. Needless to say" —he grinned— "Cyrus wasn't happy."

She laughed, but he could see the relief in her eyes.

He felt the same.

"Zeus wasn't happy either," Becca said with a chuckle. Then her mirth promptly faded. "Is he okay?"

"Yeah, he's fine. What about you? Did you have enough to eat and drink?" He mentally kicked himself for not leaving her extra supplies.

"I made do." Becca sipped her coffee again. "What were you grumbling about earlier?"

"I was greasing the wheels and dropped the mop."

"Oh... Need help butchering?"

Good grief. She must be bored. "Nah, I already did it. But you can help me roast the turkey and salt down the venison."

Becca beamed. And her smile struck him square in the heart.

How would he ever let her go, much less, hand her over to another man? Even if that man turned out to be worthy? Even if he was her betrothed?

Seth steered the wagon through a flat stretch of prairie, thankful for Sam's advice about storing water when it was plentiful to get them through these arid stretches of desert. That's all this part of the journey was—mountains and streams followed by miles of barren sand. Feast followed by famine.

Ironic how the landscape matched his state of mind. He'd go from wanting to claim Rebecca as his own to wanting to do thehonorable thing and return her to her intended. Most days, the battle between his feelings and his integrity occupied his every thought.

Feelings would have already won, were it not for his lack of assets and the wealth of honor instilled in him from an early age. It didn't matter that he wanted Becca. He wasn't in any position to give her the kind of life she deserved.

The best he could do was give her back her sense of self-worth, and then deliver her to the man who could give her everything else.

He shifted on the jostling oak seat and glanced over at her. She was bent over a mound of fabric in her lap, totally absorbed with manipulating cloth and guiding a needle and thread.

"Ouch."

"That wouldn't happen if you'd refrain from sewing on a moving wagon." She'd stuck herself at least a dozen times.

"What?" She made a face and pointed to her ear.

He slowed the team so she could hear him over the noise. "I said that wouldn't happen if you'd refrain from sewing on a moving wagon."

"I don't have a choice." She gestured at the sun. "The days are too short."

"What are you doing?"

"Altering my skirts."

"Why?"

Becca cut her eyes sideways, and a blush crept up her cheeks. "They don't fit anymore."

"Oh. I hadn't noticed."

The hell he hadn't. Rounded curves and lush, full breasts. He should be the one complaining. He could barely keep his mind off her. Much less, his hands.

She mumbled something about her ankle and poked at her waist. "This is what I get for lying around, doing nothing for two whole weeks."

That and he'd purposely fed her well.

He glanced her way again, trying not to look at anything that might get him in trouble—with her or his wayward thoughts. "You look fine, Rebecca."

"I know you're just saying that to be nice, but thank you."

He wasn't, but... "You want the truth?" He met her gaze and the fragile uncertainty in her eyes. "There's nothing wrong with gaining a few pounds. That's something you ladies dreamed up. Men prefer women with meat on their bones."

Seth ignored her gaping mouth and turned his attention back to the trail.

"Ouch."

She'd stuck herself again, but he doubted it had anything to do with the roughness of the ride.

Becca kept sewing until they made camp, but her thoughts were of Seth. For a quiet man, he could be awfully bold.

That she was attracted to someone who lived like a drifter and sometimes spoke like one, too, perplexed her. She'd always pictured herself with someone settled. A man with both goals and roots. Not anyone stuffy or overly sophisticated, but someone more restrained, more refined.

Someone—her heart sank—like Nathan.

The what-ifs loomed larger as Blackwater neared, and her growing attachment to Seth made her feel like a fraud and a traitor. Nathan was the man of her dreams. Yet Seth was the man who stirred her, body and heart.

Thankful for the break she got from him while cooking, she used the time to reason all this out. First kisses aside, the bulk of her feelings for him arose from gratitude and familiarity. That's all it was. Not only had he rescued her, they were traveling together, for heaven's sake—spending every waking moment together and depending on each other for their very survival. How could she not grow attached?

All she had to do was keep that in mind. There was nothing wrong with being friends. Even close friends. She simply had to make sure they didn't become anything more.

After serving their plates, Becca pulled her coat closed and tried to get comfortable on a cold, flat stone.

Seth scooted over and patted the space beside him. "It's warmer over here. Come sit."

She considered his offer, then took him up on it, lowering herself onto his ground blanket, a few inches away.

Seth scooped some beans onto the top of his cornbread and broke the wedge apart with the side of his spoon. "What are you going to do when you get to California?"

The bite of food she'd just taken seemed to swell in her throat. Becca balanced her spoon on her plate and took a sip of coffee. "I'm not sure. It depends on what I find when I get there."

He tilted his head and regarded her thoughtfully. "Fair enough. What do you *want* to do? With your life, I mean."

You ask that like I have a choice. "Well, if I'm welcome at my parents—" He raised a brow in dissension. "—I guess I'll spend some time with them, and then get married. To someone. Eventually."

"What about your art?"

"What about it?"

"Have you ever thought of studying to become a professional artist?"

"I've thought of it, but... I just want to settle down and have a family."

A smile curved his lips but failed to light his eyes. "You'll make a fine wife and mother."

Once they finished eating, Becca stared at the crackling logs and watched the sparks rise from the fire, swirling up to meet the stars. "I love the sky when it's clear like this."

"Me, too. There's nothing quite like sleeping under the stars."

"How do you use them to find your way?"

"I locate the North Star, then I look at the positions of the other stars around it."

"But they're always moving."

"True. But their movements are predictable." Seth lifted his arm and pointed. "See those three bright stars in a row?"

"Where?"

He put his other arm around her shoulders and leaned closer. "There."

"Oh. Now I see it."

"That's Orion's Belt. The constellation Orion always rises in the east and sets in the west."

Becca closed her eyes and savored the feel of Seth's chest against her arm. How easy it would be to rest her head on his shoulder and stay here with him, safe in his embrace. But she couldn't. She had to maintain a respectable distance, no matter the cost.

Her family probably thought she was dead, and Nathan likely did also. But what if he still wanted her? That her intended might be waiting, or at least willing, to marry her when she found him again was a possibility she couldn't ignore. She'd promised herself to him. And, regardless of her nebulous feelings, she had to stay true to her word.

Treading carefully through her tangled circumstances, Becca eased away from Seth as gently as she could.

In a flash of self-awareness, he withdrew his arm and assumed a less familiar posture.

"Goodnight," she said as she stood, unable to keep her murky emotions from dimming her smile. At his equally-formal reply, she collected their empty plates and left him for the wagon.

Seth barely spoke the next morning.

Though she longed to go to him and explain, Becca let the silent rift between them stay. Decorous distance was better than the risky alternative.

Gray clouds coated the sky as thickly as the ache of separation coated her soul, and by late afternoon, a brutal winter storm had blown in, bringing icy rain and unrelenting winds.

Seth parked the wagon near a stand of trees to shelter them from the worst, and then insisted on staying outdoors.

Becca burrowed under her blankets, but sleep wouldn't come. How could it when she lay there, dry and in relative comfort, while Seth huddled in the rain and the cold? She tossed and turned for hours, wishing she'd pressed him harder to join her, wishing—

"Becca," he called from outside.

"Yes?"

The glow of a lantern lit the space as he opened the bonnet and peered inside. Rain dripped from the brim of his hat and his lips were blue. "The rain's too h-heavy. I c-can't keep a fire going. C-can I come inside?"

"Of course."

Ushered by a gust of rain-soaked wind, he climbed inside and sealed the bonnet.

Propping up on one elbow, Becca took the lantern from him and hung it near her head as he removed his duster and lay his hat aside. Water darkened the edges of his clothes and he smelled of winter.

Seth rubbed his arms as his eyes took in the crowded space. The only place for him to lie was next to her.

With a smile she hoped would allay his doubt, she scooted

over and lifted the edge of her covers. Surely he wouldn't object. They were both fully dressed, and they'd slept together before.

Brow tightening with obvious reluctance, he lowered himself to her pallet and eased in next to her.

Becca jerked when his frigid form touched hers. There was no stemming the shiver that rattled through her body.

Seth scooted away. "I'll move. I—"

"Nonsense. You're half frozen."

"I'll b-be all right. I'll just go—"

Becca grabbed his arm. "*No.*" The force of her tone surprised them both. "Please. Let me warm you. If you take ill..."

The words left unspoken sobered him and he relented.

She pulled the quilts up around them, then took his icy hands in hers and rubbed them briskly, blowing her warm breath over them again and again and feeling lower than low. She shouldn't have left things as she had. Thanks to her well-meaning snub, he'd waited too long to seek shelter.

"I'm sorry for all this," she said, alternately kneading his hands and rubbing them, trying to restore the circulation. "I bet you're wishin' you'd never offered to take me home."

Seth's whole body quivered from the cold, but beneath that, it took on a strange stillness.

She glanced up to see him staring at her. She stopped what she was doing and stared back. "Why are you looking at me like that?"

"The time I left to go hunting and g-got stranded, you cried yourself to sleep."

She returned her attention to his fingers and began rubbing again. "I was worried about you."

Seth pulled his hands from hers and grasped them, stilling

them, then placed a cold finger under her chin and tipped her face up. "Why do I get the feeling that's not all?"

Becca chewed the inside of her lip. "At first, I worried something had happened to you, but then... I was injured, and you were forced to take care of me. I thought you decided I wasn't worth the trouble and went on without me."

The sudden glaze of compassion couldn't dampen the ire flashing in his eyes. "I wouldn't do that to you. I didn't take you from the safety of your cave to abandon you in the wilderness. I'll return you to your family if I have to *die* doing it."

She swallowed back the emotion that lodged in her chest. "Well," she said, feigning bravado when she wanted to cry, "if you don't let me warm you up, you'll die right here of pneumonia."

Becca rubbed his hands again, then scooted closer and wrapped her arms around him. She felt like a handkerchief trying to cover a haystack, but she was determined to warm him. Tiny bumps broke out and scattered over the surface of her skin as the chill of his body seeped into hers. Only half of them were from the cold.

Seth tensed and regarded her warily as another bout of shivers racked his body.

After reaching up and turning out the lamp, Becca guided his head to her shoulder and drew him close. "It's all right, Seth. Do what you need to survive."

When his quivering frame folded into hers, she lay there, listening to the storm howl and the wind buffet the wagon as tremulous streams of breath skimmed the hollow of her neck.

Cold air grazed her face, but the rain had stopped and the howling wind had died to a low drone. Becca opened her eyes and strained to see in the blackness that surrounded her—a wasted effort. It was still night.

Seth lay next to her on his back, his breathing slow and deep. At some point, they had switched roles. Now it was her head on his shoulder and his arm around her. His familiar scent filled her nose and comforted her soul.

She knew she should keep her distance, but his very presence was like air to the drowning. When they were apart, she found it hard to breathe.

Molded to his side like warm candle wax, her body came alive with tiny jolts of awareness that flickered like edges of smoldering coals. She lifted her hand and ran her finger along buttoned placket of his shirt. Smooth, even stitches guided her path like the dotted line on a map. When her fingers reached the valley of his chest, she flattened her hand over his heart. The slow, steady thump against her palm was exactly like the man.

Strong. Predictable. Dependable.

Seth's hand came to rest on top of hers before she could move it. He turned his head and buried his nose in her hair. "Are you cold?" he murmured.

"No."

"Mm. Me neither." His sleepy reply warmed her forehead, his lips brushing her skin as they formed the words.

When his easy breaths turned to deep, soft snores and the hand holding hers slid aside, she resumed her caress of his shirt until her fingers grazed his jaw. His beard framed the curve of his face like coarse corn silk. She spent several moments stroking it gently, smoothing the hair from root to tip.

The pad of her index finger skimmed the ridge of his lips. A heartbeat later, she lifted her face and planted a light kiss at the corner of his mouth. Then another.

He sighed and turned his head, mimicking her gesture, his lips eventually capturing hers in a lazy, nibbling kiss.

It was as if he'd fanned flames. Her skin ignited and her body burned. She cupped the side of his face with her hand and nibbled back. A deep groan vibrated Seth's chest. He rolled toward her and deepened the kiss, his powerful arms clutching her tight and his leg sliding up and resting on hers in weighty possession. A few more inches and she'd be pinned.

Groaning again, he kissed a fervid trail down her neck, and reality splashed over her like an icy wave. This wasn't real. Seth wouldn't behave like this if he were aware of himself. And he would regret his actions once he was.

Becca ignored the longings of her flesh and her heart and whispered his name.

His moist, warm mouth continued to draw on her skin.

"*Seth.*"

His ardent grip turned to rigid detachment in an instant.

"Becca, I—" He disentangled himself and scooted away, filling the space between them with frigid air. "I didn't mean to do that. I..."

"You what?"

"I dreamed you kissed me."

Her face burned so hot, she was surprised it didn't glow in the dark. "It wasn't a dream."

Seth didn't move a muscle. He barely breathed. "You kissed me?"

"Yes."

"Why?"

Becca tucked an errant strand of hair behind her ear. She refused to admit the depth of her feelings, but she couldn't deny the truth to herself any longer. She was falling in love with him. "Because I care about you."

The pounding of her heart marked endless moments of silence.

Fabric rustled as he scooted closer again. He gathered her in his arms and drew her into a comforting embrace. "I care about you, too."

Their sighs mingled as she slid her arm around his waist and rested her head on his chest.

He gave her a gentle squeeze. "I'm sorry for not telling you sooner. Maybe if I had, you wouldn't have spent an entire day thinking I left you."

Becca snuggled closer. "Why didn't you? Tell me, I mean."

"I figured you wouldn't be interested in someone like me."

She lifted her face and nuzzled the underside of his chin with her nose. "Why do you have such a low opinion of yourself?"

He drew back. "I could ask you the same question."

Becca pressed her lips together. She didn't feel like rehashing the thoughts that had plagued her for months.

Seth's fingers grazed her cheek. He brushed her lower lip with his thumb, then tilted her face up to his. His breath caressed her skin as his lips met hers in an easy kiss. "You're beautiful, Rebecca. You're smart." His lips touched hers again. "And talented." He kissed her a third time, and this time he lingered, resting his head against hers when he was done. "Don't let anyone tell you different or make you feel unwanted ever again. You deserve better than that."

He tugged the quilts up around them and held her close. "Morning'll be here soon. We'd better get some sleep."

Becca hugged him back and buried her face in his chest, hoping he wouldn't feel the tears soaking into his shirt.

Chapter Twenty

Five days later

Clear skies stretched out in every direction as the wagon bumped and clattered beneath them. The storm had been short-lived, and for that, Becca was thankful. If Seth's calculations were right, they would reach California in a matter of days.

What she'd find when she arrived still cluttered her thoughts, but she'd made peace with her feelings. At least for now. Hypothetical obligations weren't worth hurting Seth. And they certainly weren't worth jeopardizing his safety or his health.

Becca squinted at a dark object in the distance. "What's that?"

"What?"

She leaned in and pointed. "That."

Seth narrowed his eyes as they drew closer, then lifted his brows. "I think it's a stove."

He reined the team to a halt and set the brake. After climbing out of the wagon, they circled a black cast iron stove that sat pristinely on the prairie a few feet from the trail. As stoves went, it was pricey. And it was practically new.

Seth squatted down and opened the door to the firebox. "I guess it got too heavy to carry." He looked up at her. "Are you thinking what I'm thinking?"

"Can we?"

He rose and glanced at the sun hanging low in the sky. "It's almost time to make camp. Why not?"

Becca bounced on her feet. They'd have supper—and breakfast, too—cooked on a stove.

Seth grinned. "Gather some wood while I park the wagon."

She'd gladly do that. And stir up some bread to bake—bake!

By the time Seth unhitched the team, she had a nice collection of sticks. He brought some thicker logs from their cache and set her crates of utensils nearby. "Need any help?"

"No." She adjusted the damper and began adding kindling. "What would you like for supper?"

"Well... we've got plenty of beef."

Becca choked back a laugh. *No kidding.* Two days ago, he'd shot a wild cow. "How about some stew?"

"Sounds good."

While Seth was fetching the meat, she fanned the flames and added some larger sticks. When the stove began giving off heat, she closed the door to the firebox and adjusted the flue. She needed to get the dough mixed soon, or it wouldn't have time to rise.

As she stood, something darted out from under the stove and skittered across the ground. Then another. Brown. With tails.

Mice!

Becca leapt onto the crate, screaming and clutching her skirt. She was acting like a ninny, but she hated the sneaky little creatures.

Seth dropped the meat and ran. "What's wrong?"

"There—under the stove. *Mice.*"

He stopped a few feet away and followed her gaze, then sprang backward as three more ran out. "Ah!" He hopped on one leg and shook the other, bouncing around in a jerky dance.

Becca gasped at the string of curses coming out of his mouth, then teetered between squeamish shudders and bouts of laughter. A field mouse had run up his pants!

He swatted his trouser leg and kicked with increasing force. "Damn mouse is going up my drawers!" Seth let another string of curses fly. He grabbed the lump on his thigh with one hand and began unbuttoning his fly with the other.

Becca clamped her hands over her eyes and turned away.

At his growl of 'gotcha,' she peeked to see him pull a furry brown lump from his pants and fling it, sending it sailing through the air. He mumbled an apology for his language and moved to fasten up. She snapped her fingers shut and tried not to laugh.

What a fool's errand; she doubled over and howled.

Seth stared at her as if she'd lost her mind. Then the corner of his mouth lifted. "You think it's funny, do ya?"

She hugged her aching sides and nodded, tears leaking from her eyes.

"Well, then." He crouched and picked something up off the ground. "Let's see how funny you think it is when I put one on you."

With a shriek, Becca jumped off the crate and ran, her skirt twisting around her legs and choking her stride. She snatched it and hiked it up so she could run faster, but it wasn't enough.

He was still gaining on her.

Halfway to the wagon, Seth caught up to her and grabbed her arm.

"No!"

He swept her braid aside with the other hand and began wedging his fist into her collar.

"No! Please!" She begged and begged until she was practically crying.

His iron grip softened and he chuckled. "I was only kidding, Becca. Look." He waited for her to lift her face, then opened his fist, revealing a smooth brown stone in the palm of his hand. "No mouse."

"You— *Argh!*" She shoved him away and slapped his chest.

He laughed louder.

"C'mon," he said when she finally stopped scowling, his chest still quivering with fading laughter. "I'm sure the heat has rousted them out by now. Let's go cook supper."

Becca basked in the warmth of the campfire and admired the loaves of bread cooling nearby. She'd baked a hasty one to go with the stew, then baked two more that had time to properly rise. A third batch of dough was mixed to rise overnight and bake in the morning. Might as well make use of the oven while she had it.

Seth leaned back and propped his elbows on his bedroll. "I'm stuffed."

"Me, too." She sighed. "I guess our treat of jam and warm bread will have to wait until morning."

His brows lifted. "You didn't say anything about jam. For

that, I could make room."

Becca eyed his flannel shirt stretching across his food-filled belly. "For the love of all things sensible, Seth. If you eat any more, you'll explode."

His easy laughter made her smile.

"I suppose you're right," he said. He motioned for her to move closer. "If you're going to deny me dessert, at least keep me company for a while."

"You're incorrigible."

Becca shook her head and rolled her eyes, but it was for show. She dreaded parting every night as much as he. If not for his insistence she was safer in the wagon, she'd fall asleep next to him under the stars.

Seth draped a blanket around her shoulders as she took her place at his side. "Warm enough?"

She nodded and snuggled deeper. The storm had come and gone, but the lower temperatures it brought were here to stay.

He breathed a contented sigh as he tucked her against his side, and she echoed it. They'd finally reached a place of harmony, an unspoken understanding, it seemed. They still didn't talk much—most evenings they'd sit in companionable silence—but the awkwardness was gone.

Becca gazed at the deep indigo horizon, the sparse clouds above turned pink by the disappearing sun. "We're lucky, you know?"

"How's that?"

"Most people live their entire lives never seeing more than their own hometown. We get to see mountains and rivers and prairies across half of America." Her voice grew soft with reverence. "I'll never forget this as long as I live."

Seth looked down at her with warmth in his eyes. "Me neither."

Becca rose before dawn, but she barely had enough time to bake the last two loaves of bread. A winter storm was coming—one worse than the last—and they had to make it through the mountain pass before nightfall. She looked back at the stove as they pulled away from camp, then faced forward and prepared herself for what was ahead.

Despite bitter wind biting her cheeks, she rode up front with Seth most of the way.

His expression matched the sky, turning more dismal by the hour.

Clouds churned and flurries of snow swirled in the air. When it became so thick it whited out the landscape, she climbed inside the wagon and shivered as Seth guided them the last few miles. Thankfully, he'd spotted a rocky overhang where they could shelter the wagon and weather the storm. They'd lose a few days' progress, but waiting out the blizzard was the only thing they could do.

Becca huddled under a quilt, her teeth clattering as loudly as the wagon jolting over the rocky soil. The temperature had to be well below freezing. Even in her heaviest skirt, two shirts and her coat, she was miserably cold.

"Whoa," Seth called. The wagon jerked to a halt and boots struck the ground as he jumped down to unhitch the team.

Without the rattle of boards to compete, the moaning wind took on an eerie sound. She pulled her scarf tighter around her head and pressed her shoulders to her ears to dampen the mournful wails. Ample rations surrounded her, yet she felt bereft and forsaken. How much worse it must have been for the Donners.

The crunch of grain being scooped sounded to her left. Then, several minutes later, the creaky hinges of the wood box whined on her right.

Becca hugged her knees and rocked back and forth. They wouldn't starve, but how would they survive the cold? Even bundled together on her feather tick, sandwiched between layers of skins and quilts, there was no way they would stay warm.

She cursed her impulsiveness as tears pricked her eyes. The choice had been hers. She was the one who pressed to keep going instead of wintering in the cave and waiting until spring.

They were going to die, and it was her fault.

A surge of icy wind hit her and she jerked her head up. Seth stood at the open back bonnet, reaching in her direction. White flakes filled the crevices of his hat, and frost coated his beard. "Bring the deer skin and come with me," he called over the howl of the storm.

He took it from her and helped her out of the wagon.

Gathering up the corners of the quilt, she shielded herself behind his large frame and followed him.

He led her deeper under the rock ledge to where he'd built a fire. He spread the deer skin on the ground and had her sit on it, then headed back to the wagon. A few trips for supplies later, he joined her and started preparing a simple supper.

Becca was colder than she'd ever been, but the heat from the blazing logs began to thaw the aching numbness. Maybe they'd survive after all.

Seth made broth from some leftover turkey and served her some.

A throaty hum escaped when she wrapped her gloved hands around the steaming cup. She could barely wait for it to cool enough to sip.

"The storm is worse than I anticipated," he said as he set a plate full of pemmican and bread between them.

Becca picked up a bar, but she wasn't sure she'd be able to eat it. She searched his expression for any sign of real fear.

"The amount of wood it'll take to keep us warm is going to deplete our supply, and any we gather will be too wet to be of use."

"What do we do?"

"We'll sleep here tonight. Then, in the morning, I'll do some exploring and see if I can find a warmer place."

Warmer. That was a relative term.

Becca nibbled at her supper and sipped her broth, her throat clenching with relish as the steaming liquid slid past and heated a trail to her stomach.

Seth held the plate out to her. "Have some more."

"No thanks."

"It wasn't a request. Even with the fire, it's going to be a cold night. You need to eat as much as you can hold."

Grudgingly, she took another piece of bread.

Seth continued to hold the plate, his brows rising. Only when she'd taken two more pieces of pemmican and a third slice of bread did he relent.

"Won't do me any good if I overeat and lose my supper," she grumbled.

His cheek creased. "You'll be fine. I've seen how much you can eat, little rabbit."

She cut her eyes at him, but her glare of indignation withered under the amusement in his smile. "I don't eat *that* much."

He barked out a laugh. "You're the only female I know who can rival me at butchering game *and* putting it away."

Coming from anyone but Seth, that would have hurt her feelings.

Becca grinned. "Admit it. You've met your match."

His eyes softened. "That I have."

Once they'd eaten all they could, Seth made a thick pallet, using every piece of bedding they had.

"Take off your boots," he said as she lowered herself onto the makeshift bed.

Pulling on his leather gloves, he returned to the campfire. As she unlaced her shoes and tugged them off, he lifted a large stone from the fire's edge, wrapped it in flannel, and carried over to the pallet. He peeled back the covers at the very bottom and sandwiched it there.

Becca lay on her side, facing the fire, and stretched out her legs until her stocking feet reached the cloth-covered stone. She could barely stifle the groan of pleasure that erupted when the piping hot lump met her toes and sent a wave of heat melting its way up her frozen legs. "That feels gooood."

She opened her eyes at the sound of Seth chuckling. He was squatting in front of her, holding another flannel-wrapped stone. He set it near her waist and covered her up with a heavy layer of blankets and skins.

"What about you?" she asked as he shrugged off his duster and set his holster and hat aside.

"I'll be fine." He climbed in behind her and tucked her against him like he'd done their last night in the hut. "I have you to keep me warm."

The chill of his intrusion faded, and Becca sighed. She was wedged between a blazing fire and a warm, strong man. And she was safe. She drifted into sleep, watching firelight dance on the rocky ceiling and thanking her maker for Seth.

Becca opened her eyes to a blanket of white. The air was still, and snow covered everything as far as the eye could see. A sleepy smile spread across her face. Save being dimly aware of Seth getting up a few times to add wood to the fire and swap cold stones for heated ones, she'd slept soundly. Better than she had in days. She closed her eyes and snuggled deeper into the muscular arms that had held her all night long.

"Morning," a husky voice said from behind her.

"Good morning."

"Sleep well?"

"Mmhm. Very well... You?"

"Too well. I don't want to get up." He sighed. "But I have to. The horses need tending, and I need to find us a better place to stay."

Seth got out of bed and she started to also.

"Stay put," he said. "Let me stoke the fire first."

Once fresh logs were flaming, he donned his outerwear and went to tend Cyrus and Zeus. She stayed behind to make coffee and breakfast—more pemmican and bread per his insistence.

Seth returned and stood by the fire, his frosty beard and reddened skin a testament to the cold. He tugged off his gloves and flipped his hands back and forth.

"How'd the horses fare?"

"They'll survive. I gave them extra feed, and there's a spring where they're sheltered, so they've got plenty of water."

"Where are they?"

He hooked a thumb toward the entrance. "Just around the corner."

Becca held a cup out to him. "Have some coffee."

He joined her and they ate in silence. When they were done, he rose and tugged his gloves back on. "I'm going to be gone a while. Want me to tuck you in before I go?"

"No thanks. I'll be okay."

Seth studied her for a long moment, then squatted down right in front of her. "I'll probably be back by lunch. Nightfall for sure." He took her hand in his and rubbed his thumb across the back of it. "I'll be careful not to get hurt or stranded. You have my word."

Chapter Twenty-One

Becca followed Seth into the cave he'd found. It was small, with a low, solid ceiling, but it was deep and it would serve their needs for the next few days. They arranged their belongings and began bedding down by candlelight.

"Take off your coat."

Becca sucked in a breath and fought the urge to flee. The man who'd said it this time meant her no harm, but it didn't matter. Her body had already reacted. She willed her heart to stop its frantic pounding as her fingers clumsily worked the buttons, numb from the image Seth's words had brought to mind.

He folded back the covers and glanced at her. "You okay?"

"Yeah." She lay her coat aside and rubbed her upper arms.

Once she'd removed her boots and climbed into bed, Seth covered them up and blew out the flame. "G'night."

"Night."

She was warm and comfortable, but sleep wouldn't come.

Surrounded by still air and blackness, she tossed and turned as every frightful image her memory possessed flashed through her mind—the day she walked back from the stream and found an empty prairie... the day the cry of a mountain lion echoed through the hills behind her... the day the men found her.

The snapping of twigs underfoot was so crisp it made her flinch. Ray lunged at her, but this time he pinned her beneath him and began tearing at her skirts. "No! Don't!"

"Becca."

"Get away from me!" She shoved at the huge man on top of her, beating his chest with her fists.

His grip loosened and she heard a strange hiss. A sudden light made her squint, but she didn't stop struggling. She had to get away.

"*Becca.*" He grabbed her wrists before she could land another blow. "What's wrong?"

How does he know my name?

Becca lay there, chest heaving, heart pounding, until she summoned the courage to open her eyes. She raised her gaze to Seth staring back at her, lines of concern on his face etched deeper by candlelight. He was lying next to her, facing her. Not on top of her.

Her lip trembled when she realized where she was.

He released her wrists.

"I must've been dreaming. I thought—" She reached out a shaky hand and smoothed his shirt. "I'm sorry I hit you."

The air between them was thick and silent. "I'm sorry I led them to you, Becca."

She touched his lips with her fingers and shook her head, then cupped the side of his face and smiled at him. He'd saved her. The last thing he should feel is guilty. "It's my fault. I should have gone with you the first time. If I had..."

Becca closed her eyes at the memory of all he'd endured for her, then opened them to tortured eyes searching hers. Her gaze dropped to his lips and she lifted her face until she felt his breath on her skin. She glimpsed the turmoil once more before closing her eyes and closing the distance. Softly, she brushed his lips with hers.

Seth cradled her face with his hands and returned her kiss with such tenderness it made her cry. How was she supposed to save her heart for another when it was already taken?

Her fingers threaded through his hair as he kissed her with increasing urgency. Duty clashed with desire. She shouldn't do this, but she couldn't stop herself. His tender assault filled her with simmering heat and stripped away her restraint. Desire won.

Seth tore his mouth from hers and kissed a fervid trail up her jaw, across her forehead, down her nose. Ragged breaths stirred her lashes and lips grazed her cheek, smearing the salty drop that clung there. She turned her face, her mouth eagerly seeking his, but he wrapped her in his arms and clutched her to his chest before she made contact.

Seth held Rebecca close and willed his body to calm. He couldn't let lust overtake him. Not now. And certainly not with her.

She was pure and vulnerable, and what he felt for her was more than some base craving. She piqued his want and cooled it all at once. He'd lusted after women many times—what man didn't? But this was different. He wanted to know everything about the woman in his arms, be everything to her. Not just some shame-worthy tryst or a temporary lover.

Her precious kiss had affected more than the hunger inside him—the fire that burned for her night and day. It soothed his mind and gripped his heart. She knew his darkest secrets, yet she didn't despise him, didn't turn away. No. She looked on him with compassion. With adoration even.

Her innocent eyes couldn't hide the feelings she had for him, even though she tried. It was obvious she struggled with their situation as much as he. And they were both losing.

So how come losing felt so much like winning?

Dare he let himself hope she might choose him? Might find herself free to choose him?

Seth sighed and rolled to his back, tucking Becca against his side. He was weary of fighting a battle he had no desire to fight.

Becca ran the tips of her fingers lightly over her lips, recalling the kiss Seth had given her in the night. It had started as fine summer mist that quickly turned into a downpour. And she'd welcomed it—had willed it to wash them away, far from duty and lingering promises.

A strong arm tightened around her and muscles bunched under her cheek. Seth planted a kiss on the top of her head.

She tilted her head back and looked into warm eyes crinkled by an easy smile. The whole room glowed amber. He'd left the candle burning the rest of the night.

"How'd you sleep?" he asked.

"Better." She hadn't moved from his side. Becca rested her cheek on his chest once more. If not for human needs and chores, she could stay tucked in the crook of his arm forever.

"C'mon." He patted her arm. "Let's get breakfast, then I have something to show you."

Becca followed Seth out of the cave and around the other side of the rocky hill that housed it. The snow was melting, but the air was cold. And it only made her colder. The temperature inside the cave was tolerable, but without a fire or activity to keep her warm, a dank chill had settled deep in her bones.

Lantern in hand, Seth led her into the mouth of another cave. He glanced back at her. "Watch your head."

She gathered up her skirt and crouched as they made their way through a narrow tunnel better suited to a child. Just when she thought she might never straighten up again, the tunnel opened into a cavern.

Seth stood to the side as she stepped around him. The floor rippled in the amber glow and the scent of sulfur met her nose—the room held a spring.

Becca looked back at him. He was grinning.

"It's not quite as deep, but it's got ledges just like your old one, and it's just as hot."

She slipped off her coat and basked in the relative warmth of the room. "How'd you find it?"

"I noticed some steam rising out of the hill yesterday evening when I went to tend the horses." He shrugged off his duster, then gestured to a grouping of rocks behind her. "It'll be another day or two until we can leave," he added as they sat. "I thought you'd be more comfortable here."

She surveyed the room, now that her eyes had adjusted. "There's not enough space for the pallet."

"No, we'll have to sleep in the other cave. But we can spend the days in here." Seth drew her attention to a cloth wrapped bundle near the water's edge. "I brought towels and soap.

I'll leave if you want to bathe."

"Maybe later."

They chatted a while, then he rubbed his hands on his trousers and gave a single pat to his thighs. "If you're not going to get in, I am." Before she could register his words, much less react, he'd yanked off his boots and was leaving a trail of clothes on his way to the spring.

Becca gasped and covered her eyes. She rose to leave, feeling her way with one hand.

Water splashed. "Ahhh."

Her head struck rock. "Ouch."

"Where are you going?"

She straightened and stood primly with her back to him and her hands clasped in front of her skirt. "Out. To give you some privacy."

"Did I ask for any?"

"No. But..."

He let out a longsuffering sigh. "There's less of me showing than when you bathed me and stitched my side. You don't have to leave."

Becca turned, slowly, her gaze catching on the nearest garment and tracing the trail of them one by one. Shirt. Trousers. Woolens... No drawers. She released a breath. He was still wearing his drawers.

She lifted her eyes to meet his, feeling like a fool. She'd been in such a rush to leave, she hadn't even thought to grab her coat.

Becca settled back onto the rock, and they chatted. She was glad for the warmer temperatures, but the damp air was giving her a chill. She hugged herself with her arms.

"You cold?"

"A little."

His fingers tapped the stony edge of the pool, and his eyes narrowed, debating. He gave a tilt of his head. "Come get in."

Becca chewed her lip.

"Leave your chemise on if that makes you more comfortable, but don't sit there shivering when you could be warm in here with me."

She pressed her lips together. "Okay."

When she didn't move, he turned and faced the other way.

Becca turned her back as well. Glancing over her shoulder, she stripped herself of her shoes, stockings, shirts, and skirt, then stepped down into the spring and promptly submerged herself all the way to her chin. She groaned as the delicious heat enveloped her.

"Can I turn around now?"

"Yes."

He faced her and resettled himself on the spring's rocky ledge, sending a series of ripples skimming across the surface of the water. The steam rising in smoke-like wisps had dampened his hair so that it clung in wavy tendrils, framing his face. His cheek creased and his eyes twinkled as he studied her—he was holding back a smile.

Becca rubbed the discomfiture gnawing at her belly. "I suppose you think I'm being childish."

The spark of amusement went out. "No, Becca, I don't. Your modesty is one of the things I like most about you."

"Really?"

"Yes. Turn around and back up a little." He pulled her to him until she was sitting on the ledge in the vee of his thighs. His hands released her and the weight of her braid lifted. He must have removed the cord that bound the end, because the next thing she felt was his fingers combing through her tresses until the unwoven strands lay loose around her shoulders.

"Want me to wash your hair?"

No one had ever done that for her before, except her ma. "If you want to."

"Duck down and get it wet."

Becca did as he asked and settled herself on the ledge again. The scent of jasmine mingled with the steam.

Seth's hands smoothed her hair, then his fingers scrubbed gentle circles all over her scalp. She let her head loll back and luxuriated in his ministrations.

"Like that?"

"Mm." He'd rendered her boneless, and she was too numb of mind to speak.

A low chuckle rumbled from his chest. He pulled the lather through to the ends, over and over, then nudged her to dunk again and rinse.

She sank completely under this time and lingered, then pushed face first through the surface. As she wiped the water from her face and slicked it down her hair, she stood straight up and turned around. "That was nice. Thank you."

Seth's eyes widened and he audibly swallowed. If he'd been facing a stampeding herd of buffalo, he couldn't have looked any more shocked.

Becca followed the path of his gaze to her chest, and her eyes went just as wide. The thin, wet fabric of her chemise clung to her breasts like a cobweb and concealed little more. She might as well be naked!

She plucked the fabric loose, then clamped both arms over her chest. Her pulse raced and her face burned. She didn't have the guts to look up.

Before the tears that pricked her eyes could overflow, strong hands reached for her and pulled her close. "It's okay." Seth wrapped her in a protective embrace, shielding her body with his.

"I... I..."

"Shhh." He tucked her head under his chin as she buried her face in his chest. "You have nothing to be ashamed of." He held her for a long moment, then tipped her face up to his. His clear blue eyes held only affection. There was no judgment there.

One side of his mouth quirked up. "Me and my big ideas." When his smirk spread into a full grin, Becca smiled, too. She couldn't help herself.

Seth turned her around and set her on the ledge with him again. He wrapped her loosely in his arms and leaned back as the water lapped at their shoulders. Or rather *her* shoulders. It only reached midway up his chest.

Becca lifted her hands out of the water and examined them, front and back. "We're going to turn into prunes."

"Yes. But we'll be warm prunes."

"True." Becca shivered at the thought of getting out of the spring. She rested her head in the curve of his shoulder, absorbing the heat and the closeness.

It was obvious Seth cared about her, enjoyed spending time with her, but why? She was dowdy and naïve. He was handsome and experienced. What did he see in a simple girl like her? And, she frowned, where had he gotten his *experience*? The thought of him kissing someone else sent a rush of jealousy swirling through her veins. Not that she had any claim on him, but still.

Curiosity finally sprung the lock decency had on her tongue. "Seth?"

"Hm."

"The day you read the diary, when we... um... when you

touched me. How did you know what to do?"

There was nothing but silence behind her. And one suddenly-tension-filled man.

Becca hazarded a glance over her shoulder. Seth's face was unreadable and his lips were pressed into a straight line. Oops. She turned back around, her posture as stiff as his features looked. "Never mind. Forget I asked."

He blew out a heavy sigh. "No. After taking such liberties with you, I—you deserve to know."

Becca turned, facing him, but she swam back and sat on the opposite ledge. She sensed he could use some space. She definitely could.

Seth opened his mouth, then closed it again. He raked a hand through his hair, plowing deep rows in the damp locks. A crease appeared between his brows, and then he offered a sheepish expression. "This isn't as easy as I thought."

Becca waited patiently, ignoring the flutter of nerves. She wanted to know.

He blew out another sigh. "After I left home, I went to work on a cattle ranch. On Saturday nights, the single hands—that was nearly all of us—would go into town together and play cards at the saloon. It wasn't something I enjoyed very much, but the empty bunkhouse could be pretty boring, so I went."

Seth paused as if he were gauging her reaction.

Becca shrugged and nodded. Loneliness and boredom were things she understood.

"Anyway, I was a greenhorn. The guys gave me grief every chance they got. They figured out I was... that I hadn't." He raked his hand through his hair again as a flush crept up his neck.

"That you were what?"

The fiery glow shot across his cheeks. "A virgin, Becca. They figured out I'd never been with a woman."

"Oh." A blazing blush climbed her face faster than it had his.

"They—" He rubbed the back of his neck and shifted uncomfortably on the ledge. "I can't believe I'm telling you this. They insisted I visit one of the women who worked there. I tried to refuse—I *did* refuse—but they carried me up the stairs and dumped me in her room." He scrubbed a hand over his jaw. "I knew they'd never let up if I left, so I stayed."

"Oh." Becca lowered her gaze.

"Hear me out. It's not what you think."

A strange ache wormed its way through her heart. How could it be anything else?

Seth pushed off the ledge and reached for her hand. He pulled her back across the spring until she was standing in front of him, but his eyes were focused on her face, not her chest.

"The woman wasn't very old, but she was wise for her years. I guess that kind of life makes a person that way. She could see I was being forced into the situation. She told me I could leave and she wouldn't tell. But I knew they'd be watching, and if I didn't stay with her long enough, they'd figure it out. When I explained, the woman reconsidered. She told me the time had already been paid for and that I could stay and talk if I wanted."

Seth settled himself on the ledge again and rested his arms loosely around her waist. "When I found out she'd already been paid, I decided to make the best of the situation. Once I worked up the nerve, I asked if she would tell me how to please a woman."

"So, all you did was talk?"

He drew a deep breath. "Not exactly. It started out that way, but... well... those women are forward. She insisted I practice a few of the things she'd told me about. But" —he lifted her chin and peered into her eyes— "I only kissed her and touched her. I was raised to be faithful, and I believe that a man should be with only one woman. Holding to that hasn't been easy, but it's what I plan to do."

She searched the eyes staring into hers.

"Do you believe me?"

She wanted to. "Yes."

"Good." The relief in his tone was doubled in the force of his hug.

Becca rested her head against his chest. "So, what happened?"

"What do you mean?"

"The other men. Did they leave you alone after that?"

Deep laughter vibrated her cheek. "That's the best part of the story.

"When the lesson was over, the woman and I sat and talked for a while. I think she enjoyed our conversation so much she lost track of time. When we finally walked back down to the table where everyone was sitting, they checked their watches, grumbled, and told me I'd have to pay for the extra time myself.

"I reached for my coins, but the woman shook her head. 'Keep your money,' she said, loud enough so they could hear. 'You were so good, the extra half hour is free.' With that, she planted a kiss on my cheek and walked away. The subject was never brought up again."

Seth held her out from him and looked into her eyes. "Do you think less of me, Becca?"

"No. I'm... glad."

"Glad?"

She fought the urge to look away. "That she taught you those things."

Something sparked in Seth's eyes. He leaned down and

touched his lips to hers, tentatively, as if he wasn't sure she wanted him to.

She wanted him to.

Becca parted her lips and brushed his, their breath mingling like the wisps of steam rising off the water around them. He cradled her face with his hands, then tilted his head and deepened the kiss.

As they explored each other's mouths, he slid forward on the ledge until he was standing in front of her, heat pouring off him like an inferno. Next to the blaze of his skin, the water felt tepid. One of his hands slid down and splayed across her back, holding her firmly as his tongue took bold possession. His hard body pressed against her belly and he groaned.

Seth tore his mouth away and rested his forehead on hers. "Lord help me," he rasped. "Every part of me is screamin' for me to keep goin', but..."

"It's wrong."

She felt him nod.

Becca turned out of his embrace to leave the spring. She was turning into a prune anyway.

Seth caught hold of her arm and stopped her. He stoked her cheek with his free hand and kissed the tip of her nose. "I'm attracted to you, Becca—so much, I can hardly control myself—but I care about you too much to take your virtue from you without a future to offer in return. Do you understand?"

Becca nodded. It nearly killed her, but she understood completely. He didn't want her.

Chapter Twenty-Two

Becca put the supper dishes away and took a seat by Seth. It had been a rough two days and they hadn't traveled very far, but it was good to be back on the trail.

"How close are we to the border?" she asked, tossing a twig into the fire.

"We should get there sometime tomorrow."

"Then we cross the river, right? At Camp Calhoun?"

Seth exhaled a long breath. "It's Camp Yuma now. And, no. We won't be crossing there."

"Why not?"

"The fort fell on hard times this summer. There was a shortage of food, and most of the soldiers left. Last Sam heard, the fort was under siege."

Becca pushed the word past her tightening throat. "Indians?"

"Yes."

Visions of finding her family withered. She should have known Seth's promise was too good to be true.

He put his arm around her and drew her to his side. "It'll be all right. We're taking a trail farther north."

What good would that do? Threat of Indians aside, they needed the ferry.

Despair drained the strength from her voice. "How will we get across the river?"

Seth brushed her cheek with his thumb and peered into her eyes with concern. "There are other wagon crossings, Becca. Camp Yuma's not the only one." He guided her head to his shoulder and tucked it under his chin. "Don't you worry. I'll get you home."

Seth lay alone with his head on his saddle bags, staring up into the night sky. Sending Rebecca to sleep in the wagon was the hardest thing he'd ever had to do. But if he didn't put some distance between them, he'd never be able to let her go. Even now, the thought of living without her gutted his heart and fractured his soul.

But he was a man without means. Especially now. He'd spent the bulk of his savings on the wagon and supplies. The best he could hope for was to get her safely to California and into the hands of someone who would take care of her. Someone other than him.

A humorless chuckle resonated from within his throat. He was getting ahead of himself. They had to make it across the border first. He wasn't lying when he said there were other ferries, but they were smaller and sometimes poorly maintained. Second to unfriendly Indians, crossing the mighty Colorado was the greatest danger they faced.

"It's so big." The awe in Becca's voice was as real as the fear spreading its way through her limbs as she stood on the bank of the Colorado and stared at the expanse of water before her. They'd crossed rivers before, but none like this.

She turned to Seth. "Where's the ferry?"

He gestured to his right, where the trail turned and ran parallel to the river. "There's a scow a few yards upstream." Seth stared at the water again, his lips drawing into a frown.

The longer he stared, the more Becca's insides flopped about like a grounded fish. "What's wrong?"

He looked up as if she'd pulled him out of some deep deliberation, then lifted one corner of his mouth. "I'd prefer having another wagon or two here to help us, that's all. Don't worry," he said, tugging the end of her braid free from her fingers. "We'll make it to the other side. I just need to do some planning so we get across safely."

Seth looked at the river again, then glanced at the sky. "Go fix lunch while I scout around. I'll join you in a bit."

Becca set out the leftovers from breakfast and waited by the wagon. To pass the time, she retrieved her drawing pad and began sketching. The river was as beautiful as it was menacing, and she wanted to preserve the memory.

Shores of red dirt edged a wide current of blue-green water, and rows of purple hills stood guard in the background. Charcoal alone could never do the image justice, so she switched to pastels. The act of drawing calmed her as it always had, but reality clung to the edge of her thoughts. As she sketched and filled and smudged, Becca prayed her picture would make it across unharmed and she and Seth would live to tell the story.

Zeus whinnied. The sound was followed by a blow and a firm stomp of a hoof—probably Cyrus. She smiled. He was as petulant as they came and not shy about asserting his opinion. Seth had tied them to graze in a clearing on the other side of the wagon, and they were probably wishing to be watered again. They always got greedy when they could hear the flow of a stream.

The ruckus continued, so she set her things aside. "Settle down, boys," she chided as she rose. "I'm coming."

Becca rounded the back of the wagon and stopped dead in her tracks as the air in her lungs completely evaporated.

Cooperate. But don't show any weakness.

Chapter Twenty-Three

Seth trudged back to camp under the weight of the task ahead. The scow was in working condition and a sturdy rope already spanned the divide, but the river was deep and the current was swift. Crossing would be dangerous at best.

And how would they go about it? The scow was too small to hold both the wagon and the team. He'd have to swim the horses across, or ferry them first and come back for the wagon. No matter what method or order he chose, something vital would be left unprotected. He couldn't be in three places at once.

Approaching the wagon with a sigh, he spotted the biscuits and cheese Becca had set out. Worry had his appetite in its grip, but he'd force himself to eat. Fighting that current was going to take all his strength and more.

The snort of a horse stopped him short as he bent to pick up his lunch. The sound was too close. He'd staked the team in the clearing beyond the trees that lined the other side of camp.

One of them must've gotten loose.

Seth rounded the back of the wagon and saw Becca standing a few feet away. He opened his mouth to call her name, but closed it again. Something was wrong. Her back was ramrod straight and her hands hung, pale and trembling, at her sides. He'd only seen her this frightened one other time.

Pulse kicking into a gallop, Seth eased his hand toward his holster and crept closer.

"Iipa!"

The cry was followed by a stream of staccato words Seth didn't understand. Hooves thudded the ground as firmly as his heart against his ribs, and a savage on horseback loomed over him, poised to throw a spear.

Seth straightened and lifted his hands, palms out, hoping the brave would comprehend the gesture.

The Indian barked something at him, but Seth could only shrug.

The Indian repeated himself, this time reining his horse backward several steps.

Seth glanced at Becca who was looking at him now, her face bloodless and her hands gripping the folds of her skirt. He took a tentative step forward, toward the brave.

The Indian issued the same command and backed up some more, so Seth took more cautious steps.

A murmur of male voices to his left stole his attention, and his blood ran cold.

Six more braves atop horses emerged from the shadows of the trees, all of them stone faced and most of them armed. They carried everything from bows to clubs, and were in various states of undress. Some wore leather pants and scanty animal skin ponchos, while others had only a loin cloth. But all of them bore blue ink tattoos.

The markings—rows and rows of parallel lines—varied in pattern from one to the next, decorating their bodies and extending to cover their faces. Their long black hair flowed wild and loose, and the slant of the inky lines matched the fierce slant of their eyes.

Seth's indrawn breath grated over his throat as he regarded the threat. No matter what, he had to protect Becca. Everything else was expendable. Including him.

The brave with the spear glared at him, unblinking, as if waiting for a reason to attack.

Seth held the man's gaze and lifted his chin.

The savage narrowed his eyes, then looked to Rebecca, his lips curving to match his lecherous stare.

A growl lodged in Seth's throat as he resisted the urge to fist his hands.

One of the men spoke, another sharp string of meaningless syllables. The phrase was apparently meant for the spear-carrying savage, if the cowed look that crossed his face was any clue.

Seth focused on the man who'd spoken. The entire group was young, but he was older by several years. Perhaps he was their leader.

The older Indian spoke to him then, his cadence slow, but his words as lost on Seth as the ones before.

"I'm sorry," Seth said, turning out his hands. "I don't understand."

The older man turned to one of the others behind him. After a brief exchange of words, the brave dismounted and emerged from between the horses.

His skin was lighter than the rest—merely tan, not deep bronze—and his only tattoos were five vertical lines spanning his chin. His prominent cheekbones and sinewy frame were clearly native, but sky blue eyes crested an aquiline nose.

Was he a half-breed?

"Kumadha wishes to know why you are here." He spoke slowly, as though pulling each word from deep in his mind.

"We're on our way to California. We were preparing to cross the river."

The fair-skinned brave turned and spoke to the older man, apparently translating his answer. Kumadha gave a brief reply.

The translator glanced around, as did many of the men on horseback. "Where are the other wagons?"

Seth drew a measured breath and debated lying. "There are none," he finally said, ruing the fact he'd tipped his hand. "We're traveling alone."

"How can one man cross a river?"

"I was figuring that out when you came."

The translator had another brief exchange with Kumadha. The spear-carrying savage growled and spat out several words with disgust, but Kumadha calmly put him in his place.

Seth gnawed the inside of his lip. He and Becca were grossly outnumbered, and Kumadha seemed reasonable. Maybe they could make some kind of deal.

"My name is Seth," he said when the translator faced him again.

The Indian hesitated, studying him. "I am Hatchoq." Seth slowly lowered his hands, but kept his right well clear of his holster. "What tribe are you?"

"We are called *Mojave*."

"You speak English well."

Hatchoq's gaze darted away. "It is my mother's language."

Kumadha spoke to Hatchoq, his voice low but with an edge of authority.

Without looking back, Hatchoq nodded. He lifted his chin,

his blue eyes keen yet cold. "What will you give us to cross?"

Seth glanced at Rebecca. Her face was still pale, but she'd stopped shaking. He crinkled the corner of his eye in a barely-perceptible wink, then focused on Hatchoq and mentally tallied what he could barter. "I have extra corn and beans."

"How much?"

"I can spare ten pounds of corn and twenty pounds of beans."

Hatchoq relayed the offer to his leader. "What else?"

"Well... I can give you a peck of dried apples."

Hatchoq said something in his language without even turning around. "What else?"

Seth rubbed his chin and exchanged a look with Rebecca. He was reaching the end of their surplus.

"Clothing," she whispered. For the purpose of salvaging fabric and fasteners, she'd packed extra clothes from her stash in the cave. It was worth a shot.

"Good idea," he replied. "Bring out what you can spare."

Becca turned to climb into the wagon, and a chorus of clicks disturbed the silence. Save Hatchoq and Kumadha, every brave had drawn a weapon and aimed it at her back.

She glanced over her shoulder and froze, her hands gripping the box and her foot on the rail.

"She's getting some clothes to trade," Seth explained.

At Hatchoq's retelling, Kumadha spoke and his men lowered their weapons—a few of them reluctantly.

Hatchoq inclined his head.

Seth gave Becca another reassuring look. "Go ahead. Just don't make any sudden moves."

Becca climbed in. After rummaging through a trunk, she handed a stack of odd shirts, skirts and trousers to Seth who turned them over to Hatchoq for inspection. Amid murmurs of approval, Hatchoq passed them to one of the men who then tied them to his saddle.

The spear-carrying brave said something while Seth helped Becca out of the wagon.

Seth looked slowly from Hatchoq to him and back. "What did he say?"

"Mahwat wants one of your horses." The interpreter gave no guidance and Kumadha's face was impassive.

"I can't give you that," Seth said.

Hatchoq glanced back at Mahwat and shook his head.

The denial brought a more demanding comment. When Hatchoq didn't respond, Mahwat addressed Kumadha. The words were foreign, but the meaning was clear.

Kumadha listened, and then drew his thick brows as though he were considering the plea. With a mix of authority and resignation, he spoke to Hatchoq.

"Mahwat wants a horse or he won't agree."

Seth's patience slipped to the ground along with his stomach. "I can't give him one. I need both of them to pull the wagon. Your leader seems to be a fair man. Surely Kumadha can convince him to see reason."

"I could appeal, but it would do no good," said Hatchoq. "Every member of our group must agree. It is our way."

Seth looked at Rebecca. The defeat in her eyes deepened that in his heart. They wouldn't be allowed to cross the river if he didn't give up a horse. And without the team, they'd never make it farther than the opposite bank.

"Interpret for me," he said as he angled to face Mahwat.

"I found her in the wilderness," Seth began, indicating Rebecca. "She got separated from her family when they were traveling west. She was starving and alone."

Hatchoq hesitated, then spoke in the same calm tones.

"I told her I would help her find her family. I spent all the money I had on the wagon and supplies." He paused while Hatchoq repeated his words. "I need two horses to pull the wagon, and I can't afford to buy more. If I give you one, we won't be able to complete the trip.

"Please," he added when Mahwat's scowl failed to ease. "Don't prevent me from taking her home."

The spear-carrying brave sat tall on his stallion, eyes dark and unreadable.

At a shift of his gaze, Seth glanced behind. Rebecca had held up her hands and was easing toward their forgotten lunch. After squatting down for moment, she lifted something and carried it toward Mahwat.

"You don't have to do this," Seth murmured to her as she passed. "We'll find something else."

"We don't have anything else."

Moving slowly on shaky legs, she approached Mahwat and lifted the wooden box she held in her hands—her precious pastels. "Will you accept these instead?"

She held them out to him for what seemed like minutes, but—despite Hatchoq's translation—he didn't respond.

Becca lowered the box and opened the lid. "They're for coloring. See?" Her trembling fingers lifted out the sapphire blue one, her favorite, and stroked it along the pale skin of her forearm until some of the color rubbed off.

When the stone-faced savage refused to acknowledge her, she replaced the beloved stick and closed the lid. Her disappointment was palpable.

Seth gritted his teeth and resisted the urge to spit on the heartless bastard. But his anger quickly turned to embittered despair. They were going to end up stuck on the trail—or worse—and there wasn't a damned thing he could do about it.

Damn it all! Why can't these people see reason!

Hatchoq said something in his peoples' language and brows rose throughout the group. Even Mahwat's harsh veneer was affected.

"What did you say?" Seth asked.

A wan smile curved Hatchoq's lips, spreading the lines on his chin. "I reminded them of another one of our ways."

Kumadha looked at Mahwat expectantly.

The brave's jaw clenched, causing muscles in his cheeks to bulge and twitch. Eyes shuttered with rancor, he gave a curt nod, then looked straight ahead and fixed his gaze on the horizon.

Once the bartered food was portioned out and given to the Indians, along with Becca's precious pastels, the men pulled the wagon to the edge of the river and rolled it onto the scow. They removed a few crates and ration barrels from the bed and placed them around it to spread the load and make the narrow barge more stable. As the braves finished shoving the containers into place, Seth walked up the bank and took Becca aside.

"I'm going to swim the horses across while you ride on the scow. I wish I could ride with you, but I need to keep an eye on the horses. I don't want to be on the opposite bank from either them or you. The safest thing is to stay together, to reach the other side together."

She stood tall and nodded, but fear radiated from her in waves. He was frightened, too. So many things could go wrong, and there wasn't enough time to prepare her. His mind raced as he worked to keep his cadence slow and his voice calm.

"Stay near Hatchoq. And hold on tight, but don't get in the wagon. If the scow starts to capsize or sink, jump clear of it and swim to safety." He drew her into a hug and whispered in her ear. "If we get separated, go to the other side and go downstream. Hide yourself and wait. I'll come find you. Understand?"

"Yes." Her arms slipped around his waist and she clung to him. "Be careful."

"I will." Seth memorized the feel of her as he inhaled her sweet scent and gave her one last squeeze. "Be brave, little rabbit."

After gazing up at Kumadha sitting on his horse and watching from a nearby hill, Becca turned toward the river and stepped onto the scow. It wobbled, sloshing the shallow muddy water. She bent her knees and held her arms out in an effort to gain her footing. Two ropes stretched from the raft's upstream corners to the long rope spanning the river to keep the small ferry on course, but they didn't do much for stability. Spreading her feet to give herself a wide base of support, she eased forward, grabbed onto the left, rear corner of the wagon, and positioned herself so she could see around the side.

The four Indians traveling with her had already boarded and taken their places with ease, walking as if they were stepping on solid stone. One manned the front, two held long poles at either side, and the one called Hatchoq stood near her, in back. The native at the front of the scow called out to the others on the bank, then went about his final preparations.

Becca's hands began to ache. She was squeezing the wood so hard, her knuckles blanched. Forcing breath into her constricted lungs, she eased her grip and willed her pounding heart to slow.

She could do this. They'd make it. Everything would be fine.

Hatchoq stood a few feet to her left, his shoulders square, his back straight, and his hands not holding onto anything. Clad in only a pair of leather pants, he was facing south, observing his surroundings without a word. She tried not to look at his bare chest and the lines on his chin, but she found it hard not to stare.

A slight breeze lifted his shiny black hair off his shoulders as his piercing blue eyes scanned west and lit on her. Becca's breath caught in her throat. Crystalline irises regarded her with uncertainty... curiosity. Then, with the humble courtesy that marked everything he did, their silent owner drew them away.

"Thank you for helping us," Becca said once she'd found her voice.

Hatchoq turned those striking eyes on her again. After regarding her until her lungs seized up again, he answered with a slight lowering of his lids. "You're welcome." They silently studied each other. He started to look away, then stopped. "May I ask you a question?"

Becca swallowed. "Yes."

"How long were you alone before Seth found you?"

Her gaze fell slightly at the memory, but she lifted it again. "More than a year."

A look of surprise wove its way through his brow as his golden chest rose with an undisciplined breath. He quickly regained his impassive face and stoic composure, but a look of admiration lingered in his eyes. "You have much courage."

Becca chewed her lip. "May I ask you something?"

Hatchoq gave a single nod.

"The other men have lines all over their bodies. Why are yours only on your chin?"

A distant look stole the light from his expression. "My

252

mother is white and my father is Mojave. Like my mother, I am a slave."

The shock of his confession left her speechless.

"Ready," Seth called.

Hatchoq turned and said something to the other men, then crossed behind her and placed a single hand on the wagon.

Several yards downstream, Mahwat swam his stallion out to a sandbar midway across the river while Seth mounted Cyrus and waited on the bank. Zeus's lead line in hand, Seth spoke softly to Cyrus and urged him down the sandy slope and into the water.

Still stunned by the Indian's answer, Becca looked back and forth from Hatchoq to Seth. She wanted to know more, but she'd run out of time. The horses were in the water and the braves were preparing to float the scow. She needed to focus all her attention on keeping her balance and making it to the other side.

The Indians holding poles dug them into the dirt and began pushing away from shore. Their muscles bulged, and they grunted and groaned with the effort, but she couldn't feel any difference. How could they possibly move such a heavy load?

Long moments later, the scow eased forward. Her hands closed like a vise on the wood as the raft lifted and rocked and surrendered its will to the current.

The ropes pulled taut and the scow leveled out. Other than a gentle rolling motion and the lapping of water, it felt as if they were slowly sliding across ice. Becca didn't let go, but she released her bated breath. This wasn't so bad. Maybe they would make it after all.

Seth was keeping pace, now in the river to his knees. She wished he'd turn and look at her, give her reassurance—if only with his eyes—but his focus was entirely on his team.

Cyrus' neck gleamed as he held his head high and glided through the water, the flare of his nostrils the only clue to his exertion. Zeus followed a few feet behind, riderless, and looking as majestic as his yokemate.

Becca sighed, wishing she still had her pastels. They were a found treasure she'd given up freely, but it would likely be years before she could obtain another set.

One of the Indians yelled. Something struck the scow, jolting them and pitching them sideways. Becca's pulse pounded in her ears and she gripped the wagon with all her strength. The scow listed right, toward the ropes. Frigid water washed up over the side, swirling around her ankles and seeping into her shoes. She tried to keep from sliding, but the angle was growing too steep. Her boots slipped on the wet wood and her fingers clawed oak. They stung from gathered splinters as she struggled to keep from falling into the river.

Hatchoq grabbed her and yanked her toward him. He caged her with his arms and flattened her against the back of the wagon with his rock-hard body. Panic hit and she tried to shove him away. She couldn't jump free if he pinned her like this. Natives shouted all around her. Something splashed to her right and she shrieked. God help her, she was trapped. They were all going to drown!

"Becca!"

The distressed shout rising above the din was undoubtedly Seth's, but the lump of terror in her throat prevented her from answering. Water kept grabbing at her feet, and the Indian held her so tightly she could barely breathe. The ropes began to creak and whine under the strain. If one of them broke...

She begged Hatchoq to move, but he didn't budge. Her pleas were sucked back down by a gasp when the scow righted itself, nearly throwing them off in the other direction. It listed back and forth, rocking so far she feared the wagon would tumble off. But then it settled into a gentle glide as if nothing had happened.

Becca shoved at Hatchoq. "Let me up." She was glad now he hadn't let go, but she needed to tell Seth she was okay.

He released her, allowing her to move back to the corner of the wagon.

Her blood turned from hot to cold, and her mouth opened in a silent scream. A huge limb was floating away from the scow—headed directly for Seth!

Cyrus' eyes went as wide as his master's. He began thrashing and trying to rear. Seth worked to get control of him, but the horse was far too spooked. Muddy water churned around them as the branch closed in. Cyrus stumbled and plunged beneath the surface of the river, taking his rider with him.

"*Seth!*" Becca's throat closed up as soon as she'd screamed his name.

Please, God. I need him. Don't let him die.

A lasso flew. Rope landed on the limb with a slap. Mahwat jerked his arm back, cinching the loop around a protruding stub of a branch and yanking it tight so it held. His horse tossed his head and backed up as Mahwat growled and fought to change the course of the log. Its path began to shift and its gnarled, leafless hands passed just west of the whorl marking the fallen horse and rider.

Cyrus surfaced with a splash. Alone.

Becca's body ached with dread. Where was Seth? Was he unconscious or injured? Had he been crushed?

Numbing seconds ticked by as images of his fate shot icy barbs straight through her heart. Her lungs shriveled. She was surrounded by miles and miles of fresh air, but Seth was engulfed in suffocating darkness. Was he scared? In pain?

Was he even alive?

She choked on a sob. "*Seth.*"

Becca started toward the edge of the scow to jump in, but Hatchoq grabbed her arm and stopped her.

"Let me go!" She jerked against his iron grip. "We have to help him!"

He shouted something to one of the men on the bank. The brave promptly threw off his poncho, waded into the shallows, and dove in.

Something burst from the water near Cyrus' hip. Pale hands clawed at his saddle, pulling a gasping, dripping Seth halfway onto the horse's back. He lay there, coughing, his chest heaving.

"Are you hurt?" Hatchoq called.

Seth shook his head. After looking Cyrus over and locating Zeus's lead line, he hoisted himself into the saddle and took up the reins. "Let's go."

He caught up and kept pace with the scow. The river grew so deep in the middle, he had to slide off Cyrus and swim, hanging on to his tail, but they made it across.

Rebecca gasped when Hatchoq caged her again, this time wrapping an arm around the front of her waist, between her and the back of the wagon. She was about to object when the scow hit the bank with a bone-jarring thud. His arm took the brunt of the blow.

"Thank you," she murmured, grateful they'd struck land before she could protest and make a fool of herself.

The narrow raft rocked as the men began hitching the team and releasing the wheels, but not so much she couldn't keep her balance. Why hadn't he let her go? Hatchoq leaned closer and she stiffened. His body heat seeped through her clothes, and his breath stirred the hairs on her neck.

"When you leave here," he said softly near her ear, "do not

camp for many nights. Camp only in the day, and only as long as you must to eat and rest your horses. Mahwat is ready to take a wife, but the woman he wants has a high price. Her father asks three horses. I fear Mahwat will not keep his word."

Apprehension prickled the surface of her skin and her lungs had shriveled again, but she managed to squeeze out a, "Thank you."

Hatchoq backed away and escorted her to the shore.

On her way up the bank, Becca stopped and looked up at Mahwat towering above her on his horse. His eyes were dark, and his menacing expression hadn't changed.

She swallowed, the movement scraping her dry throat. "Thank you for saving Seth." If what Hatchoq said was true, he'd acted to save the horse—not its rider—but if he hadn't changed the course of the limb, Cyrus and Seth *both* would be dead.

Hatchoq repeated what she assumed were her words. She prayed they would get through to the brave, but Mahwat ignored her. He turned and rode away.

Becca bid Hatchoq farewell and trudged her way up the slope, then stood and watched the men reload the wagon. Her body shook from her ordeal and it ached with fatigue. By the time the shaking had stopped and her muscles had turned to mush, the Indians were gone and Seth had driven the wagon up the slope and parked it on the trail.

He hurried back to her and captured her in a fierce hug, clutching her so tightly she could scarcely breathe. "Thank God you're all right. When the scow shifted and I heard a splash—"

His body shuddered against hers as he pressed his lips to the top of her head.

Becca hugged him back. The muddy water saturating his

clothes was seeping into hers, but she didn't care. "We lost the corn."

"I don't care about the corn." His hand splayed across her shoulder as he molded his body to hers.

"I was so frightened." She pressed her cheek to his muscular chest. "I thought you were going to drown. If something had happened to you—"

"Shh." Seth ran his hand soothingly up and down her back. "I'm all right. I just got tangled in the tack." He gave her one last squeeze and pulled away. "I'm getting you all wet."

Drawn by the vulnerability in his eyes, she rose up on her toes and touched her lips to his. Warmth spread across her cheeks as he cradled her face and kissed her back.

"We made it," she said when he pulled his lips away. "I can't believe we're in California." Becca lifted her face to kiss him again, but he stiffened and backed away.

The tenderness was gone, replaced by hard lines and a shuttered expression.

"What's wrong?"

"You shouldn't be kissing me. You're betrothed to another man."

Seth turned and stalked away, leaving her standing at the bank of the river, alone and shivering.

Chapter Twenty-Four

Two and one-half weeks later

The December wind, whipping through the bonnet and invading her coat, barely chilled her numb skin, and the jostling of the box could never bruise it as much as Seth's rejection had bruised her soul. After changing his clothes, he'd listened to her as she relayed Hatchoq's warning, and then he'd sent her to ride in the wagon without another word.

For more than a week after crossing the river, they traveled at night and stopped for brief rests in the day, taking turns keeping watch while the other was sleeping. She told herself his mood and his silence were due to the danger combined with fatigue, but she knew better. It was her. Her unfaithfulness disgusted him.

Even after resuming their old routine, Seth made it clear he didn't want her. He made sure her basic needs were met, but he avoided her as much as he possibly could. No more noontime chats over lunch or evening cuddles by the fire. If she noticed him looking at her, he'd look away.

It hurt, but it was for the best... wasn't it? She needed to prepare herself in case Nathan still wanted her. No matter how painful it was, she had to estrange herself from Seth and pray the act wouldn't totally destroy her heart.

Becca finished packing her valise and carried it with her as she climbed through the front of the bonnet and onto the wagon seat. Today was the day she'd been waiting for. In a matter of minutes, they'd arrive in Blackwater.

Unsurprisingly, Seth did nothing to acknowledge her presence. The lines in his face were as deep as the ruts in the road leading into town, and his jaw was as stiff as the north wind. Becca watched him out the corner of her eye, trying not to be obvious, but his stern expression made it hard not to stare. Anxiety rising, she clasped her hands in her lap and forced her attention away.

Wooden sidewalks and clapboard buildings lined the main road. It was only nine in the morning, but the town already hummed with activity. Wagons and men on horseback stirred up dust in the street, while ladies in bonnets and hats walked along the storefronts and went about their day.

Seth stopped the wagon in front of the general store and set the brake. "Grab your valise. You can wait for me in here while I take the wagon to the livery." He reached for her and helped her down, barely making eye contact, then let go of her as soon as she had her footing. "I'll come back as soon as I'm done."

She took him at his word, but a spot in the center of her chest stung as he drove away. Very soon, that would be the last image of Seth she'd ever see.

The sounds of footsteps and voices drew her back out of her thoughts. Gripping the handle of her bag with a damp palm, Becca smoothed her hair and reentered civilization.

A bell tinkled as she walked into the store. The man behind the counter looked up and smiled, but the well-dressed lady in front of him had the bulk of his attention.

Thankful for the reprieve, Becca closed her eyes and inhaled. The scents of fabric, soap and leather blended with the smells of a kitchen pantry. It reminded her of all the times she'd ridden into town and shopped with her ma.

I miss you, Ma.

Her hands dampened again. She desired the truth more than ever, but opposing visions—one of her mother greeting her with open arms and one of her scowling and sending her away—had invaded her dreams for weeks.

Could she handle a second rejection? One that was certain, not softened by doubt and speculation?

Becca sighed. If there was any chance her parents still wanted her, she had to find them. She wouldn't be content to live the rest of her life and never know.

A feminine gasp made her open her eyes. She gaped. The well-dressed lady at the counter stood in front of her now. "Charlotte?"

Eyes wide and face leeched of color, her friend stared at her as if she drawn a gun and held up the store. "B—B—Becca?"

Joyful tears burned the backs of her eyes. "It's me."

"But— But you..."

"Should be dead. I know."

Charlotte swallowed, and her skin turned a faint shade of gray.

Becca's breath hitched. "I've missed you." She stepped forward and gave Charlotte a hug, hoping the trail dust that clung to her garments wouldn't taint the emerald taffeta dress her friend was wearing.

Charlotte's body stayed rigid, and Becca regretted her

impulsiveness. She should have known better than to go near her in such grimy clothes.

"I've missed you, too," her friend whispered. She lifted her arms and patted Becca on the back. It wasn't a hearty hug full of feeling, but it was familiar. It was Charlotte.

"Well," Charlotte said, pulling away and brushing the front of her dress, "You probably have quite a story to tell. How long have you been in town?"

"Not long. Seth and I just arrived."

"Who's Seth?"

"Seth Emerson, the man who found me and brought me to California."

"Where is he?"

"At the livery."

Charlotte fingered her fiery, upswept hair and eyed Becca from head to toe, making her feel like a street urchin in her mended clothes and adolescent braid. She chewed the edge of her lip, then glanced around the shop. The starched bow on her flat-brimmed hat barely shifted with the movement. "You and I should talk." She took Becca by the hand and led her to a blue velvet settee located in an out-of-the-way corner. "Have you seen your parents?"

"No," Becca said as they sat down, thankful they were the only ones in the store. "I haven't found Nathan yet either. Do you know where they are?" Charlotte shook her head. "Nathan and his family settled in another town. I'm not sure which one. And I haven't seen your parents since shortly after we arrived in California. They broke off from the train and went their own way."

"Oh." Becca's heart sank. "I was hoping to find them by Christmas."

"I still can't believe you're here. What happened?"

"I returned from my walk and found the wagons gone. When no one came back for me, I used the junk people left by the trail to make a shelter, and then I sifted through the trunks and crates until I found the things I needed to care for myself." She exhaled a breath and shrugged. "I made do."

"How long were you there?"

"A little over a year."

Charlotte's lips parted in a look of reserved horror.

"Seth found me in September, and then we left in October. It's taken us over two months to get here."

"I didn't think trains traveled this time of year."

"They don't. We traveled alone."

"You spent months on the trail—alone with a man?" Charlotte stared at her with such stunned revulsion, Becca suddenly pictured all the passengers of the train glaring at her the same way.

She hid her discomfiture behind a neutral expression. "Yes. But we... we're friends. Nothing more."

The tilt of Charlotte's head and the set of her mouth said she didn't buy it.

So what? Becca didn't really care. She straightened her spine and bolstered herself. Charlotte might not know the whereabouts of Nathan or her parents, but she'd traveled with them all the way to California. It was time for answers. "What happened that day? Why didn't you come find me and tell me the wagons were leaving?"

Charlotte's air of superiority vanished. Despite her elegant posture and fancy clothes, she looked decidedly uncomfortable. "The men cleared the rocks off the trail faster than expected. As soon as I realized we were packing up to move, I told your ma where you'd gone."

"Was she angry?"

"No. I expected her to be upset with both of us, but she just thanked me and said she'd take care of it."

Becca's gaze grew unfocussed. It didn't make any sense. Her father might have kept his feelings to himself, but her mother would have been livid.

"There's more." Charlotte's slender fingers touched the jewel-encrusted brooch at her throat. Her hand returned to her lap and grasped the cinch of her beaded reticule. "This isn't easy to tell you, but it's something I feel you should know.

"When it was time to leave, your pa told us to go ahead without them and they would catch up. My mother sent me to take some bread to Mrs. Godfrey. She needed help looking after her daughters, so I stayed and walked with them a while. When we passed your parents' wagon, your ma was unloading ration barrels and moving them to the side of the trail."

Becca pushed words out, but they were a strangled whisper. "Where was my pa?"

"I don't know. I assumed he went to find you."

No. All the air in the room evaporated.

"I'm sorry, Becca," Charlotte said as she reached out and touched the tattered sleeve of her coat. "I didn't make the connection until later."

Becca pressed a hand to her stomach. The coffee and biscuits she'd eaten for breakfast were about to come up. Why had she let Seth convince her to hope? She should have believed what she saw all along. She should have stayed in the cave. "I think I'm going to be sick."

"Oh dear." Charlotte scooted a few inches away. Her hands twisted the strap of her purse, and she shifted on the cushion as though she might bolt.

Becca swallowed back foul-tasting liquid as waves of pain and anger surged up her throat. "What did they say?"

Charlotte stared at her with big round eyes. "Who?"

"My parents. What excuse did they give for my disappearance?"

Charlotte blinked and fingered her brooch again. "Well, when they caught up with the train later that evening, they said you were asleep in the wagon. I figured you were tired from exploring... and probably shamed by a good scolding," she added with a sheepish look, "so I didn't give it a second thought. No one else did either. The next morning, your ma *discovered* you were missing when people started asking after you."

Tears begged for release, but Becca wouldn't let them fall. "Did anyone go looking for me?"

"Of course! The captain sent out scouts two days in a row. When they didn't find you, he organized a search of the entire train."

"And?"

"Well..." Charlotte's lashes lowered along with her voice. "Some of your belongings were found in Melvin Cantwell's wagon."

"What? How did my things—" Becca's heart stopped as realization hit. Her parents must have put them there.

"Your parents just stood by and watched. They didn't even speak up when Mr. Cantwell was accused. When word got around he had some of your things, a few of the men carried him off. No one ever saw him again."

Her stomach lurched. "Nathan wasn't involved, was he?"

Charlotte fingered the ecru lace adorning her cuffs. "No."

"What about my Pa?"

"No."

Becca released a breath, then squelched the derisive note rising up her throat. It was perfectly all right to leave your own daughter to die in the wilderness, but not to kill a man to cover your crime. Some honorable set of values that was.

As the crippled walls of her childhood ideals crumbled, her anger disintegrated with it. She should be angry and hurt and sad, but all she felt was empty.

"Becca...? Is there anything I can do?"

"No." Becca pasted on the best face she could. "Thank you for offering."

The bell above the door rang, and a man dressed in a black morning coat over gray waistcoat and trousers stepped into the store. He looked like something out of a catalog, and he looked right at Charlotte. "You've been here quite a while, dear. Need I fear the bill?"

Charlotte blushed as she and Becca rose to their feet. "No, no. I bumped into a friend of mine." She gestured politely. "Rebecca Garvey, this is my husband, Harrison Bradford."

Harrison smiled—the way a learned person regards a simpleton—and then he bowed to Becca's proffered hand, but didn't let it touch his lips. "A pleasure, Miss Garvey."

"Likewise, Mr. Bradford." Becca withdrew her hand and smiled back. He obviously regarded her as inferior. At least he had the decency to pretend.

With eyes the color of ice, he gave her the same critical assessment his wife had. "You must be new in town."

"Yes. I—"

"Rebecca just arrived," Charlotte cut in. "She's been traveling for quite a while and she's exhausted. I'm sure she'd rather we didn't delay her any longer."

Becca closed her mouth, perplexed by the interruption, but thankful for it all the same.

"I hate to rush off," Charlotte said to her, "but the town council is meeting this morning. Harrison's father is the mayor of Blackwater and Harrison is the treasurer, so we're expected to attend." Her failed attempt at humility announced it wasn't a hardship. "Perhaps we can get together later for tea." Her failed attempt at hospitality wasn't lost on Becca either.

"Perhaps."

Harrison tipped his hat. "Good day, Miss Garvey."

Becca managed to hold a smile in place until they left. Then her heart deflated and she sank back down on the settee. She and Seth had made the arduous trip for nothing.

Well, maybe not *nothing*. There was still Nathan.

Seth sifted through his coins and handed one to the livery worker, hoping Becca's search wouldn't last much longer. He was running out of funds.

Another part of him hoped it would last forever. Despite the callous way he'd been treating her for weeks, he didn't want to ever let her go.

"Is that enough for tonight?" he asked the rangy young man.

"Yes sir, Mr. Emerson."

Seth glanced at the wagon and the team, the bulk of his earthly possessions. "Can I be assured my things will be safe here?"

"Oh, yes sir." The lad's head bobbed up and down along with his Adam's apple. "I'll guard them personally."

"If a lady by the name of Rebecca Garvey stops by, allow her access to anything she needs."

"Garvey. Will do, sir."

Seth cursed his next words, but he had a bad feeling about how things would go. Bad for him. "If for some reason I don't return, give her everything—the wagon, the team—everything."

"Uh, yes sir."

Seth watched the youth lead Cyrus and Zeus to their stalls, and then he left for the general store. For now, at least, Becca needed him.

A bell tinkled overhead as he walked inside and removed his hat. Women milled about, oohing over this and gossiping about that, but none of them was Rebecca.

The storekeeper smiled as he approached the counter. "Can I help you?"

"I'm looking for a young lady I dropped off earlier."

"Light brown hair? Dark wool coat?"

"Yes."

He pointed to a spot near the corner of the store. "I believe she's over there."

Seth made his way through the tables of goods to a small sitting area to the right of the door. His throat tightened.

Like a lost child, Becca sat with her hands in her lap and her shoulders slumped, staring at a spot on the floor.

"Becca?"

She lifted her head and smiled, but the pain behind the mask was so plain, it hit him like a hoof to the chest.

God, he was a bastard. After treating her no better than the dirt on his boots for weeks, he'd dumped her here like a load of rotten trash. She probably thought he hated her. But, hell. What other choice did he have? They'd grown too close—developed too many feelings for each other. Driving that wedge was the only way to honor the commitment he'd made and push her into the arms of her intended.

Seth held out his hand to help her up, but she rose without his aid. "Did you do any shopping?"

"No."

"Why not? You used up your soap, and I'm sure you'd like some new clothes." He could scarcely afford it, but he'd buy them for her anyway. It was the least he could do.

"Thank you, but I don't want anything."

"Are you sure?"

"I have a change of clothes in my bag, and we have plenty of soap."

Yeah, but it doesn't smell like jasmine. "At least let me buy you a dress to wear when we find your parents."

Was that a wince?

Shit. Did she really dread traveling with him that much?

Becca drew a deep breath and offered another pasted-on smile. "You've spent enough money on me already. The clothes I have will suffice."

Seth scratched his jaw, then smoothed the furrows he'd made in his beard. "All right, then. Let's start asking around and see what we find."

The storekeeper and the blacksmith weren't of any help, and he'd already questioned workers at the hotel and the livery. He'd even stopped several random citizens on the street. They were running out of options.

Oddly, Becca was unfazed. She just followed along and let him ask all the questions. She offered information at times, but she rarely showed any emotion. In fact, she seemed more interested in news about Nathan than getting word of her folks.

Seth glanced her way and sighed. That was what he wanted, right—the reason he'd pushed her away?

It was. But it still hurt like hell.

At the first break in traffic, they crossed the street and headed for the mill at the edge of town. The sound of rushing water blended with the whine of a saw in the distance, and the scents of oak and cedar grew more pungent with every step.

"If we don't have any luck here," Seth said, "we'll take a break for lunch." He hadn't expected to hit a dead end so soon. He needed a chance to think and decide what to do. And he needed to talk with Becca. She had every reason to despise him—he wouldn't dare argue that—but something had changed. Something about her closed off demeanor wasn't right.

The throng of people and conveyances had thinned and disappeared by the time they reached the sidewalk edging the lumber yard. New boards clattered as they were loaded into the back of a farm wagon up ahead. Then parting words rumbled as the worker disappeared back into the mill.

Becca halted and stared as the customer stepped from behind the bed.

So did Seth. He'd know that face anywhere. It belonged to the man in Becca's crumpled drawing.

"It's Nathan," Becca whispered. She looked up at him with big round eyes. "I..."

"You should go talk to him," Seth supplied, his chest aching with every word. "Want me to hold your valise?"

"No, um. I should— I'll keep it."

She looked at Nathan again, then back at him.

"Do you want me to go with you?" *Say yes.*

"No. I..." The indecision on her face, the mix of apology and gratitude, was a momentary balm.

Seth forced a smile. As much as he wanted to interrogate the jackass who'd left her behind, this was something she wanted to do by herself. "Go on." His words fell like salt on his wounded heart. "Catch him before he leaves."

Becca wet her lips and drew a shaky breath. She turned away from him and walked toward her intended.

Fate sucked the air from Seth's lungs as he backed away and obscured himself in the shadows. He wanted to run to the woman who'd stolen his heart and tell her he'd changed his mind, but he fisted his hands and forced his feet to stay put.

Long before they met, she'd made someone a promise. He needed to let her go.

He needed to let her keep it.

Becca's boots dragged in the dust as she neared the man who held the fate of her future in his hands. She tried to call his name, but her voice wouldn't work. That didn't keep the word from rushing through her mind in a swirl of longing and anger and pain.

Nathan.

He was as handsome as she remembered, tall and lean beneath the work clothes he wore. His hair was shorter and hidden by his hat, but the few strands that showed gleamed the same coal black as the locks that used to fall across his forehead when he would walk with her and talk on the trail.

What would she do if he didn't want her anymore? And what would she do if he did?

By the time he'd secured his load and checked his team's harness, she stood almost close enough to touch him. Her feelings were so jumbled, she didn't know what she wanted anymore, but she couldn't walk away. She'd survived her parents' rejection and she'd survived Seth's, too. She wouldn't turn her back on this last chance for happiness. "Nathan."

He turned around. "Yes?" His eyes flew open wide and his chest seized mid-breath.

Becca's lungs halted as well. She'd best get used to people's reactions coming face to face with a ghost.

"Rebecca?" His expression melted. "Oh, Rebecca." He gathered her into his arms and clutched her to his chest. "I—" His voice broke. *"Dear God."*

Nathan squeezed her with a force that matched the emotion of his words. He held her so tightly, the buttons of his coat pressed painfully into her face and she couldn't lift her arms to hug him back. She wasn't sure she wanted to.

After a long moment, he let go. His hands slid down the sleeves of her coat, and then the right one lifted to touch her cheek. It never made contact. He withdrew it and lowered it to his side. "How... How are you?"

"I'm alive." That was all she could claim for now.

Nathan removed his hat and glanced around. He gestured in the direction of a bench on the mill's porch, and she sat with him there.

Becca placed her valise on the plank at her feet, and then she folded her hands in her lap and waited for him to speak.

As his deep blue eyes took her in, feelings played across them like clouds racing by before a storm. Relief. Regret. Guilt. Shame. Sadness. "I searched for you day and night when you went missing. I begged the captain to keep looking for you, but he made us stop. I... I thought you were dead," he said quietly.

She blinked in acknowledgement, then held his gaze and kept her counsel. His distress looked real and he seemed to be telling the truth, but she wanted to be sure. More than a year's worth of pain and bitterness wasn't easily washed away.

"Did he hurt you, Becca?"

"Who?"

"Melvin Cantwell. Did he—"

"No." She drew a breath and chose her words. "Mr. Cantwell wasn't involved."

Nathan swallowed and looked almost sick. "Not at all?"

Becca shook her head.

He closed his eyes and whispered what sounded like a prayer, and then his lashes lifted, revealing bleak eyes. "They killed him. They killed an innocent man."

"I know."

"If it wasn't him... What happened to you?"

"I— There was a miscommunication. I went for a walk, and when I returned, the wagons were gone." She winced at his look of abject horror. "I managed to survive until I found someone willing to bring me here."

"I searched for you, Becca. Believe me, I did. I wanted to keep looking—even after they found your things—but by then, there were Indians in the area and the captain refused to let us search any longer." The anguish pouring out with every word put her doubts to rest and doused the angry embers she harbored.

"I believe you." She tucked an errant strand of hair behind her ear and thought of a way to change the subject. There was no use rehashing the past. Her only concern now was the future. "I'm surprised to see you here. I was told you didn't settle in Blackwater."

"I didn't. My farm is in Dorland, about fifteen miles west. I'm here because the mill broke down. I need one more load of lumber to finish my house."

Becca tried not to appear too hopeful.

He took one of her hands in his. "I waited for you, Becca,

long after people told me it was time to forget about you and move on. I couldn't believe you were actually gone. I meant what I said when I asked you to marry me." Her heart thudded against her ribs as his work-worn fingers squeezed hers gently. "But when you didn't show up after nearly a year, I—" He swallowed. "I began courting someone else. Hannah and I were married last week."

Becca slid her hand from his as the last of her hope slipped away. She clasped one set of fingers with the other to keep them from trembling as her heart broke and her dreams disintegrated.

"I'm so sorry," Nathan said. There was a tremor in his voice, and tears lined the edges of his lids.

"Don't apologize," she managed along with a watery smile. "I'm happy for you." No matter how painful it was to say, it was the truth. Nathan was a good man; he'd done nothing wrong.

He composed himself and cleared his throat. "Have you found your parents?"

"No. The only person I've spoken with is Charlotte."

He grimaced. "She set her cap for me shortly after you went missing—said she was worried about me and wanted to offer me comfort, but I knew better."

"Why would she be interested in you?" Becca's hand flew to her mouth. "I didn't mean it that way. You're a fine, well, you— She—"

"I know what you mean. She likes fancy things and thinks she's better than everyone else. What would she want with a farmer?" His sardonic smile faded and his boots shifted on the planks. "My family is wealthy, Rebecca. We had to pretend we weren't as long as we were on the trail, but I think Charlotte knew."

"Oh." Becca blinked. She would have never guessed. "Why

did you have to pretend?"

"My father wasn't claiming land, he was buying it—a much larger portion than the federal grants. He had already paid and received the deed, but he had to keep it a secret, for fear someone might kill him and steal it.

"I was going to tell you," Nathan added with regret, "but I never got the chance."

"Did you tell my father?"

"Yes. I told him when I asked for your hand."

Becca rolled the end of her braid between her fingers. Her parents would want her to marry well... wouldn't they?

"I wish I knew where your parents were so you could find them and let them know you're alive. Your mother was in such a state, I thought she was going to die of grief. And your pa—" Nathan shook his head and sighed. "Everyone did what they could. We helped them, and they managed to keep up with us as far as the Colorado; but once we crossed, they fell behind."

She dropped her hand to her lap and suppressed the urge to scoff. They weren't grieving. They fell behind so they wouldn't have to keep up the act anymore.

"Do you have a place to stay?"

"Yes." It wasn't a lie. At least not for tonight.

Nathan glanced at the sky. "I wish I could talk with you more." He stood and helped her up. "I hate leaving like this, but I have a long journey ahead. If I don't go now, I won't make it home before dark."

"I understand."

He reached for her face, and this time the tips of his fingers grazed her cheek. "If you ever need anything..."

His offer was as genuine and heartfelt as they come, but the things she needed he was no longer free to give. "Thank you."

Filled with renewed admiration and love for a man she could

never have, Becca watched him ride away. With the last of her strength, she picked up her bag and prepared herself for a long discussion with Seth.

She turned, expecting him to be bearing down on her, brimming with all kinds of questions, but the path was empty. "Seth?"

He didn't answer.

She lowered herself back onto the bench, pressed down by the weight of her circumstances. Her parents didn't want her, and she'd been turned away by the only two men she'd ever loved. She had no future, no way to support herself. She didn't even have the means to rent a room for the night.

Her stomach rumbled, attesting to her human fragility when food was the last thing on her mind, and tears of bitterness wet her face. Seth had encouraged her to trust again, to hope. He had coaxed her out of her blessed numbness and made her *feel.* Now pain consumed her heart and singed her entire body. At least at the cave, she could bury the past and care for herself, have a tolerable existence. Now she hurt like she'd never hurt before. And she had nothing.

Resisting the urge to swat her valise off her lap, Rebecca choked on Seth's name and cursed the day she met him. She hugged the bag to her aching chest and sobbed.

Chapter Twenty-Five

"Rebecca?"

She lifted her head to Seth standing before her, his brow wrinkled with concern and confusion. Her breath hitched with the snuffles of a sniveling child, but her eyes bore into him with the contempt of a full-grown woman.

"What's wrong? What happened?"

"As if you care."

"Becca, I—"

"Don't call me that." She rose, shifting her valise to one hand and swiping away her tears with the other.

"Did Nathan hurt you?"

"Not the way you did." The impact of her words was plain and, for a moment, she regretted them. "No."

"Why did he leave?"

"He had to go home to his *wife*."

The color drained from Seth's face, but heat rose in hers. Becca bit her lip to keep it from trembling. "You should have left me in the wilderness," she blurted before emotion could overtake her again. "I wish we'd never met."

She pushed past Seth as fresh tears began to flow. She didn't know where she would go or what she would do, but she was educated and able. Surely she could find a respectable way to provide for herself.

A sob caught in her throat.

Who was she kidding? She was a woman with no family and even less means. She'd end up a beggar—or worse, a soiled dove selling her body in some saloon.

Seth made a grab for her arm and she jerked it away.

"Rebecca."

She spun around and glared at him. "What!" She practically shook with rage and despair. "I tried to tell you no one wanted me, but you wouldn't listen. You dragged me here. You made me h—*hope*. Now—" Her breath hitched again. "Now I have *nothing*."

"You still have your parents."

"No. I don't!" she cried as the open admission loosed all her pent-up pain. "They're the ones who left me there!" Becca clamped a hand over her mouth as roars of anguish clawed to get out. She wished she'd never been born.

Seth took hold of her. "I'm so sorry, Rebecca."

She wanted to scream at him and pound him with her fists, but the enormity of her loss had drained all her ire. A sob tore its way up her throat, followed by another, and she crumpled in his grasp.

With strong, gentle arms, he led her back to the bench and let her pour out her grief on his shoulder.

As her shudders dwindled to whimpers, he handed her his handkerchief and murmured words of reassurance, his rich voice soothing her as it vibrated through his chest. Her bout of weeping eventually ceased, but then her stomach growled, causing her to release an errant sob.

Seth put some space between them and tilted his face so he could see hers. "The hotel has a restaurant. Let me take you to lunch."

She nodded and rose, hoping the chilly wind would cool her face before she got there. It always turned splotchy when she cried.

As they reentered the bustling town, she handed Seth his handkerchief and reached for her bag, thankful he'd had the presence of mind to lift it from where she'd dropped it and bring it along.

He shook his head. "I'll carry it."

His kindness melted more of her resentment. She looped her hand around his proffered arm instead.

Seth paused at the entrance of the hotel and looked down at her, his penitent eyes shaded by the brim of his hat. "I shouldn't have let you do that alone. I'm sorry."

Her world was falling apart, yet she couldn't keep the corner of her mouth from lifting. "Feed me and you're forgiven."

After scanning the busy dining hall, Seth helped her off with her coat and hung it on a rack with his duster and hat. Becca smoothed her hair and looked herself over. Her clothes were plain and worn, but they were clean. Her coat had shielded all but the bottom half of her skirt from the dust. She unobtrusively eyed the haze that circled the dark brown fabric. Maybe no one would notice in the dim light.

A young man of no more than sixteen, dressed in a white shirt and dark trousers, approached them and smiled. "Welcome to Aubrey House."

"Could you seat us someplace quiet?" Seth asked.

"Certainly, Sir." The youth led them to the rear corner of the room where several tables stood empty and readied a small, square table covered in crisp white cloth.

Seth helped Becca with her chair, and then he sat across from her and ordered for them as though he did this every day.

He lifted his glass and took a sip of water as the waiter walked away. "Are you pleased with what I chose?"

"Yes. I love roast beef."

"I figured so. You practically drooled when he mentioned it."

Seth was trying to cheer her and Becca faintly smiled at the attempt, but nothing could lift her out of the pit of hopelessness that had swallowed her whole.

"Today for dessert, we have apple pie," the waiter said as he cleared their plates. "Shall I bring you some?"

Seth raised a brow at her.

Becca gave a small shake of her head. "No, thank you."

"Are you sure?"

She nodded. Despite her hunger and the fine food, she'd done well to force lunch down.

"Just one, then," he told the waiter. "And two coffees."

The number of patrons had dwindled, and Becca welcomed the reduction of curious eyes. But the silence gave unwelcome rein to her thoughts. Before she knew it, Seth's pie was gone and her coffee was tepid.

"Rebecca," he said, gaining her attention.

She readied herself for the interrogation she'd known all along would come. At least he'd let her finish eating first.

Seth's chest rose and fell with a heavy breath. "I owe you an apology."

The unexpected turn further shook the fog loose. "I meant what I said—apology accepted."

"No, I'm speaking of how I treated you on the trail these last few weeks. I was rude and harsh. You didn't deserve that."

He was right, but she wasn't sure what to say.

"I thought—" He sighed. "It doesn't matter what I thought. It was wrong."

She traced the ring of moisture left by her glass. "I'm sorry you wasted your savings and your time bringing me here."

He reached across the table and stilled her fingers with his. "My time and my money are mine to spend. And giving you a chance at life was worth it."

Even if I'm out of chances?

Seth released her hand and leaned back in his chair. "Will you tell me what Nathan said?"

Becca returned her hand to her lap. "He lives in a neighboring town. He got married last week."

Her quiet words barely reached his ears, but they held his chest in a startling grip. By hiding from him, she delayed their arrival by more than six weeks. If she'd left with him the first time...

Seth willed his lungs to fill as Becca cleared her throat and went on.

"He told me they looked for me for two days, but then the captain called off the search."

"Did he say anything about your parents?"

She lifted a shoulder. "He said they were upset."

"Does he know where they are?"

"No." She reached for the end of her braid and stared at the table. "They fell behind after crossing the river into California. Charlotte said the same thing." Her fingers stopped twisting, and she looked up. "She was in the store when you dropped me off. We talked for a while."

That explained a lot. "Have you spoken to anyone else?"

"No."

He took a sip of coffee, and it churned in his stomach. This wasn't looking good. "What else did Charlotte say?"

Becca's eyes were aimed at him, but her attention was a hundred miles away. Her fingers started moving again. "The rocks that blocked the trail were cleared sooner than expected, so Charlotte told my ma where I'd gone. She assumed they were going to look for me when Pa told her to leave with the train— that he and Ma would catch up later—but then she saw my ma removing the barrels from the wagon when she passed by. She didn't understand why at the time.

"When my parents rejoined the train that evening, they told the others I was sleeping. Then, the next morning, when people began asking about me, Ma *discovered* I was missing."

Seth's whole frame sagged as Becca's bleak admission further weighted his heavy heart. He'd been so sure she was wrong.

"Well, that explains why the scouts didn't find you," he said, sitting forward and returning his cup to its saucer. "You could have been sitting in plain view the entire time and it wouldn't have mattered. They were looking in the wrong place."

Conscious occupancy returned to her eyes. "You're right. I didn't even think of that." Her gaze dropped to her lap. "There's something else... When the scouts didn't find me, the captain ordered a search of the train. They found some of my things in Melvin Cantwell's wagon."

"That doesn't make sense. How—" He sighed. "Your parents planted it... made him the scapegoat."

Becca nodded. Her eyes were damp, and her skin was as pale as the porcelain cup that sat untouched in front of her.

Seth grimaced, his teeth set on edge by the logical conclusion. The trail had its own set of rules. "Let me guess. He never made it to trial."

She didn't respond, but she didn't have to.

"Was Nathan involved?"

Her head shot up. "No!"

"What about your father?"

"No." Her hand dropped from her braid. "Not with... *that*, anyway."

But his actions, and possibly her mother's, led to an innocent man's demise.

Well, damn it all, if this wasn't a holy mess. He'd planned to leave the choice up to Becca, but now he would be forced to involve the law. The mere thought of it made him sick—both the crime and what turning her own parents in would do to her.

She glanced over her shoulder at the nearly-empty dining room, then aimed an unfocused gaze in the direction of her cup. "I grew up thinking my parents were such good people. I knew they weren't perfect, but I don't understand how I could have been so wrong about them. They did things they taught me not to do—worse. They did things I would never even *think* to do." Haggard eyes lifted and stared into his. "They're the people who raised me, and I feel like I don't know them at all."

Seth ached for her. He'd never met the Garveys, but the impression he got from Becca's drawings and her recollections reminded him of his own ma and pa. Her disappointment was shared.

A sad smile ghosted across her face. "At least I was right about Nathan."

"You still love him, don't you?"

She looked down at her fingers picking at a nub in the weave of the cloth. "Part of me still cares for him, yes. I mean, if my parents hadn't left me behind, Nathan and I..." Her lip trembled. "We'd be married."

"Do you think you could find a place in your heart for someone else?"

She looked up at him with liquid eyes.

Seth took her hand in his and hated himself for what he was about to do. He was a bastard as much as a saint. "I don't have much to offer, and I'm probably not the kind of man you dreamed of spending your life with, but I'll spend the rest of my days taking care of you and giving you the best life I can. Will you marry me?"

Becca's mouth fell open, and then she closed it and swallowed as confusion claimed her brow. She pulled her hand from his and shook her head. "You don't have to do this. I'm grateful to you for bringing me to California, but you don't need to rescue me anymore."

"I'm not rescuing you. I'm asking you to marry me because I love you."

A derisive note left her throat. "Don't confuse love with pity and make a promise you'll regret just because you feel sorry for me."

"I don't pity you, Rebecca. I love you. I have for a long time. I just didn't want to admit it to myself, or you." He grasped her hand again and brushed her knuckles with his thumb. "I wanted better for you than someone like me, but I can't stand the thought of you with anyone else. I'm selfish. I want you all to myself, forever."

She stared at him, and then at their hands.

The silence stretched on until it grew painful, and Seth ignored the growing ache in his heart. "I know you don't have the highest opinion of me, and I plan to change that; but if you don't love me, if you don't think you could grow to love me in time, then I'll let you go. It'll kill me, but I'll give you your freedom and walk away."

She lifted her face, tears edging her lids.

Rejection.

Seth mustered the strength it would take to back his words with action. He wasn't sure he could do it.

"I care about you..." Becca began.

"But you don't love me."

She shook her head. "No," she whispered, "that's the problem. I *do* love you."

"You do?"

She nodded, causing a tear to break loose from her lashes and roll down her cheek.

"You want someone better."

"No."

"It's all right." He let go of her hand. "You don't have to lie to spare my feelings."

"I'm not. You're one of the bravest, most honorable men I've ever met. It's just—" She wiped the tear from her face and a second one took its place. "I feel like a traitor. I was betrothed to someone, and I fell in love with someone else."

"Nathan *married* someone else. He gave up on you."

"Yes. But I gave up on him, too."

Seth pulled the handkerchief from his pocket, still damp with her earlier tears. He'd scarcely placed it in her hand when a murmur of insistent voices drew his attention to a group of people standing just inside the door.

The waiter glanced back at him, then continued to speak to them in hushed tones.

Three men and a woman, all but one of them dressed to the teeth, kept peering over him, their heads bobbing up and down in turns like a nervous clutch of chickens.

The oldest of the men, a distinguished fellow with graying hair, shouldered past the waiter and led the group right up to their table. "Are you Seth Emerson?"

"I am." He held the man's gaze long enough to challenge the dominance in his eyes, and then scanned the other three sets that were inspecting him. He paused when he got to a feminine green pair that looked oddly familiar.

"I'm Judge Tate," the man said, regaining Seth's attention. He indicated the young, affluent couple to his left—the man dressed like some wealthy easterner, and the woman trussed up in an outfit as vainglorious as her expression and as starched as her spine. "This is Harrison Bradford, treasurer of Blackwater, and his wife, Charlotte."

I knew it.

When the judge didn't introduce the other man, Seth hooked a thumb toward the modestly dressed quinquagenarian. "And him?"

Tate cleared his throat, though from irritation or chagrin, Seth couldn't be sure. "That's Reverend Bell."

The potbellied preacher offered a kind-but-shaky smile and murmured a greeting. *Hmph.* For a man whose job it was to assemble and care for a flock, he looked none too at ease with people.

Judge Tate eyed Rebecca, then locked gazes with Seth. "We need to have a word with you."

Rude or not, Seth remained seated. The skin on his neck had prickled the moment the group walked in, and he wasn't about to leave Becca. "Anything you have to say to me, you can say right here."

Tate glanced at her again. "I had hoped to spare the young lady some embarrassment, but if you insist." He smoothed the front of his waistcoat and lifted his chin. "It has come to our attention that you're traveling alone with *Miss* Garvey and, according to the proprietor of the hotel, you've only reserved a single room for the night."

Seth's blood boiled. He wanted to knock these people off their collective high horse and tell them to mind their own affairs, but he didn't, for Rebecca's sake. That, and it would likely be a waste of breath. "I'd planned to let *Miss* Garvey have the room to herself and go stay at the livery." He'd also planned to sneak in after dark and bed down like a surly guard dog just inside her door, but they didn't need to know that.

"Be that as it may, you've been traveling without a chaperone, casting suspicion on Miss Garvey's reputation. The residents of Blackwater place great value on moral integrity. We don't allow loose behavior in our town."

That explained the lack of a saloon.

Propelled by his rising temper, Seth stood, causing the entire group to tilt their heads and look up. "Miss Garvey—who happens to have the most *moral integrity* of any lady I've ever met—was left behind by a wagon train. She was living in a cave."

"Circumstances don't matter," Harrison Bradford said coldly.

"What are you saying? That I should have left her in the wilderness to die?"

Reverend Bell wrung his hands. "Well, no, uh, of course not. It's just that, well, her reputation is compromised and, uh—"

Bradford waved the stammering away. "As I said, circumstances don't matter. What's done is done."

"Charlotte?" Becca said, her voice thready with disbelief. "You agree with them?"

For a moment, Charlotte's smug exterior faltered. Then she resumed the bearing of her husband—glaring down as though Becca were a smear of dung on her fancy shoes.

Reverend Bell tugged at the front of his collar. "Like Mr. Bradford said, what's done is done. But there's a simple solution to this," he added quickly, with a nod and a hopeful smile.

"And what would that be?"

"Why, just marry the girl. That'll set everything to rights."

"You've got to be kidding me."

Eyes wide with candor, the preacher shook his head, jiggling his jowls and causing a few strands of his thinning hair to shake loose.

"And if I don't?"

Tate didn't blink. "Then you and Miss Garvey will be escorted out of town."

"Unbelievable," Seth muttered.

He drew a deep breath before speaking again. Keeping the contempt out of his voice wasn't easy. The smugness either. "Well, you're a little late. I already proposed."

That got a gasp and a few raised brows.

Bell sputtered. "What did she say?"

"She *didn't*. I was waiting for her answer when you interrupted us."

Seth turned to Becca and bit back a curse at the sight of her tear-streaked face. He wanted her to marry him more than he needed to draw his next breath, but he wanted her to do it for the right reasons.

He sat back down and took her hand in his. "Don't let these people sway your decision. The choice is still yours. I meant what I said, but if the answer is no, we'll spend the night someplace else. No matter what, I won't abandon you."

More tears ran down her cheeks.

"Yes," she choked out. "The answer is yes."

Chapter Twenty-Six

Becca turned a slow circle, taking in the lacy curtains, quilt-covered bed, and simple elegance of the room she'd been left in. A soon as she'd accepted Seth's proposal, she'd been ushered to Reverend Bell's home and introduced to his wife.

Dressed in a high-neck white blouse and plain gray skirt, the diminutive woman had greeted her with a smile and promptly sent her upstairs to wait, assuring Becca she would take care of everything.

Not knowing what else to do, Becca sat on a trunk at the foot of the bed, still reeling from the day's events. She'd faced her parents' desertion, lost her betrothed to another woman, and been publicly humiliated by someone she used to consider a friend. And now she was getting married—to Seth. The river of pain that had filled her until she thought she would burst had largely seeped away, leaving the sand soft and shifting under her feet.

Someone knocked on the door and she jumped up. "Come in."

The door opened and a wreath of grizzled brown hair led the way as Mrs. Bell slipped inside, carrying a brown paper package that was bigger than the woman herself. She closed the door and hurried over to the bed.

"What is that?"

"It's your wedding clothes."

"My what?"

"Your *wedding clothes*."

"Oh, Mrs. Bell, you shouldn't have."

"I didn't. And call me Lottie," she added, squeezing Becca's hand. "Seth sure is a generous one," she chirped as she untied the string. "Just wait till you see what all's inside." The tiny woman lifted out a lacy white chemise—the likes of which Becca had never seen—and held it up, peeking out from behind it with a grin.

Becca gasped. "He picked that out for me?" she squeaked.

"Goodness, no, dear. He left money with the storekeeper. I was the one who chose your things." One by one, she held up a set of drawers and two petticoats that were lacier than the chemise. And then she drew out a flowing, frilled nightgown, her eyes twinkling with unholy glee.

Becca wished the floor would open up so she could fall in.

Lottie laughed. "Now don't go looking like that. This is right proper for a new bride." She fished around again, rattling the paper. "And so is this."

A silent breath of awe filled Becca's lungs as folds of cornflower blue calico tumbled open into a readymade dress. The bodice was modestly fitted, and the cut of the sleeves and the skirt was surprisingly generous. She'd never owned anything so nice.

Lottie held it up to her and smiled. "It brings out the blue in your eyes."

Maybe so, but it was the exact color of Seth's when the early morning sun lit his face.

Becca pressed the dress to her chest with one hand and examined it with the other, marveling at the delicate buttons and the tightness of the weave. A garment made from fabric this fine must've cost a week's pay. "It's beautiful."

"You know what they say. *Married in blue, you will always be true.*"

Lottie checked the length and tugged at the edges, testing the fit. "Perfect. I've always had a good eye, if I do say so myself." She laid the dress across the bed and placed the bundle of white in Becca's arms. "Take these underthings behind that screen, freshen up with the basin, and put them on."

"Why two petticoats?"

"Together, they'll give a nice fullness to your skirt; then you can wear them separately for every day."

They were too nice for every day, but Becca chose not to argue.

A few minutes later, she reluctantly eased out from behind the screen. She felt completely at ease around Lottie, like she'd known her all her life, but her cheeks still flamed.

"Well, well. Aren't you a sight? You remind me of my Esther. She was wed in mid-December, just like you." Lottie helped her on with her dress, then patted the stool in front of a small cherry vanity. "Come fix your hair."

Becca loosened her braid and began running a brush through the wavy locks. She met Lottie's gaze in the oval mirror. "Thank you for opening your home to us."

"You're welcome, dear. When Zebulon told me what that bunch was up to, I made up my mind—right then and there—

that I would make things as pleasant for the two of you as possible. I considered beseeching Judge Tate not to force you to wed, but then I learned Seth had already proposed."

Lottie rested a hand on Becca's shoulder. "I hope you don't think too poorly of our town. Things didn't used to be this way. Zeb and I moved here because Blackwater needed a preacher. We liked it at first. It's full of God-fearing people—a wholesome place to live. Unfortunately, a few of its members carry things too far."

Becca stopped brushing. "Why do you stay?"

Lottie tilted her head to the side, then her lips formed a smile that was short on humor and long on humility. "The rules our Lord gave us are good and for our benefit, but we're broken beings living in a fallen world. Someone has to be the voice of mercy."

Becca laid the brush aside and swept her hair over her left shoulder. She hesitated, then divided it into three sections and started to braid.

"Would you like to wear it up?"

"I would, but I don't have any pins."

Lottie opened a small drawer on the right side of the vanity and drew out a handful of metal hairpins. "I have plenty. Take as many as you need."

After trying, unsuccessfully, to arrange her tresses, Becca gave up. "I've never done this before. I don't know how."

"It's not difficult. Let me show you." Lottie smoothed the hair and gathered it into her fist, then twisted it into a rope and coiled it on the crown of Becca's head. Before securing the first pin, she paused. "Do you like it this way?"

"Yes, very much." The bun was neat, and the hair around it formed a fluffy wreath that framed her face.

"What's bothering you, then?"

Becca almost laughed at the scope of the question. She handed Lottie a pin and chose the most pressing thing. "I'm worried Seth is marrying me because he feels sorry for me."

"*Pft.* That's a wasted worry."

"You think so?"

"Land sakes, child. I haven't seen a man more smitten with a woman since Zeb courted me. The way Seth speaks of you—" She shook her head. "He's completely besotted. You couldn't get rid of that man if you tried."

"I hope you're right," Becca murmured.

"I am." Lottie patted her shoulder. "What else is bothering you?"

Becca picked up two more pins and handed one over. "I'm nervous about tonight," she finally admitted. "This is all happening so fast. There wasn't time to plan or prepare."

"Is it your woman's time, dear?"

"No, that happened last week." Becca ran her thumb along the edge of the hairpin still in her hand, grazing her skin back and forth across its bumpy ridges. "I don't know much about being a wife."

Lottie reached for the pin and Becca relinquished it. "Men are easy to please," she said as she worked the metal prongs into the hair and slid it into place. "I'm sure Seth is no different. Just keep his belly full and his bed warm."

"The first part I can do. It's the last part I'm not sure about."

Lottie studied Becca's reflection, then cupped her shoulders with lean, work-worn hands. "Seth strikes me as a gentle soul who'd sooner die than bring you harm. A desire to please him is all the knowhow you need."

The skin around Lottie's eyes crinkled at the nudge of a

warm smile, and she gave Becca's arms a pat. "We'd best head downstairs. I'm sure your groom has paced a permanent grove in my hardwoods by now."

Becca paused at the upper landing and pressed a damp palm to her fluttering stomach. All that stood between her and a life-changing act was her own judgment and a single flight of stairs. Her mouth went dry and her heart flailed like a trapped bird against her ribs. She didn't doubt her love for Seth, but she needed more time to be sure of her motivations—and his. Vowing to marry someone was largely irrevocable. And success depended on more than just love.

Lottie appeared at the base of the stairs and smiled up at her. "We're ready." The hem of her skirt brushed the bottom step as she turned and hurried away.

This was it.

Becca's heart pounded faster as she lifted her foot and took the first step. She gripped the banister and steadied herself, then descended the stairs on shaky legs.

Her breath caught and her knees threatened to buckle when the lower room came into view.

Seth stood in the parlor with his back to her, leaning down, listening to something the preacher was saying. His flaxen hair was slicked back neatly, the ends of it curling just above his collar. The dark brown pants he wore were familiar, but the crisp white shirt that spanned his shoulders was new.

Lottie stood next to them, beaming. She whispered something to the men, and they promptly turned around.

Seth's eyes widened. He swallowed so hard his neck corded and his throat rippled.

Becca's heart skipped a beat and she froze. He didn't look pleased. Her chest tightened around the fear he regretted his choice.

She drew a scraping breath to tell him he could change his mind, but the words died on her tongue as the corners of his mouth lifted into the most heartfelt smile she'd ever seen. He held out his hand, and her anxiety fled. With much surer steps, she walked through the archway and into the room.

Becca turned her head left when a clump of green brushed the edge of her vision. Her chest tightened again.

Charlotte and her husband stood by the door, looking on with the same disdain they'd shown at the restaurant.

Becca shared a wordless exchange with her former friend, then put the two of them out of her mind and joined her groom. The mere sight of him restored her smile.

"You shaved," she said, reaching to touch Seth's bare face. Heat rose in hers when she realized what she'd done.

Seth winked at her. He took her hand in his and faced Reverend Bell, who was smiling as heartily as his wife. "We're ready."

Zebulon cleared his throat and lifted a worn, leather-bound book. "Dearly beloved..."

Becca stole glances at *her* beloved as the words *love, honor,* and *cherish* flowed past her ears. By the time the reverend reached *better or worse and richer or poorer,* Seth's adoring gaze was locked with hers. The warmth in his eyes melted away the hurts of the day and filled her heart with enough hope to last a lifetime.

She still couldn't believe she was standing here, marrying him. Not only did he stir her senses and turn her boneless with desire on sight, he was the one she wanted. The blatant love she felt for him banished all doubt. "I do."

"What therefore God has joined together, let not man put asunder." Reverend Bell closed the book. "You may kiss your bride."

Seth framed Becca's face with his hands and lowered his mouth to hers. His lips brushed and nibbled with a gentleness that belied the passion beneath. She had to restrain it, and she knew he did, too.

Much too soon, he pulled away, his eyes searching hers once his face came back into view. "You're beautiful," he whispered.

A sudden draft chilled her back and she turned.

Charlotte was gone.

Harrison's icy gaze lingered, touching on each one of them with unhurried regard, and then he left the way of his wife, closing the door behind him.

Lottie stepped forward and gathered Becca into an exuberant hug. "Congratulations. I'm so happy for you."

"Congratulations is right." Zebulon shook Seth's hand with the zeal of a man newly freed. "It was an honor to marry such fine people as yourselves. I hope you'll stay for supper."

"Yes, do," Lottie said. "Several ladies in town heard about Rebecca's ordeal and insisted on providing a meal to celebrate your nuptials."

Seth looked to Becca and raised a brow.

"Please stay," Lottie entreated. "They'll be so disappointed if you don't."

Becca hoped she wouldn't live to regret any of the words she said in Lottie's parlor, including the next. "We'll stay."

Chapter Twenty-Seven

"That was a nice supper," Seth remarked as they walked from the Bell's house to the hotel.

"Yes, it was," Becca replied.

"Did you enjoy yourself?"

She'd feared being a spectacle and an object of gossip. Thankfully, Lottie's friends were as kind and loving as she. They asked about her trip and listened with rapt attention to her tales of survival, but they didn't pry. "I did."

She wrapped her hand around Seth's arm and leaned closer. The sun had disappeared and the air was growing cold.

Keenly aware of his muscular frame brushing hers with each step, Becca drew a slow breath in hopes of calming her jangled nerves. She was on edge in both good ways and bad. The scent of Seth's leather duster, mixed with the woodsy aroma of his skin, drew her like a honey bee to a field of spring flowers, but the potency of his presence was as daunting as it was beguiling.

He opened the door to the hotel's lobby and followed her inside.

The proprietor looked up from his ledger and smiled. "Congratulations on your wedding, Mr. and Mrs. Emerson."

"Thank you," Seth said. "Is the tub available?"

"Yes. I'll have it brought right up."

Seth offered his arm again as they climbed the stairs to the second floor. "I arranged for a hot bath. I figured we could both use one after the day we've had."

Becca's muscles melted in anticipation, but her pulse sped faster than a hare being chased by a weasel.

Seth stopped outside the door to their room, his profile bathed in amber light from the sconces that lined the hall, and withdrew a key from his pocket. With hands that looked much steadier than hers, he unlocked the door and pushed it open.

He followed her inside.

The room was simply furnished, but it was clean and neat. A dressing table stood to one side, while an upholstered chair and settee formed a grouping on the other. Light from two sconces flickered on the walls, warming the browns and blues of the damask. The same colors were repeated in the window curtains and the gathered cloth panels of the dressing screen in the far corner.

"Will this do?" Seth asked.

Becca jerked her attention to him. "Yes. It's very nice."

Someone tapped on the doorframe behind them, and Seth turned around. "You can come in."

Two men carried in a large copper tub and set it on the floor. After making several trips with buckets of steaming water, they placed the dressing screen in front of the tub, nodded a polite farewell, and left.

Seth closed the door and locked it, then faced her, rubbing the back of his neck as she willed her hands not to wring themselves raw. "Go ahead." He handed over her valise and indicated the tub. "You first."

She gave him a shaky smile and hurried around the screen with her bag.

After lighting the lantern that sat on a small table next to the tub and draping her nightgown over the screen, Becca removed her shoes and unfastened her buttons with trembling fingers. She wished Lottie had told her what to expect.

The soft scuff of boots on wood marked the seconds as she removed her petticoats and slid her chemise over her head, and the creak of a chair overshadowed the whisper of her drawers falling from her hips and puddling at her feet. Totally naked, she stepped into the tub and lowered herself into the heavenly water.

Crystal clear ripples turned milky as she soaped herself, and the temperature began to cool as she rinsed. "I'm almost done," she called, feeling guilty.

"No rush. Take your time."

She swirled her hand through the water, recalling the time they'd soaked together in the spring. Why should he have to settle for seconds?

Her heart fluttered. "There's plenty of room... You could join me." Becca stilled her hand and listened. If silence were money, they'd be rich.

"Are you sure?"

A thrill shot through her veins. "Yes, I'm sure."

Boots scuffed the floor again and the light from the sconces went dark.

Becca scooted forward and hugged her knees, her heart beating like the wings of a hummingbird. She glanced over her shoulder as Seth rounded the screen, tugging his shirt free of his pants, then she faced forward again and waited. She didn't need to see him to know what he was doing. She'd heard his evening routine a hundred times.

First came the pause while he unbuttoned his shirt, then the clicks of pewter on wood as he draped it over the nearest object—usually the wagon. Next, a masculine grunt... the sucking sound of his boot sliding free of his foot... his sigh of relief. The thunk—one, then the other—of the soles as he set them aside.

Neatly. She smiled. *Always neatly.*

Becca's smile disappeared and she closed her eyes. Next came the sound that riddled her body with need and filled her mind with carnal thoughts.

Jolts of awareness pulsed through her as Seth flicked open the buttons of his trousers one by one, and smoldering tremors ignited as he slid them off and lay them aside. On the trail, it would have stopped there, but not tonight. Tonight his drawers and woolens would follow.

Her breathing ceased and her fingers gripped her legs as she waited for him to strip and step into the tub.

Tiny waves broke against her back, and then the level of the water rose to her shoulders as his knees bracketed her and his feet slid past her hips on either side.

"Ahhh."

Sounds of him washing met her ears as more waves lapped at her skin. God help her, but she wished the hands washing him were hers.

Warm, wet fingers grasped her shoulder and tugged gently. "Lean back."

Becca turned to the side and reclined against him, thankful the milky water concealed her breasts.

Seth's arms left the rails and wrapped her in a wall of velvety muscle.

For a long time, he simply held her, his chest rising and falling easily and his heart thumping steadily under her ear. It was as if he'd been waiting to comfort her all along—to surround her with his whole being and shut out the world.

His protective patience was welcome, and she relished the blessed reprieve. But the needs of the body rarely bowed to the will of the mind or the heart, and a deeper part of her hungered for something she didn't understand.

Longing thrummed through her veins with every whiff of his virile scent and every caress of his breath on her hair. Seth had to feel that way, too. How he held his passion in check was as much a mystery as what he would do once he set it free.

He pressed a soft kiss to the top of her head. "What are you thinking?"

When she didn't answer, his torso stiffened and he loosened his hold. "Are you sorry you married me?"

"No." She lifted her head and looked at him. "Are you sorry you married me?"

Warmth returned to his eyes and the corner of his mouth lifted. "No." He trailed a finger from her temple down to her neck, grazing the damp wisps of hair clinging to her skin. "So, will you tell me what you're thinking?"

Shame heated her cheeks and she looked away. "If I do, you'll think poorly of me."

"I doubt it." He planted another kiss on her hair. "Tell me."

She reluctantly met his gaze. "I was thinking about the times I listened to you undress on the trail... how I wished I was watching instead of listening. And just now, while you bathed, I wished it was my hands washing you instead of your own."

Seth blinked and his eyes flared an intense shade of blue. She waited for him to chastise her for her wanton thoughts, but he just stared at her.

The shock of his response emboldened her. "Every night of our trip, I lay in my bed unable to think of anything but you. I'd close my eyes and remember the times we kissed, the time you touched me in the cave. Even on the coldest nights, my skin heated as if a summer breeze had blown over it, and my insides tingled and throbbed. I knew it was wrong, and yet I lay there, wanting you to do those things again."

His nostrils flared. "Becca..." He wrapped her in his arms. "You tempt me, too. You've tempted me from the first day we met."

Seth lifted her face so she was looking at him. Hunger simmered in his eyes, but it was cloaked in love. "Don't be ashamed of what you feel for me. I promise you, I lay in my bedroll wanting the very same things. Thoughts of you assailed me constantly. It took every ounce of will I had to keep from giving in to those urges."

"Truly?"

The skin at the corners of his eyes crinkled. "Don't you remember me making a beeline for every stream and creek we came to? You didn't think I actually *liked* bathing in water so cold it turned my skin blue, did you?"

She hid a laugh behind her hand. She'd assumed he liked being clean.

"Speaking of icy streams, we should get out. This water's gone nearly as cold."

Becca nodded and shivered as tiny bumps scattered across her flesh. She'd been so shamelessly single-minded she hadn't noticed.

Seth pushed himself up and stood, turning away to reach for a towel. Tiny rivers ran down his body and into the tub as her eyes traced every curve and valley from his shoulders to his knees.

A wonderful panic swept through her. Electrifying. Exciting. She lifted her gaze and swallowed when it met his.

He tucked the towel around his waist, then held out a hand. "Stand up." His eyes were dark with want again, and his voice was husky and low.

Becca placed her hand in his and rose from the milky water. She held her breath as her husband's gaze swept over her, then crossed her arms over herself.

As if pulling himself from a trance, Seth slicked the water from his hair and reached for another towel. He draped it around her shoulders and drew her into a warm embrace. Heat blazed from his skin like a blacksmith's furnace. No wonder he was shrouded in wisps of white vapor.

"I love you, Rebecca," he said as he loosened his hold enough to see her face. "I'm not worthy of you, but I'm glad you chose me anyhow."

She opened her mouth to argue and he claimed it with his own. The same emotions she'd heard in his voice invaded his kiss. All at once he was tender and fierce—his mouth both asking and demanding.

His soapy scent assailed her senses. His tongue entwined with hers as his hand splayed against her back and pressed her body more firmly to his. He clung to the kiss a few moments more, then tore his lips away.

Seth rubbed his hands along the cloth he'd draped over her and blotted the water from her body, but she barely felt it. Her hot, swollen lips had the bulk of her attention. She'd never dreamed a kiss could feel like that.

"Step out of the tub," he said, offering his hand once more so she wouldn't fall.

Using a third towel, he dried himself off, then patted dry the parts of her that hers didn't cover while she stood there like a fool, too dazed to care for herself.

He studied her for a moment, then picked up the lamp and led her by the hand around the screen. "The clerk said they wouldn't need the tub till morning. They won't be coming back tonight."

Seth set the lamp on the bedside table and bent to blow it out.

"Don't."

He straightened back up. "I thought you'd be more comfortable without the light."

"I've spent the last two years in the dark—at night, anyway. I'm tired of being at the mercy of the sun. Can we leave it on? Please?"

"Of course, we can. Want me to turn the flame up?"

"No. Just leave it high enough it doesn't go out."

He grinned. "You got it, Mrs. Emerson."

"Mrs. Emerson... I like the sound of that."

A glaze of sober intensity replaced his smile. "I pray there will never be a time when you don't."

Seized by a sudden bout of nerves, Becca glanced around the room. Her frilly nightgown still hung over the screen. "I should put on my gown."

"Suit yourself, but you won't be in it long enough to make it worth the effort."

She looked up at him through her lashes. His grin was back.

Seth's expression softened. He leaned down and touched his lips to hers as gently as the first time they'd kissed. His mouth left hers and he planted a kiss on her nose and her forehead, his warm breath stirring the tiny hairs on her skin.

Drawing away, he reached for her hair. He carefully withdrew the pins and laid them aside. Once all of them had been removed, he ran his fingers through her hair and gazed into her eyes as the wavy locks fell loosely about her shoulders.

Seth brushed a strand of hair back away from her face. His finger touched her skin with a stroke so light, she wouldn't have believed it possible from a man his size if she hadn't felt it herself. It traveled down her temple, over the curve of her cheek, and along her jaw, his eyes following the slow, deliberate movement. When his caress reached the side of her chin, the pad of his thumb grazed her lips. He turned his wrist and his index finger warmed a path from one corner of her mouth to the other, along the plump, ridged bow.

His attention lingered there as his hand fell away. She lifted her face, anticipating a kiss, but he didn't meet her halfway. She withdrew, uncertain.

"This night will change you, Becca. I'll love the woman you become, but I also want to remember you as you are... the way your skin turns the color of a rose at the slightest touch... the way your eyes shine with trust and curiosity and optimism. I know you probably don't understand, but thank you for indulging me this." He released her to turn back the covers, and a battle with herself ensued. She wanted to wrap herself in a hundred towels and never turn loose her grip. But another part of her longed to feel her husband's skin against hers.

Drawing a bolstering breath, Becca dropped her towel to the floor. She scrambled into bed and dove under the covers—as much from the cold as from nerves. Seth followed quickly after and burrowed nearly as deep. The heavy quilts sealed them in, and the scent of sun-dried cotton surrounded them.

"You're hands are like ice," he said. "Snuggle up to me so I can warm you." He tucked her fingers in the valley of his chest and drew her close, enveloping her in his arms so they were facing each other. One last shiver left her as she melted against his hot skin.

The feel of their bodies touching from head to toe without clothing in between was even better than she'd dreamed it would be. "Mmm. Heaven."

Seth chuckled. "Not yet, but soon."

Becca ducked her head into the hollow of his neck.

"Are your nervous?"

"A little."

He hooked a finger under her chin and urged her to lift her face. "Seems like more than a little. Want to talk about it?"

Not really.

He pinned her with his gaze, wouldn't let up.

Looking everywhere but his eyes, she forced out barely audible words. "I don't know what to do."

"Look at me, Becca." It was difficult, but she did. "We can talk about things first if it'll make you feel better, but there's really nothing you need to do." His thumb caressed her cheek, and then he pressed a kiss to her lips. Sweet. Undemanding. "We'll take it slow. You do whatever you feel like doing and tell me if you don't like something I do. Okay?"

"Okay."

Seth swept her hair aside and caressed her neck. "My body is yours, now, and yours is mine." He pressed his lips to the sensitive patch of skin just below her ear. "God gave you to me to enjoy... for us to discover each other. This is the way it's supposed to be."

Rolling her to her back, he lifted her hand to his lips and planted a kiss on her palm. Then he eased her arms aside, baring her chest to him, and gently traced the swell of one breast. When he pressed a trail of kisses along the path his finger had made, she could hardly keep still.

"Every part of you... is beautiful," he said between soft brushes of his lips. He traced his finger over her skin again, then skimmed the peak and curve of her breast with his palm, as if he were admiring a coveted possession. "Ever since that day in the spring, the image of your body has been seared like a brand on my mind. All I could think about was running my hands over your bare skin, touching you and kissing you in places I could only dream about." He pressed his nose to her flesh and inhaled deeply, his eyes closed in the most exquisite look of tortured bliss. "You're perfect—you're all I need."

Scooting lower, Seth slid his arm under her pillow and drew her nipple into his mouth. A jolt of pleasure shot through her like a flash of summer lightning. With each tug and swirl of his tongue, heat sizzled to the deepest parts of her. It wasn't long until she felt the sensations more down low than at her breast where he actually was. "Seth, please."

He lifted his head. "Want me to stop?"

No. Gosh, no. Becca shook her head.

He planted a kiss on her nose, then went for her other nipple.

"Oh." That made it worse. Better. Whatever. Just— "*Ohhhh.*" She felt him smile against her skin. She also felt him grow hard against her hip. Harder than ever before.

Her body sobered.

Seth lifted his head. "You all right, Becca? I'm not being too rough, am I?"

"Yes— I mean no. I mean... it feels good." Why did saying that make her feel so decadent?

Seth's electric blue gaze locked with hers. It slid to her lips and his mouth followed. He nibbled a few times, then tilted his head and deepened the kiss.

She didn't resist. She opened for him automatically and

anticipated his strokes as he moved. Her hands reached for his head, and her fingers threaded through his silky hair.

His kiss grew urgent and he arched into her, pressing his shaft into her hip until it hurt. His whole body was taut, so hot it burned like fire.

He tore his lips from hers and buried his face in her neck, panting. As he nipped from her ear to the curve of her shoulder, his hand cupped her breast and his thumb brushed her beaded nipple. Sparks shot to her core again, and that strange liquid heat pooled low. Becca moaned.

Seth closed his mouth over her breast once more. He drew and drew on her sensitive nipple until she thought she'd go mad, and then his hand flattened over her stomach and slid downward until his fingers brushed her patch of curls. He lifted his head, meeting her hooded eyes with his as his fingers parted her folds.

Becca longed to close her eyes and hide from the soul-baring intensity of his regard, but she couldn't. The intimacy of doing such a thing face to face was as intoxicating as it was disconcerting.

The dark centers of Seth's eyes expanded and his fingers began to move. Just like before, he started slow, then gradually increased his ministrations until she was defenseless against him. Utterly and totally defenseless. Her legs parted of their own accord and her hands fisted the sheets.

"That's it, Becca. Open for me." His fingers slowed to a stop, leaving her bereft.

"Don't stop," she moaned. She was shocked at her own desperation, but she wanted him too much to care.

He pressed a flat hand over her curls and made a few slow circles, but it wasn't enough. Her hips rose to no avail. He drew her nipple into his mouth again, somewhat banking her fire, then his hand slid lower and his finger slipped inside.

Her thighs clamped together and her muscles clenched like steel around his hand. It didn't hurt, but she hadn't expected it.

"Relax," he murmured. "Open your legs."

When she did, he slid his finger in and swept it side to side. The movement felt good, mostly, but in a different way than before—the sensations satisfying, but not as intense.

Seth withdrew his finger almost all the way and added a second. As he pushed them in together, her skin stretched uncomfortably. Air hissed through her teeth and he stilled.

He removed the second finger and touched her point of pleasure with his thumb, this time giving the place the attention it needed. She relaxed and her muscles eventually squeezed his finger of their own accord.

Her pulse began to pound and her world began to shrink. She was losing touch with everything but the blessed torment inside—her pleasure building. She could hear herself moaning, but she couldn't make herself stop.

Seth took his hand away.

"Nooo," she whimpered.

"Trust me, Becca." His words were gentle, but his voice was husky again.

He slid his arm from beneath her pillow and knelt between her parted thighs. Scooting closer, he sat back on his heels and draped her legs over his.

He leaned forward and kissed her, slow and deep, then he sat back again and reached for the place that ached for his touch.

The fingers of one hand started rubbing her again while a finger of the other slid inside. The position she was in—so open to him—and his hands working together set her ablaze. It wasn't long until she was writhing against him, begging and calling out his name.

A second finger went in, stretching her even more, but she no longer cared. Pleasure overrode pain. A few more moments and she'd be there—shudders rippling through her body like before. Just a little longer... a little more...

A cry of release slipped out as her body fell into a storm of pleasure.

Seth wrung every drop of ecstasy from her, making her clench his fingers over and over. When she finally went limp, his hands left her completely and her eyes flew open. He was hovering over her, his gaze locked with hers. Hot and firm, his shaft pressed into her, confirming her suspicions. She tensed against the intrusion.

"Trust me," he murmured again.

Becca held his gaze and searched his eyes. She'd trusted him with her future. And, on the trail, with her very life. She could trust him with this.

She willed her body to soften to him.

The stretching sensation returned as he started to enter her. She gripped his shoulders and scrunched up her face.

Seth stilled. His rock-hard body shook—the lust in his eyes betraying his patience—but he didn't rush, didn't drive himself into her like she knew he wanted to. She relaxed again.

He pushed all the way in.

Becca gasped, more from surprise than from pain.

Seth drew a tremulous breath. He levered himself above her, his lips tight and a faint line between his brows cast in shadow. He slid slowly out and eased back in, filling her until she ached. "Ahh, Becca," he groaned. "You feel so good." His eyes drifted closed and shudder rippled through him as he withdrew and filled her again. "Good... so good."

This joining, it *was* good. By the third slow thrust, she'd grown accustomed to him.

He moved within her a few times more, and then he opened his eyes and looked at her, his gaze taking hers in, questioning.

Heaven. He was right. It was heaven.

She pulled his face to hers with both hands and kissed him hard. "Don't stop," she rasped into his luscious mouth. "Please, don't stop."

Passion flared in his eyes, darkening them even more in the flickering lamplight.

Taking his weight on his elbows, Seth gripped her shoulders and gave himself over to his want. She could see it in his face as he moved. His hooded eyes drifted closed, and she knew he was nearing the edge just like she had—his world shrinking and his focus centered on the place where their bodies joined.

Becca closed her eyes and savored the feel of him—his muscular body pressing her into the mattress, his slick hot shaft slipping in and out of her body, his spicy scent ripe with the smell of their love. Without his hand touching her, the feelings were different, but the steady grind of his hips was enough. She wrapped her legs around his waist and dug her fingers into his back as she let him take her to the peak again. If she fell again or not, it didn't matter.

"*Mmm*," his voice rumbled in her ear. "Heaven."

"Yes." She kissed his neck.

"Trying to wait for you," he gritted out.

Her body tightened around him. She was teetering on the edge.

His tempo increased. The part of him inside her swelled. His movements lost their rhythm and their grace. "Becca... I—"

His guttural groans mingled with her cries as muscles tensed, bodies shuddered, and bursts of heat spurted inside her. Their clinging form was all she knew—all sense of time suspended. She didn't want to let go. Never wanted to let go.

Seth caught his breath and kissed the side of her neck, but he didn't withdraw. He lifted her up—legs still wrapped—until she was sitting on his lap, enfolded in his muscular arms. His possessive grip echoed the word growing louder with every beat of her heart.

Mine.

Seth clutched his angel to him, so glad he'd waited for the one who'd be his bride. He'd felt the force of their union all the way to his toes, and all the way to his soul. A better woman he couldn't have found, and now they were one. Forever bonded.

He nuzzled Becca's sweet-smelling hair and gently rocked them back and forth, enjoying the sensation of being inside her. Her arms encircled him, and her head rested sideways in the curve of his shoulder. She sighed, the sound muffled by his neck.

"I love you, Becca."

"I love you, too," she murmured—contented words that eased his mind. He'd been so afraid he'd hurt her, and he had, but she didn't seem to mind.

For so long, he'd viewed his encounter with the girl at the saloon as something worthy of shame. And maybe it was. But if it hadn't been for that, he would have hurt his bride more.

The other woman meant nothing to him. The woman in his arms meant everything.

He ran his fingers up and down her back and breathed a sigh of his own. The sight of her tempted him beyond measure. And the feel of her next to him practically lit him on fire. Her body was a perfect blending of lines and curves. She still fussed about gaining weight, but he didn't mind. He liked the new softness beneath his hands and the fullness when he cupped her breasts. *Mmm.* The very thought of it was making him—

"Seth?"

"Hm?"

"Are we going to love each other again?" Despite what had just transpired between them, sweet innocence laced her voice.

"No."

She lifted her head and looked up at him. "Why not?" The shift caused her warm channel to slide against him and her muscles to tighten. He almost groaned.

He drew a deep breath and willed his body to be calm. "Because it wouldn't be right." He brushed the hair from her face and peered into her questioning eyes. "This was your first time. You're probably sore. It would be selfish of me."

"But I'm not. I feel fine."

Seth held her hips in place and pushed his forward, sinking himself deeper.

She winced.

"You're not fine. I barely moved and I hurt you." That did it. His passion abated.

"I'm sorry," she said as she lowered her gaze.

He kissed her forehead and hugged her close. "You have nothing to be sorry for. You're everything I want in a bride. We have our whole lives to love each other."

Seth held her close a few minutes more. He slowly lifted her away and instructed her to lie back and wait for him while he went over to the tub.

Once he'd washed up, he returned and pressed a wet cloth to her swollen folds. She winced again and he frowned. "I'm sorry the water's so cold."

The lines of her face disappeared as her features smoothed. "It's all right. It feels good."

Seth lifted the lantern with his other hand, shining enough light to be sure her injury was only minor. It was. He blew out a breath, then shifted his gaze to meet hers, worried his boldness had made her uneasy.

It apparently hadn't. She lay there relaxed, staring up at him with placid eyes.

He set the items aside and climbed into bed. Becca shivered as he drew her into his arms and tugged the covers up around them. Their warmth had faded right along with the heat of their passion.

She readily laid her head on his arm and tucked her delicate hands between them. And he felt their bond to his soul yet again.

The thought of anyone harming a woman ignited his ire, and the act itself could send him into a murderous rage. But the image paired with the precious wife he held in his arms had the power to steal the air from his lungs. If he ever lost her, it would tear out his heart.

Seth cleared his throat of emotion. "Do you need anything?"

"No."

"Are you warm enough?"

"Mmhm."

"Goodnight, sweetheart."

She snuggled deeper into his embrace. "Goodnight."

Chapter Twenty-Eight

A smile spread across Seth's face as he opened his eyes. Rebecca's body was pressed to his in a warm, soft tangle of limbs. Save slipping out of bed to use the chamber pot sometime in the wee hours, she'd slept molded to him all night long.

Her cheek rested on his chest, and the fringe of her hair glowed in the early morning light. The words he said to her the evening before were true—she *was* beautiful. And even more angelic in sleep.

He stroked the curve of her back, recalling how the sight of it stopped him cold when he'd joined her in the tub. Her slender torso rose like alabaster out of the pool. His blood had heated in an instant.

Somehow he'd managed to hold his urges at bay and hold *her*. She'd been deeply hurt, repeatedly, and forced to bend to everyone's will but her own; her wedding day was also the worst day of her life. He no longer doubted her love for him, but he would rather she have had time. Time to get over her intended and time to come to terms with what her parents had done.

When he'd asked her what she was thinking, he expected it to be that. He'd even prepared himself that she might not be ready for him to consummate their vows and make her his wife, and he was willing to set his own needs aside until she was. When she revealed frank desire for him instead, he'd had to beat lust into submission and stop himself from taking her right there in the tub.

Hmph. That didn't take long. The truth behind her words had cooled his raging need quicker than the douse of an icy stream.

For months, he'd felt such pride over rescuing her, felt so *honorable* taking her to find her betrothed. Yet he'd been turning her heart toward himself from the very first kiss. The intimate touch he'd bestowed should have been saved for her wedding night and her husband. He'd taken something that wasn't rightfully his—even though circumstances ended up making it so—and he was too ashamed of himself to laugh at the irony.

Seth abandoned his critical musings and looked down at his wife. He couldn't change the past. He needed to focus on the future.

He caressed her back again. As his fingers glided over her smooth skin, Becca arched into his touch and purred like a contented feline. Her eyes remained closed, but a dreamy smile tugged at the edges of her lips.

He pressed a kiss to her forehead and kept stroking until she roused to wakefulness. He knew the very instant that she did. Her eyes came open, and the pliant form under his hand stiffened with ingrained propriety.

"Good morning, Wife," he offered with gentle emphasis on the last word. Perhaps the endearment would remind her and set her at ease.

Blue-gray irises slowly lifted until they were gazing into his. A true blush deepened the flush of sleep that colored her cheeks. "Good morning."

Seth smiled sweetly, but it took effort. One look at those plump, pink lips and he was battling urges all over again. "Did you sleep well?"

She sighed and relaxed against him. "Better than I have in a long time."

"Me, too."

He relaxed his head on the pillow for a few more minutes of rest. He'd love to while away the hours curled up with his tempting wife, but he needed to find work.

Becca snuggled closer and slid her arm around his waist, the simple movement leaving blissful sensations in its wake.

His eyes fluttered closed. Finding work could wait. For a while, anyway.

"I could stay like this forever," she murmured against his skin.

"Mm. I was thinking the same thing." A carnal thought curved his lips. "If we did, though, we'd miss out on ever doing again what we did last night."

Her head rested in the crook of his arm, but he could see the mound of one cheek. The color of it deepened.

Seth tilted his head so he could see a little more of her face. "I know not everything was pleasant for you, but did you enjoy it...? Did you like the things I did?"

"Yes." Becca's answer was little more than a whisper, but it was a satisfied one. Bashful with an undercurrent of desire.

The extra color left her skin and she stayed quiet, so he closed his eyes and did the same. She needed time to adjust to the loss of her innocence, and talk of it would only weaken his resolve. He focused on the soft crackles of the coal-burning heater in the corner and the sounds of the town coming alive below.

"What about women?" Becca asked.

"Huh?"

"Women... Are there things we can do to please a man?"

A few notes of dry laughter left his throat. "Women don't have to *do* anything. They please a man just by bein'."

She got quiet again.

"Seth?"

"Hm."

"Did you mean what you said last night?"

He ran his fingers slowly up and down the back of her arm. "About what?"

"That your body belongs to me now."

"Yes."

"Does that mean I can touch you?"

His hand paused. "Yes."

"Any time I want?"

"Yes. Although, depending on the kind of touching you mean, you had best save it for when we're in private. We wouldn't want to scandalize the good people of Blackwater."

Seth winced. He'd said the last in jest and with a mocking tone but without an ounce of tactful thought. Thankfully, she humored him with a smile.

He lifted her hand from his waist and brought it to his lips. After planting a kiss on the curve of her thumb, he placed her hand palm down on his chest and covered it with his. "My body became yours last night, but you've always had my heart."

The gracious levity in her eyes melted into deep contentment. If he was blessed to see that look half the rest of his days, he'd be a lucky man.

Becca returned her attention to his chest. She wiggled her

hand from beneath his and nudged it aside. With the lightest of touches, she ran her fingers along the ridges and valleys of his muscles. She rose up on her elbow and lightly touched one of his nipples with her tongue, then nibbled gently.

"Mm-ahem." He'd cleared his throat to mask a moan.

She froze stock still. "Did I hurt you?"

Hell, no.

He smiled and shook his head. "Frog in my throat," he croaked.

She abandoned the sensitive brown disk to pluck and swirl the patch of hair in the center of his chest with her delicate fingers. She traced the trail southward, pushing the covers down as she went.

Seth closed his eyes as heat simmered through his veins. He'd have to stop her before things went too far—he'd meant what he said about waiting—but she needed to explore.

He looked down at her again. Even with her face turned away and her hair spilling sideways like a veil, he could sense her fascination. It was evident in her posture and her shallow, bated breaths.

When she got to his scar, she stopped and stared at the puckered pink line. He hated that he was marred, that she would have to see the stark reminder for the rest of her life. She'd done a good job of stitching, but the blemish was unsightly; it would never go away.

Becca lifted her hand to her mouth and planted a kiss on the tips of her fingers. She gently touched them to his wounded flesh and said, "Thank you," then continued her descent.

Seth held perfectly still as she kept tracing his attributes and touching his skin. Her inquisitiveness was beautiful. And maddening. He kept a firm grip on restraint, but here was no willing away his arousal that tented the sheet.

Her hand paused just below his navel, the edge of the covers riding low on his hips, and then, slowly, she lifted the fabric.

Sharp cracks echoed through the room as knuckles rapped on the door.

Becca stiffened and squeaked. She dove for his shoulder, yanking up the covers and sealing them completely over her head.

Seth groaned. And then he chuckled. "Relax, Becca," he said, freeing his chin from the fortress of cotton. "No one's coming in. I asked the night manager to wake us."

The rapping sounded again. "Mr. Emerson?" a male voice called. "Are you awake?"

"Yes," he called back.

"Very well, sir. I'll be back in half an hour for the tub."

Seth sighed. He planted a kiss on Becca's forehead. "We'd better get up." He slid out of bed. "Stay here where it's warm. I'll bring your chemise."

He pulled on his drawers and rubbed the chill from his arms, then fed some coal to the heater before gathering Rebecca's things and bringing them to her. He busied himself with his morning routine and she did the same, exchanging an occasional smile as they tried not to get in each other's way.

She'd packed her new dress in favor of one of her old outfits, and he rued the choice, even though he understood the practicality. Would she also choose a braid over an upswept style? He hoped not, but it really didn't matter. She would be beautiful to him no matter what.

Seth carried his socks and boots over to the bed. The mattress sagged as he sat on the edge.

Becca swept past him, her loose hair grazing her waist as she walked. He was glad his hands were occupied. They itched to touch her so badly, he could hardly resist. She carefully raked the hairpins from the nightstand into her hand and carried them to the dressing table. Her eyes met his in the mirror as she sat, then she focused on her reflection again.

She gathered her hair together until it hung from her fist like a horse's tail. The uncertainty creasing her brow deepened into a look of pure determination as she wound it like a lariat high on her head. It took three tries before she was able to hold the coil in place and work the pins in without parts of it falling, but she didn't give up. And he didn't interfere.

Seth walked up behind her as she slid the last pin into place. "You sure are pretty when you wear your hair like that. I don't know whether to show you off or hide you away. The minute we set foot on the street, you'll cause every man in town to break the tenth commandment."

Becca scrunched up her lips as if to call bull on a line of flattery, but her eyes gave her away. Her well of self-worth had run dry, and her heart soaked up every word.

He bent down and kissed her cheek. "On second thought, Mrs. Emerson, I'll show you off over breakfast."

Becca smoothed imaginary wrinkles from her clothing for the third time since she and Seth left their room, then placed a clammy hand over her pounding heart. She wasn't sure which part of facing the other diners made her more nervous—them suspecting she'd lain with Seth on the trail or them knowing she had last night.

Seth's fingers curled around her hand resting in the crook of his elbow. "Relax," he whispered, leaning down so only she could hear. "Most everyone thinks very well of you, and those who don't—their opinions don't matter."

That took care of worry number one.

"But they... they'll *know*," she whispered back.

He stopped and looked at her with a sideways smirk. "That's what you're worried about? Them knowing what we did last night?"

Becca's face heated and she nodded.

"Well, don't be," he said. "I'd lay money more than half the couples in that room were doing the very same thing. And the others wish they had."

Her cheeks grew even hotter, but she couldn't stop the smile. Raising her chin, she ignored the churning mass of worms in her middle and walked with her husband under the archway and into the room.

Several diners looked up, but they didn't scoff or smirk. Most of them nodded a polite greeting and turned back to their food.

"See. I told you," Seth whispered as they followed the waiter to their table.

Despite his assertion, he was thoughtful enough to seat her so that her back was to most of the group. Seth was the only one she wanted to see anyway. His easy smile and the way his eyes regarded her with frank satisfaction warmed her more than the coffee swirling over her tongue and sliding down her throat. The last time they'd sat in this room, she'd doubted his motives and his love. Not anymore. His proposal had been genuine.

"There's something we need to talk about," Seth said once the waiter had brought their food. His bearing remained pleasant, but the tenor beneath it had changed.

Becca's stomach knotted as she unfolded her napkin and laid it in her lap. Seth had a strong sense of ethics and duty. He must be planning to turn her parents in. She nudged the steaming mound of scrambled eggs on her plate with her fork and waited for him to elaborate.

"I, uh..." He cleared his throat, and hers grew tighter. "Things happened rather quickly and, well, I wasn't prepared to take on a wife."

She looked up at him and blinked.

"Aw, Becca, don't look at me like that. You're not a burden—that's not what I meant." He reached across the table and wrapped her hand in his. "I'm looking forward to planning a life with you, but I'm running low on funds. I need to find work."

"Oh." She sat back, relieved.

He eyed her a moment, then picked up his knife and fork. "I know there are a lot of details we need to work out—where we want to settle and such—but those issues are moot until I save up some money."

Becca swallowed a sip of coffee. "What about a land grant? Could you get one?"

"Probably. But it takes money to build a house and stock a farm."

The worms churned again, but this time from guilt. "What about your plans... your ranch?"

He gave a weak smile and sawed at his ham. "Plans change."

Becca nudged her eggs again. He'd given up so much for her. It wasn't fair.

She set down her fork. "I'll go with you anywhere. And I don't need fancy things to be happy—we can live in the wagon if we have to. Or I'll find another cave. If owning a cattle ranch is your dream, I'll do whatever it takes to help you achieve it."

Seth's chest rose sharply. He blinked several times and reached for her hand. "My dream is to spend my life with you."

His fingers tightened around hers. She smiled and squeezed back.

His eyes suddenly brimmed with mischief. "I wonder what the neighbors would think if we invited them to a cave."

A giggle bubbled from her throat at the same time a chuckle rumbled from his.

They reached for their forks and went after their food with renewed vigor.

When they'd polished off the last of their meal, Seth sat back in his chair. "One of the ranchers I worked for after I left home recently relocated to California. His place is only a half a day's ride from here. He's a good man to work for, and he pays a fair wage. I thought I'd start there."

Becca didn't relish staying in Blackwater alone, but she'd make do. "When will you go?"

"I'd like to go today, if you're up to it." Seth scanned the area around them. "It'll mean a full day's ride with only a break for lunch," he said, leaning in and lowering his voice. "If sitting a horse is too uncomfortable yet, we can wait another day."

Warmth filled her cheeks and her heart. "I can ride."

Chapter Twenty-Nine

Becca tied the tails of her new knitted scarf under her chin. She turned toward Cyrus and prepared to mount.

"Face me," Seth said. "Let me help you."

She was capable of ascending the saddle herself, but she braced her hands on his shoulders and let him lift her onto the seat.

He'd hovered and doted all morning, buying her a new coat and scarf, even insisting she wear a set of his woolens under her clothes. Now he was standing in front of her, shielding her body from strangers' eyes as she hooked her leg over the pommel and adjusted her skirts.

Becca wished she could ride astride, but only brazen women did that. She'd had her fill of people calling her brazen.

"Are you comfortable?" Seth asked, handing her the reins.

Comfortable enough. "Yes."

Cyrus shifted on his hooves and answered Zeus's blow. The horses were as anxious to leave as their riders. Seth swung into his saddle, bid farewell to the liveryman, and led them on their way.

Becca relaxed and breathed deeply as they cantered across the countryside. Clear skies spanned the horizon, and sunlight warmed her everywhere it touched. The heat of it was welcome in calm cold air.

When the sun was nearly overhead, Seth stopped at a stream. He surprised her by stealing some kisses, saying he was getting his fill while the horses drank theirs.

She gently chided him as a proper lady should, then abandoned that insanity. Her fingers gripped his nape and her tongue sought his, turning his chaste kiss into something darker. They both groaned. Hands groped and bodies ground together in a futile effort to get skin against skin. Seth's hat was knocked from his head, but he gave no notice.

He finally pulled away, panting. "Damn." A smile curved his luscious lips. "I shoulda gone swimming instead."

"That must be the place," Seth remarked as they topped a hill and surveyed a sprawling ranch below. A grand farmhouse stood to the right, near a grove of leafless trees, surrounded by acres and acres of rolling pasture.

Becca kept her horse in step beside his, but her attention was on the men working in the many corrals. Some trained horses while others tended beeves. A few sat on the rails, watching.

"Stick close and keep control of your mount," Seth said. "The fact I have a woman with me should allay some of their fears, but they're going to be wary of us. We need to take it slow."

Sure enough, two armed men approached on horseback, reins in one hand and rifles in the other.

"Stop," one of them called once they were close enough to be heard.

Seth reined Zeus to a halt and slowly raised a hand in greeting.

"You're on private land," the other said with a hard edge to his tone. It matched the callous regard of his narrowed eyes.

Seth gave an acknowledging nod. "Name's Seth Emerson. I'm here to see Peter Dixon."

The men glanced at each other.

"He's not expecting anyone," the first one said.

"There wasn't time to get word to him before my visit," Seth replied, "but he knows me."

Becca shivered when the brusque man shifted his gaze and stared at her.

"Who's she?"

"She's my wife." Seth waited long moments. Neither man spoke. Did the air around him feel as heavy as it did to her? "All I ask is that you let him know I'm here."

The solemn man said something to the surly one.

His lips curled back over his teeth as though he'd eaten something bad. He spun his horse around and rode away.

The remaining man eased his horse closer and laid his rifle across his lap. "I'm Amos Yates. I apologize for Percy's manners, Mr. Emerson... ma'am." He tipped his hat to Becca. "Tensions are still running high from the war. We've had everything from raids to rustlers. Everyone is suspect."

"I understand."

"You said you know Peter."

Zeus snorted and Seth gave him a pat. "I worked for him a few years ago, in Ohio."

Yates lifted his chin in acknowledgement, but said nothing more.

The unwelcome silence dragged on. Becca smoothed her skirt, then patted Cyrus on the neck. Her fingers brushed along her shoulder, seeking a familiar tuft of hair but finding only the point of her coat collar. She lowered her hand to her lap and plastered on a pleasant expression.

Percy finally returned, the same bad taste twisting his mouth. "Dixon says let 'em come."

A tall man, whose gray eyes matched the patches of hair above his ears, crossed the yard as Seth helped her down from her mount. "Good to see you," he said as he shook Seth's hand. "I couldn't believe it when Percy told me you were here. And married," he added, looking to Becca with a delighted smile.

"Peter, this is my wife, Rebecca."

"Pleased to meet you, Mrs. Emerson."

"Thank you. It's good to meet you, too, Mr. Dixon. Seth speaks very highly of you."

"Oh he does, does he?" Peter chuckled "He gave you the bowdlerized version, then." The mirth faded as he lifted his head and looked past them, scanning the horizon. "Nicky'll see to your horses." He indicated a towheaded youth who was already gathering reins. "Let's get you folks inside."

Peter led them up the porch's steps and into the parlor of the ranch house. The interior was large and furnished, but rustic— all iron and leather and wood. It lacked a woman's touch.

After taking their coats, he gestured to a grouping of chairs near the fireplace and invited them to sit. It was obvious Peter knew this wasn't a social visit, and just as obvious he'd been called away from his work, but he was mannered enough to make small talk for a time.

"So, how'd you two meet," he asked, leaning back and resting the ankle of one boot on the opposite knee.

Seth glanced at Becca and she gave a small nod. "Quite literally, I found her," he said. "She'd gotten separated from the wagon train she was traveling with and had managed to survive in the wilderness of New Mexico Territory for over a year."

Peter gaped.

"I was traveling alone and got thrown," Seth continued as his friend recovered. "She graciously took me in and put up with me long enough to nurse me back to health."

A grin split Peter's lips. "She must love you, then, Emerson. When you're hurt, you're a surly sonuvagun."

A throat cleared to Becca's left. A young man stood in the archway leading to the kitchen. He was dressed like one of the hands. "Lunch is ready," he said to Peter. "I brought some sandwiches and set the table for you and your guests."

"Thank you, Lucas."

Lucas nodded and appraised the group, his deep blue eyes lingering on Becca long enough to raise a tingle of alarm. Dragging his gaze away, he reached for his hat, settled it over his shiny black hair, and walked out the door.

Becca stared at the exit for a long moment after he left. Had his undue attention caused the flutter in her stomach and the sudden weight on her heart, or was it the fact he looked so much like Nathan?

"Where's Ruth?" Seth asked Peter. "Is she well?"

"She's fine. She's still in Ohio. I'd planned to send for her once I got the house built, but things here are still too unstable." He and Seth exchanged a look. "Mrs. Emerson,"

Peter said, rising, "if I set out the things you need, could I impose upon you to make us some coffee?"

"Certainly. I'd be glad to."

Once he'd settled her in the kitchen, Peter excused himself. Becca watched through the window above the sink as he walked with Seth to a spot across the yard. She wished she could hear what they were saying.

Peter spoke to Seth for a while, then listened intently, nodding his head from time to time. His expression was not unkind when he replied, but his overall bearing was serious. When Seth's shoulders sagged, so did her spirits. He'd been turned down for the job.

Becca turned away from the window and pasted on a smile.

Peter waited with her on the porch while Seth readied the horses. She tugged on her gloves and tied her scarf around her head. "Thank you for lunch, Mr. Dixon."

"You're more than welcome." He glanced in Seth's direction. "Your husband asked me for a job," he said in a lower voice, "and I don't want you to think any less of him for me telling him no. I'd hire Seth on the spot if I could. Not only is he a good friend, he's one of the best hands I ever had.

"As I told him, things are still dangerous in California. Towns are fairly safe, so are small homesteads. But big operations like mine are targets because the ranchos see us as a threat. I've been forced to hire more men to provide security than I have working the livestock. I simply can't afford to hire anyone else."

"I understand."

He offered his arm and walked with her into the yard. Armed men on horseback now formed a loose circle around the house.

Fear slithered through Becca's veins at the same time guilt swept her conscience. They'd been moved here to protect her, but they were also here *because* of her. By visiting, she'd made the whole of Peter's ranch less safe.

"Thank you for the hospitality," Seth said as he shook his friend's hand.

"It was good to see you." Peter pulled him into a backslapping hug that was a heartfelt as his words. "Lucas will ride with you as far as the creek," he said as the two of them released each other. "After that, you'll be close enough to town to travel alone."

"You don't need to send—"

"Save your words, Seth. I do, and it's done."

Seth pressed his lips together and drew a slow breath. "Thank you." The set of his jaw eased. "Give Ruth our best."

"I will, next time I write. She'll be so sorry she missed your visit." Peter's warm eyes settled on Becca. "She would have loved meeting you, Mrs. Emerson."

"I would have enjoyed meeting her, too."

Seth helped her to mount as he'd done before they left town. He climbed on Zeus and flanked her right side as Lucas took his position on her left.

As the horses began to walk, Becca looked back at Peter standing in the yard, his broad shoulders squared and his eyes fixed on them as they left. He'd treated them with the manners of a nobleman while wearing farmer's clothes. His bearing was no less refined. He was undeniably a gentleman—a spot of elegance and culture amidst a savage land.

She faced forward again, staying between her escorts and letting her mount have his way. Their ambling pace didn't change, even after they reached the edge of Peter's land. If the men were holding back on her account, they needn't bother. She was tired and sore, but she was no weakling. The events of the day—of her life, for that matter—were piling up and kindling a flare of rebellion. She wanted control. And she wanted to get back to the safety of town as soon as possible.

Becca urged Cyrus into a gallop and silently dared the men to keep up.

Moments later, hooves pounded the ground behind her, and they flanked her again.

Ignoring them, Becca leaned forward and tightened her thighs on the pommels as Cyrus leapt over narrow streams and fallen logs with a grace that belied his size. Despite the danger of their location, she reveled in the exhilaration of flying over the land. She might not ride astride, but she could ride. Well.

"Rebecca," Seth called, breathing as hard as the horses.

"Ma'am, slow down."

A half a mile later, she growled in the back of her throat and complied. Seth was frowning at her; so was Lucas.

"Are you scared?" Seth asked.

She was, but she gave him a look to the contrary—more like made a face.

"Ma'am." She turned her head in Lucas's direction. "Going too fast can be as dangerous as going too slow."

Becca bit the inside of her lip to keep from rolling her eyes. "I'm capable of keeping myself in the saddle."

"I have no doubt of that, ma'am. That's not what I meant. I was sent along to protect you. I can't watch our surroundings if I'm racing through them at breakneck speed."

He had a point.

She faced forward and resigned herself to letting the men set the pace.

About a half a mile later, Seth turned a less than friendly look in Lucas's direction.

Out the corner of her other eye, she saw Lucas studying her. She faced him full on and he looked away. A few minutes later, he did it again, and then a few minutes later, again.

For a man who was supposed to be keeping an eye on things around him, he wasn't doing a very good job.

Becca shrugged inwardly. It didn't matter. The creek lay over the next rise.

Zeus slowly dropped back half a length. He shot forward and whipped around in front of her so fast, Cyrus snorted and tossed his head. By the time she'd calmed him, Zeus stood nose to nose with Lucas's horse.

Seth glared at its rider with an expression so fierce, it could melt solid steel. "Would you like to tell me what you find so interesting about my wife?"

Lucas held up his hands. "I meant no offense." He looked at Becca, then thought better of it and averted his gaze. "Truly, ma'am, I apologize. I..."

"You *what?*" Seth practically breathed fire.

Lucas drew a breath so deep, his shoulders sagged with the exhale. "Ma'am," he said, raising his eyes to Becca's, "is your maiden name Garvey?"

She blinked.

"What business is it of yours?" Seth growled.

Lucas held her gaze. "Is it?"

"Yes." She swallowed.

He gave Seth a tentative look. "I overheard you tell Mr. Dixon your wife had been left behind by a train. That was the only reason for my interest, I swear. I just wondered if she was the one."

Seth looked from Lucas to Becca and back again. He stared

the man down for a whole new reason. "What do you know?"

Lucas's horse shifted under him as he sized up his audience. "Mid-August last year, I was hired to provide extra security for a train headed for California. The captain said there'd been trouble, that a young woman had disappeared under suspicious circumstances."

Seth shot Becca a look. "Did they ever determine who was at fault?"

Becca clutched fistfuls of skirt to keep her clammy hands from shaking.

"I heard some of her belongings were found in a man's wagon, but..."

"You were traveling with them," Seth pressed. "Surely you know more than that."

"I heard a lot of things—true, but hearsay isn't proof." Lucas grimaced and shook his head. "You know how it is on the train. There was more rumor and innuendo flying around than dirt in a dust storm. I didn't know who to believe."

Seth frowned. "What about her parents?"

"What about 'em?"

"How did they seem to you?"

"Well..." Lucas's horse shifted under him again. "I spent most of my time on forward patrol, but the few times I saw them, they looked" —he lifted a shoulder and let it fall— "sad."

Becca couldn't stop the derisive note that slipped from her throat.

Lucas briefly narrowed his eyes. He looked down at his gloved hands resting on his saddle horn, like he was wrestling with his thoughts, then he raised his head and looked right at her. "One night, when I was on watch, I came across your father out in the woods. He was sitting on a fallen log, grieving. I'd never seen a man cry like that before.

"I figured he went out there to have some privacy, so I left without disturbing him; but I'm telling you, he was a broken man."

Becca closed her eyes as some of the ice around her heart fell away. What if it was true? What if her father was innocent? But there was no way to know. He could just as well have been grieving the state of his own soul rather than hers.

She opened her eyes and kept her heart hard. If she didn't, she'd fall apart.

"Do you know where they are?" Seth asked.

Lucas shook his head. "They made it as far as the Colorado. They fell behind after that."

Chapter Thirty

Relief and gloominess settled in Becca's chest as she and Seth ambled into town. Putting her past behind her and making a fresh start wasn't going to be as easy as she thought.

The news about her father was equally comforting and disturbing. She didn't know what to make of it, and the doubt nagged. It was enough to give her pause, but would it be enough to keep Seth from turning her parents in? He hadn't said anything one way or another, but he was a man of integrity. The knowledge had to be eating at him just like it was at her. Becca knew she should report them herself—in the heat of angry moments, she hungered for revenge—but she couldn't bring herself to do it.

Groaning, she shifted in the saddle. Her back ached, her legs cramped, and her bottom was part painful, part numb. "Stop," she called to Seth when they reached the middle of town. "I'm getting off here."

His left cheek creased and his lips formed a thin line, making her fear he might refuse. Instead, he gave a single nod. He dismounted long enough to help her do the same, then climbed back on Zeus, holding Cyrus' lead line. "I'll be back shortly. Be sure to lock the door."

Becca nodded and slowly took the steps of the hotel. If she could get away with rubbing more than her lower back in public, she would. Maybe Seth would arrange another hot bath. Then again, maybe not. Money was in short supply and he didn't have a job.

A large, work-worn hand reached for the door, and she lifted her head to thank its owner for the chivalrous act. The sentiment died in her throat when she saw the stern face staring back at her. Her eyes tracked along a stiff arm, back to the man's hand. It was pressed flat against the door, not curled around the handle to pull it open.

"Are you Rebecca Garvey?" His voice was gruff, and his tone was as curt as the set of his slate-colored eyes.

"I was." She took a wary step back. "I'm Rebecca Emerson now."

"Were you traveling with the Pittman train through New Mexico Territory last August?"

"Yes."

"Are you the daughter of Levi and Martha Garvey?"

Her lungs drew a dread-filled breath. "Yes."

"In that case, you're coming with me."

"Why? Who are you?"

"I'm Sherman Hicks, Sheriff of Blackwater." He withdrew a short length of rope from his back pocket. "Hold out your hands. You're under arrest."

"Me? There must be some mistake."

He leveled a dissenting gaze so dark it brooked no argument. "I said give me your hands."

Becca's heart flailed against her ribs and a chill swept over her skin. She lifted her arms. The sheriff looped the rope around her wrists as casually as if he was tying shoelaces. He seemed oblivious to the gathering crowd.

She wasn't. She was mortified. Faces of people she knew dappled the cluster of spectators. Women who'd welcomed her at her wedding supper looked on in horror.

Becca turned her eyes away and stared at a spot on the ground. What would they think of her now?

"Sheriff Hicks," one of the ladies said. "Is that really necessary?"

His fingers stilled, and he looked up with a mixture of irritation and confusion on his face. "I don't have a choice. I have to arrest her."

"But she's cooperating, and she's so slight compared to you. Must you bind her like that?"

Supportive murmurs followed, male and female alike.

The sheriff scanned the crowd. He looked back at Becca with slitted eyes and a scowl. "If I untie you, will you run from me?"

Becca swallowed and shook her head.

He removed the rope. As she rubbed the burn from her wrists, Hicks rested his palm on the butt of his revolver. "Don't give me any trouble."

He wrapped a hand around her upper arm and squeezed so hard she thought he'd snap the bone. She offered no resistance as he led her down the boardwalk, doubling her steps to match his long strides, but he didn't let up.

Some of the townspeople hurried away while others followed along in the street. "She seemed so nice," one of them said. "What did she do to get arrested?" another pondered.

Becca wondered the same thing, but she dared not ask now. Not while so many eyes and ears were trained on her.

The sheriff hauled her into his office and shut the pine door on the crowd. "Are you armed?"

"No. Um, just my knife."

Becca gasped when his fingers went for the buttons of her coat. He crudely divested her of the garment and hung it on a rack near the door. Next, he reached for her waist. Her pulse shot as high as her arms. He tugged loose the tether and tossed the sheath aside, knife and all. Then, breeching all bounds of decorum, he ran his hands down the sides of her skirt, lifted the hem, and examined her ankles.

Becca's impulse was to scold him for accosting her, but she clamped her jaw shut and pressed her teeth into her tongue. The stab of fingers digging into her arm affirmed she'd made the right choice. With a viselike grip, he steered her toward the empty cell on the other side of the room and swung open the door.

Becca's knees locked, and her boots dug for purchase on the dusty wood floor.

Hicks' fingers curled painfully into her flesh. "Don't fight me, woman. The *only* reason I untied you was because the people who voted me into office seem to think you deserve mercy. I don't share that opinion."

"Please," Becca said, quaking under the glare of the ruthless man towering over her, "at least tell me why you're doing this."

His lips scrunched as if he'd eaten something sour. "Among other things, your actions on the trail led to an innocent man's death. I don't know the way things are where you come from, but here in California, murder's a hanging offense."

"Bu— But I didn't do anything."

"You didn't steal from other people's wagons?"

"No."

"You didn't steal rations and hide from your family?"

"No."

"You didn't put some of your belongings in Melvin Cantwell's wagon to throw suspicion off yourself?"

Her eyes rounded. She shook her head to emphasize the point. "*No.*"

"Well, if you didn't, then who did?" Hicks' brows were raised in question, but his lips held a smug curve.

Becca stared at the steely eyes boring into hers. She forced a swallow past the lump in her throat to keep the contents of her stomach from coming up.

"If you have information that can clear your name, tell me." He gave her arm a shake. "Well, Mrs. Emerson?"

Her parents' names nudged her lips, but she couldn't force her mouth to speak. Her knees turned to jelly and her spirit drained from her chest. "I don't."

"Hmph. Figured as much." He shoved her into the cell and locked the iron door behind her with a fatal clang.

Holding a river of tears at bay, Becca surveyed the tiny space. The sheriff's office was sparse, but the six-by-six room he'd confined her to was bleak. A few rays of light passed through a single, barred window high above her head in the concrete wall. A chipped chamber pot sat completely exposed in the left corner, and a filthy, tattered cot lined the wall to her right. The emotion clogging her nose and throat dimmed the smell, but the foul, musty air made her wretch.

Becca turned around and stared through the bars. Her bladder had been begging for release since two miles out of town, but she squeezed her thighs tight and held her water. She refused to lift her skirts and squat where the sheriff—and anyone else who walked in—could plainly see. She considered sitting on the cot, but the lines of the striped tick wiggled as if they were alive, and stains she couldn't identify covered more of the surface than the dingy spaces in between.

Crossing the room, Becca hugged herself and leaned against the far wall. She ran her hands along her arms to rub away the chill and winced when her fingers brushed the place Hicks had squeezed. She'd have bruises tomorrow.

The sheriff removed his dark brown sack coat and sat at his desk. After slipping on a pair of spectacles, he shuffled through a stack of papers and began writing as if he were penning invitations to a soiree. His calm confidence only heightened her fear.

The door to the office flew upon and light rushed in along with Seth. His eyes went wide and his mouth fell open.

Becca's heart thrilled at the sight of him, but that comfort faded faster than a winter sunset. She hugged herself tighter and looked away. He'd surely regret marrying her now.

"What's the meaning of this?" Seth's voice was low and seemingly calm, but she knew better. The words had been all but growled.

"I..." She didn't know where to begin.

"Your wife's under arrest."

"For what!"

Becca lifted her eyes. Seth was glaring at Hicks, not her.

Hicks rose. "Well, theft, for starters."

"What in blazes did she take? And from whom?"

"She stole from other travelers, last year on the trail. It'll all be sorted out at her arraignment. I sent word to the marshal. He should be here sometime next week."

Seth paled. "You called in a US Marshal?"

"The crime happened in a territory, not a state. That makes it federal."

Seth rubbed the back of his neck. His throat bobbed with a

swallow. His hand slid from his nape, and he sighed. "Can I see her?"

Hicks glowered for a moment. "Fine. But give me your weapons." He pointed to Seth's sidearm and held out his hand.

Seth pulled the Colt from its holster and handed it over butt first.

"I want everything." Hicks pointed to his boot.

Seth propped his foot on the worn seat of the chair between him and the sheriff's desk. He slid his knife from its sheath and gave him that, too.

Hicks set the items next to Becca's knife. "I said everything."

"That is everything."

Hicks narrowed his eyes and glowered some more.

Widening his stance, Seth held his arms out from his body and turned his palms to the ceiling. His posture was submissive, but his expression didn't yield.

"Go ahead," Hicks grumbled, giving a flick of his head.

Seth swiped off his hat, crossed the room, and stared through the bars. "Becca? Are you all right?"

She nodded and closed the distance between them, dragging her feet when she wanted to run. Looking up into his questioning eyes, she forced hoarse words from her throat. "I didn't do it."

His lips curved into a troubled smile. "I know you didn't." He stuck his hand through the bars and wiggled his fingers in invitation.

He didn't have to ask twice. She latched onto his hand with her own.

"We'll get through this. Don't worry." His words were spoken in good faith, but doubt lingered in the shadows. "Do you have the key to our room?"

"No. I never made it inside. He arrested me right after you dropped me off."

Seth cursed softly. "I shouldn't have left you alone."

Becca crossed her legs and squeezed her thighs as tightly as she could. She was about to embarrass herself worse than hiking her skirts in front of a stranger. "Will you stand between me and him? I need a private moment."

Seth looked in the direction of the chamber pot. His gaze shot back to her, flaming like a fresh torch. "I'll do you one better." He turned and strode to Hicks' desk, muscles coiled and boot heels pounding like thunder. "Step outside with me."

"I'm not going anywh—"

"Yes you are. My wife needs privacy. *Now*. Step outside."

Hicks tossed his glasses down and rose amidst a loud scrape of chair legs, but a strangled noise in his throat betrayed the bravado. Maybe he did have a speck of decency under all that crassness.

Becca nearly wept with relief when the door closed behind them. She rushed through her task, but she didn't need to. Seth gave her plenty of time.

He returned and grasped her fingers through the bars like before. "I'm going to retrieve your things from our room and get you some supper. I'll be back as soon as I can."

Becca paced the filthy floor, casting occasional glances at Hicks hunched over his desk, absorbed with paperwork. She hated being alone with him.

Seth finally walked back in, arms loaded, and she sent a prayer of thanks heavenward. The half hour he'd been gone had felt like a year. He spread everything on Hicks' desk.

"What's all this?"

"Her belongings and her supper. I figured you'd want to search it first."

Hicks sifted through the loose items. He opened Becca's valise and peered inside. "This really isn't necessary. I planned to feed her, and she's got everything she needs in her cell."

"She doesn't even have a blanket."

"I would've given her one," he said tiredly.

Seth hung his duster and hat on the rack, then gathered everything back up and headed for the cell. He walked in when Hicks opened the door, and Becca had to twist her hands into a knot to keep from throwing her arms around him.

"Well?" Hicks said. "What are you waiting for? Put it down and come back out."

"Lock me in. I'm staying with my wife."

Hicks shook his head and sighed. "Suit yourself."

Seth eyed the cot and frowned. "You got a sheet for this filthy bed?"

"Hang on. I'll get it."

Hicks reached inside a small, freestanding cabinet next to the cell and shoved a wad of tattered cotton through the bars. Becca spread it over the cot, trying not to touch the smelly mattress as she tucked under the edges. At least the sheet was clean.

She and Seth sat side by side and nibbled on the roast beef sandwiches he'd brought. She wasn't sure what occupied his thoughts, but she knew what plagued hers. "They think I hid on purpose and implicated Mr. Cantwell," she said in a soft voice.

"I know." Seth looked past her to Hicks. "I pried a few details from him while we were outside."

Her insides prickled with a flutter of nerves. "Did you tell him about my parents?"

"No." A troubled expression ghosted over his brow as he turned his attention back to her. "I was planning to turn them in, at first. But after hearing what that lookout said, things don't seem so black and white anymore."

They finished their meal and sat in silence.

The office door opened and a rather scraggy young man came in. He glanced at them as he removed his coat and hat, then walked over to the desk and spoke with the sheriff.

"Who's that?" Becca asked Seth.

"Probably his deputy."

Hicks cleared his desk and tugged on his coat. He crossed the room to the cell as the young man settled into his vacated chair. "Arnold's in charge while I'm gone. Don't give him any trouble."

The implied threat combined with the sheriff's stern glare turned the food in Becca's stomach to stone.

Seth seemed unfazed. "Innocent people don't make trouble."

"Hmph." Hicks frowned as he spun on his heel. He headed for the door, grabbed his hat, and left.

Seth scooted to the end of the cot and turned sideways, resting one boot on the mattress and leaving the other on the floor. Urging her closer, he nestled her in the vee of his thighs and guided her head to his chest. The concrete wall he was leaning against had to be cold and hard, but that didn't seem to faze him either. He shook out the blanket he'd brought and wrapped her in wool.

Becca closed her eyes and inhaled her husband's familiar scent. Despite the long ride, he smelled far better than anything else in the cell. The warmth seeping through his flannel shirt and the steady thump of his heart began to soothe her fears.

Seth slid a finger along her jaw and tilted her face up. "Are you angry with me?"

"For what?"

"For wanting to turn your parents in."

She thought about it for the space of a breath. "No. Your

345

integrity is one of the things I love about you. I can't expect you to forsake that just because it affects me or someone I care about."

He gazed into her eyes for a long, heartwarming moment, with such bare appreciation that it nearly stole her breath.

His grateful smile turned cocky. "You said that's *one* of the things. What else do you love about me?"

Becca grabbed his finger and twisted it playfully. "You can mark humility off the list."

He chuckled.

She glanced over her shoulder at the pock-faced deputy leaning back in his chair, watching them. He pressed his feeble lips together and rolled his close-set eyes.

"Let him scoff," Seth murmured when she turned her face back. "He's just jealous. I mean, look at him—he's homely and he works nights. I'd lay odds his bed is empty."

"Seth Lawrence Emerson!" She slapped his chest.

He shook with a deep, rumbling laugh—the scamp—and his twinkling eyes withered her indignation. The way they always did.

"Ah, Becca," he said, wrapping her in his muscular arms. "Life with you is anything but boring."

"I'd welcome *boring* right now." She slid her arms around his waist. His body was as solid and unmovable as the trunk of a tree, and she clung to it. "I'm scared."

"I know." He held her tight. "But don't lose faith. That lookout—what was his name? Lucas?—he had it right. Rumor isn't proof. We just have to be patient and give the truth time to sort itself out."

Becca snuggled closer and stared into the gathering dark. *I hope you're right.*

Chapter Thirty-One

Becca blinked at the pale morning light filtering down through the tiny barred window. Seth's arm rested heavily across her waist. Sometime in the night, he'd stretch out behind her on the cot and tucked her against him. Warmth from the coal-burning heater near the sheriff's desk barely reached the inside of the cell. And strangely, she didn't mind. She preferred Seth's heat to any other source.

His embrace grew more intentional and his breath brushed her ear. "Mm. Mornin'."

"G'morning," she whispered back.

A strange noise came from across the room.

Becca lifted her head and looked past her feet. The deputy was slumped in the desk chair with his head lolled back and his eyes closed. Slow, deep breaths sawed in and fluttered his lips on the way out.

Some guard he was.

Seth rose up on his elbow. "Wanna make a break for it?"

Becca jerked her gaze back and turned it on him. A sleepy grin lit his eyes with mischief.

She let out a breath. For a moment, she'd thought he was serious.

He nudged her onto her back, then leaned down and nuzzled her neck. "On second thought, I have a better idea." He kissed a languid trail from the lobe of her ear to her collar bone, sending shivers rippling over her flesh. His hand slid up her side and grazed the underside of her breast. Even through layers of clothing, the simple touch set her on fire.

The potent mixture of affection and desire was heady. She loved this man so much. She'd looked forward to coupling with him again from the moment he'd made her his wife. But now, what could she do? Instead of a cozy hotel room, they were stuck in a filthy cell like animals on display in a zoo.

Becca fought a sudden rush of emotion and tears. What if she was found guilty? They might never be together again.

Seth lifted his head. "What's wrong?"

She tried to speak, but words wouldn't come. Her chest seized up like a rusty pump.

Seth's eyes darted back and forth, searching her face. He shoved himself into a sitting position and scooped her onto his lap, blanket and all. "I was only playing, Becca. I— He was asleep. I was just—" He clutched her tight and buried his face in her hair. "I would never take you in front of anyone—*ever*."

"I know," she croaked out.

He pulled back and looked at her. "What has you so upset then?"

"I..." She dragged in a ragged breath and tried not to burst into tears. "I want to be a good wife to you."

"You *are*."

Becca shook her head. He didn't understand what she was

trying to say. "You—" She forced air into her burning lungs and made words come back out. "You married me and I made promises. Now I may not be able to keep them. When the Marshal takes me away, if they find me guilty, you— you'll be all alone."

The deep lines of concern on Seth's face melted away. He hugged her and settled back against the wall, running his fingers soothingly up and down her spine. "Don't go getting ahead of yourself. Remember? I made promises, too—to love you and protect you, for better or worse." He shrugged. "So we're having the *worse* first. Let me do the worrying. And the protecting. I've braved outlaws, rivers, and Indians to get you. I'm not giving you up without a fight."

The deputy snorted and jerked forward in his chair. His startled gaze skidded around the room and settled on them with a look of relief.

"Relax," Seth told him. "I won't tell Hicks about your nap. It'll be our secret."

Arnold pressed his lips into a grimace and smoothed his clothing.

Boots clomped the boardwalk outside and the door to the office swung open, sending a blast of cold air into the space. Sheriff Hicks stepped inside. He shut the door and removed his hat and overcoat, giving the place a quick perusal. "Any trouble?"

Arnold shot up and rubbed his palms down the front of his trousers. "Na—" He cleared the sleep from his throat. "No sir."

"Fetch coffee and breakfast for these folks, then you can go."

Arnold nodded and hurried out.

"Maybe this isn't so bad," Seth whispered as Hicks reclaimed his chair and hooked the wires of his spectacles over his ears. "Not only do we get free food, Rip Van Arnold has to serve it to us."

Becca couldn't help it. She smiled.

Hicks paused from his work and looked at them, his lip curling in disapproval.

Her smile faded. She eased off Seth's lap and sat beside him.

"Do you need a private moment?" Seth asked quietly.

"Not yet."

"After breakfast, I'll find you some water and a basin and get Hicks out of here for a while."

Becca nodded and managed another smile, but her attention was dominated by the surly sheriff. And the uncertain fate that awaited her.

Lunch was less appetizing than breakfast and sat in her gut like a big lump of dough.

Becca couldn't sit any longer. She pushed to her feet. The movement shifted the tray of dirty dishes on the end of the cot, making them clink.

She wrapped her arms around her middle and paced. Waiting to learn the fate of your future was torture, but doing so in the confines of a tiny cell was a hundred times worse. Her chest felt as if someone were squeezing it, and her stomach kept tying itself in knots. The anxious idleness was about to drive her insane.

Seth studied her with a worried frown.

Her stride paused and her eyes lingered a moment. He'd

been loving and loyal, but it hurt to look at him—at all she might lose. She forced her eyes back to the floor and kept pacing.

The office door swung open and Becca spun around. A tall man walked in, all windblown and covered in dust. The shorter, stouter man who shuffled in behind him was even grimier. The taller one hung up his hat, then swiped the hat off the other man's head and placed it next to his. As the pair approached the sheriff's desk, the second man's hands came into view. Rope bound his wrists, tugging him along like a reluctant farm animal.

The tall man looked over at Becca and Seth. His brow dipped in the middle as his gaze settled on her. Then, as if he'd shaken off some kind of trance, he pulled his attention away and turned it on the sheriff. "I'm John Murdock."

"Sherman Hicks. What can I do for you?"

"I need to house a prisoner."

Hicks stood and planted his hands on his hips. "That's going to be a problem. My only cell is occupied."

Murdock frowned. "This is Quinton Cooley, wanted for murder and counterfeiting. Since I caught him a week ago, he's nearly escaped twice. I need your cell." He pulled aside the lapel of his dusty black coat. Sunlight glinted off silver and Becca's knees went weak.

Hicks eyed the US Marshal's badge on Murdock's chest, then glanced at her and Seth. "Well... I suppose we could work something out." He hooked a thumb in her direction. "She's wanted for theft in New Mexico Territory. I sent for a Marshal to take her to the federal judge, but the letter only went out yesterday." Hicks drew a longsuffering breath. "If you'll take her for me, I'll rescind my request and secure your prisoner."

"I'm not in the habit of transporting women. I'll need proper documentation of the charges, including statements from witnesses."

Hicks shifted on his feet. "I'll get it for you."

Murdock tilted his head in the direction of the cell. "Who's that in there with her?"

"Her husband. He insisted on staying with her."

The Marshal eyed her and Seth again, looking them up and down. He turned back to Hicks. "Fine. Let's make the switch, but I'll have to leave them with you for now. I need to go see Judge Tate."

Murdock's prisoner backed away, his eyes like large white eggs on his dirty face. "Not Tyrant Tate!"

"I'm afraid so, Cooley." The Marshal tugged him toward the cell. "Should've paid better attention to where you were when you committed your crimes."

Hicks unlocked the door and motioned for them to come out. Becca's legs shook and her shoes felt as if they were nailed to the floor. When Seth came up behind her, carrying their belongings, she forced herself to walk.

Hicks pointed to a wooden bench along the adjacent wall. "Sit there and don't move."

She quickly obeyed and took her place on the bench before her quivering legs gave out. Seth placed their things in a pile on the floor and sat next to her.

Becca stifled a gasp when Murdock shoved his prisoner into the empty cell and drew his revolver. He aimed it at Cooley. "Untie him and lock him in," he said to Hicks as his eyes narrowed on his charge. "One wrong move, and you'll be limpin' to your trial."

Thankfully, Hicks removed the rope and locked the man in without incident.

Murdock then turned and faced *her*, gun still in hand.

Becca stared wide-eyed at the Colt. Her blood rushed to her feet and her breath left her completely. Was it possible to faint sitting down? She lifted her eyes to the hazel ones staring back at her.

Murdock's lower lip twitched. Never breaking his gaze, he swept aside his coat revealing a worn leather holster riding low on his hips, then slipped his gun into it as easily and soundlessly as if he were putting a pocket watch away. With one last glance at Seth, he turned and headed for the door.

Becca sucked in a breath. The spots clouding the edge of her vision faded.

Seth slid his hand over and threaded his fingers through hers as the Marshal retrieved his hat and left. He tightened his grip in a comforting way, but his skin was as cold as hers. She waited for words of reassurance. None came.

A sense of finality slithered like ice through her veins. The sheriff had charged her with a crime and summoned a Marshal. He said he had witnesses. Seth couldn't save her from that.

Becca longed to look at her husband, to search his eyes and find comfort and hope, but she kept her face forward. The ambivalence in his grip was enough. Her heart would crumble if she saw the same doubt in his eyes.

The longer they sat there, the more mercurial her emotions became. Beneath the suffocating layer of sadness, a growing surge of anger clawed to get free. She wasn't perfect, but she was a good person, kind and honest and chaste. All her life, she'd worked hard and followed the rules. And for her trouble, she'd been defamed and deserted. Then—when she had finally been rescued and fallen in love—falsely charged with a crime. The part of her that wasn't grieving her losses wanted to clench her fists and scream.

Hicks returned to his desk. He paused to glower at her over top of his spectacles before immersing himself in his work.

Cooley paced the cell for a while, grumbling. Then he lay down on the cot and rolled over, facing the wall.

Becca wished she could pace, too. The mindless, repetitive motion would help her cope. But she didn't dare move.

With a sigh of defeat, she closed her eyes and wished she were back in her cave.

About a half an hour later, the office door opened and Charlotte's husband walked in. As soon as he saw her, one edge of his mouth lifted, changing his expression from icy and hard to cold and smug.

"Harrison," Sheriff Hicks said, rising from his chair.

"Sherman," he replied with a nod. "I see you made the arrest."

"I did, but something's come up. I need to talk to you."

The two men eyed her in unison, then leaned toward each other and spoke in low tones, garbled words she couldn't make out. From Hicks, she thought she heard 'short notice' and 'complicate things.'

Harrison straightened. "Not a problem. I'll make sure you have what you need." His eyes cut to her, gleaming blatant victory; and, as quickly as he'd come, he was gone.

Seth's frame had already hardened beside her. His hand squeezed her fingers so tightly, the tips were turning blue. "What was that about?" he growled near her ear.

Becca wiggled her wrist and tried to tug her hand free. "Seth. You're hurting me."

He apologized and released her hand, but angry trepidation rolled off him in waves. "What's going on, Becca? Why did he look at you that way?"

"I don't know," she whispered.

"Was he with you on the trail?"

"No." She paused and looked at Seth—really looked at him. His reaction wasn't one of jealousy or doubt. Beneath his ire, the emotion creasing his face and flooding his eyes was fear. "Char—" It took effort to push the words past her dry throat. "Charlotte married him after she arrived here. He's the mayor's son."

Seth muttered an oath and raked a hand through his hair. His eyes closed as the back of his head met the wall with a hopeless thud.

Becca hugged herself and hung her head. She was doomed. She was well and truly doomed.

Wrapping herself in the silence, she began walling off the part of her heart where feelings for Seth resided. Being torn from him would be easier if she started the process now. At least that's what she told herself. She knew it was a lie.

The office door opened, sending a gust of wintery wind her way. Two men stepped over the threshold and lingered at the entrance. They twisted the brims of their hats with grimy hands, and their eyes darted around like skittish colts. They didn't seem of a criminal element, more like laborers, but the tattered clothes hanging from their gaunt frames convicted them of poverty.

One of them looked at Becca, then quickly drew his eyes down and away. Something about him was familiar. A chill settled deep in her chest when she realized why that was. She'd seen him on the train.

Someone prodded the men from behind. They shuffled forward, and Harrison Bradford appeared. "Go on," he said to them. "Tell the sheriff what you know."

The pair approached Hicks' desk like paupers approaching a king. The man on the right, the rougher-looking of the two, mumbled something to the other and elbowed him in the ribs. The second man reluctantly started speaking.

Becca couldn't hear every word that was said, but she heard enough—the irreverent lout was claiming she stole from him during the trip west. Her teeth ground together with the effort it took not to shout in defense of her innocence.

The sheriff pulled a paper from his desk and dangled it in front of the man who'd borne false witness against her. "Can you write?"

He muttered a denial and shook his head.

"Figures," Hicks huffed. "I'll write it and you can sign it."

"Write one for me, too," the other man said. "My story's the same as his, 'cept for the things she stole."

Becca fumed. The second heathen wasn't even on the train! But it didn't matter. It was her word against theirs.

The pine door creaked open again, and Charlotte stepped in, dressed head to toe in in deep blue velvet. She took in the room, her eyes growing wider with each person her green gaze touched until her brows were fully raised and she was staring at Becca. She dragged her stupefaction to her spouse. "Harrison, what's going on?"

"I'm helping Sheriff Hicks with a small matter that came up."

"What small matter?"

Harrison approached his wife, wearing a self-satisfied smile that was dimmed with a touch of discretion. "After you told me what your friend did, I decided it shouldn't go unpunished. Mrs. Emerson has been arrested for her crimes on the trail."

Charlotte looked taken aback. "I didn't want her *arrested*." She fingered a fiery red ringlet near her ear and leaned in. "I told you those things in private. I never intended for you to take them any further than our room."

"I know," he said, sounding genuinely repentant. "But we

can't overlook things like this, if we want to maintain the standards of our town."

Gone was Charlotte's haughty confidence. Instead of joining him in a sanctimonious victory cry, she chewed on her lip and worried her white lace cuffs with pale, anxious fingers.

"Don't fret," Harrison said, patting her arm. "Other witnesses have come forward. We should be able to keep your name out of this."

Charlotte glanced at the two scraggy men, then nodded, staring at the floor.

Something flickered in Harrison's eyes, a quizzical look paired with the barest scrap of compassion. "It will be over soon, my love. As luck would have it, a US Marshal is in town and he has agreed to transport Mrs. Emerson. She'll be gone by morning."

Some of the tension in Charlotte's shoulders eased, and she looked up at him with a pasty smile. "Thank you, Harrison."

"How was your visit with your mother? You weren't due back until supper. Did something happen?"

"No. I'm feeling a little under the weather. That's all."

"Go home and have Henrietta fix you some tea. I'm nearly done here. I'll be along soon."

The pine door opened again, and Becca shivered from the chill. Two men dressed in dusty farm clothes walked in, pausing at the threshold until Hicks motioned to them. They removed their hats and approached. A thin white scar extended from beneath the nearer man's forelock to just above his left eye. A familiar scar.

Thick tendrils of defeat wove their way through Becca's chest. *More witnesses.*

"We're here to speak to you about Miss Garvey," the scarred one said. He wasn't reluctant like the first two. This bold slanderer tossed a smile and a nod in her direction before telling his lie.

"She's Mrs. Emerson now," the sheriff corrected, "but go ahead."

The man opened his mouth to speak, but closed it and turned when the office door swung open. Five more people came in—two of them women and most of them familiar.

One of the men stepped forward. "We heard you arrested Rebecca Garvey. We came to give our accounts."

Hicks threw a questioning look at Harrison.

Harrison shrugged.

He apparently didn't recruit them, and that knowledge multiplied Becca's shame. These people had come forward of their own accord. They must truly hate her.

The rising hum of a gathering crowd came from outside. Charlotte backed up and lifted a handkerchief to her nose as more people pushed through the door, but Becca barely noticed the acrid smell of sweaty bodies. Her spirit was so beaten, her senses were dulled.

When the marshal cut a path through the throng, she sagged from the jolt of finality.

Hicks puffed out his chest. "These are your witnesses, Murdock. It'll take me a while, but I'll get their statements."

Murdock studied the crush of people, then turned his keen eyes on her. Thankfully, not for long. There was something about his regard that reached straight into her mind and squeezed, as if he could extract her very thoughts.

Of course, he couldn't. If he could, he'd know she was innocent.

The first two witnesses scribbled their signatures and left. Next, the man who'd smiled at her stepped up to the desk.

"What did she steal from you?" Hicks asked.

His scarred brow shot up. "Nothing."

"Nothing?"

"No. Nothing. That's what we came to tell you." He waggled a thumb back and forth between himself and his companion. "George and I traveled with Miss Gar— I mean Mrs. Emerson on the Pittman train. We heard she'd been arrested for theft, and we came to speak on her behalf."

Hicks frowned. "Just because she didn't steal from you, doesn't mean she's innocent."

"Maybe not." George said with a mild voice and steady brown eyes. "But she's a good person. What I saw of her during the trip—she was kind and she helped a lot of people. That ought'a count for something."

A ripple of nodding heads and affirming murmurs skimmed over the crowd.

"He's right," one of the men behind him said. "She was willing to help any time she was needed, and did so with nary a complaint. She cooked meals for my family five days in a row when my wife took ill."

Seth rose from the bench.

Becca did likewise. She couldn't believe her ears.

"She helped my wife, too," another man said. Phil. Phil was his name. "When Wilma caught her skirt in the fire, Miss Rebecca tended her wounds and took over her chores. She did all that and sewed my Wilma a brand new skirt without asking anything in return." He dipped his balding head in Becca's direction. "We're mighty grateful, ma'am, much obliged."

Becca bit her lip to keep it from trembling.

"I traded her a box of jelly for some corn," yet another man said. Liam. "I didn't know my wife had hidden our money inside. Mrs. Emerson returned the cash to us before Esther even knew it was gone—every last cent." His eyes sharpened on the sheriff. "I ask you, would a thief do that?"

A few people near the edge of the group began whispering among themselves and casting glances. The oldest man among them lifted a thin, gnarled finger. "That's your thief. I'll swear out a statement against her right now."

He was pointing straight at Charlotte.

"What's the meaning of this," Harrison blustered. "My wife didn't steal anything."

"Oh yes she did." A short, scrappy wisp of a man pushed his way to the edge. "I seen her myself. She took a tin of tea from my wagon. I didn't report her because I could manage without and I didn't need no trouble on the train—but she took it. I seen her snatch it with my own two eyes."

"Come to think of it," one of the women said, "I saw her loitering around quite a few wagons." Murmurs of agreement went up again.

"I also seen her snooping through the Garvey's wagon," the short man added. "She 'uz friendly with them, so I didn't think nothin' of it at the time, but now I wonder."

Murdock hooked his thumbs into the belt of his holster. "Better start taking those witness statements, Sheriff. I'm going to need them when I transport Mrs. Bradford."

Charlotte's jaw dropped as far as her husband's. "Harrison, do something."

Harrison pressed his lips together, and fire flashed in his eyes. "You're not taking my wife anywhere, especially with nothing more than the word of these—these *commoners*. My father is the mayor—"

"Save your breath." Murdock nudged his lapel aside, exposing his badge. "I don't answer to you."

Harrison's mouth gaped again, and then it clamped shut. His jaw bulged, and squiggly veins popped out along his temple.

Hicks held up two papers. "What about the signed statements accusing Mrs. Emerson?"

Murdock stared at them for a moment. "Send those, too."

Becca's heart sank.

"*If*," he continued, "the complainants will stick with their stories, *when pressed*, and their travel with the train can be verified."

The sheriff looked to Harrison.

He scrunched his lips into an annoyed knot, then sighed and gave a small shake of his head.

Murdock grunted.

Charlotte's peachy skin turned the hue of used wash water. Next to her husband's florid face, the peaked shade of gray looked almost white.

A scruffy young man emerged from the crowd, dressed in a tattered blue shirt and pants covered with worn leather chaps. Piercing blue eyes peered from under shaggy brown, hat-dented hair and over a moustache and beard that looked no less unkempt.

Murdock's eyes narrowed on the newcomer.

Charlotte's eyes widened, twin black dots expanding to fill the green, and she grew even paler.

After a cursory glance around the room, the man headed for the sheriff's desk, his gate rolling and easy, and his spurs clinking as he walked. "I'd like to add my statement, too," he drawled with a heavy Georgian accent.

Hicks threw an uneasy glance at Harrison. "I think we have enough witnesses from the Pittman train."

"I'm not from the train. And Mrs. Bradford's crimes on the trail are the least of her worries."

"Really," Murdock said. "How's that?"

"She hired me to get rid of these folks." He gestured to

Becca and Seth. "Wanted me to lay in wait and ambush them, then dispose of the bodies."

A collective gasp came from the crowd as Becca's breath froze in her lungs.

"You can't trust what he says," Charlotte blurted. "That man's a criminal."

"No, ma'am." The corners of the newcomer's mouth twitched with a smile that was trying to break free. "I just look like one."

Murdock lifted his chin in Charlotte's direction. "Take her into custody, would you, Josh?"

"J—what?" she sputtered. "You know him?"

"Yup. Hired him myself, as a matter of fact. He's my deputy."

Harrison looked on the verge of apoplexy. "You can't arrest her for murder. She didn't kill anyone!"

"That's true," Murdock said, "but we have her on theft. That's enough to get her in front of the judge."

His deputy smirked. "Maybe we should save ourselves some time, John. We could turn her over to the mob outside and let *them* decide what to do with her."

"You wouldn't!" Charlotte screeched. "You can't put my fate in the hands of those people!"

"Why not?" Josh said evenly. "It was good enough for Mr. Cantwell."

Charlotte sucked her outrage back in on a gasp.

A couple of the men from the train lowered their gazes. Becca didn't draw attention to it, though. They had come to her aid. That was penance enough.

Josh kept his eyes trained on Charlotte as he slowly circled her, like a cat stalking a grounded bird. "You thought you got away with that, didn't you? I know quite a lot, Mrs. Bradford.

Ever since you approached me two days ago, I've been doing some snooping of my own. It's amazing the things a man can discover if he asks the right questions."

Murdock's cheek creased, adding a look of annoyance to the permanent grimace he wore. "I wondered where you were when you didn't meet back up with me," he grumbled. "I coulda used your help with Cooley."

"I know." Josh flicked a grin at his boss. "But when this prim and proper *lady,* in her East Coast clothes and her five-dollar shoes, lured me into the shadows and beseeched me to commit a double murder, I figured you'd want me to turn over a few rocks and see what crawled out."

Murdock grunted again.

Josh clasped his hands behind his back and kept circling. The slow, steady clank of his spurs rang like a knell, and Charlotte's shoulders twitched with each step. "Here's what I think happened. I think you wanted something that belonged to Miss Garvey, but as long as she was around, you couldn't have it. When you discovered an avalanche had blocked the path, you saw your chance.

"Tell me, *Charlotte,*" he said, leaning in near her ear. "Did you tingle inside when you told her the rocks were going to take all day to clear? Did you enjoy the shiver of danger when you lied?" He leaned a breath closer. "Of course, you did."

Harrison bristled. "Stop insulting my wife."

"Shut up." The deputy resumed his methodical pacing. "All you had to do was get Miss Garvey left behind. You knew the train was splitting up. Even if she ran after it, she wouldn't know which way to go.

"And by concealing her absence until the next day, thus altering the location of the search, you made sure the scouts' efforts were useless."

Charlotte moistened her lips and shifted uneasily.

"Your fellow travelers never put the pieces together." He tapped his head. "But I did."

Josh turned his eyes on Becca. His brow dipped and his gaze eased at the sight of her tears. When he focused on Charlotte again, his body hardened like that of a predator. "Those people aren't stupid," he told her, "just misled and distracted. You made sure of that.

"First, you had to keep them from missing Miss Garvey too soon. The story you told her mother—that she'd gone to help Mrs. Godfrey with her children—was perfect, wasn't it? Telling her that, and saying Rebecca had gone to bed early, kept her from looking for her daughter for nearly a whole day. Then, while everyone was out searching, you went to work hiding Rebecca's things in Melvin Cantwell's wagon, throwing them off your trail."

The deputy stopped in front of her and glared, just inches from her nose. "You must have a godforsaken pit where your heart should be. You left an innocent girl to die, and then you cast suspicion on an honest man and said *nothing* when you could have spared his life. You had best hit your knees tonight and pray for the fate of your worthless soul."

"You're wrong about me," Charlotte cried. "I didn't know they planned to kill Mr. Cantwell. I thought they were just going to beat him up—you know—teach him a lesson. And I didn't leave Rebecca to die. I made sure she had a canteen and a knife. I even left some of her rations behind so she'd have food."

Becca clapped a hand to her mouth.

Charlotte turned her pleading eyes on her. "Why did you stay there, Becca? I never meant for you to stay. You were supposed to get rescued. All you had to do was ask for a ride with someone on the next train."

"You didn't mean for her to die," Josh said from beyond Charlotte's far shoulder.

"No. Never."

"That's why you hired me to kill her."

Charlotte snapped her eyes to him, quivering.

"Time to go, Mrs. Bradford," Murdock interjected. "I suggest you change into something more comfortable. We've got a long ride."

She grabbed the sleeve of her husband's coat with both hands. "Harrison, *do something.*"

He shook free, his face stiff and his eyes glacial. "I'll have the maid bring you your traveling clothes."

Charlotte whimpered as if he'd struck her.

She spun her head around so fast, her hat tipped sideways and some of her fiery curls tore free. "Look what you've done," she spat. *"Miss Rebecca's so kind, Miss Rebecca's so good*—you're nothing but a glorified peasant."

Her wild eyes suddenly narrowed and raked Seth up and down. Charlotte fixed her gaze on Becca and curved her lips into a wicked smile. "It's fitting you ended up with a penniless drifter. You wouldn't know what to do with a rich man anyway."

Becca reached for Seth's hand and found a fist. She rubbed the bulging muscles of his arm with her fingers. As Josh brought Charlotte's hands together and bound her wrists with rope, the lumps began to soften.

One by one, the witnesses began writing their statements.

A man who had squeezed in the door earlier with the crush of people removed his hat. When he turned and straightened to his full height, Becca's heart clenched. *Nathan.* She was wholly devoted to her husband, but she would never forget her first love.

Seth's arm snaked possessively around her waist, and she was glad for it. Her wobbly legs had grown so weak, she feared they'd give out.

Nathan scanned the room until he found her. A slurry of emotions churned in his cobalt eyes—the most notable of which was pain. Whether it arose from seeing her wronged or seeing her with another man, she wasn't sure.

Seth tightened his grip and lifted his chin, drawing Nathan's attention to him.

Nathan's lids lowered briefly. When they opened again, pain had given way to resignation and wordless appeal. He didn't have to say a thing. The message *take care of her* was heartrendingly clear.

Becca's throat burned with bittersweet pride as Nathan made his way through the crowd. He stood tall and self-assured, like a single sunflower amidst a field of wheat.

"Mr. Murdock." His rich baritone infused the room as he extended his hand. "My name is Nathan Keating," he said as the marshal gave a cursory shake. "I'm here on behalf of Mrs. Emerson. I traveled with the Pittman train."

"You'll need to give your statement to the Sheriff."

"I will." Nathan reached into his coat pocket. "But first I'd like to give you this." He handed Murdock a small card. "My uncle is a senator. Everything needed to contact him is there. I'm sure he'd be grateful if you passed this on to the federal judge."

"Why would I do that?"

"My uncle has been working to gain support for a change of law—a bill that would expand the felony statue to include solicitation of murder. Mrs. Bradford's case would be perfect for his cause."

Murdock smiled for the first time since he'd arrived. He slid his hand under the lapel of his jacket and tucked the card away. "Thank you, Mr. Keating. I'll see that he gets it."

Nathan cut his eyes to Charlotte. The brokenness that had muted them earlier was gone. His humanity was still there, but it was eclipsed by the cold precision of justice.

As witnesses signed their statements, they trickled over to wish Becca well. Nathan caught her eye again, but only to exchange a small smile before leaving. Anything more would have been too painful, for both of them. Becca watched him go, and then she tamped down her grief and gave her supporters the gracious reception they deserved.

When the crowd finally thinned, a faintly familiar man approached them with tentative steps and his hat in his hands. "Miss Gar—" He nodded in deference to Seth. "Beg your pardon. *Mrs. Emerson.*" He had a deep voice that made Becca think of moss-covered gravel and weathered gray eyes that had seen at least twice as many years as hers. Wrinkles fanned out from their corners like cracks in drought-hardened farmland.

"You may not remember me," he continued. "My name is Frank Sanders. I traveled a few wagons back from yours in the train."

"I remember you, Mr. Sanders. How have you been?"

"Very well, ma'am. Thank you for asking. I don't wish to impose on your courtesy, but I have some information I think you might want." His eyes twinkled as his lips lifted into a smile. "I know where your parents are."

Chapter Thirty-Two

As soon as they rounded the curve leading to the house, Seth knew they'd found the right place. The sharp rise of Becca's chest and the tremble of her lips told of recognition—not of the house, but of something resting on its porch. Whatever the object was, her eyes were locked on it.

The modest farmhouse stood eerily still. A straight-back chair and two rockers sat to the left of the door, and a water barrel to the right. Other than that and curtains barely visible through dingy windows, the place was bare. No rose bushes adorned the yard like the ones in Becca's drawings of her childhood home, only a weed-riddled vegetable garden that had succumbed to winter.

Seth drew the wagon to a stop and surveyed the rest of the property. The barn and the fields weren't much better. If not for the presence of livestock, he'd have thought the place abandoned.

He dismounted the wagon and helped Becca down. "It'll be

all right," he assured, planting a kiss on her temple and taking her hand in his.

The barn door opened. A man came out and headed in their direction. He wasn't Becca's father—he was too young—but he held his shoulders square and strode with authority.

Seth raised a hand in greeting and the man did likewise, stopping a few feet away, his expression guarded.

"I'm Seth Emerson and this is my wife."

"Ma'am." The man tipped his hat, his face softening. It hardened again as he returned his attention to Seth. "Augustus Lassiter. What can I do for ya?"

"We're looking for Levi and Martha Garvey. Have we found the right place?"

Augustus frowned, his mouth matching the curve of his horseshoe-shaped moustache. "You might've. What do you want?"

"We want to speak with them. My wife is their daughter."

The man's thick brows lifted to the brim of his hat. He narrowed his eyes and studied Becca.

"Well," Seth said. "Is this the Garvey's place or not?"

"It is," Augustus finally admitted, still eyeing her. "Stay here." He walked over to a small shack near the paddock and stuck his head inside. He hooked a thumb over his shoulder and shifted on his feet. A few moments later, he backed away.

Becca made a strangled noise when her father emerged. Her grip tightened as he crossed the yard.

The corners of Levi's mouth drew down. At first it looked like a scowl, but as he neared, the quiver of his lips and the sheen in his eyes made it clear the man was struggling to control his emotions.

"Pa?" The word was spoken so softly, Seth wondered if Levi heard it.

He had. His arms lifted, and shaky, work-worn hands turned out in welcome.

Becca let go and moved toward her father with tentative steps. Her steps quickly gained strength, and she ran to him with the candid devotion of a little girl.

Home. She was finally home.

Becca buried her face in her father's coat and filled her lungs with the smell of hay and leather and tobacco, all the things she associated with him. "Pa..."

"*Rebecca.*" He hugged her so tightly, his arms squeezed the air from her lungs. "When we couldn't find you, I thought—" His voice broke and he held her tighter. "I can't believe it's really you," he whispered.

"It's me," Becca choked out, clutching him just as fiercely. "It's me."

They held each other for a long time, her fingers gripping fistfuls of his coat and his arms wrapping her so completely, they blocked out the light. His breathing eased, and then it roughened again. He turned his face into her hair, and his teeth ground together. "Did Melvin..." He swallowed audibly. "Did he hurt you?"

Becca's heart broke. Not only had her father lived all this time thinking she was dead, he'd lived with a worse lie, too. "No one hurt me, Pa. Mr. Cantwell had nothing to do with my disappearance."

He pulled back. "But we found your things in his wagon."

"I know." She drew a deep breath and gave him a watery smile. "It's a long story. I'll tell you everything over supper. That is, if you'll have us."

"Of course, you can stay." He hugged her again, then lifted his head and looked over her shoulder.

That simple gesture sent Becca's mind racing right along with her heart. What would her father think of Seth? Would he be angry that she married without asking him first?

Steeling herself for a possible scolding, she led him to the other two men who were blinking and clearing their throats. "Pa, this is Seth Emerson... my husband."

Seth smiled and extended his hand. "It's a pleasure to finally meet you, Mr. Garvey."

Her father didn't move.

"Pa," she prompted, "Seth is the one who rescued me and brought me to California."

The starch left his shoulders. He clasped Seth's hand and wrapped it with his other. "Same to you, Seth," he said as they shook. Moisture gathered along the edges his lids. "Thank you for—" He cleared his throat. "Thank you."

Becca glanced at the house and tried to quell her growing apprehension. Her mother had always been vigilant, with senses that bordered on preternatural. Even from the farthest reaches of the cellar, she could hear a wagon long before it reached the yard. The fact she hadn't been the first one to greet them... "How's Ma?"

Something in her pa's expression shifted. His eyes took on a pitying curve, the way they had when her favorite colt took ill. "Your ma has been through a lot, Rebecca. She's not the same woman you remember. Your return is going to be a shock to her. I'll need to prepare her before she sees you."

At her father's urging, she and Seth followed him to the house, careful to soften their steps as they ascended the porch. Silently, they filed into the foyer and hung up their coats and hats.

Becca's spirit sagged at what she saw. A layer of dust coated every surface, and the windows were so dingy she could barely see out. The rugs were caked with dirt, and the floor looked like it hadn't been scrubbed in months. The mother she knew would never neglect her house like this.

She turned back to her pa.

"Stay here," he whispered. "I'll call for you when she's ready." He touched an index finger to his lips and went through a doorway on her right.

Becca eased forward in the direction her father had gone. She clamped a hand over her mouth and blinked back tears when she laid eyes on her mother.

Wearing a faded brown dress, she sat at the kitchen table, totally motionless. Her back was to them, but her face reflected in the window above the sink—a murky portrait of graying hair, lifeless eyes, hollow cheeks. Something more brutal than time had aged her.

Fighting for control of her emotions, Becca retreated. Her back met Seth's solid chest almost immediately, and she turned into his waiting embrace.

"Don't cry," he murmured near her ear. "If the effect you had on your pa is any indication, your return will render healing to your ma."

If the shock doesn't kill her first.

Becca blinked and looked up into her husband's face. She so wanted to believe him.

She dried her cheeks and crept back in time to see her pa round the table and pull out a chair.

"Oh... Levi," her ma said, emerging from her daze. "Is it time for supper already?"

"No, no." He lowered himself into the seat. "I came in because I have something to tell you, some news." Her father had always been a devoted husband, but the way he looked at her mother ruined all Becca's attempts to stem the flow of tears. When he took her ma's hand in both of his and smiled, his loving tenderness was as undeniable as the salty rivers running down her face. "Do you remember when our daughter went missing?"

"Emily?"

His chest rose and fell with a measured breath, but the love in his eyes never faltered. "No, not Emily." The softness of his voice didn't either. "I'm speaking of Rebecca, the daughter we lost on the trail."

Becca waited for a word, a wail, a hitch in her mother's breath—*something*.

Nothing but apathetic silence filled the room.

The woman who'd borne her and raised her for nigh eighteen years sat there as though he'd mentioned something insignificant.

The hope Becca had clung to for months drained away, and her throat went as dry as the dirt on the trail. Rejection wasn't the worst thing she faced.

Seth's hand closed over her shoulder, and, for the first time since this odd conversation began, her father's countenance wavered.

"You remember Rebecca," he said, regaining his composure. "She got lost while we were traveling to California. She..." Something glimmered in his expression—the look he got whenever he conceived the solution to a problem and his thoughts abruptly changed course. "She found a way back to us, Martha."

"She did?"

"Yes." He leaned closer, conspiratorial almost. "Would you like to see her?"

"Well, I..." Her mother tucked a stray lock of hair behind her ear and glanced at the cluttered counters. "I'm not fit to receive guests."

Seth's fingers tightened and Becca pressed a hand to her trembling lips.

"Rebecca won't mind," Pa said. "She's not pretentious that way. Never has been."

"Oh, all right," her mother relented.

He lifted his head. "Rebecca, would you come in, please?"

Seth squeezed her shoulder once more. He slid his hand downward and flattened it against the small of her back. "Go," he whispered. "I'll wait here."

The legs of her father's chair scraped the floor, and he stood, waiting.

Becca swiped the moisture from her face and straightened her spine. However her mother received her, she'd make the best of it.

She treaded softly as she entered the kitchen. Her hands tingled and numbness weighted her limbs. Her throbbing heart lay heavy in her chest, but she managed to lift the corners of her lips as she walked to the end of the table and turned around. "Hello, Ma."

Her mother slowly rose. A crease formed between her brows, and her tired eyes regarded Becca like those of a long lost acquaintance struggling to place a face. "Something's... different."

Becca glanced at her pa, but his expression gave nothing away.

She looked down at her clothes and brushed her fingers over the cloth. The brown wool skirt and white cotton blouse were garments her mother had made—the same ones she was wearing the day she was left. The skirt had been mended in places and the sleeves of her blouse had thinned at the elbows, but the outfit was still recognizable.

Her fingers traced upward from her waist, along the line of tiny buttons, and closed around the tip of her collar. "It must be my hair," she said, meeting her mother's gaze. "I've started wearing it up."

Her ma tilted her head, still lost in her musing. A smile curved her lips and further crinkled the skin around her eyes— eyes that suddenly glowed like newly sparked kindling. "*Rebecca*. I've been looking all over for you, child. Where have you been?"

Becca choked back a sob and stepped into her mother's outstretched arms. "I was lost for a while," she whispered, trying not to cry. "I— I've been looking for you, too." That battle was forfeited the moment she felt her mother's bony frame through the muslin of her housedress. Did she also forget to eat?

She wept softly into her mother's shoulder until the kitchen rumbled with the masculine clearing of throats.

Becca drew away and dried her face. "Ma, there's someone I'd like you to meet." She motioned to Seth, who still lurked in the hall. Cautiously at first, he entered the room and came to stand at her side.

"This is Seth," she said simply. The rest could wait.

Her mother's face lit up again. "Hello, Seth."

His smile was equally warm. "Hello, Mrs. Garvey. It's nice to meet you."

"Martha," Pa said, gaining her mother's attention, "I invited them to stay and have supper with us."

Her ma's eyes lost their sparkle. "How am I going to cook for everyone, Levi?"

"I'll come back in a couple of hours and help you."

Becca pinched folds of her skirt and worried them with her

fingers. "That won't be necessary." She eyed her husband in silent question. "Seth got a deer yesterday, and we still have rations from the trip." At his nod of approval, she looked back to her pa. "Let me make supper. I'll help with the kitchen, too."

Her father's lips pressed together. He despised the taking of charity. But they were family, so it wasn't really charity. His face eased. He'd apparently drawn the same conclusion. "Thank you, Rebecca." He pushed his chair under the table. "Seth, let's go stable your team. Daylight's a wastin' and I've got work to do."

"Yes sir." Seth followed her pa out of the kitchen. Footsteps trailed off as the men retrieved their outerwear and exited the front door.

Becca smiled at her ma, then stared at the grimy, disheveled kitchen. How she was going to clean it in time to cook the evening meal, she didn't know.

Levi dabbed his mouth with his napkin. "Excellent meal, Rebecca."

"Yes. Very good, Ma'am," Augustus seconded.

Both her pa and his hired hand had tucked into their plates and shoveled food into their mouths like starving men. Seth wasn't far behind. The lot of them had barely sat down and said grace before serving spoons began scraping bottom.

"Thank you. I should have made more," Becca said for the sake of courtesy. She'd made a feast. "There's pie," she added with a lilt in her voice and a lift of her brow.

A chorus of requests went up.

She placed a hand on her mother's arm to stop her from rising. "I'll get it. You rest." Her mother had helped with both the cleaning and the cooking. She was capable of simpler tasks as long as she had someone to remind her of things and prompt her from time to time. Even so, the extra activity had taken its toll.

The conversation remained light through dessert, as it had during supper. Her father's eyes held endless questions, but he didn't give them voice. The truth would ravage his heart and kill his appetite. He seemed to know that as well as she.

Once the pie was gone, Becca summoned her courage and told her story. Emotions assaulted her pa as she recounted the last sixteen months of her life. She knew his rigid posture and distorted face showed but a fraction of the pain and rage he felt inside. She grieved her mother's affliction. But, for this, it was a merciful protection.

Becca reached across the table and covered her father's fist with her hand. "I've been wronged—we all have—and my life didn't go as planned, but I found you again. And" —she managed a smile for Seth— "a good man found *me*."

Seth had been holding her other hand under the table the whole time. His work-roughened fingers squeezed hers.

Outwardly, her father's ire cooled, but embers of hatred smoldered in his eyes. Just as with her, his hunger for vengeance would burn for a very long time.

"Levi?" her ma said in a quiet voice. "I'm not sure what to do?"

"About what, sweetheart?"

"About our guests. I readied the spare room for Rebecca, but where is Seth going to sleep?"

Augustus choked on his coffee.

"One room is enough," Becca murmured to her ma. The men sported bright pink cheeks. If the feel of hers was any clue, they must be absolutely flaming.

Her father shoved his chair back. "C'mon, Gus. Let's finish up evenin' chores."

Gus was on his feet before the last word was out. Seth was already standing. She'd never seen three men in such a rush to quit a room.

Gus paused in front of her, his embarrassment replaced with a different kind of unease. "You're a brave woman, Mrs. Emerson—braver than a lot'a men I know. I'm sorry for all you went through." He looked down at the toe of his boot, then struggled to meet her gaze. "And I'm sorry for the way I treated you when you first arrived. You, too Mr. Emerson. I, uh..."

"You were protecting my parents, Mr. Lassiter. No apology necessary."

Soft lamplight cast shadows in the valley of Seth's back as he peeled his undershirt off over his head. Becca paused from turning down the bed when he bent forward and rinsed in the basin. The expanse of shifting muscle was both arousing and mesmerizing. She'd never tire of the sight.

Gathering the folds of her nightgown in one hand, she braced herself for pain and climbed into bed. Her body listed like a falling tree and landed on the mattress with a poof. She groaned.

Seth twisted around, water dripping from his hair. "You all right?"

Becca clenched her teeth as the sharp spasms in her back and limbs began to fade to cramping aches. "No. I hurt all over."

He eyed her from underneath the towel as he dried himself, a grin slowly forming. "What happened to my tough little rabbit?

You used to work circles around me."

She stuck out her tongue at him and regretted it. Even that simple movement hurt.

He chuckled and removed his trousers. His chest still quivered with a deep rumble as he crossed the room and climbed in next to her.

Becca poked out her lower lip. "It isn't funny."

"No, it's not." Then why was he still laughing?

He reached for her and she pulled away. *Ouch.*

Seth tilted his head and gave her his most irresistible look of contrition.

She tried to steel herself against his charms, but it was no use. She sighed and forgave him with her eyes.

He reached for her again, but instead of gathering her to his chest like he usually did, he nudged her shoulder as if to push her away. "Turn and face the window." With a frown and a groan, she did as he said.

His large hands wrapped around her shoulders and his strong fingers began kneading her muscles. One by one, he turned them from stubborn lumps of dough to pats of melting butter.

Ohhhh—mmmmmmm.

His chest rumbled again. She must've moaned out loud.

He nudged her on over to her stomach and moved his ministrations to her lower back. Her eyes drifted closed.

"Don't fall asleep. I'm next."

"I thought big stromng men didm't get sore mufsles," she mumbled into the pillow.

"When they're trying to please their new father-in-law, they do."

She turned her face to the side. "Is that why you were in such a rush to help with evening chores?"

"Huh?"

"You jumped up from the table faster than Gus." Out the corner of her eye, she glimpsed him shake his head in amusement.

"That wasn't bootlicking, Becca. It was self-preservation. Your ma had just brought to mind the image of the two of us in bed together. I *jumped up* so I could get out of the way in case your father took a swing at me."

Becca frowned and rose up on her elbow. "Why would he do that? We're married."

"Trust me." Seth patted her backside. "When it comes to a man's daughter, that doesn't always matter."

He stretched out on his stomach and crossed his arms, hugging his pillow and wedging it under his chest. Becca placed her hands on his back. She tried them at different angles, but none of the positions gave her any leverage.

There was only one thing to do. She'd just have to sit on him.

Bunching the hem of her gown, she rose up on her knees and straddled Seth's narrow hips. They were surprisingly thick. She tried to give his muscles the same treatment he'd given hers, but her hands were sore. Besides cooking and cleaning the kitchen—both before and after supper—she'd swept the floors and dusted the parlor. It was going to take a solid week, at least, to properly scour the house... if Seth was willing to stay.

He squirmed underneath her, lightly bouncing her on his behind. "I like you there, rabbit. It gives me all kinds of ideas."

Wha—! "You're incorrigible."

"Yes, I am. And I'm facing the wrong way for what I have in mind."

She swatted the bulge of muscle just below his shoulder blade and scolded him again; but, in truth, she liked his playful side. Their wedding night had been overshadowed by doubt and fear and the distressing events of the day, and all their couplings since had been tender but solemn. She was ready for happier times, both inside the bedroom and out.

Becca climbed off his sturdy frame and stretched out on her side, smirking at his groan of disapproval. "What if my father were to hear us?" she teased. Not likely—they were upstairs and her parents were down. "He might bust in and punch you."

The corner of Seth's mouth lifted, but not for long. He sighed and flipped to his back. "He may hang me from the highest tree, but it won't be for that."

"What's that supposed to mean?"

He glanced at her sideways. "Nothing. Come here." He slipped an arm under her neck, then he nudged her closer and tugged the covers up over them. His lower body smelled of horses and hay, but the scent of soap lingered on his chest. "How'd things go with your Ma?"

Becca adjusted her shoulder and head until she was comfortable. "Better than I expected."

"That's good... isn't it?"

He must've noticed her frown. "Yes, but— It's strange. At times, she seemed like her old self. She'd get busy drying dishes or peeling potatoes and do a fine job. She'd even talk to me and carry on a sensible conversation. Then she'd change. She'd forget where something was or how to perform a task she used to be able to do without thinking. But she wouldn't ask for help. She'd just stand there, looking lost."

"Maybe, now that you're here, she'll improve."

"Maybe... I'm sorry she embarrassed you."

He looked at her with warm eyes and an easy smile. "Your ma may occasionally say things that send us men running for the barn, but she's not an embarrassment."

Becca squinted one eye and looked at him through the other.

"Can we stay here a while?"

"Yes. In fact, I think we should. Your ma's not the only one who needs help. Your pa is struggling, too."

"He's not ill, is he?"

"No. He's as keen as a fox and as strong as a mule. Your pa's problems have to do with the land and the livestock." Seth shifted so he was facing her. "The reason your folks fell behind on the trail was that your ma took ill. At first, she was just grieving... slowing things down. But after they crossed the river, she had some kind of episode. Your pa couldn't make it to Blackwater. He had to stop here and settle for a second rate claim.

"Then he had a run of bad luck. Rustlers stole his oxen right after he got here—one of the reasons he hired Gus. His plowing was delayed until he got a new team, and then the water went bad. He had to put off planting to dig another well. All that made for a poor harvest.

"Your pa is a smart, hardworking man. But even with Gus's help, he can hardly run the place, much less prosper. Even if the land was choice, there aren't enough hours in the day. Both of them have to sacrifice work time to help your ma. Gus takes up slack with her chores, and your pa comes in early for meals and helps her make whatever they can throw together in a short time."

Becca stared past Seth at the jagged, bare limbs outside. This wasn't the life she'd envisioned at all. And she doubted Seth would want to settle down and make a permanent home with her parents. "What happens when we leave?"

Seth rolled to his back and tucked her against his side. "Let's stay put for a while and see how things go. If we share our rations and if Gus and I can manage a few good hunts, the five of us can make it through winter. Besides, there's not much chance of me finding gainful employment until spring."

His plan made sense, and he sounded completely amenable. But later, when she awoke, chilled, to his empty side of the bed, Seth was standing alone in the dark, staring out the window.

Chapter Thirty-Three

Seth walked out of the kitchen, and Becca flinched when he closed the door. He hadn't slammed it. In fact, he'd closed it quietly. Too quietly. Less than two weeks had passed since moving in with her parents, and her husband barely made a sound anymore.

Everyone got along. Her pa had nothing but praise for her mate. But something was eating at Seth, and all her attempts to coax it out of him had been fruitless.

Becca chuckled ruefully in the empty room. She had gotten her wish—she'd made it home before Christmas—but the holiday hadn't been anything like she'd dreamed. A modest spread of food was consumed in subdued ambiance, and there were no gifts to exchange.

After the meal, the men had retired to the parlor to speculate on the coming year. She'd walked in on dour expressions when she went to serve coffee. The frowns had quickly been replaced with smiles, but she wondered if the future of the farm was bleaker than the men let on. She'd already surmised that Seth would have to choose between helping her pa and leaving him shorthanded to take a paying job. One option would extend Seth's sacrifice; the other would increase everyone's hardship.

He had told her on their wedding night that he didn't regret marrying her. Now she feared he'd changed his mind.

Becca put the last of the breakfast dishes away and went upstairs to help with chores. Her mood lifted at the sight of her ma snapping a sheet and floating it onto the bed. Today was a good day. Her mother's eyes twinkled and she hummed like old times as she deftly smoothed the wrinkles from the cloth and tucked the corners.

Becca scooped the folded quilt out of the chair and assisted her mother to center it on the bed.

"Your husband offered to plant my kitchen garden as soon as we're past the last freeze."

So he hasn't gone mute after all. Just as quickly as the scornful thought came, Becca squelched the urge to be bitter. Seth had been nothing but kind to her ma. "That's nice."

"Seth sure is a fine man."

The honest declaration snuffed the guttering wick of resentment. "Yes, he is."

Her ma reached for a pillowcase and paused. "He's been awful quiet lately. Have you two had a falling out?"

"No. Not that I'm aware of." They each slid a pillow into its case and place it on the bed. "I've tried to get him to tell me what's bothering him, but he won't."

"Well, you know what Aunt Bertie used to say—God made woman from one of Adam's ribs, but when He made man, He used the dust of a mule."

Becca couldn't hold back her laughter.

Her ma hugged her to her side as they walked toward the

door. "Your pa used to have sullen spells, too. I'd just keep trying until I found a way to pry it from him. Usually, whatever was vexing him wasn't nearly as bad as he made it seem."

Becca sighed. "I'll talk to Seth again, when he gets back home."

"Back from where?"

"The men all went into town."

"No, just Gus and your pa. Seth's around here somewhere." She patted Becca's arm. "Go find him. And this time, keep pressing him until you get an answer. Don't give up."

Becca searched the barn and the fields with no luck. Maybe it wasn't such a good day for her ma after all. On the way back, she stopped again at the tack room. She'd called to him from outside before and gotten no answer, but they could have crossed paths while she was searching. Or...

She didn't announce her presence this time, just opened the door and stepped inside.

Seth rose from the crate he was sitting on, abruptly shifting from his defeated posture into a stiff, stone-faced man she barely recognized. "What are you doing here?"

She took a step forward. "I came to find you because I'm worried about you."

A muscle ticked along his jaw. "Well, you needn't have bothered." He turned away and walked across the room, bracing hands on the workbench and staring out the small window above it.

Becca closed the door behind her. "What's wrong with you?"

"Nothing."

"Why are you acting this way?"

He didn't answer.

"Have I done something to make you angry?"

"No." The steel left his voice with the word.

"Then why are you treating me like this?"

"I don't know what you're talking about," he muttered.

Becca crossed the room until she was standing right behind him. "You never smile anymore, and you go about your days barely saying a word."

He kept staring out the window, hands splayed on the wooden table, muscles taut and bulging under his shirt.

"You haven't touched me in days... not even a kiss." She felt more unwanted than when she'd been left behind on the trail. She placed a tentative hand on his shoulder. "I love you. I miss the husband I married."

A humorless chuckle echoed in the musty space. "And after years of living with a man who has no means to support you, will you still love me then?"

Becca wrapped her arms around him and pressed her cheek to his back. "I'll love you no matter what."

He straightened and his hands left the table, but he made no move to touch her. "Thanks for trying, but like I've told you, you're not a very good liar."

"*I'm not lying.*" She clung to him tightly and fought back a sob.

He didn't react. Just stood there like a tower of stone.

A surge of anger pushed back her tears. If he didn't want her, he was going to have to face her and say it. She wasn't giving up this time.

Becca let go of him and stepped back. "If you regret marrying me, then turn around and tell me so."

She gave him plenty of time to respond, but he didn't move.

Didn't speak.

Embracing him again, she splayed her hands across his chest. She stood on her toes and grazed her lips across the back of his neck.

A shudder rippled through him and raised little bumps on his skin. Her tower of stone was beginning to crack.

"You can push me away and act like you don't care," she whispered, her breath skimming his ear, "but I'm not giving up. Do you want to know why? Because I'm not the one pretending." Becca slid her hand lower and molded her fingers around the evidence of his arousal. "You are."

Seth ripped her hands from his body and spun around with a growl. His lips were on hers before she could suck in a breath. He banded his arms around her, crushing her to him, and ravaged her mouth like a man possessed.

"You picked the wrong man to love," he rasped when he came up for air.

"No I didn't!" she shot back as his mouth came down on hers.

Seth's hands roamed her body, matching the desperation of his kiss. And she gave it right back, groping and clawing as if she couldn't get enough. She never would.

Without breaking their kiss, he picked her up and plopped her gracelessly onto the table. His lips went for her neck and his hands went for her blouse. He freed a few buttons and cursed her chemise, then pushed her shirt aside and closed his mouth over her breast anyway.

Becca tunneled her fingers into his hair and moaned as he drew on her nipple, laving it through the warm, wet fabric. "Touch me," she begged.

Switching to the other breast, Seth fumbled with her skirts until he had them up over her knees. His hand was on her so fast she cried out. He twisted it this way and that, trying to get a better angle. He finally sank two fingers inside her as his thumb pushed into her folds and moved in jerky circles.

The smell of hay and leather assailed her along with Seth's heady scent. She was so near the edge of ecstasy, she wanted to jump, but she couldn't. He was being too rough.

"Hurry, Becca," Seth panted near her ear. "I want you so bad, I can't wait."

She turned his face up with both hands. "Then don't."

He shook his head, but then he yanked his hand free, grabbed her, and pulled her hips forward. After fumbling with his fly, he palmed the small of her back and pressed himself against her with his other hand. He swallowed her moan with his own as he pushed all the way in with a single thrust.

He braced his hands behind her and pounded into her, bumping the table and jarring her father's tools with each strike of his hips. After dislodging her and shifting her back into place several times, he growled in frustration.

Seth threw her arms around his neck and demanded she hold on. He lifted her without even withdrawing, spun them around, and pinned her with her back to the wall.

Becca dug her fingers into his rock-hard shoulders as he gripped her thighs and drove himself into her, thankful for the ropes and bridles behind her that softened the blows. With each relentless slam of his hips, she could feel his shame and his anger. And his love. He couldn't hide it. He was clinging to her just as fiercely she was to him.

She closed her eyes and lost herself in the storm of a man who was her lover. The stretch and bite of each thrust kept her on edge, each plunge forcing air from her lungs. The way he savagely claimed her. Filled her. She wished it could go on without end.

Unintelligible words rumbled from Seth's throat and his eyes clenched shut. He buried his face in her neck and shuddered his release with a guttural groan.

His chest heaved, and his iron grip on her thighs loosened.

"Feel better?" she murmured as his passion ebbed.

He lifted his head, revealing dark eyes swimming with vulnerability.

Becca nuzzled his face and brushed a kiss against corner of his mouth. "I love you."

He withdrew and lowered her feet to the ground. "I don't know why."

Seth righted his clothing, then wrapped her in his arms and clutched her to his chest. "What's wrong with me?" he croaked. "I just took you in a filthy tack room like a whore."

"I'm not fragile. Stop treating me like I'll break."

"You're my wife. You deserve better."

"There *isn't* anyone better." Becca framed his face with her hands. "When are you going to get it through your head, you stubborn man? You're the one I want. Your gentleness, your passion—all of it. All of *you*. "

He searched her eyes, hope and disbelief warring in his.

"My body is yours and yours is mine," she said as she traced his brow with her finger. "My future is yours and yours is mine."

Seth caught her behind the knees and lifted her into his arms. He settled onto the crate and cradled her in his lap. "Please tell me I didn't hurt you."

"You didn't."

A deep sigh left his lungs as he rested his head on hers. "Still, I was a selfish lover."

"So," she said, caressing the skin exposed by the vee of his shirt, "make it up to me."

Seth brushed the fallen strands of hair back from her face and took her lips in a gentle kiss. With the reverence of the first time he ever touched her, he slid his hand beneath her skirts and up her thigh.

The warm scent wafting from the depths of the bed covers made Becca smile. Cotton and skin smelled different after amorous acts, especially multiple ones. Her and Seth's encounter in the tack room had thrown open the love gate and stampeded the herd. He had whisked her off to bed as soon as night fell and coupled with her for hours. They'd both be exhausted come dawn, but it would be a good kind of tired.

Sated to the bone, Becca dropped off to sleep until the rooster's crow roused her to wakefulness again.

She and Seth groaned in unison.

He pulled her into a sleep-warmed embrace. "I'm going to strangle that bird."

Becca nuzzled his chest. "You can't. We need chicks. Besides, the hens would probably gang up and attack you."

He drew back, wearing a lopsided grin. "Oh they would, would they?"

"Well..." Her cheeks heated—marriage had made her indecently bold. "*I* would track down and wallop anyone who took you away from *me*."

His eyes danced with levity and beamed with pride. "Good thing I'm not a polygamous rooster, then."

Becca grabbed a patch of his chest hair and twisted it until he winced. "Yes, good thing."

"Ouch." He disentangled her fingers and rubbed at the spot.

She decided to broach a subject she'd been saving for the right moment, even though it would probably sour the mood. Not only had recent events handed her the perfect prelude, she'd grown bold in other ways, too. "Mrs. Perkins came to pay Ma a visit yesterday."

"Perkins... They own the farm to the east, right?"

"Mmhm. She brought Ma some canned fruit. She said it was a welcoming gift for you and me, but I think she brought it to help us make it through winter." Her parents hadn't made many friends since moving to California, but they had a few. And word of their troubles had gotten around. "She stayed and visited a while."

"I'll bet," he said dryly. "Did she grace you ladies with any earthshattering news or tawdry stories?"

Becca giggled. Cordelia Perkins was friendly and generous. She was also the biggest gossip this side of the Colorado. "Not any I can repeat," she teased.

"I hope you didn't give her any fodder," he said more seriously.

"I didn't." Becca bolstered herself and pressed on. "She told us of several families that settled around the same time they did, near Clearhaven, a town about fifty miles to the northeast. She said one bore the name Emerson and asked if they were your kin."

Seth's face fell and he looked away.

Becca softened her voice but not her resolve. "I know this is a difficult subject for you, but is it possible? Could they be relatives of yours?"

He stared over her shoulder at the window for quite a long time. "They are."

"Cousins...? An uncle?"

His gaze dropped to between them, but he still wouldn't look her in the eye. "My parents."

She wasn't sure what to say. Seth claimed he'd had no contact with them for five years. How—

"I kept in touch with a couple of friends after I left home. One of them wrote to me when he moved west. On his way through my hometown, he discovered someone had bought my parents' farm. The new owner told him where they'd gone."

"Did he say if... Did he have news of your sister?"

Seth shook his head. "He didn't mention her. He didn't *know* to mention her. I never told him about— For Rachel's sake, all that was kept quiet."

Becca nuzzled his chest again and slid her arm around his waist.

He hugged her back. "I want to make a good life for you, but I don't know what to do. If I don't stay and help your pa—hell, maybe even if I do—he won't be able to sustain the farm. If I find work, I'll have to give him most of my earnings instead. It'll take years to save enough to build a place of our own." Seth made an exasperated sound. "If I thought he would speak to me, I'd go see my father and ask him for a loan, but I know that would be a waste of time and breath.

"I love you so much, I ache with the depth of it," he said, his cheek pressed to her hair and his heart pouring out with his words. "But sometimes I wish, for your sake, you'd married Nathan. I should have searched for you longer. If you'd have come with me the first time, your intended might still have been free."

Becca sharply inhaled at the familiar flash of longing. When she learned that Nathan was so newly married, she'd had the very same thought. But the sensation today was fleeting and, more importantly, irrelevant. She could honestly claim she no longer harbored that regret.

Gripping Seth's chin between her thumb and forefinger, she angled his face towards hers and looked him square in the eyes. "This is the last time we will have this discussion, so listen well.

"It touches my heart that you care enough about my future to wish me with another man, but I don't ever want to hear you speak this way again. I believe things happen for a purpose. I wouldn't change the course of my life, even if I could.

"I used to think Nathan was better suited to me than you, but I don't think that anymore. He's a fine man, and had we married, we would have had a good life together—of that I'm certain. But Nathan isn't you. He's kind and honorable, but he doesn't have your sense of humor. He's handsome and wealthy, but he's never looked at me the way you do—like you can't wait another moment to kiss me, like you'll die if we don't touch. Like—" Her voice wavered. "Like I'm the center of your world."

Becca drew a steadying breath. "You are the one I want, Seth—you and only you. I'll gladly live here with my parents if that's what you choose, but I'm married to *you*. Wherever you go, I'll follow. Whatever choices you make, I'll stand by your side. However easy or hard our life turns out, that is how it will be. So stop letting regret and fear and doubt keep you from making plans and being happy."

He stared at her with watery eyes, and his throat bobbed with a swallow.

Becca released his chin and planted a kiss on his stubbled jaw. "You sacrificed everything you had to save me. I'm not going to hold it against you now."

He held her close for several minutes before drawing their

upper bodies apart and looking at her again. "Why did you hide from me?"

She didn't want to answer, but the image of him calling to her from the base of that snowy canyon invaded her mind and crumbled her defenses. "I told myself it was because I didn't want to be taken somewhere just to be abandoned again. But that was only part of the reason. The truth is, I didn't want to be rescued at all."

She placed a finger on his parting lips. "When you first convinced me to go to the outpost with you, I planned to get some supplies for my cave and send you on your way, alone. I didn't want to find Nathan or my parents, because I was too angry at them... too hurt by them." She lowered her hand. "And going someplace else just to be left again wouldn't have solved anything. Not on the inside, anyway. I believed no one wanted me, that I was ruined and unlovable. I didn't care if I lived or died."

"Becca..." The misery filling his eyes pricked her heart.

She offered up a small smile. *Be careful what you ask.* "During the months before you found me, I often climbed to the cliff overlooking the trail with plans to throw myself off. I'd stand at the edge, watching the pebbles dislodged by my boots tumble to the ground below. But I could never do it, never take that last step.

"I'd end up sitting there for hours, unable to make a decision. Then, come dusk, I'd trudge back to my cave, perturbed with myself for being such a coward."

His eyes closed for a long moment, then opened again. "I'm glad your stubborn streak chose those times to leave."

Her smile was stronger this time. "I don't think it did."

"No?"

She shook her head and focused on the tap of his pulse near the hollow of his throat. "Even though I believed I'd been rejected by the people I loved, that all the evidence pointed to that, I couldn't be certain. Deep inside, I clung to that tiny scrap of hope.

"And, either way," she said, looking up at him again, "I didn't really want to die. I just wanted to stop hurting."

Seth closed his eyes again and clutched her to his chest.

Becca held him, too. She pressed her ear to the space over his heart. The rapid pounding slowed, then quickened again.

"What if I hadn't come back?" he rasped. "You might've—" His grip tightened as a strangled sound swallowed the rest of his words.

"But you did. And now I have you."

He planted a lingering kiss on her forehead. "You'll always have me."

The steady rise and fall of his chest lulled her, but her mind wouldn't rest. "It's strange to think I almost ended my life over something that wasn't true."

She drew back enough to see his face. "What about you? You and your parents...? You should at least pay them a visit and speak with them, Seth. What if you're making choices based on wrong information?" He looked away with an expression of irritation and pain, but she didn't back down. "Even if you aren't, you'll be haunted by it the rest of your life if you never go."

Chapter Thirty-Four

At the first break in the early January weather, Becca helped Seth pack the wagon for the four-day journey to his father's house. It was with no small amount of ambivalence that she said goodbye to her parents, though she'd see them again very soon. As the two of them drove away, she was thankful for the cold air that blanched her face and dried her threatening tears.

Seth had offered to make the trip alone, but she would never have let him. She was the one who'd urged him to do this—she would be there to support him if things went well and to console him if they did not. At best, she expected a mixed resolution. Even if his parents held no ill will, he likely faced confirmation of the loss of his sister.

That fact plagued Becca most and relentlessly tugged at her heart—along with gaining the truth of his parents' feelings toward him, Seth would lose any hope that Rachel might still be alive.

During the next three days, Becca helped with chores,

cooked the meals, and tried to be good company. During the nights, she wrapped Seth in her arms and held him close, hoping to impart strength and peace along with her warmth.

He was stoic, even grim faced at times, but he'd planned the trip without further prompting from her. And she took comfort in that. Seth teased her about being stubborn, yet he was the truly obstinate one. He wouldn't be doing this if he didn't want to go.

Midafternoon on the fourth day, they topped a hill and spied a sizable farm below. A stately, two-story house crowned a smaller rise, surrounded by acres of plowed land and rolling pasture. Winter had dulled the colors and stolen the leaves from the trees—and still, the place was impressive. It had to be magnificent in spring.

Seth stopped the wagon and stared.

"Is this it?"

"Yes." His voice was as flat as his expression, but it didn't fool her. He was knotted more than a fisherman's net on the inside. His arms were casually bent, and his gloved hands cradled the reins with practiced ease, yet he rubbed the straps with his thumbs as if he aimed to wear clean through the leather.

Becca still remembered, vividly, how she felt facing her parents after all that time. And she'd had some indication of how things would go. Seth's situation was far less favorable, and he had nothing. She placed a hand on his forearm and offered a small-but-reassuring smile.

He smiled back, but it was weak and weary.

Becca scooted closer. She looped her arm in his and pressed a chaste kiss to his cheek. Such familiarity in broad daylight was highly improper, but no one was present to see.

Seth shifted the reins into one hand long enough to place his other on top of hers and squeeze. He studied the house again, then snapped the straps and urged the team forward with a sharp click of his tongue.

Becca gripped Seth's shoulders as he swung her down from the wagon seat where he'd parked in the yard. A few horses milled about in a nearby paddock—the only apparent witnesses to their arrival. Seth gazed out over the land. When he turned and faced the house, she did likewise and stood by her husband in silent support.

A tall, slender woman eased out the door and onto the porch. Her hand lifted to conceal parted lips. A long moment later, it slid to the base of her throat. Becca wasn't sure, but she thought she saw the trace of a tremulous smile.

Seth exhaled, and some of the tension in his shoulders went away. He offered Becca his arm, and they cautiously approached.

The middle-aged woman moved to the edge of the porch, her dun-colored skirt softly rippling in the breeze. Her hair was the color of Seth's, but she had green eyes.

Seth stopped at the base of the stairs. His chin was level and his shoulders were, too, but the muscles of his forearm bunched so tightly, they quivered. "Hello, Ma."

His mother clutched her fine-boned hands at her waist. She didn't look angry and she seemed to be shedding happy tears, but she wasn't rushing forward to embrace him. "Hello, Seth."

Seth cleared his throat. "Ma, I'd like you to meet my wife, Rebecca."

A spark of surprise shot across her face. She recovered and smiled politely. "It's good to meet you, Rebecca."

"It's good to meet you, too, Mrs. Emerson."

A bit more warmth crept into her smile. "Please, call me Abigail."

The narrow nose and high cheeks of his mother's face reminded Becca of a statue she'd once seen. Abigail Emerson looked to be one of those women who was beautiful no matter what—whether happy or sad, ill or well. She was pretty when she cried, that much was so, and she would likely keep her looks when she grew old.

Seth lowered his arm. Becca released him, but kept her hand close to his. He discretely threaded his fingers through hers, among the folds of her skirt. When he drew his next breath, she readied herself for anything and gave his hand a gentle squeeze for luck.

"I came to speak with Pa... if he's willing to speak with me."

Abigail's fair brows knitted slightly. "He's out riding the fence line right now. I won't answer for him, but I think he will."

Seth released a breath and nodded. "We've been traveling since first light. Would it be all right if Rebecca warmed herself by your fire?"

"Yes, of course." Abigail reached out to Becca and took her hand as she ascended the porch. Then she turned a pair of softening eyes on Seth. "I'll make coffee. Come inside once you stable your horses."

Seth paused at the entrance to the barn. It was twice the size of the one at his childhood home and half a country away, yet heinous memories assaulted him as ruthlessly as the men who'd attacked his sister. He'd apologized to Rachel a million times in his mind. Now, it seemed, the best he might do is visit her grave.

"C'mon, boy." He led Cyrus to the first unoccupied stall, then opened the next one for Zeus. Seth took in his surroundings as he tended his team. The structure was generous and the equipment, first-rate. His pa had done well for himself.

The prospect of facing his father weighed on Seth as he made his way back to the house. He hadn't been turned away, but he hadn't been greeted like the prodigal son either. His ma's nature was to be quiet and respectful; she was a walking, breathing lesson on discretion. But with that, she was keenly observant and sharp of mind. That she wasn't sure enough of his pa's wishes to answer for him didn't bode well.

At least she'd been kind to Rebecca.

Seth climbed the steps at the side of the porch, took the corner, and headed for the front door. The presence of a woman standing in his path ground his feet to a halt. His gaze took her in from her wreath of auburn hair, down over her dark green calico dress, to her prominent belly that was heavily swollen with child. His eyes met hers and his heart turned inside out. "Rachel?"

A sweet smile spread across her face, making the moisture clinging to her lashes glisten.

Seth fisted his hands at his sides as he worked to squelch the spasms in his chest that threatened to unman him. He wanted to throw his arms around her to assure himself she was real, but touching her would completely do him in.

His disbelieving eyes drank her in one more time. "You— You look well."

"I am." She glanced down at her burgeoning middle when his gaze wandered there again. "I'm Rachel Evans now. I married two years ago, before we moved west." She clutched the tails of her cream-colored crocheted shawl in one hand and gestured toward the north with the other. "Jacob and I live in a house on the back half of the land."

Seth lifted his chin in acknowledgement, then shifted on his boots. Not only was his sister alive, but she was well and apparently happy—the only denouement that had never played out in his mind. He was at a loss for words.

Rachel smiled at him again. "Welcome home."

The joy that had flooded him dimmed. "Thank you. But I'm not sure *welcome* is what I am. Ma's greeting was tepid, and she wasn't sure if Pa would even talk to me."

"You showed up out of the blue. Give them time."

Seth sighed. "I will, but I don't know what good it'll do. They hate me."

"No they don't."

"Yes they do. They barely spoke to me after— They blame me, and rightly so."

"No they don't. They blame themselves. I..." Her voice softened, and a shadow ghosted across her face. "I was in the barn alone because Ma sent me."

"Why would she—"

"Just listen to me. It's not your fault." Rachel led him to a grouping of chairs on the porch and urged him to sit. He did so, but only after helping her into one of the chairs.

"When Pa went out to call the men to breakfast, they were

gone. Their horses, everything, gone. He was surprised t̲ didn't stick around to eat—even checked to make sure they hadn't stolen from us. He finally admitted he was wrong about them and said they must have wanted to get an early start.

"Ma was perturbed because she'd cooked so much food. She started grumbling about how she was going to keep it all from spoiling before it got eaten and told me to find you. Pa didn't object. Both of them thought I'd be perfectly safe or they wouldn't have sent me. You have to believe that, Seth. You know how they are."

She was right, but it didn't assuage his guilt much. "I didn't even try to help you."

"Yes you did."

Seth pounded the arm of the chair. "I should have tried harder," he growled. "I should have fought them."

"No." Fresh tears glistened in her eyes as she clasped her hand over his fist. "The man behind you was twice your size, and they both had knives. If you had fought them, they would have killed you."

"Do you wish they had?"

Her eyes went wide. "Killed you?"

He nodded.

"No. Never! I didn't blame you then, and I don't blame you now."

Rachel's long brown lashes lowered, grazing her cheeks. Then a pained gaze met his. "For a while, though, I wished they'd killed me. I thought my life was ruined and I wanted to die. I couldn't get those images out of my mind, no matter how hard I tried." Her voice had dwindled to a whisper. "I didn't have to be asleep to have nightmares."

"And seeing me every day didn't help," Seth muttered.

"You're wrong. Having you with me when... Your presence

.ough it. And then afterward, every time I saw

.d the attack."

you did, and I didn't want you to."

Se.   .t his brow crease and his sister's cool fingers as she rubbed it away.

"I left because I thought you'd be better off without me," he said.

"I know. And in a way, I was." She rubbed away another crease. "When you left, it forced me to think of someone other than myself. I realized I was hurting the people around me by giving up. I started eating the next day.

"It hasn't been easy, and I'll never be the same, but I've made my peace with it. I have a man who loves me, and now a child. They give me a reason to keep going when the bad days come."

"Is your husband good to you?"

"Yes. Jacob's very kind, and he's the most patient person I know. He's had to be." She looked up at him through her lashes, splotches of pink dotting her cheeks. "I'm not always the kind of wife I should be, the kind he deserves."

"You're a fine woman, Rachel. He's lucky to have you."

Now the crease was between her brows. "Jacob tells me the same thing."

"He'd better. And he'd better be good to you."

"He is." She patted Seth's hand, then leaned back and pulled her shawl up around her shoulders. "Jacob lost his first wife when she gave birth. His firstborn, too. It was horrible and he still grieves, but it changed the way he views life." An introspective smile drifted across her lips. "We're an odd, broken pair, but we're good for each other."

Seth sat for a moment, thinking about all she'd said. "We should go back inside. It's too cold out here for you." He rose and helped his sister up. Before he could offer her his arm, she embraced him and hugged him tight.

"I'm glad you came back."

"Me, too." Emotion clogged his throat. "I've spent the last five years thinking you were dead."

Rachel drew away, a smile crinkling the skin around her moist eyes. "No. Just learning how to live."

The air in the foyer smelled of new wood and old scents—yeast and apples and onions, like his childhood home. After hanging up his hat and coat, Seth followed his sister and the melodious sound of female voices into the sitting room. His wife and his mother shared a settee near the fire. Their amiable postures and pleasant expressions set his mind a little more at ease.

His mother looked up, her gaze bouncing back and forth from him to his sister. Her bearing relaxed and she settled her clear green eyes on him. "Your wife has been telling me the story of how you two met. Mercy, Seth." She laid a palm on her chest. "It's a good thing I learned of your harrowing journey after the fact, with you standing alive and well before me."

Becca beamed up at him. "I told her what a wonderful son she raised and how lucky I am you found me."

Seth flushed under her praise. She was trying to smooth things over for him, but the frank esteem in her eyes struck him deep in the heart and nourished his love-starved soul. He'd probably never admit it to anyone other than himself, but he couldn't have faced his family without her by his side.

As soon as he'd eased Rachel into a comfortable chair, his mother rose and crossed the room to where he stood. "Rebecca's right. You're an honorable man—the kind of man I always hoped you'd be." She gathered him into her arms. "My heart has ached for you all these years, and I've prayed every night for your return." She squeezed him firmly and pressed her cheek to his. "I feared we'd never see you again when we left Ohio."

Seth clung to his ma and hid his wet eyes in the swell of her upswept hair. He'd prepared himself so well for rejection, he hadn't considered how overwhelming her welcoming arms would be.

The floorboards quivered beneath his feet and a door opened somewhere at the back of the house.

"Abigail?" his father called.

Apprehension dried Seth's tears instantly as his mother pulled away and dabbed her eyes. Something told him his father's reception wouldn't be nearly as warm.

"Abigail," his father called again as he came up the hall, a sharp edge of concern tempering his voice.

"In the parlor," she replied.

"I saw a strange wagon," he said as he rounded the corner. "Who's h—"

Seth swallowed as his father's gaze landed on him. Though he still looked up to the man figuratively, they now stood eye to eye, his pa thinner and his once-dark hair salted heavily with gray. Seth held his breath, his chest throbbing with each pound of his pulse.

His father's expression of shock hardened into an angry scowl. "How dare you show your face here," he growled, his blue eyes flashing and his hands fisting at his sides. "You—" His chest rose and fell with several seething breaths. "Get out of my house." He turned and stalked away, leaving the bitter dictate hanging behind him in the silence.

Seth released a slow breath. Rachel had misjudged the situation. She'd always been the optimistic one—the one who looked for the good in everything and everyone... no doubt the reason she'd fared so well after what she'd been through. And she was too honest, too sincere, to ever purposely mislead him. No matter how much his wounded pride stung, he wouldn't fault her for her idealism. He gathered what was left of his dignity and held a hand out to Becca. "Let's go."

The look on his lovely wife's face lay somewhere between disbelief and devastation, and that wounded his heart. He'd lost his past, but she'd lost her future.

Becca quickly composed herself and rose from the settee. "Thank you for the coffee, Mrs. Emerson."

His ma looked at Becca. Then him. She looked at the empty archway through which his pa had just passed. She turned back, her eyes brimming with tears and her hands pale and clutched at her waist. He'd never seen a woman more torn.

There was no remedy for it. Lawrence Emerson was an ethical man, but he'd already decided the matter and he was the source from which Seth's own stubbornness flowed.

Seth squatted down and cradled Rachel's hand in his own. "It was good to see you again."

She looked at him, tears returning to her eyes. "You, too."

"May I write to you?"

"Yes. Please, do."

He rubbed his thumb across her knuckles and managed a smile.

As he stood and faced his mother, he drew a grating breath. The prideful part of him wanted to run from the room before he completely broke down, but these were the last moments he'd have in the presence of the woman who'd given him life and raised him with kindness and love. He refused to squander the time.

Enfolding her willowy frame in his arms, he pressed a kiss to her cheek. "I love you, Ma."

She hugged him back, then took his face in her hands and kissed him between his brows the way she had so many times when he was a boy. She rested her forehead on his and wept softly.

Seth lingered there, too, no longer caring about the salty drops wetting his face.

He pulled himself away and swiped at his eyes.

His ma glanced at the archway again, then placed a staying hand on his arm and another on Becca's. "Don't leave yet. Let me go speak to him first."

"Thanks, Ma, but—"

"Please," she entreated. "You've come all this way. Let me try."

Seth relented with a feeble nod. He knew his father too well to believe she could sway him on something like this, but it was late in the day and the temperature outside was dropping faster than the January sun. Maybe she could gain permission for them to stay the night.

Both his sister and his wife offered words of encouragement while he waited for his mother to return, but he barely heard them. He was too busy listening to his better judgment regarding his pa.

Still, whatever the verdict, the trip had not been for naught— seeing Rachel content was worth any amount of humiliation and hardship.

Feminine footsteps echoed from the hall. Seth looked up, bracing himself for a second and final rejection. His breath stilled in his lungs at the sight of his ma's face—more specifically, her smile.

She held a hand out to him. "He agreed to talk to you."

Seth's thoughts spun as fast as the blood surging through his veins. His father may have acquiesced to his wife—she rarely failed to find the soft spot in his heart—but his dealings with males were another thing entirely. Drawing a deep, steadying breath, he wiped his clammy palms on his trousers and followed his mother out of the room and down the hall.

She stopped outside a closed door and paused, lips parting and closing, brows knitted in thought. "Your father's a proud man," she finally said, "but he's a good man. Be patient with him."

Seth watched her walk away until she disappeared through the entrance to the parlor. Praying for mercy from his father—and forbearance for them both—he knocked on the door.

"Come." The reply was muffled but gruff.

He opened the sturdy door and stepped into the dim interior of his father's office. Heavy brocade drapes covered the windows and a large mahogany desk filled a third of the room. A single kerosene lamp glowed from one corner of it, casting shadowy amber light on his father's back as he stood, staring out one of the windows.

"Your mother thinks you deserve a second chance," he said without turning around. Moving only his head, his pa looked at him, his expression sour. "I don't." He turned his face back to the window, and Seth counted ten breaths as they stood there, neither saying a word.

He counted three more rises of his chest as he weighed the value of speaking versus remaining silent. "I'm sorry I let you down. If I had obeyed you and kept an eye on Rachel..."

His father's shoulders lost some of their starch. "I blamed you for that for a long time. But the truth is, it's my burden to bear." His pa faced him then, pain and anger deepening the lines of his face. "As damnable as that is, what you did was worse."

Seth swallowed with a dry throat and braced for the verbal lashes he knew were about to come—a grown-up version of a trip to the woodshed. One thing hadn't changed. The disappointment in his father's eyes still hurt worse than the strap.

"You deserted us at one of the most difficult times our family has ever faced," his father said, his eyes hard and his voice harder. "Rachel started eating again, but she was far from well. I had to hire help just to manage the daily chores. Had to trust an outsider with our secrets and bring a stranger onto the farm right after—" He twisted his lips as though he'd tasted something bitter. Then his nostrils flared as he drew a sharp breath. "How do you think that made your sister feel?"

A burning ache ignited deep in Seth's chest. He'd been so mired in guilt and grief, he hadn't given much thought to how his family would fare without him. The only image he'd pictured—besides them giving voice to their condemning thoughts—was them burying his sister.

"Doc Bennet..." His neck bent and his spirit wilted. "I thought she was dead."

The desk chair creaked as his father lowered himself into it. He rubbed his face with both hands, then dropped them limply to the table. He no longer looked angry, just very, very tired. "I've spent five long years hating my only son. I don't want to live that way anymore."

With the aid of the light cast by the lamp, Seth got a good look at the toll those years had taken. His father had never been bulky, but he'd been muscular and fit. *Rawboned* now described his lean frame. The color of his lips had faded like weathered wood, and deep-gray shadows occupied the hollows beneath his eyes and cheeks. There was barely any blood in his skin.

"Why did you come?"

Seth took a moment to catch up with the change. "Because I couldn't live with the uncertainty. And... because I need help."

His father eyed him skeptically, then gestured to a chair opposite the desk. "What sort of trouble are you in?"

"Not *trouble* really," he said as he sat. He had shown forbearance and gotten it in return. Now he hoped for mercy. "I found a young woman who was stranded and spent all my savings bringing her west to find her family. I didn't worry at the time, because I figured I could work and save up again, but then we married—" Seth halted, realizing how odd his story must sound. He released his pent up breath when his father's eyes twinkled with amusement.

"I should have known there'd be a woman involved." Schooling his features, he gestured with his hand. "Go on."

"We're staying with her parents. They're good people, but they got a bum claim and fell on hard times. No matter whether I work for her pa or find a paying job, the lot of us'll do well not to starve. I want better for her than that.

"I'm willing to work my own claim, but I have no means to buy the materials I need. I came to ask you for a loan."

Lawrence leaned back in his chair and steepled his fingers, tapping their tips together, his expression contemplative.

Pulse thrumming and palms sweating, Seth waited, trying to keep his face neutral and his racing thoughts from running away with his mind.

After a period of excruciating silence he'd swear was longer than the prophesied millennium, his father sat forward again. "The money's yours if you want it. Whatever you need... we can work out the terms."

Seth sat there, flummoxed and speechless.

"But I hope you decide not to take it."

He dug through growing layers of bewilderment to find his voice. "Why not?"

His father's steady gaze wavered, and a bit of color entered his face. "You're not the only one who needs help."

Wealth surrounded them—prosperity met him at every turn. "I don't understand."

"I'm sick."

All Seth's puzzlement burned away, leaving nothing but dread. "How sick?"

Lawrence grimaced. "One doctor says it's my heart, another says it's my lungs. All I know is I can't put in a full day's work anymore."

"Is there anything they can do?"

His father shook his head. "They've tried all manner of treatments and concoctions to no avail. The only thing that seems to help is rest." He rubbed his face again, then propped on his elbows and folded his pale hands on the desk. "Rachel's husband and I made an agreement when we moved west to work the land as a team. In exchange for his help, I gave him half. The last few months, he's been doing his work and part of mine, too. I had planned to hire an extra hand in the spring, but I'm willing to offer you the job instead, let you earn back your inheritance. I can't give you everything, but I can offer you my portion."

Seth couldn't believe his ears. The total spread was at least six times the size of a grant. And it was prime. Even half was a settler's dream.

"The entire estate could have been yours, had you stayed, but Jacob stepped in when I needed someone and worked in your place. I won't go back on my promise to him."

"I understand."

"If you agree to this, the two of you will be working side by side. I'll expect you to deal fairly with him."

The admonition rankled, but Seth kept his counsel and gave a single nod.

"And I suppose it goes without saying, but I'll expect you to look after your mother, should anything happen to me."

"You're right. That doesn't need saying."

Eyes narrowed briefly at his sharp retort.

Seth reigned in his pride and softened his tone. "Regardless of what I choose, I'll take care of Ma. You have my word."

His father's features smoothed into an unmistakable look of relief. He blinked a few times and blew out a breath. "I suppose you'll want some time to think this over," he said as he rose.

Seth stood. "I'll need to work out a few details with you before we set it in stone, but I know what I want." He stuck a hand across the desk. "I want to earn back my inheritance, and your trust."

Staring at his proffered hand, and then him, Lawrence Emerson met him halfway and shook. The clasp lingered until a wave of emotion threatened to tumble them both.

Seth waited as his father circled the desk, then walked with him toward the door.

"Did you bring your wife with you?"

Damn. Single-minded fury *was* blind. "Yes."

"Good." He clapped Seth on the back. "I want to meet the woman you spent your life's savings to rescue. She must be something special."

"She is." *She most certainly is.*

Chapter Thirty-Five

Lying beside her on the bed in one of his parents' spare rooms, Seth swept Becca's hair aside and nibbled the slender column of her neck.

"Not only are you incorrigible," she said in a husky, amused voice, "you're insatiable."

"Mmm." He nibbled some more. "Only because you're irresistible." She was. And he had a lot of making up to do—to Rachel and his pa and his ma—but most especially to her.

He'd gotten started on his restitution the minute they'd excused themselves for the night. It was well past one, and he still wasn't done.

"*Irresistible* or not," she mocked, "it's in your best interest to get some sleep. I don't think your pa will take too kindly to you strangling any of his birds."

She was teasing, but she was right. Even in the dead of winter, morning came early. He nudged her away from him, onto her side, then tucked her soft, curvy backside against him and gazed out the window.

"You made a good impression on my family," he said. "By the end of supper, the whole lot of 'em was ready to adopt you. Especially my pa." When she'd told her story—and a watered down version at that—Lawrence's face had looked nearly as stricken as her own pa's.

"I like them, too. Though Jacob scared me a bit at first."

Seth stifled the urge to chuckle at her understatement. He'd felt the same way. Jacob was the biggest man he'd ever seen—tall and burly, and gruff-looking, to boot. As soon as he'd watched his brother-in-law in action, though, his intimidation had fled in favor of respect. Not only did the man ooze integrity from every pore, he was as protective and soft-hearted as they came, especially toward Rachel.

If his mother was a walking lesson on discretion, his brother-in-law was a walking reminder not to judge a person's temperament or heart by their appearance.

"Jacob's a very large mother hen. But don't tell him I said that."

Becca snickered.

"Do you see that hill in the clearing over there?" he asked after a while.

"Which one?"

Wrapping his arm around her middle, he scooted her up a little higher in bed, then pointed across the moonlit landscape that glistened with a thin layer of new-fallen snow. "That one. That's where I plan to build our house." He propped on his elbow so he could see her reaction. "Do you like it?"

"Yes." She'd smiled, but sadness lurked in her big gray eyes. Just as she'd promised, she had accepted his choice to stay without complaint, but she'd done so at a great sacrifice.

Seth rested his head on the pillow again, just above hers and focused on the reflection of her face in the window. "There's a stream nearby that's perfect for a spring house and a nice slope on the far side where I can plant you a kitchen garden.

"I also have some ideas for the house. To make things easier on you, I'll put the well as close as I can to the washroom and the kitchen, and I'll build a split plan with bedrooms on both ends. That way we'll have our privacy... and your parents will, too."

Becca's lips parted. She turned in his arms until she was facing him. "You'd do that for me?"

"I returned you to your family, only to take you away again. It's the least I can do."

Uncertainty stole her excitement so quickly, it gouged his heart. "Do you think they'll come?"

"It'll be up to your pa, but I think he will. There's work and lodging for Gus, too."

"You're so good to me."

"You deserve it, Rebecca."

She brushed his jaw with the tip of her nose. "Say it again."

"What?"

"My name."

"Why?"

"I love the way it sounds when you say it."

"Rebecca."

A satisfied smile spread across her face, and she closed her eyes. "Say it again."

"Rebecca."

"Again."

"Becca-becca-becca-becca."

Her sleepy giggle tickled the hairs on his chest.

Seth dipped his head and planted a kiss on her forehead. "I love you."

"I love you, too."

Tiredness and satiety had woven their way into her voice, so he tucked her under his chin and held her in silence—his arms filled with a far better future than any he could have planned for himself.

Once her breathing had slowed, well-deepened by sleep, he closed his eyes and touched his lips to her hair. "I'll call you any name you want," he whispered, "but you'll always be my Angel... the angel who rescued me and brought me home."

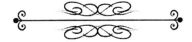

Thank you for reading *Come Back*.

To receive important updates and notice of new releases by Melissa Maygrove, subscribe to the author's newsletter. You can do that from the home page of her website: www.melissamaygrove.com.

Goodreads:
www.goodreads.com/author/show/8103285.Melissa_Maygrove
Writer's blog:
www.melissamaygrove.blogspot.com
Twitter:
@MelissaMaygrove

CPSIA information can be obtained at www.ICGtesting.com
Printed in the USA
LVOW07s1522230715

447374LV00003B/672/P